1

For my granddaughters, Sutton and Isla. I hope you love great Christian Fiction when you grow up!

Banished

A young adult novel

By Tammy Bowers

KDP Publishing, 2018
Exclusively on Amazon
Copy Rights Reserved
https://authortammybowers.blogspot.com

This book has not been professionally edited.
Please excuse the mistakes.

Acknowledgements

Thank you, Wordsmiths—Karen Barnett, Patricia Lee, Marilyn Rhodes, and Heidi Gaul for your excellent critiques and edits of *Banished*. You made my story better!

Thank you to Bill and Colleen Wall for your thought-provoking Precepts Bible Study lessons of Genesis and Revelations. They stimulated this story idea and various elements of *Banished*. God always leaves a remnant.

Thank you to my sister-in-law, Teresa Bowers, for your words of encouragement when I first started writing two decades ago. You said I was smart enough to write novels, and I believed you.

Most importantly, thank you to my husband, Dan Bowers, for believing in me and encouraging my writing dream. None of my stories would be possible without your support and faith in me. I love you forever.

Banished

CHAPTER ONE

Jordana hid behind a rainbow eucalyptus trunk, her body concealed in the shadows. Steps away, baboons scavenged for fallen fruit in the mango grove. A large male sniffed the air and turned her way. She held her breath, as his flashing eyes pierced the dimness. Jordana dare not move—detection could mean death. Would her pounding heart give her away?

After a long moment, the massive creature dipped his head and snuffled through the grass once more.

Jordana released a noiseless sigh. During the past three years, some of the beasts had grown to tolerate her, but as the end of the hot season neared and the trees' produce waned, the troop became more protective of their territory. She had to stay upwind from the unpredictable creatures, and hidden from the females carrying babies on their backs. If threatened, the mothers would kill to protect their family.

Family. Jordana's heart clenched. If Mamu hadn't fallen, Jordana would still belong to a family. She sunk her fingernails into the eucalyptus bark. If her cherished mother were still alive and on the throne, Jordana never would have been banished from the Tree Warrior Village. She'd have a family of her own by now, instead of living alone in the jungle—competing with wild animals for food. Or fighting from becoming their prey.

Forehead pressed against the trunk, she forced her fingers to relax and her lungs to exhale slow and steady. After shoving the longing away, she focused on the baboons. Each one busy with their loot.

The scent of fresh mango filled the air, overpowering the eucalyptus fragrance. Jordana's stomach growled. The outer trees were picked clean. She'd have to harvest from an interior tree. Fruit gave her energy to hunt meat—a constant competition with her fellow omnivores for antelope and hare, rare finds so close to the Forbidden Falls Territory.

Toucans in the jungle chirped loud enough to drown out the rushing Azul River. Would their racket help conceal her crawling through the reeds? Time to find out. She sunk into the grass and crept forward, green blades closing around her shoulders as she crawled past two trees. At a third, she inched upright and plucked several ripe mangos.

Shrieks sounded. Baboons stomped and uprooted ferns.

Jordana took off for the jungle, sprinting as fast as she could pump her arms and legs. Once she reached the tree line, she glanced over her shoulder. None of the beasts had moved past the center of the grove to pursue her. Several males charged forward, then skidded to a stop. Their screeches filled the air, but it was only for show. Perhaps the troop had accepted her more than she realized.

At a fallen log, Jordana slowed her pace and stepped over. The popular destination attracted many animal species. Most posed no threat. But what hunted the fruit-eaters— cheetahs, jaguars, and panthers—would be happy to settle for her.

She smiled at the large ripe mango in her hand. "Thank you, Elohim, for a successful reaping." Two mangos tucked into her satchel, Jordana bit into the third, pulled back the peeling and chomped into the fruit. Juice slithered down her fingers. Eyes alert, she ate while picking through the jungle toward her favorite spot near the forbidden river. When she finished eating the mango, she deposited the pit into her satchel. Tomorrow she'd plant it an hour north. Or maybe west. Her diligence should lead to mango trees producing fruit all over the rainforest just like with the wild plum trees, coconut, and banana.

At a white neplar trunk, she climbed to a strong branch thirty feet off the ground, and stretched out on the snow-colored limb. Back nestled against the smooth trunk, she crossed her ankles and glanced around. No sign of intruders. As usual. Most people stayed clear of the forbidden river, making it a perfect place for her. A gust of wind rustled the sapphire leaves above as she pulled out a second mango.

As soon as she bit in to rip the skin back, a putrid taste touched her tongue. She spit the peel out and inspected the inside of the mango. Black veins ran throughout the interior of the orange fruit. "What on Tzuri?" A rotten mango, how could that be? Had someone violated a sacred palm? Jordana glanced at the perimeter of the clearing below her perch. Several purple palms swayed, their black rubbery bark sparkled as their amethyst fronds danced in the breeze. They showed no sign of desolation. Where had the holy law been violated?

Why are they sacred, Mamu? As a child, Jordana's appetite for knowledge seemed unquenchable, and her late mother never grew impatient when explaining things.

Because Elohim designated them holy for a special purpose. Mamu's loving face filled Jordana's memory—auburn hair framing pale eyes.

What purpose? And why the purple palm and not a pear tree or kapok?

Perhaps Elohim will one day reveal His answer to you.

One day hadn't come and Jordana still waited.

A twig snapped in the distance and Jordana froze. At the crack of another stick, she searched in each direction as she dropped the fruit into her satchel. She wrapped one leg around the branch, squeezing it between her calf and hamstring. Dry leaves crunched beyond the clearing like faint footsteps approaching. Certainly not a lion or a puma. Both were far too furtive for such a rowdy gait. Would a person dare to travel this deep into the rainforest? Most people stayed clear of the gateway to Elohim's Holy Land. Even the animals.

Unless…

Jordana's pulse quickened. Had someone finally come for her? Father? Benjura? *No.* She dismissed the foolish hope. No one would come for her. Not ever. Besides, evidence of someone defiling a sacred palm had reached the mango grove. Her mouth ran dry. Anchored to the bough, she unsheathed a blade from each harness encircling her thighs below the hem of her tunic. Weapons raised, she poised them above her shoulders and studied the forest below.

She focused on the distance between her and the threat. Roosted high in the neplar, her tanned skin and flaming red hair would make her stand out. Against the pure white bark and indigo leaves, she sat vulnerable. The distance to the closest rainbow eucalyptus was too far to jump. Did she have time to climb down, run over, and scale one? The peeling bark of the rainbow would help conceal her, thanks to their brilliant slashes of orange, red, and green.

Jordana closed her eyes and strained to hear the footfalls. At the swishing of vegetation, her lids shot open.

A giant stepped into the clearing below her wielding a sword larger than any she'd seen before. He paced the perimeter, searching the jungle with weapon ready, his legs and shoulders bulged with thick muscles. Streaks of gray lined his mane.

The man's face looked nothing like Jordana's ex-tribesmen when their hair grew striped by age. Unlike her beloved kinsmen, the giant's skin contained no wrinkles, except for a deep scowl-line between his thick, black brows. Distinctive spots like dried blood covered the giant's hands, leather pants, and bare chest. The markings on his scabbard were foreign to her. From what tribe had the behemoth come?

Another twig snapped in the distance. The warrior didn't turn toward it, and neither did she as adrenaline shot through her veins. Held to the limb only by one leg, she dare not move to wrap both around for better balance.

A second giant passed her trunk and eased into the clearing directly below her perch. His approach from behind her had been silent. An arrow sat nocked in his tall bow—taller than her. The stealthy giant joined the first stranger in the clearing, each turning back to back as they scanned every direction. Except up.

Across from her, dry leaves continued to crunch as the noisy one drew near.

A shiver snaked up Jordana's spine and coiled around her lungs, holding her breath. *Please, Elohim, let not their eyes see me.* She held her weapons ready, moving nothing except her gaze to search as far as her peripheral vision allowed.

At last the noisy third fighter entered the area. He grasped a huge spear and joined the other two in scanning the jungle. All three failed to search upward. A tree warrior would never make such a fatal mistake.

Each giant stood eight feet tall or more, with varying degrees of dark hair. Long and course like a horse's tail, their massive manes hung down their wide backs.

The first giant, a gray-haired goliath, stopped moving and sheathed his sword. "Doesn't look like we were followed. Bring in the last two men. We'll rest and eat here before crossing the Azul."

They spoke her language, so why had she never seen these giants before? Jordana's heart rate picked up speed, for they were the first humans she had encountered since her two banishments. Weeks after the tree warriors exiled her, she'd gone to the garden tenders. A month later, the garden tenders banished her, too. What was wrong with her? Would she ever belong to a family again?

Jordana shrugged the longing away and focused on the mammoth men below her. Their bronze skin seemed almost golden. *Beautiful.* Perhaps the giants were friendly and would accept her…if they worshiped Elohim.

Without lowering his bow, the stealthy archer blew out a

sharp whistle.

The gray giant motioned at the third warrior who had entered the clearing. "I heard you approaching, Boar. Tromping like a war horse."

The noisy third fighter smiled. "Good, old man. We'll let you raid with us until you can no longer make out my footfalls." Boar's grin revealed black rotting teeth.

Jordana cringed at the man's disgusting mouth, and at the word *raid*. Who had these brutes plundered? Not friendly after all, she must put space between her and the threats. A branch hung within reach. Could she ascend without notice? Or would it be better to wait until after they ate, and maybe fell asleep?

The stealthy archer motioned with his bow and two new men entered the clearing.

Oh, bats! Five giants now stood below her.

The newcomers carried large packs. They were dressed the same as the other three, except they carried no bow or sword. Only a single hatchet hung from each one's waist belt.

If she had to, Jordana could take out the first two raiders before the third got off a shot. But his one weapon might be enough to pick her out of the tree. If not dead from the piercing, she would be crushed upon hitting the ground. She dare not breathe heavy or move an inch. Waiting in utter silence might be her only hope. She squeezed the branch under her, a position she could hold for hours and had done so many times before while hunting. Or being hunted. Her throat clenched as moisture drained from her mouth. Never before had she been hunted by people.

The two newcomer giants swung the massive bundles off their backs and dropped them to the ground. A high-pitched wail sounded when one of the packs landed on the forest floor.

The gray-haired warrior stormed to the packers, yanking up the smallest one—probably a mere seven and a half feet tall—and gripped his throat with a grimy hand. "Hoag, what have you done?"

The packer struggled for air. "I took a babe during the

12

raid as a gift for the king. I'm sorry, Lord Joice. Do you wish me to slay it?"

"Yes." Lord Joice released Hoag, shoving him away. "A baby will not remain silent for our journey across the forbidden territory." The gray warrior swiped Hoag upside the head with a heavy forearm encircled by a wide leather cuff. The rest of Lord Joice's bare arm revealed massive biceps.

A shutter raced up Jordana's torso. Surely they wouldn't harm a child. *And cross the Forbidden Territory?* These beasts dared to disobey Elohim's decree?

Hoag dropped to the ground and scrambled to the pack. He yanked the drawstring open and pulled a baby out, swaddled in a blanket, and held it at arm's length. The babe wailed, and seemed dwarfed inside Hoag's huge hands as he dropped the blanket.

Jordana gaped at the sight of the child's red hair—a babe from the Tree Warrior Village. She couldn't let Hoag murder the innocent thing. Jordana scanned each giant. All had dropped their guard, except the archer. Jordana would sink her first knife into him and aim her second dagger at Lord Joice. If the favor of Elohim befell her, she'd down the third fighter before he spotted her in the jungle canopy and fired his weapon. It would leave Hoag and the other packer for last. No doubt her slender knives could reach them before their heavy hatchets flew her way. The four knives secured around each thigh, smallest to largest, outnumbered the giants by three. She mustn't miss—shouldn't be a problem with such large targets. If rabbits and quail were easy at this range, the giants should fall in five throws.

But her hands trembled. As she tried to steady her aim, her stomach dropped to her knees. Did Elohim lead these men straight to her so she could rescue the babe? Jordana gulped hard and willed her fingers to relax. She must do whatever it took to save the child.

"Wait!" Lord Joice twisted back to Hoag, his deep voice carried over the infant's cry.

Jordana stilled as Hoag obeyed and cradled the child.

13

Immediately it quieted.

The elder Joice pulled the diapering rag down. "Tis a girl." His voice rose as if in awe.

The other warriors gasped.

Jordana soaked in the look on each man's face. Why were they so shocked to see a girl?

Hoag said, "Tis why I thought the king would want her."

"I will buy the female and raise her to become wife to my son." Boar flashed a sickening grin as he reached for the child.

"No." Stealthy sheathed his arrow. "The first girl must be given to the king. But let us go back and gather more females for our own sons to marry."

"Yes!" The men cheered.

"Silence." Lord Joice held up both hands. "We must deliver this baby to the king and return with our army. If the tree people are still birthing girls, we shall take every female of childbearing age and younger for our own tribe."

The other braves nodded their agreements.

Boar slapped Lord Joice on the back. "Someday you'll make a wise king."

Lord Joice punched his fist against his open palm. "Our army shall wipe out every living male from amongst their people. No man will be left alive in their village."

"Father." The breathy sound escaped Jordana's lips.

Boar's head jerked her way, his hand raising his spear.

The archer pulled an arrow from his quiver while searching the jungle.

"There." Lord Joice pointed at her and went for his weapon.

Boar's spear flew through the air and struck into the trunk inches from her head.

Adrenaline surging, Jordana flung a blade. It landed in the chest of the stealthy warrior just as he released an arrow. It swooshed by her head, whipping up a wisp of hair. She looked back at the clearing, as a second arrow shot her way. Jordana jerked to the side and released a second dagger at the archer. It sliced into his thick neck and the brute fell.

Her focus shifted to Boar, who ran to her tree truck and scrambled up, pointing his spear at her.

Jordana didn't hesitate to fire her next blade straight into his heart. She didn't miss. No scream escaped Boar's mouth as he plunged to the forest floor.

An arrow sliced across her arm, and Jordana winced.

Lord Joice had picked up Steathly's bow and fired at her.

Jordana didn't think as she released knives four and five, then dropped to hug the branch. Arrows skimmed over her back, as her blades spun downward. At the sight of a massive hatchet, she slid around the branch. The hatchet struck the bough, lodging into the white limb.

She scanned the clearing below. Her last two shots had hit their marks—the necks of Lord Joice and one of the packers. Now only Hoag remained, frozen as if in shock. Jordana sat up and pointed at him with her dagger. "Set the baby down, and I shall let you live." Secured to the bough and gazed fixed on Hoag, she reached over to the hatchet and tried to wiggle it free.

The giant shifted the child to one arm and went for his weapon.

In an instant, her long slender pick released from her grip and flew into Hoag's forehead, well above the little girl. As hoped, the brute fell straight back with the babe landing on his chest. Jordana shimmied down the trunk, whispering a prayer of thanks to Elohim for protecting her and the child. She rushed to snatch up the baby, and cuddled her while retrieving her weapons. Only one of the hideous brutes survived, though incapacitated.

A line of blood spilled from the gray giant's mouth. "I am son of the Chinzu King." The evil prince sputtered. "If I do not return, my father will send his army." He coughed up blood. "You have brought war upon your people."

Jordana stood over him. "Better to be prepared for battle, than slaughtered for our women. Why would you steal another man's child or wife?"

15

"No Chinzu…has borne a female…" He fought to push words past his bloody lips, "…in fourteen hot seasons."

"Fourteen years of only boys and not a single girl?"

"We…need…wives."

"You could try courting girls from other tribes." Jordana's throat clenched over the man's struggle to suck in air. Was there anything she could do to help him?

"We are mighty…Chinzu Giants." Blood gushed from his mouth. "Small men and—and women are on…Tzuri…to serve us."

"Did you destroy one of Elohim's sacred palms?"

"I know not what you are…talking about, woman." His voice turned soft. "Help me."

She bent and pulled her knife from his neck. As soon as it slid out, blood gushed, making it worse not better.

The giant gasped for breath, and his massive body convulsed. Seconds seemed like minutes until at last he stilled. The man's eyes glazed over.

Jordana bolted to the edge of the clearing. Babe secured on her hip, she bent over and retched. As a skilled hunter, she'd slain animals for food her whole life. But never a man. If only she had remained silent and they hadn't seen her.

Straightening, Jordana marched all the way to the Azul and waded out to her hips.

Lord Joice's declaration tore through her mind. *You have brought war upon your people.* His father, the King of the Chinzu Giants—a foreign tribe—would send an army to avenge the prince. The Chinzu kingdom must dwell on the far side of the Holy Land. Even though they were mighty giants, how dare they defy Elohim's decree and enter the Forbidden Falls Territory. And why did he not understand about the sacred palm tree?

Jordana must go back and warn her former tribe. But as a banished maiden, she'd be run through for attempting to enter the village. Should she even bother to risk her life for a people who had rejected her? She squeezed her eyes shut. Granna was there. Father. Benjura and good people she'd known her whole life.

16

Jordana settled herself and eased open her lids. No matter the cost, she must alert the Tree Warrior Village, return the baby to her mother, and stop the giants from defiling the Holy Land.

It'd take two days to reach her former village. Once there, how could she get an audience with the Arrdock before someone attacked her? Perhaps if she approached from the northeast during Benjura's watch, he'd provide escort. *Benjura.* Her stomach dropped to her knees.

Excited cooing from the child drew Jordana's attention. The baby jerked her feet, tiny toes splashing the warm water. Hot springs merged upriver with mountain runoff, keeping the Azul warm all year long. The girl giggled as she kicked in the tepid liquid.

Joy on the baby's face melted Jordana's heart like rays from the morning sun. "So what's your name little one? Are you about seven months old?" Jordana tickled the child under her bright strawberry curls. "You're just as rosy and delicate as a pink zinnia. Shall I call you that? Pretty Zinnia?"

She smiled and reached up to Jordana's cheek. The child's poor mother must be tortured with grief. Or had the giants orphaned the little one? Jordana must quickly return the baby to her mother.

Despite standing in a warm river, ice shot into Jordana's veins. Might she be an orphan now, too? Was Father with Mother in Elohim's paradise? What of Granna—had the giants slain her matriarch in their raid? And Benjura… A moan escaped Jordana's lips—would he even be alive when she returned?

Benjura's hazel eyes, wavy auburn hair, and heart-stopping smile filled her memory. The music of his deep laugh sang in her ears. No one in their tribe could jump as high as Benjura. At nearly six foot four, the boy stood taller than most in their village. But Lord Joice would have towered two feet taller.

From where had the mammoth men come?

Yes, she must find Benjura and make him take her to the Arrdock. But would Benjura be willing to help her? Despite being her betrothed, the man never stood up for her at the

Banishment Rite. By now, the toad was probably married with wee ones of his own.

Fire filled her belly once more. Alone and banished, Jordana would never be a mother to a precious baby like the one in her arms.

Perhaps she shouldn't approach from the northeast after all, in case tempted to bury one of her daggers into Benjura's cold heart.

No. She shook her head. She must forgive the man. Again. A breathy sigh escaped her lips. How many times had she spoken words of forgiveness only to have her fury reignited with a mere thought? When would she fully forgive him, despite never knowing why he did what he did?

CHAPTER TWO

Jordana shifted Zinnia to her hip and bent to the Azul's surface. Using one hand, she splashed water on her face, and rubbed. She cupped water onto her leather tunic, and scrubbed it clean. Blood spatter anywhere on her caused her stomach to curdle. One at a time she swooshed her knives through the river's current, washing all kill evidence away. If only she could rinse away the hideous memory of the dying giants. Their death tore through her gut like a rhino busting out of the brush. But they had left her no choice.

As the excuse tried to take root in her mind, the truth pushed it out. She had made a noise. If she had just remained silent, she could have slipped down after nightfall and rescued the baby. A wave of dizziness twirled through Jordana's mind, and she sank down in the water. *What have I done?*

How much time before the Chinzu King dispatched a search party for his son? A week? Two? And when they found the men slain, the king would seek revenge. Perhaps she should hide the corpses to provide time to warn the Tree Warrior Village. Then they could prepare for battle. Yes. This she must do.

She exited the river and hung their clothes on a bough to dry in the evening breeze. Sopping wet in her undergarments, she picked back through the jungle carrying the naked baby. At the clearing's edge, she withdrew her machete and whacked branches down, slicing off their leaves. She stabbed the long sticks side by side in the ground, forming a three-foot circle, and then retrieved Hoag's pack. Contents dumped onto the ground, a rolled up skin caught her eye. Twine cut, she shook it loose. A black and white striped fur rolled out. She spread the zebra skin on the bottom of the make-shift baby stall and set Zinnia atop.

Jordana must hurry, as the child would only be content a short time. From the neplar, Jordana brought down her belongings and donned her extra tunic. She cut a large corner of her blanket, and fastened it around Zinnia as a diaper. After chopping down several coconuts and hacking them open, she filled her water-skin.

The last of her baby-caring tasks stole her breath away. Was there any other option? She paced the clearing, her gaze darting from plant to plant, and over to inventory the supplies in the giants' packs. Nothing. She forced herself to pause in front of a purple palm. A roll of nausea passed through her gut as she poised a knife against the trunk's bark. "Please, allow this, Elohim, for the sake of the baby. I don't want to be like the giants and destroy a sacred palm. Let not my damage cause any serious harm."

A flick of her wrist and a small section of the stretchy black bark sliced off. Jordana used it to fashion a nipple over the wineskin opening, and propped up Zinnia to drink. No leaking appeared, so she must have done it right.

As she strode back to the clearing, a gust of wind rustled the rainbow eucalyptus, twirling scents through the air. Jordana took in a deep breath, as if it could soothe her contemplation over hiding the dead bodies. Dumping them in the river would make them easy to find downstream. Digging five deep graves would take too long. The Garden Tenders burned their dead and spread the ashes in their fields. Perhaps it would be smart to cremate the giants. A shudder ricocheted through her over the gruesome task. But it must be done.

Too risky to build a fire in the trees, she'd have to drag the corpses to the riverbank. Despite the short distance, she'd need help for the heavy job. An elephant or horse would be best.

Jordana raised her face to the sky. Hues of pink and orange filled the air. Dusk-light would be gone in an hour. "Please send help, Elohim." Jordana whistled her late mother's animal tune. Growing up, she had repeated it often. It never worked before and the tree warriors had long since dismissed the stories. But Granna and Mamu never stopped believing. That was good enough for her. She whistled the call for animals to come and help her as loud as she could.

While gathering wood, chopping long bamboo poles, and dragging everything to the river's edge, she whistled the tune over and over. Soon the horizon concealed the sun and both crimson moons shone overhead, their rings not yet visible.

Inside the tree line, she checked on Zinnia. The baby's sleeping face appeared peaceful and content. Her lips rose in a smile as if dreaming. Jordana's breath caught. Never before had she seen anything so precious. A yearning shot through her. Would Jordana ever be a mamu? She shook off the reckless idea, for to raise a child in the wild would only bring an early death. Yet gazing at Zinnia now filled Jordana with a new longing. "Oh, Elohim," she whispered. "Help me return this child to her parents. But if they do not live, may I raise her?" Jordana soaked in the view one last time, before moving to the dead bodies.

The gray prince looked the largest, so she'd start with him. A leg tucked under each arm, she marched forward dragging the man behind her. Dig in, pull, breathe. Dig in, pull, breathe. She stopped a second to whistle Mamu's animal call, and then began anew.

At last she reached the river and dropped Lord Joice's legs. Her throbbing muscles screamed at her as she raced back to check on Zinnia. Still asleep. Jordana trudged back to the cremation site and rolled Lord Joice up several bamboo poles. She piled brush around him. It wasn't like the Garden Tenders did it, but she didn't have time to build a four-foot platform. Once she set it to blaze, smoke billowed into the sky. Both moons' rings now shimmered in the star-dotted firmament.

Although sitting by the Azul for a quick cry appealed at

the moment, she had no time. Jordana glanced across the river, and gasped. Many sets of green eyes pierced the darkness on the far edge of the riverbank. They crouched low in the brush. As she dropped to her knees, she unsheathed two blades

"Who are you?" A soft voice echoed over the sound of the current.

Jordana's thundering heart calmed at the voice's melodic tone. How odd that it could ease her turmoil. The words did come from the forbidden side leading to the Holy Land, and no human's eyes shinned so bright. Perhaps the creatures were Seraphim? Her pulse accelerated anew. Still, she stayed low and kept her knives poised. "I am Jordana of Arrie. Who are you?"

"I am Lainey. My brothers and sisters are with me. I'm the oldest. We heard your call. Do you bid us to cross the river to help you?"

"Hello, Lainey. From what tribe do you come?" If she said Chinzu, Jordana would aim her blades at each set of glowing orbs.

Eyes like two sparkling emeralds moved forward, but they stayed low and did not stand up. Perhaps they were as leery of her, as she was of them.

The same voice spoke again. "We have no tribe. We live in the Forbidden Falls Territory. We're descendants of the Great Tarbu. From what tribe do you hail?" Lainey's words purred at Jordana.

Tarbu? There was nothing about him in the ancient scrolls. Or about any people allowed to live in the Forbidden Territory. "No tribe for me, either. I used to belong to the Tree Warrior Village, but not anymore." Perhaps Tarbu had been banished decades ago along with his wife, and they begot many descendants, founding their own small village. Until Lord Joice and Zinnia today, Jordana had not spoken to another human since her banishments. Three years alone was long enough. Could Jordana join the Tarbu clan? At last she might find a place to belong.

"May we cross to you?" Only Lainey spoke, her siblings

22

had yet to utter a word.

"Yes." Jordana stood.

"We can't move until you put your weapons away," Lainey said.

Jordana had forgotten about her knives and holstered both daggers. "Sorry. Please join me." How did they see her knives from all the way over there? Did the bonfire's flames glint off her blades? Or did Lainey have special eyesight? *Wait.* "How did you know I needed help?"

At her right, a male voice cut through the night. "We heard your whistle."

Jordana snapped around. Two guppy-green eyes sparkled under some brush not ten feet away. First Stealthy entered her clearing undetected, and now this stranger had drawn close without giving her the slightest inkling. Could she be losing her skill of early detection? Banished and alone, acute awareness was crucial to survival.

The male crawled toward her without standing up. Or perhaps Lainey's people were even shorter than the Garden Tenders.

Seconds later, from out of the darkness stepped the biggest black panther Jordana had ever seen. "I'm Ojai."

Jordana shrieked and scurried back, tripping over a bamboo pole and landing on rocks. Adrenalin surged into her veins, as she tried to scoot away.

The panther sprang to her side. "Are you hurt?" Slanted eyes blinked inches from her face. "Grab hold of my fur and see if you can stand."

Grappling for words, and still as a stone, she couldn't even reach for a weapon. A panther spoke to her? Movement drew her attention. Several cats closed in around her, each having various shades of green irises—lime, chartreuse, jade. Jordana zeroed in on the emerald spheres in the center of the group. Then water droplets flung at her face.

All heads turned toward a large feline shaking its fur. The cat stilled, head inching around. "Oh, sorry, Lainey. I probably shouldn't have done that. You know I hate the water. It's—"

"Silence." The emerald-eyed panther swung back to Jordana. "I am Lainey. Are you injured? Have you broken your sticks?"

"Sticks? What?" Jordana pushed up, and brushed herself off.

"Your stick-legs are skinny like snapping twigs—not powerful like a leopard's."

Ojai moved even closer. "I do not know how humans can run on those things."

"My leg muscles are strong." Jordana flexed a quad.

The pride moved in, planting their noses on her skin, sniffing at her legs and knees. One cat ran its tongue across her ankle. The tickling sensation made Jordana giggle.

"Enough." Lainey commanded. One by one, each feline inched back. "Forgive us, Jordana of no tribe, but we have often wondered how humans can survive on thin sticks for legs. We have never spoken to a human before. We've only seen them from afar." She plunked her bottom down and blinked up at Jordana.

Ojai nudged under Jordana's dangling arm. "Sorry for frightening you." He kept walking so her hand ran along the length of his spine.

The panther's silky fur delighted Jordana's fingertips. Maybe later she could bury her hands in his shinny coat. For now, she kept still.

The pride parted and another feline sauntered forward. Each huge paw placed in a slinky crisscross pattern. The shade of the cat's eyes reminded Jordana of the moss hanging near the swamps. The panther turned before reaching Jordana and sashayed away while swaying her long, thick tail across Jordana's neck. "I'm Tanga." The feline purred.

"Stop showing off, Tanga." A tall and skinny cat pranced forward. "She's hoping you'll notice her tail. It's the longest in our pride." This panther had a high-pitched voice. "I'm a fast and graceful jumper so they call me Zelle, as in gazelle." She bunted her head on Jordana's thigh, and rubbed it back and forth.

Jordana giggled. "I've never heard of a panther named after a gazelle. Of course, I've never talked to animals before."

"We're not panthers." A low growl sounded from the back of the group. "We're black leopards."

The deep voice rattled Jordana's bones. "My mistake. Sorry." She searched for the one who spoke.

"Tis fine, child," said Lainey. "Under the moons, you cannot tell. But on the morrow, you shall see we have brown spots under black tips."

"I've never touched such soft fur before. Your glossy coats are fantastic. Even in darkness, your fur shimmers like the bark of a purple palm."

"Yes, our fur is magnificent like the sacred Tamar." Above her head, Tanga's tail whipped back and forth.

"I've never talked to a human before. Why do you do this?" Zelle's lips curled up revealing sharp white fangs.

Jordana laughed. "It's called a smile. It's how humans show joy. But on you it's a little scary."

"Outta the way, Zelle." The same deep voice from moments ago chased the jovial moment away. A stocky leopard with thick legs and huge paws, bore down on her. He stopped a foot short, and tipped his head. "I am Beast." He let out a powerful roar.

All moisture drained from Jordana's mouth. She could almost see the muscles flex in his powerful jaw.

"You need not be frightened of me, if you're a follower of Elohim." Beast's gaze seemed to search into her soul.

"I am," she whispered. In awe of the wonderful news or from the dangerous creature in front of her, she did not know. Of course, she shouldn't be surprised to learn the leopard pride followed Elohim. Who else could make animals talk and allow them live in the Forbidden Falls Territory? She swallowed hard. "Are all of you worshipers of Elohim?"

"Yes, human. We're His gatekeepers. Tis why we've come." Beast trotted away. "Finish the introductions, so we may get on with it."

"Twins. Stop playing and come meet the human." Lainey peered at Jordana. "Please forgive the yearlings. They do not understand what an honor this is."

"The honor is mine." Jordana struggled to keep her mouth from hanging ajar as she conversed with the leopard family.

Bounding forward, two small cats blinked eyes the color of limes and rushed to Jordana's legs. They flanked her, wrapping their tails around her calves, and snuggling into her bare skin. Their whiskers tickled.

"I'm Tut." One of the yearlings said.

"And I'm Simi. We're twins, but he's a boy, and I'm a girl."

"I can tell." Unable to resist the temptation any longer, Jordana bent and buried her hands in their napes. She rubbed their ears like she had done so many times to the village kittens back home.

Tut and Simi purred and closed their eyes.

"Enough." Beast chased the twins off. "Why did you bid us to come, human?"

Jordana frowned. "I whistled the animal tune of my mamu. Is that what you mean?" She puckered her lips and blew it out again.

"Yes." Lainey's ears twitched toward every jungle sound, but her gaze stayed glued to Jordana. "We heard your whistle and came to the Azul. Tis forbidden to cross unless summonsed by a human for Elohim's work. Only Ojai is allowed because he's our scout. He followed your whistle to make sure it was safe."

"Oh my." Jordana raised a hand to her mouth. She wished Mamu could see this. "No one's actually seen the animal call answered before."

"You've never seen animals before?" Graceful Zelle glided forward.

"Yes, yes, but none of the animals on this side of the

Azul speak. And I've never been across to Elohim's Holy Land."

"Are there others with you?" Beast's deep voice caused her to jump. His tone was the complete opposite of Lainey's soothing melody.

"No, I'm alone." Jordana froze, then gasped. "Zinnia." She sprinted into the jungle, ignoring the ferns and bushes whacking her shins as she raced the short distance, her path illuminated by the glowing orange fungi.

Inside the baby-stall, Zinnia slept with knees curled up under her tummy, and bottom in the air.

"She's okay. Praise Elohim." Jordana clutched her heart. If she were to keep the child, she had a lot to learn about parenting. A good Mamu would never leave her baby alone in the woods without a watcher. Snakes. Baboons. Jaguars. A shudder ricocheted through Jordana over what could have happened. Instant tears pooled in her eyes as her throat swelled. *Thank you, Elohim, for protecting Zinnia. Forgive my failure.*

A half dozen leopard heads leaned over the baby-stall and sniffed the air.

"I rescued her." Jordana extended her arm and pointed at the clearing. "From the evil giants over there. They plundered my village and kidnapped this baby." Jordana dropped her hand. "They planned to return to my tribe and kidnap all of our women. I had to stop them."

Beast growled and bared his teeth. "You said you have no tribe. Why do you lie?"

Ojai leapt between Jordana and Beast. "Let her explain."

"I'm not lying. I used to belong to the Tree Warrior Village, but not anymore. Tree warriors are a people of red hair like me and this baby." Her hands trembled atop her weapons, but she didn't withdraw any. Yet. "I had to save this girl, and I must warn my former village."

Each leopard blinked at her. None uttered a word.

Once again Jordana's stomach churned. Would Elohim's gatekeepers understand what she did? She sucked in a deep breath and jutted out her chin. "I killed the giants. Five men lay

27

slain because of me. One of them is the son of the Chinzu King. He will send war to avenge his son."

CHAPTER THREE

Jordana stood still, waiting for them to judge her. She deserved whatever guilty verdict the leopards would render. Could it be worse than her own condemnation? Another stab pierced her heart over killing the giants.

Lainey chased the strained silence away, her slanted emerald eyes shining in the dark like green candles. "So you rescued the child and wish to save your people. How may we be of aid?"

"This child stinks." Tanga broke the tension. "Zelle, go fetch Ariel and the nursemaid."

Zelle bounded away, but Beast and Ojai had yet to move. They stared each other down.

Jordana licked her lips, thankful for Ojai's defense of her. But could he best the massive size of Beast?

The twins skidded into the area. "Come quick. The men we saw last week are lying dead in a clearing."

Jordana's heart raced like it had been all day. First the baboons, then spying the men, slaying them, dragging one to the riverbank, then facing a pride of panthers—nay—black leopards, and defending herself to a talking beast. Now she must show them the evidence of her dastardly actions. She should be used to life or death fights in the wild. As she gazed around the silky black faces, Jordana filled her voice with a false bravado. "Follow me. I shall show you." Without waiting for their reply, she spun and strode into the clearing.

As straight as she could make herself stand, Jordana pointed. "I killed these men. I must burn their bodies at the riverbank. Can you help me drag them down there?"

Beast circled the giants, sniffing, and inspecting their wounds. At last he stood in front of her. "You are a fine warrior. These men are much larger than you. I am impressed with your skill."

"I'm not. I've never killed a human before. Tree warriors live in peace with the Garden Tenders, trading goods and honoring each other's territory. From time to time, a band of outcasts might raid a village, and the Arrdock would dispatch a hunting party. Only the best of the tribesmen go. Never a woman, even though I've never lost a knife challenge to a man. I've only killed animals before, never a—" She stopped mid-sentence, realizing what she just said. *Oh bats!*

Silence filled the air, until at last, Tanga swished her tail in front of Jordana's face. "Us too. Animals only. Never a human."

Beast emitted a low sputter. Laughter perhaps?

Jordana let out the breath she had been holding, and nodded.

"Let's get to work." Lainey barked instructions to her siblings. "Everyone sink your fangs into a leg. We'll drag the men to the banks of the Azul. Jordana you go on ahead and prepare the fires."

The lime-eyed twins pounced on one of the giants, and omitted squeaky growls.

"No, Tut and Simi." Lainey stepped in and nudged them away with the top of her head. "Go to the river and wait for Ariel and the others. Bring Nurse up to tend to Jordana's baby."

She stopped cold. *Jordana's baby?* If only Zinnia could be her baby. She shook her head, as she veered by the baby stall to check on her charge. She ought not to wish for another woman's child. Zinnia's family must be heartsick over losing such a precious jewel. Did the woman die protecting her daughter? *Elohim, if Zinnia's mother is wounded, please heal her. If she lives, lead me to her.*

Zinnia whimpered and squished up her face to cry.

Jordana lifted the child and patted her back while bouncing her.

In an instant, Zinnia quieted and leaned back to gaze at Jordana.

Tut sat on the path watching them.

Simi strode close. "She's so beautiful. Can I smell her?"

"She's about the prettiest thing I've ever seen." Jordana squatted and held out the child, while leaning back on her haunches.

Both cubs closed in, planting their noses on Zinnia's perfect skin.

Round rosy cheeks and angelic eyes blinked back. The child's dark lashes reminded Jordana of Benjura's lashes. All Tree Warriors had varying shades of red hair, strawberry blond, to dark auburn and pale eyelashes. But not Benjura. His dark lashes and rich auburn hair made him stand out. As if he needed any help. Queen Brin had dark lashes too, but only because she colored the tips with black kohl.

Heat surged into Jordana's veins. It took work to keep her mind away from the woman who had stolen so much from her. Jordana shook off the evil woman's image and gazed back at the midnight blue eyes of sweet Zinnia. Trusting and innocent. Jordana kissed the baby's forehead, and prayed again for Zinnia's safe return to her mother's arms. But if Zinnia were now an orphan, Jordana would keep her and raise her to worship Elohim. Would the Arrdock permit it? A wave of dizziness passed through Jordana and she reached out to the closest tree trunk to steady herself.

Zinnia's strawberry curls shimmered and freckles could already be seen across the bridge of her nose. She reached for Simi and wrapped her arms around the cat's neck.

Chuckling, Jordana fell in love with the child that very second. Perhaps hiding her before entering the village would allow Jordana to search for grieving parents. She could make

31

discrete inquiries to see if the parents lived. If not, she'd keep the baby without asking the Arrdock's permission. Banished, alone, no way to meet a husband, this might be her only chance at motherhood. And the baby's only hope to learn the worship of Elohim alone. Yes, Jordana must keep this baby if her parents are gone.

She stood up, hugging the baby close. "Please, Elohim, let not this child's mind absorb any of what happened today. Give me safe passage into the Tree Warrior Village. Help me find Zinnia's family. Grant me audience and favor with the Arrdock." Jordana bowed low to the ground, supporting Zinnia's head. "We pray only to you, the Great Creator. May it be so."

"May it be so." Both twins chimed in.

Mind settled, Jordana straightened. As long as air filled her lungs, she'd only worship Elohim. And if the baby's parents were gone, she'd teach Zinnia to do the same.

The baby closed her eyes and sucked her fist.

Jordana laid her on the zebra fur. "Simi, will you stay here and watch Zinnia for me?"

"Yes." The kitten spun a circle and panted. "Can I climb in with her?"

Jordana frowned. "It would help to keep her warm. But no licking. That will keep her awake, and Zinnia needs to sleep."

Simi nodded.

"What can I do?" Tut licked his chops.

"Will you escort me back to the river and help me find the nursemaid that Tanga talked about?"

"Oh yes, I forgot about Lainey's orders to do that." He popped up and bound away. "Follow me." Tut's coat shimmered in the moons' light, reminding Jordana of dark water sparkling under the stars.

The orange glow of fungi helped light the path. The rainforest came alive at night, with neon mushrooms and blue pollen puffing out from the orange flowers they brushed against while passing. Tonight might be the first night since her banishments that Jordana walked close to the plants and admired their beauty. Most nights were spent on a high perch, weapons ready, and covered in mud to conceal her scent.

At the Azul's bank, Jordana squinted at the scene. Near the river's center, a big leopard stretched its neck up above the water line. A cub dangled motionless in the leopard's jaw, the cub's bottom half drug in the water. Next to her, an upright patas monkey waded forward, water up to its chin, arms stretched high overhead, a little cub in each hand.

"Don't just stand there gawking." The monkey barked at Jordana. "Wade out here and help me before I go under."

"Sorry." Jordana scrambled in, waded out, and reached for the cubs.

"No." The monkey moved the babies away from Jordana's hands. "Turn around and squat down. I need to climb on your back."

Jordana obeyed, not questioning the monkey spouting orders at her. Of course the primate would want to ride on her back. Why had Jordana not realized that? She smiled as wet fury legs wrapped around her waist and two arms hung over her shoulders. Jordana held the monkey as she stood and waded to shore, then crouched to let the monkey scramble down, all while clutching a cub in each hand.

"I'm Kamali. I'm a patas monkey and nursemaid to these triplet cubs." She set the two down, and the cubs clambered away.

The rest of the pride emerged from the tree-line dragging the remaining dead men. They dumped the bodies near the burning embers around Lord Joice's cremated remains.

"What next?" Lainey faced Jordana.

"More wood for—" She stopped mid-sentence as flying water pelted her face. Again.

Still holding the cub in her jaw, the newest leopard shook her fur clean of all water. She set the cub at Jordana's feet, and came up licking her own nose. "So, you're the human who called us. I'm Ariel. These are my triplets."

"I'm Jordana. It's an honor to meet you." Jordana didn't

33

know if it was appropriate, but she curtsied. "Thank you for coming to my rescue."

"You don't look like you need rescuing. Except..." Ariel's gaze fell to Jordana's legs.

Lainey interrupted them. "The rest of you drag in wood, sticks, and fallen bamboo." The pride scampered away.

The patas monkey wobbled to stand next to Ariel. Her orange head bobbing, along with her white face and mustache as she ambled.

Jordana rested her hand over her heart. "I'm honored to meet all of you, and am thankful for your help. Kamali, I hope you can teach me how to properly care for a child."

Lainey tipped her head at the rainforest. "Jordana has a human child. Kamali, please look after her while we take care of important work. Come, let me show you." Lainey leveled her emerald eyes at Jordana. "Fire. Now."

"Yes, ma'am." Jordana set to work, while Lainey led the rest of them away. Now alone on the riverbank, she marveled at the miracle she'd witnessed this night. Animals who spoke like humans helped her. *Amazing.* These animals guarded Elohim's Holy Land. Perhaps when their crusade had ended, Jordana and Zinnia could join Lainey, Kamali, and the pride.

Jordana hacked down tall bamboo trunks. When both arms were full, she followed the orange fungi back to the riverbank. After dropping her load, she arranged the poles in a crisscross pattern, trying to build up the platform enough to get air under the fire.

The twins pranced to Jordana with mouthfuls of sticks. Beast, Zelle, Tanga, and Ojai emerged dragging large boughs in their powerful jaws. They spit out their haul near the bodies. Tanga set to licking her paws and cleaning her face.

Zelle sprang to Jordana's side. "What's next?"

Her high-pitched voice made Jordana question the Leopard's age.

"I'm almost two," Zelle answered as if she read Jordana's mind. "How old are you?"

34

Jordana winced. "This hot season marks my nineteenth year."

Jordana moved to the crowd of leopards. "I'll need two long poles to roll the bodies up to top of this platform. Then we must pile wood around them. Once it's set up correctly, I'll set it on fire."

"You heard the human." Beast echoed from behind them. He tromped over to a bamboo log, bit in, and pulled it over.

Ojai brought a second one, and the rest of the pride lined up. Using their heads, they helped Jordana roll the first body up—the archer, followed by Boar, Hoag, and the final packer.

She built a fire around all four corpses, piling brush under and atop them. It was a nauseating job, but it must be done. She swallowed the bile bubbling up her throat. Would the bamboo poles suffice? Or would the platform collapse into the sand with the cremation only half finished? She shoved more and more sticks into any open spaces. Soon the massive platform blazed with flames and rising smoke.

No desire to watch the cremation, Jordana strode back to the clearing and riffled through the giants' packs. She set aside their weapons and any supplies she could use later. Once the baby reunited with her family and the Chinzu army was stopped, Jordana could use some of the giant's things to improve her solitary life...unless she saved the Tree Warrior Village and they invited her to return. Jordana shrugged off the foolish hope.

Of the giant's things she could not use, Jordana marched back to the water's edge and tossed them into the bonfire.

Stench from the fire filled her nostrils, gagging her once more. Flames blazed high, at least ten feet above the massive pile of brush. Not many people ventured near the Azul's banks on the far edge of the Great Eucalyptus Forest. The crossing point into the Falls Territory elicited fear in most people. Thus, no one should be around to investigate the great bonfire. Still, it was nice to have darkness and a pride of leopards on her side.

Jordana pivoted to the river to wash her hands, and discovered each pride member standing in two or three inches of water. Their various shades of green eyes sparkled in the fire glow. None spoke as they stared at the flames.

"What's wrong?" Jordana asked the group.

Zelle fell in next to her. "Fire's about the only thing that frightens us. We have faith, but standing in the water helps too."

"I understand." Jordana grinned at the young cat.

The corners of Zelle's lips curled up revealing her sharp, three-inch fangs as she tried to smile back.

Jordana chuckled. How will that go over when they enter the Tree Warrior Village?

CHAPTER FOUR

Jordana waded into the Azul behind the pride and washed soot from her face and hands, all the while, she praised Elohim for sending her a miracle. Once finished, she moved next to Zelle.

Lainey emerged from the trees. "Kamali wants one of your baby's diapers. She's not happy with you."

"Uh oh." Jordana rushed over to the branch where her clothes and Zinnia's diaper lay drying near the fire. She pulled everything down, and hustled up the short path with Lainey trailing behind.

"Are there any more urgent tasks to be done this night? I wish to hear your plan."

"Just one." Jordana hollered over her shoulder, which seemed silly, given the superior hearing cats held over humans. "Also, I have many questions and need your wise counsel."

Jordana strode straight to the baby stall, but it was empty, even the zebra skin was gone. She sprinted to the clearing.

"There you are." Kamali tromped in a back and forth waddling motion. She ripped the small cloth from Jordana's hand. "There are welts on this baby's bottom. How long did you leave her in a dirty diaper? And what is the meaning of this?" Kamali shook her finger at the zebra fur spread out next to the campfire.

"Isn't it cruel?" Jordana motioned in the direction of the river. "It belonged to those evil giants."

Kamali harrumphed and made quick work of diapering Zinnia, then raised the baby to nurse from Kamali's own breast. And yet, the primate didn't have an infant monkey with her, only Ariel's triplets. Jordana would ask Lainey privately what happened to Kamali's baby patas.

Human milk, coconut milk, and now monkey milk. Jordana hoped variety would make Zinnia stronger and not cause an upset tummy.

Jordana stepped close to Lainey. "Can your pride help me dig a deep hole? I have no shovel or claws." Jordana held out her hands, palms down, displaying the shortness of her fingernails. "I must bury the men's packs and weapons, and conceal all evidence of their passing through this area. Then we should all get some sleep. Tomorrow will be a long day of travel. Can you and I can talk when everyone has settled in?"

Lainey frowned. "Why not burn their possessions in the fire?"

"Some items are very valuable and will greatly assist me in war."

"War? You?" Lainey's big cat eyes dropped to gaze again at Jordana's legs.

"Yes. I'll explain once everyone goes to sleep." Jordana turned and explored the ground under some brush and vines. "This area should work for digging."

Soon Lainey had Tut and Simi scratching in the dirt while Beast supervised. Zelle and Ojai dug as well, forming a long trench-like hole.

Jordana first laid the men's bows at the bottom, then stuffed all the weapons of Lord Joice and his men into the pack Hoag had carried. Except one of the hatchets. After wrapping it in a leather cloth, she placed it at the bottom of her satchel. Anything else of value—golden goblets, a large metal pot, leather poncho, and water skin—were stuffed in the packs and cast into the hole. Jordana turned to Tut and Simi. "Can you cover it up with dirt and leaves so no one can see it?"

"Yes," they purred in unison.

While they finished the chore, Jordana pulled up all the sticks for the baby stall and tossed them in the remaining fire. She grabbed a bamboo pole to churn the embers, making sure all evidence of Lord Joice and his men, were destroyed.

Tasks complete, Lainey instructed her pride to settle down for the night.

Jordana lost sight of each dark figure as they disappeared into the tree tops, Kamali too, as she clutched Zinnia and swung high into the jungle's canopy. Only Jordana and Lainey remained in the clearing.

"Come." Jordana led Lainey to her favorite white neplar. She swung her satchel over her head and one shoulder, then climbed back up to the large branch where she had been when her peaceful day had come to a screeching halt. Again, she secured the pack at her back, and nestled into the crook of the snow-colored trunk.

Directly above, Lainey plunked down on a heavy limb, her massive paws straddling the branch and dangling inches above Jordana's head. Lainey's chin rested on the branch, her slanted eyes peering down.

Jordana had never seen an emerald as beautiful at Lainey's eyes—eyes that pulled her in. "I don't know where to begin. I have so many questions about the Falls Territory and Elohim. I'm not sure which task is most prudent—should I hurry in the morning to warn the Tree Warrior Village of a coming war, or wait here while you cross back and ask Elohim for instructions? Is it far to His home in the Holy Land?" She inhaled a deep breath. "Do your eyes glow brighter than any animal on this side of the Azul because you are in Elohim's presence? What is He like? Do any other animals speak like humans? Why did Elohim allow the Chinzu's army to pass through His Forbidden Territory? Who destroyed a sacred palm?"

Lainey's purr grew louder and came in spurts. It sounded similar to the noise Beast emitted earlier in the evening. Jordana wanted to ask if it was laughter, but Lainey's words stopped her.

39

"Elohim does not dwell in the Holy Land."

"What?" Jordana sat up, bumping her head on Lainey's dangling paw. Good thing the cat's claws were retracted. "Why's it called Elohim's Holy Land if He does not live there?"

"Elohim visits often, but His home is not on this planet, child. He lives in the paradise He created for His followers. One day, when we move away from Tzuri, we will dwell there with Him. Some of our family is there already. Twill be wonderful to reunite."

Lainey's voice soothed Jordana, like a lullaby her mother would sing.

"Elohim's Holy Land is only a small area in the center of the Falls Territory. It is sacred because Elohim visits often. I do not know all of what it contains, as I have never been invited to enter. Many times I have gazed through the gate at its beauty— its flowers and fruit are far superior to ours. The Holy Land contains springs, pools, an altar, and other duplicates of the real paradise."

"I've heard those stories."

Lainey said, "All of the land was sacred at one time, but after the great fall, Elohim set aside that area as His holy remnant. He assigned sentries to guard its entrance and crafted mighty waterfalls around the holy place as a reminder of mankind's dreadful fall from His presence. Elohim placed many types of animals in the Falls Territory as gatekeepers to the Holy Land. All the prides guard at night. Mountain sheep and rams keep watch during the day. Many species of birds soar above the land. Eagles, bamboo partridge, and hawks patrol by day, with owls and bats keeping watch at night. There's always a multitude of flying creatures spying at all times."

As Jordana settled in, she committed to memory the details Lainey shared.

"Elohim set up different animals with specific duties and territories to protect. All the gatekeepers speak. But most animals in the Falls Territory do not. We are only allowed to hunt non-speakers. All the speaking animals work together to guard the

Holy Land in the center of the waterfalls. We worship Elohim at the Holy Land's entrance during the Season of Atonement."

A stab sliced through Jordana's heart. Her village had stopped honoring the atonement season when Father married Brin. Perhaps the Arrdock would resume it after a successful war against the Chinzu army.

A mighty roar cut through the night, startling Jordana.

"Don't be frightened, child. Ojai is sounding off our nightly ritual."

A deep roar exploded and Jordana's bones rattled. "That was Beast."

"Very good," Lainey stretched her paw out, and flexed her toes, sharp claws appeared, then retracted.

A long high roar sounded and Jordana shrugged. "I have no idea who that was."

"Twas Ariel, and Tanga will be next."

A sharp but loud roar echoed, followed by another, then two young howls screeched through the night.

Jordana chuckled. "Let me guess. Tut and Simi."

"Correct. And now Zelle will sound."

"How can you tell them apart?"

"Same as you learn to distinguish between the voices in your family, your parents and grandparents. Tis no different in an animal pride."

A roar echoed that could only be described as elegant. *Zelle.* "I think I understand." Jordana rested back against the tree.

The hoo-hoo of a monkey echoed through the trees. Kamali. Then a giant roar rang out directly above Jordana's head, shaking a sapphire leaf above her. Lainey's mighty sound was fierce, yet beautiful and comforting—a protector perched above her. Jordana sighed. Perhaps she'd get a peaceful night's sleep for the first time in three hot seasons.

The magnificent leopard's head resumed its position on the limb and she gazed back at Jordana. "Now we know exactly where everyone is at and where to go if there's a growl of trouble."

"I love your care of one another. Can I join your pride?" Jordana blurted, half serious.

Lainey omitted a staccato purr.

Feeling safe with the black leopard matriarch, Jordana dared to ask. "Did you just laugh? Is that what I heard?"

"Amusement yes, but leopards do not laugh."

Jordana's mind raced. She wanted to ask why they didn't laugh, along with a thousand other questions—did they marry, who was the father of Ariel's triplets, where was Kamali's monkey baby, and would it be permissible for Jordana to cross into the Fall Territory if she did not venture into the Holy Land? Also, why did the Holy Land need a gatekeeper if Elohim did not dwell there? But Jordana's eyes grew heavy, and she didn't yet have a plan for the morning. Best to seek Lainey's advice, pray, and sleep before devouring everything she could about life across the Azul.

"Lainey, the warrior I killed was named Lord Joice. He was the son of their Arrdock."

"What is Arrdock?"

"It's the leader of their tribe. Lord Joice called him their king. Everyone in my former tribe obeys the Arrdock and the queen, or they might be put to death. Or banished." Jordana stifled a yawn.

"Lord Joice told me his father, the King of the Chinzu Giants, would send his army to find his son. I bet the king knew exactly which way his son journeyed, which means he'll know where to send his army to search. And when the prince isn't found, the king will seek revenge."

For the first time since it happened, tears welled in Jordana's eyes. "Lord Joice said I brought war upon my people. I must go and warn them. I need to return Zinnia to the family from which she was stolen." The lump forming in her throat grew thicker. "But if Zinnia's family has been slaughtered, I wish to raise the child myself. If my Arrdock permits it."

"Admirable," Lainey said. "But seek Elohim's will on the matter first."

42

"Yes, I am, of course." Jordana licked her lips and forged on. "I've never heard of a Chinzu King of Giants. I know not from which direction across the Azul they came. We cannot let their army sweep through the Falls Territory, defiling it. And..." Jordana fell silent. What she needed to tell Lainey next might change the leopard's mind. What would Jordana do if Lainey took her pride back to the Forbidden Falls Territory, without helping her unworthy Tree Warriors?

"Go on, child. Finish."

As usual, Lainey's purr soothed Jordana. What kind of miracle quality did it hold?

Jordana spit out the last. "The Tree Warriors will not care about defending the Forbidden Falls Territory. They will only care about saving their village. They'll want to wait for Chinzu's army to cross onto this side of the Azul so they can fight from atop the trees. I don't know of any army on the ground that could defeat the Tree Warriors in their own forest. We must convince them to go out and stop the Chinzu giants from defiling Elohim's Holy Land."

Except for the cacophony of frogs and crickets, silence followed Jordana's proclamation. An occasional owl sounded in the distance. Jordana prayed Lainey would not abandon her. "I'm sorry. I wish my Tree Warrior Village would be more concerned about protecting the Holy Land than their own forest, but because of the Arrdock's wife, they will not."

Lainey said, "Elohim is more than capable of protecting His own land, child. You need not worry about that. He has an army of gatekeepers and could create more with one word."

Jordana let out the pent up breath she'd been holding. "Praise be to Elohim. I worried you'd leave me if you knew the wrong priorities of my people." Her mind raced across Lainey's words. "If Elohim will protect the Holy Land, does that mean I should not warn my village?"

"I believe your job is to alert your people. Perhaps Elohim can use this as a way to turn them back to His ways. Tomorrow, I want you to march into your camp and tell them everything that has happened."

"Well," Jordana cleared her voice. "There's a little problem with that, too. It will take two days to arrive, and when I enter the Tree Warrior Village, I shall be pierced with many arrows."

Lainey gasped and her paws moved up onto the branch. "Why? Surely they'd not do that to one of their beloved." Lainey blinked at her, and when Jordana did not reply, Lainey hissed. "Out with it, child."

Belly churning, Jordana closed her eyes. "I'll be killed if I try to enter the village because I've been banished. By the Arrdock...who is my father."

CHAPTER FIVE

A high pitched growl ripped through the forest, jolting Jordana awake. She sat up and scanned the area. Lainey no longer slept on the limb above her. In the clearing below, Ariel had sprawled out and nursed her cubs while Ojai stood on a stump. He scanned the west side of the forest. Tut and Simi growled at one another, playing tug-of-war with a leafy branch. Their snarls must have been what woke Jordana.

Morning rays sliced through the branches and leaves, casting beams of light through the sparse jungle canopy all the way to the forest floor. The sight awed Jordana.

Up from the direction of the Azul River, the tip of a black tail swished back and forth above the bushes.

Just then Zelle pounced into the clearing. She leapt over a fallen trunk clutching a rabbit in her mouth. Near the twins she dropped it. "Tut and Simi, eat your breakfast." Zelle darted back into the jungle.

Tanga sauntered into the clearing carrying a bloody turkey in her mouth. She laid down, the large bird between her heavy paws, and tore into its flesh—a gruesome sight. The hunters were very skilled to find game in this area of the Great Eucalyptus Forest.

Perhaps Jordana should wait until they finished feasting before climbing down. The blood dripping from Tanga's fangs and the sound of snapping bones, kept Jordana motionless until a rustle in the adjacent trees drew her attention.

45

Kamali swung from branch to branch by one paw, two feet, and her sturdy tail. Only one hand held Zinnia to her chest, as Kamali swung at tremendous speeds.

Jordana held her breath, until they arrived safely on her branch.

"Got any fruit trees close by?" Kamali thrust Zinnia into Jordana's arms. "I'm hungry."

Jordana clutched the child and pointed in the direction of the nut grove bordered by banana trees and wild plums.

Kamali swung away without a word.

Below her, Beast, Ojai, and Lainey drug a wild boar into the clearing. All of the remaining leopards circled the fresh kill and feasted. Lainey ripped off a large back leg and gave it to Ariel, then went about eating the other rear quarter. Soon Zelle returned with another slain rabbit and kept this one for herself.

"I guess its breakfast time." Jordana dug in her pack and retrieved the remaining mango from yesterday. Its fruit was clear and she dug in while gazing upon Zinnia's precious face. "How'd you like that monkey's milk? Is your belly okay?" Jordana tickled Zinnia's tummy.

The baby giggled and flapped her arms, reminding Jordana of a baby bird.

Just then, Kamali wobbled into camp alternating bites between the plums she held in her right hand, and two peeled bananas in her left.

Jordana secured Zinnia in a wrap around her chest and inched down the tree. She greeted the leopards as she passed them, "Good morning." All the way to the Azul she paced. At the burn pile, Jordana fashioned a broom from a leafy branch and swept the evidence into the river. While Zinnia remained cocooned to Jordana in the wrap, she did everything possible to eliminate any trace of the ghastly grave.

Task complete, she unwrapped Zinnia and waded into the sparkling blue water to wash. She untied Zinnia's diaper, swished it in the water, and laid it across an overhanding branch. Next Jordana cupped water onto the child's shoulders and hair, bathing her.

Zinnia wiggled and laughed in the warm river water as Jordana swam and played with her. The Azul and various creeks throughout the Great Forest were fed by hot springs. Lainey had described snowcapped mountains overlooking the Great Falls Territory. Were their rivers and pools icy cold? She'd never seen snow or touched freezing water before. A gaze across the river to the falls side, increased her desire. *Please, Elohim, if permissible, I would love to cross over and see some of Your creation.*

Washing complete, Jordana spun around to exit the river. The entire pride sat on the bank and studying her, while licking their paws and rubbing their faces.

Lainey sat in the center of the group. Sunrays hit her back, highlighting brown spots and swirls under glossy black tips. At night, the pride appeared as black as panthers. But in the daylight, their leopard spots were distinct and magnificent. In the dark, each cats' eyes seemed to glow. During the day, they appeared like any other animals' eyes. If the leopards did not speak, no one would know they were special and set apart from other big cats. A villager might throw a spear if they spotted one of the gatekeeper-leopards striding toward a human. This side of the Azul, the pride wasn't safe.

A chill ran through Jordana as she waded out of the water. "I didn't hear you come. Sorry to make you wait for me."

Zelle's lips curled into a smile. "Why do you go in the water so much?"

Jordana couldn't help but chuckle at Zelle's happy disposition and curiosity. "Well, my tongue isn't very long, so I can't lick myself clean like you can. I have to wash off in the water."

Several cats nodded. Her answer must have made sense to them.

Jordana stood on the rocks, struggling to pull on her moccasins with one-hand while holding Zinnia on her hip with the other.

"We should get going, Kamali and your baby will come

with us, along with Beast." Lainey moved next to Jordana and issued orders to her pride. "Ariel and Tanga, I want you to take the cubs back to our side of the Azul River to wait. Ojai, you will also cross the river and travel to the outer rim. You need to find where the giants crossed into the Falls Territory. Zelle, I want you to sprint back to the dens and warn the other gatekeepers. Tell them to set sentries around the perimeter of the Falls Territory, and send more scouts to help Ojai. We must determine from what direction the Chinzu army will come."

One by one, Jordana rested her gaze on each pride member. "Thank you for helping me. I'm not sure what will happen next, but the Chinzu army must be stopped."

"How long will you be gone?" Zelle leapt up on the rocks near Jordana.

"Two days journey each way," she said. "One or two days in the village of my Tree Warriors. Plan on a week."

Tanga's ears perked. "What should we do if we see a group of humans trying to enter the Forbidden Falls Territory?"

"Hide. Listen for any words of plotting, but mostly hide." Jordana raised a hand. "The five warriors I encountered were awful men. What they had planned for my tribe..." Jordana shook her head. "They were strong and cruel, with mighty weapons. Even with your prowess, we'll need a great number of fighters to defeat the Chinzu giants."

"We're not afraid." Tut's chest puffed out. "If you can slay five from atop your skinny sticks, we can each kill ten."

Jordana raised her voice. "I have no doubt. The problem is you won't get ten men separated from packs of hundreds of men. Against a massive number, you can't win. I must enlist the help of the Tree Warriors. Together, we will defeat the enemies of Elohim."

Several members of the pride roared or growled, as if to cheer her. Jordana's hopes soared. Now if she can just convince the Tree Warriors.

Within minutes, the pride separated into two groups heading in opposite directions. Jordana stretched up and waved goodbye to Tanga, Ariel, and the twins. Ojai and Zelle had already sprinted off. In her group, Lainey walked beside Jordana, with Beast and Kamali behind them. Kamali rode on Beast's back, her toes digging into his fur, and her tail wrapped around his stomach. The Pastas Monkey coddled Zinnia at they rode.

* * *

Late the next day, Jordana stopped on the edge of a large meadow. She led the small group into a cave carved through granite boulders. "We're approaching the edge of the Tree Warrior Territory. I'd like Kamali to wait here with Zinnia. Beast, would you stay and protect them? I need to sneak to the outpost across the meadow. If my old friend is on duty, I think he'll give me safe passage to the Arrdock."

Jordana faced Lainey. "I'm hoping you'll come with me, but at a distance. I don't want you to show yourself unless necessary. Stay hidden. If you're spotted, they may see you as a threat, firing dozens of arrows your way. They won't realize you're not a wild beast hunting near their village."

"I'll stay hidden in the trees. No one will see me." A straight line of fur down Lainey's back stood on end.

"Remember, they're in the trees too." As Jordana wrung her hands, she paced. "I need to find the couple missing their baby, and send for Zinnia. But if the child's parents were killed in the raid leaving no relatives, I shall keep her hidden from the tribe and raise her to worship Elohim."

"Why?" Kamali climbed off Beast's back.

Jordana shot a look at Lainey. She had told the leopard leader about her plight. Should she now tell the others?

Lainey locked eyes with Jordana, then veered to Beast and Kamali. "The Tree Warriors will want the baby raised in their ways and inside the safety of their village. They would not allow Jordana to keep Zinnia in the wild if the child has lost her parents."

Beast's gaze darted between Lainey and Jordana. "Is that

49

not better for the child? Why doesn't Jordana return to the Tree Warrior Village, and raise the human child in the ways of her people?"

Jordana blinked at him. If Beast knew how far the Tree Warriors had fallen from Elohim, would he still want to help? Would he understand how much she loved her tribesmen, despite their banishment of her and abandonment of Elohim? She didn't even understand, but couldn't let them get wiped out by giants.

"No more questions. It'll be dark soon. Let's go, Jordana. It would be nice if you could meet with your Arrdock tonight so we can return tomorrow. I don't want to be separated from the rest of the pride any longer than we must." Lainey trotted away.

Beast's eyes narrowed at Jordana, but he said nothing. He probably sensed something. She just nodded before spinning away. "May Elohim keep you safe." Jordana jogged to catch up with Lainey. Partway across the meadow, she glanced over her shoulder. From afar, Beast stood watching, and probably still glaring at her.

Meadow crossed, they entered the tree line. Black spider veins covered the ground and coiled up many trees. More evidence of someone defiling a sacred palm. Jordana led Lainey through thick vegetation toward the outer post. When first banished, she had stayed in that area for weeks, watching Benjura from afar. She never approached him. Too great a risk for them both.

It took many moons for her to dig up the courage to leave the area for good. She had waited for the Garden Tenders to arrive for the annual trade gathering, then followed them back to their village. She asked if she could live and work with them. The Garden Tenders had welcomed her, but the first two weeks were strained. Things soured the third, and by the fourth, she would have left on her own if they hadn't kicked her out. They told her never to return. She had no trouble leaving them.

Jordana had met the Garden Tenders many times during the trade gatherings. But she had no idea their ways were so different and primitive. Everything she did was wrong, every suggestion offensive, and when they caught her cooking meat from a quail she had killed, they thought her a cannibal. They banished her, too. At least the Garden Tenders didn't conduct an official, humiliating ceremony like she had endured from her beloved kinsmen.

A familiar stab sliced through Jordana's heart. No one in the tribe came after her. Not even Benjura. Only Granna asked to join Jordana, but was denied. Life in the wild would be too difficult for someone of her grandmother's age. Jordana glanced heavenward. Thanks to Elohim alone, she survived these last three hot seasons. She did not need a people who didn't care what happened to her. She only needed the Creator.

Jordana returned her focus to the task ahead. After traveling another mile in the woods, she crouched over to Lainey's ear. "We're very close now. The post is concealed up ahead in the shorter treetops. You should take to the trees back here. I'll move up ahead and scale one of those tall moose trees." Jordana pointed and Lainey's gaze followed her motion.

Jordana whispered more to the pride leader. "Moose trees are connected by thick entwining limbs. They'll allow me to crawl pretty close, but at a turtle's pace. If even a twig snaps, the guard will pounce. At sunset, Benjura should come on duty. If he's alone, I'll make contact. If I scream for you, come. Otherwise stay back here no matter what. When everything is set, I'll sneak back to let you know if Benjura will take me to see the Arrdock."

"I'm going with you. I wish to speak to your leader as well."

"It's too dangerous. Please trust me on this."

"No child," Lainey whiskers twitched. "Elohim wishes it."

Jordana studied Lainey's eyes. Perhaps this was the answer to her prayers. A talking black leopard might be the miracle she needed to present. Jordana gasped. Why hadn't she remembered the ancient decree? Heart soaring, she almost dropped to wrap her arms around Lainey's neck when another

51

thought hit her. She couldn't return if bowing to Elohim was still forbidden. But might the Arrdock reinstate Elohim worship after speaking to one of His gatekeepers? Oh, to reconcile her village to Elohim… *Please let it be so.* She kissed the top of Lainey's head, then whispered in her ear. "Bless you."

"And you, child." Lainey's gritty tongue licked Jordana's cheek.

CHAPTER SIX

Jordana inched across the wide, fuzzy branch of a moose tree. Each movement slow and delicate to insure a soundless crawl to the outpost.

The obscure structure had been crafted into a tree. Bark covered the outside walls, with leafy boughs concealing the roof. Near impossible to see if one didn't know where to look, the outpost circled the tree forty feet off the ground. It had enough room to house several people and a bevy of weapons. Twelve evenly dispersed outposts surrounded the Tree Warrior Village. A single guard patrolled the huge gaps between each station. Twenty-four sentries around the village seemed like overkill, as they lived in peace with their only neighbor. On the other hand, it would be easy to slip into the village between stations at night. Jordana could do it—had done it when first banished, just for a glimpse of Granna or Benjura.

Her throat clenched. What would he say when he saw her again? Could she hold her tongue?

Jordana's noiseless motions ended about ten yards from his outpost—if it was the one Benjura still manned. Purple and orange streaks filled the sky, evidence of the sun's descent. It wouldn't be long before the nightly guard rotation. Crouched on a sturdy branch, she leaned forward on her haunches, inched open a thick curtain of cascading vines, and crawled inside. From there she could view whoever strolled up the path.

She slid her hand into the leather pouch and pulled out a

slice of dried antelope. Slow and quiet, she chewed on the jerky. As she finished it, footfalls sounded on the forest floor. Dusk encased the area. Jordana squinted at the path below, her pulse picking up speed.

A tall figure emerged from the brush line with a large falcon balanced on his shoulder. The man's gait mimicked Benjura's, but she'd never known him to have any interest in birds. The figure drew closer, dressed in the typical Tree Warrior garb of a sleeveless leather tunic to his hips and breechcloth. The warrior had dark auburn hair like Benjura, with a bow on his back, and a harness of five knives strapped to each leg. Each large leg. The man's shoulders were also wide and muscular, with bulging biceps.

Jordana's heart sunk. Although the same height and walk as Benjura, this man was more heavily muscled. It couldn't be him. Now what was she supposed to do?

A low whistle escaped the man's lips and his falcon took to flight, swooping to the top of the outpost roof. "Come down, Tubow. I'm here."

Every hair on Jordana's body stood up as a shiver raced across her skin. The familiar voice brought tears to her eyes. Jordana blinked them back, not knowing if they had appeared out of relief or longing. She buried the emotions. Now wasn't the time.

"You're late, Benjura." The warrior at the outpost shimmied down the tree.

"Naw. You're just anxious to get home to your new bride." Benjura smiled at the other man, his perfect teeth gleaming white under the rising moons.

"That's right, so hustle up so I can take my leave."

Benjura sped up the tree trunk. As soon as his feet hit the outpost floor, the other man trotted down the path.

"Goodnight." Benjura called, as he set his bow down and circled the outer deck. He scanned each direction before extending his arm. The falcon flew from the atop the watch tower, to Benjura's cuff. "Stand guard now." Benjura fed something to his pet.

Jordana studied the man she hadn't seen in three years. He had changed so much. He filled out. His dark auburn hair hung lower too. But his face had changed not. Clean shaven, sturdy jaw, straight nose, and golden brown eyes. In the dark she could not see the honey flecks filling his hazel irises, but she remembered them well. He'd always been her buddy and training partner who pushed her farther than any teacher could. Until one day his warm gaze fell on her in a way that made her insides come alive. The memory of his radiant face had both warmed her and haunted her these last three years.

She wanted to cry. She wanted to hit him. She wanted to run into his arms. Instead Jordana didn't move. Still as a rock, she watched the man for a good half hour. No sweetheart came to visit him, like she'd done so many dry seasons ago. He turned twenty this year, surely he had a wife and children by now.

Her fists clenched and she leaned back into the trunk of the tree. Far more important issues were at hand than her personal feelings. Eyes closed, she forced her fingers to relax, and forgave him all over again. *Forgive my bitterness and help me let it go, Elohim. Grant us favor in the Arrdock's sight. What I must ask Benjura to do could cost his life and mine. Protect us both, I pray, amen.*

Jordana leaned through the vines, unable to delay any longer. The night sky had turned black. She whispered, "Benjura." Her voice barely audible even to her own ears.

The falcon on his arm turned her way, head cocked, and eyes fixed onto Jordana's hiding place.

"What is it, girl?" Benjura spoke to the bird.

Jordana raised her voice. "Benjura."

"Who's there? Show yourself." He unsheathed one of his blades.

"Benj, it's me."

"Who are you?"

"I used to be the only one who called you Benj." In an instant, the blood in her veins boiled.

"Jor—"

"Nay. Do not say my name. Tis forbidden."

"I don't care. Show yourself." He leaned her way, searching through the darkened woods.

"I need to speak to the Arrdock." Jordana didn't trust herself to crawl over to the outpost. There one of her impulses might win over, and she had no idea which one it would be.

"Ladybug, find." Benjura sent his falcon to flight.

The bird soared straight at her, cawed, and landed on a branch close by. No doubt it would have dive-bombed her head if not for the thick vines encircling her.

Jordana stretched a leg to the limb below her, climbed all the way down the tree, and stood under the guard tower. "Something has happened. I must speak to the Arrdock."

"It's too dangerous. You will be killed. Get out of the open, climb up here to me." Benjura motioned for her. "We can talk inside the guard tower."

Jordana didn't move. As she stared up at him, her heart thundered, but not from the falcon now circling her head.

"Please come up here. You'll be hidden and safe."

"Why? Are you expecting someone from the village to visit you?" Jordana couldn't help asking, so many questions rushing through her brain.

His voice calmed. "There's no one, Jordana." He slid down the tree, covered the ground between them in a few long strides, and pulled her into his arms. "I've missed you. Where have you been?"

She wanted to melt into his embrace. Instead she stiffened. How had he read her mind so easily? Did he think she'd been pining for him all these years? He could have done something to keep them together three years ago, but did not. His rejection obvious.

Her heart throbbed in her chest. "I need you to take me to see the Arrdock. It's urgent."

Benjura pulled back, sliding his hands up and down her arms. "No. They'll kill you. I can't bear to lose you again. I've been miserable without you."

Her heart tore at his words. His action at the banishment ceremony did not match his sentiment. She jutted out her chin. "They'll not kill me. I have a miracle to present."

Eyes wide, he stepped back and gazed over her as if searching for evidence of the miracle. Finally he grabbed her, slamming her into his chest, and hugged her tight. A low chuckled resonated. "You've come back for good, then. To be readmitted into the tribe. My prayers have been answered."

Jordana pushed away and stepped back, way back— putting distance between them. "No. I'll never return to the Tree Warrior Village as long as…." She couldn't say it aloud.

"I don't understand." Benjura ran a hand over his head. "Why perform a miracle if you do not wish to return?"

"I told you," she snapped, unable to keep anger from coloring her tone. "Something has happened. You must take me to the Arrdock. I will present a miracle. Not because I want to return to the tribe, but because I want them to fight."

"Fight? Who?"

Jordana chose not to explain, and lifted her chin another notch.

The falcon cawed above her and Benjura held out his arm. "Ladybug, land."

When the bird swooped down, she flapped her wings back, slowing her descent. The falcon landed with grace and dug her talons into the leather cuff around Benjura's forearm.

"You named your falcon Ladybug?"

"Yes. She was so tiny when I found her. I rescued her and trained her myself, with Avakian's advice of course." Benjura pet the falcon's chest.

"Avakian. The old birdman is still alive?"

"Yes."

Jordana's voice softened. "And what of my Granna?"

"She lives. For a long time after you left, your grandmother was brokenhearted. Last year your cousin grew pregnant with twins. Joy and purpose returned to your granna."

57

Jordana nodded and bit back words. She hadn't left by choice, she'd been banished with the assurance of death if she ever returned. The ancient law allowed a banished person to return if they could present a miracle. No one ever had. Did the handful of banished people before her experience physical pain deep into their heart, like she did? Her own father had been the one to banish her and at such a young age. How could he do that to his only child? How could the ones who supposedly loved her the most turn their backs on her? Jordana's throat grew as parched as a dry creek bed during the hot season.

Benjura stepped closer, imploring her with his gaze. "I'll do everything in my power to help you. You deserve my trust and allegiance. I swear them both to you. Please come up to the tower, so we may sit and you can start at the beginning." He motioned for her to climb the tree ahead of him.

She stormed to it, releasing her clenched arms, and raced up the tree. Her feet barely touched the outpost floor before his noisy foot falls sounded behind her. She spun around and followed him inside the small building.

"You've grown even more beautiful, Jordana."

"Don't call me by my name. Tis forbidden. I don't want to cause you any more harm than necessary. Please call me the Banished One, as the law requires."

"Never. You will always be Princess Jordana of Arrie to me. I have missed you."

The words he said were right, but why did her spine stiffen and her hands shake? "Let me tell you what happened, so we can get moving. I wish to see the Arrdock tonight."

Before she realized it, they sat on the floor in the same position they always had—backs to the walls opposite each other, legs outstretched side by side. She ignored their familiarity, and started at the beginning. After sharing about her encounter with the five giants, and saving the baby, Jordana said, "I must warn your leader of Lord Joice's threat. We must thwart the Chinzu Army before they cross the Falls Territory. They will defile it, and we can't chance them discovering the entrance to

Elohim's Holy Land. The Tree Warriors must come against them." She did not tell him about the gatekeepers. For now, she held that part back.

"But we haven't been attacked." Benjura motioned. "There have been no raids on our village."

"What? Are you sure?" She bolted to her feet. "The baby has red hair, fair skin, and freckles like the tree people."

"Of course I'm sure. Where's the baby now?"

She paused, realizing her failure to keep the baby secret until determining if the child's parent lived. It left a gaping hole in her story. She had to tell of the baby—why else slay the men? How else would she know the giants plan to kidnap more women? Jordana folded her arms across her chest. "Somewhere safe." It was the only answer she gave.

Benjura stood and paced the small enclosure. "I wonder if there's a small village somewhere comprised of banished warriors. Maybe they birthed children, and grew into a small community. The baby could have come from them. I had hoped you found such a place to live." He paused in front of her, his voice dropping an octave. "I feared I'd never see you again."

She ignored his underlying question. "If such a village exists, those giants have raided it. But, I know not where it is. I've never seen evidence of another tribe during my travels."

He moved closer, raising a hand to her cheek, and rubbing his thumb across her jaw. "You've been alone this whole time?"

She gave a firm nod before stepped away. "Please don't touch me like that. Much has changed." Out of the watch tower she flew and away from the intimate room with too many memories. She clasped onto the outer rail, gripping it tight as her mind raced. When he came alongside, she faced him. "My plan stays the same. The Chinzu King might not know which tree village his son and warriors raided. They may stumble onto ours...yours by mistake. They must be stopped before they enter the Falls Territory and defile it. I know not how to stop them without entering the Falls Territory myself. We must beseech

59

Elohim for guidance."

"I'm sorry for hurting you."

She squeezed her eyes shut. "Stop, Benj. Just stop. I don't want to talk about any of that right now. Let's go to the Arrdock tonight. We must focus on the difficult task ahead."

Benjura stepped back, his brows cinching together. A tense silence swelled between them. Finally, he spoke through his scowl. "You must wear your ceremonial robe when you enter. It will be a sign of your intentions. No one will shoot you or me if you're wearing the royal attire."

"It was destroyed. Ripped off me and stained at the Banishment Rite, remember?"

"Your granna picked it up and made repairs. She's been saving it in hopes of your return." He folded his arms across his chest. "Show me the miracle."

"No." Jordana wasn't about to bring Lainey to see him. Not yet anyway. "Will you get the robe? Where shall I meet you?"

"Meet at our tree in the center of the west outposts. But not tonight. We must follow the custom."

Jordana nodded. "Okay." Gratitude propelled her to speak. "Thank you for risking your life for me." *This time.* She stopped short of saying it aloud, wishing he'd done it three years ago. She shook off the thought, not willing to drudge up the past. Gaze locked onto his. "Thank you. Midmorning, then?"

"Yes." Benjura had yet to unclench his arms, his biceps bulging. So much bigger than she remembered.

Jordana tore her gaze away and swung up to an overhanging moose limb and crawled several steps away before twisting back. "Do you think you could bring me a fine sash like one on a ceremonial robe? Long and adorned with many jewels or feathers. And a head dress. The finest possible, with pins to secure it. Can you ask my granna to come up with those things?"

Benjura's chin dipped, his face emotionless.

"Good. Thank you." Jordana waited for him to reply, but he only stared at her, so she bid him goodnight once more. "See you midmorning." Head snapping around, she extended her arm to another limb when his whisper reached her.

"Have I lost you forever?"

I don't know. She couldn't bring herself to say it aloud and kept moving as if she hadn't heard him. Tears welled in her eyes, but she refused to give in to them. Or to glance back. She continued to crawl away when another whisper touched her. This one penetrated deep into her soul.

Don't let your pride get in My way.

Jordana squeezed her eyes shut and nodded. She twisted back and called out. "Does Queen Brin still live?"

"Yes," Benjura answered.

She softened her voice. "Then I can never stay here, Benjura. I'm sorry." She swung away from the one she loved so long ago, her fists tight around a thick vine. As long as the queen lived, Jordana would choose exile.

CHAPTER SEVEN

Vibrant green, blue, and orange feathers draped Jordana's shoulders and hung down to the small of her back. Below them and all the way to her calves, rare white peacock feathers fanned across the middle of the amazing princess cape. Multi-color peacock feathers of teal, purple, and blue completed the bottom and train. Magnificent!

Father and mother had presented Jordana with the regal cape on her fourteenth birthday. At the celebration, Jordana's official title had changed to Princess of Arrie. The following year things began to change with Benjura—a crush blossomed into an all-encompassing first love by her sixteenth year.

Engagements were long in the village. If she completed her Shedock studies by her seventeenth year, they could marry. None of her dreams and goals happened. Instead, Mamu fell and broke her neck. She died within an hour. Less than two months later, Brin, a lovely maiden only a handful of years older than Jordana, sunk her evil talons into father. Four moon cycles later, they married.

Brin's narcissistic changes in their village came fast. First, tribesmen were no longer permitted to say her name. Brin insisted everyone call her Queen. Not even Shedock was good enough. Then Brin made it illegal for the people to speak directly to her, even when standing a foot away. Villagers could only address the Queen through her attendants, as if everyone else was beneath her. No Arrdock or Shedock before her had dared to request such an egotistical thing.

One day Jordana left on a hunt, returning to find Brin's sister living in Jordana's tree house. Jordana and Granna had been moved farther out in the village, along with the rest of mother's family. Brin brought her own kin into the Arrdock's fortress. Father only laughed, as if entertained by his young wife's antics.

When Brin insisted the tribesmen curtsey to her in the same way as they did the Arrdock, it didn't seem as bad as her other requests. But it was just a step to her ultimate goal. Soon Brin created a law forcing everyone to bow to her in the same low-to-the-ground manner reserved for worshipping Elohim. Brin put a stop to the Atonement Service because it coincided with her birthday. Instead of repenting, singing, and bringing sacrifices to Elohim, the villagers were ordered to bring Brin gifts, sing songs to her, and bow low like they did to Elohim.

Jordana could abide by all the ridiculous changes except this last one. She tried to speak to her father about Brin's blasphemy, but he did nothing to stop his wife, claiming it was just a birthday celebration. Couldn't he see it was so much more than that? Jordana refused to attend Brin's sacrilegious party, and held her own Atonement Service instead. Dismayed over the lack of mutiny by her entire village, Jordana alone stood up to Brin. And had been banished for it.

Her fingers trembled as she secured the princess cape at the neck. The train didn't drag as much as when she was fourteen. But, oh to wear it again. She rubbed her hands across the smooth feathers. Brin had torn it off Jordana during the Banishment Rite, flinging it to the ground. She even defaced it by pouring a goblet of grape wine onto the white peacock feathers. Jordana would never forget the devious smirk on Brin's face as the beautiful garment made by her mother's precious hands, lay in shreds. Refusing to weep in front of the evil queen, Jordana pivoted and took slow deliberate steps out of the grand hall—waiting for her father to stop the nonsense. Or Benjura to rescue her. Neither did. No one in the tribe sided with her.

After crossing the threshold, she ran to Granna's bedside, and melted into her arms, telling her what just happened. Granna had been sick in bed, or surely she would have stood up for her grandchild. The old woman said she would leave too, but Jordana couldn't let Granna end her life like that, and sprinted away. She climbed, crawled, and ran some more—continually moving until dawn the next day when she collapsed.

Banished and betrayed at sixteen, she would forever be on her own. From that day forward, she stopping thinking of the Arrdock as father. Many full moons had passed with Jordana on her knees, asking forgiveness for her hatred of Brin, and her anger the Arrdock. And at Benjura. Why did he not come to her aid? He never showed signs of cowardice before.

Today Jordana would return at nineteen unmarried, with no children to present. Once again, she'd disgrace her father. She closed her eyes and sucked in a deep breath. Letting it out as slow as she could make her lungs move. She twisted around to gaze down the back of cape. No grape stains and no bald spots. How did Granna repair the damage? Jordana squared her shoulders and faced Benjura. "Do I look okay?"

Eyes wide, he nodded before thrusting the headpiece and adorned cord at her. "Your Granna sent these as you requested."

"They're exquisite. Toucan feathers, rubies, emeralds." She clutched them to her chest. Oh to see Granna again. Jordana smiled. "Thank you."

"Are you ready to show me your grand phenomenon?"

"Yes. But I want you to face the other way and close your eyes. Promise not to cheat. Do you swear it?"

"Yes."

"I mean it. For your safety, do not look."

He squeezed his eyes closed, shoved his fingers over his lids, then spun away from her. "I never break an oath."

Jordana cocked her head at him, considering his words, but let it drop. She paced to his front and waved one of her knives before his face.

He didn't flinch. "I feel you near me." His breath touched

her face.

"I'm making sure you aren't peeking."

"Um-hmm." He smiled, white teeth peeking out from his perfect lips.

Jordana sheathed her blade and moved behind him, searching the brush. She motioned Lainey forward. In soundless steps, the regal cat slinked forward and sat in front of Jordana. Lainey's lip twitched as Jordana secured the feathered headpiece behind the cat's ears. Bright feathers stood up like a crown on Lainey's flat head. The feline sat still as Jordana tied the adorned sash loosely around her neck. Jordana spoke over her shoulder. "No peeking. Not quite done." She gave Lainey a quick kiss on the cheek, and whispered in her ear. "Thank you for doing this. You look magnificent."

Lainey's long lashes blinked at Jordana, and she tipped her head.

Jordana moved next to the she-cat, held one end of the sash like a leash, and faced the Tree Warrior.

"I don't want you to be frightened, okay?"

He harrumphed.

"Keep your eyes closed, but go ahead and circle around to me." When Jordana grinned at Lainey, she lifted her shoulders a notch, then dropped them as Benjura spun around. "Okay, you can open your eyes."

Benjura released his fingers. His eyes widened as he raised a hand to cover his open mouth. "Whoa. You tamed a panther?"

"Not a panther. She's a black leopard."

Benjura lowered his arms. "I'm impressed. She's very beautiful. But I don't think taming a leopard will constitute a miracle. Did you find her as a cub or something?"

A giggle escaped Jordana's lips. "I did not tame her. Elohim did. Let me formally introduce you." Jordana cleared her throat and added primness to her tone. "Benjura, son of NeBo and high watch guard of Arrie, this is Lainey, leader of the gatekeepers to Elohim's Holy Land." Jordana's gaze fell to

65

Lainey, then bounced back up to Benjura. She fixed her stare on him—not wanting to miss a second of his reaction.

Lainey stood. "I am honored to meet you, Benjura, Son of NeBo."

He jumped back, eyes rounding like the two full moons in the night sky. He gaped at Jordana, his gaze volleying between her and the feline.

Jordana laughed aloud, dropped the sash, and clapped her hands. "We surprised him, Lainey, we did."

The black leopard let out a staccato purr. "Thank you for calling me beautiful, Benjura." She tipped her head. "Jordana tells me you are quite handsome too, but I'm not good at judging humans."

Jordana shot the leopard a look, cleared her throat, and picked up the sash.

Still bouncing his gaze between her and Lainey, Benjura blew out a whistle. "I do believe you have a bona fide miracle." A smile split his face. "I am honored to meet you, Lainey. Are you really a gatekeeper to Elohim's Holy Land? May I talk to you about Him? I have many questions."

"Let us visit as we journey. We've dallied long enough. I'm quite anxious to speak to your Arrdock and return to my pride."

Benjura motioned to the path, and the group fell in beside him. "Are all the gatekeepers animals? Do all of you speak?"

"Yes to both questions." Lainey walked between them, her ears flicked toward each sound the forest made.

Benjura locked gazes with Jordana. "No wonder you do not wish to return here. What awesome adventures you must live every day."

Heat rushed to her checks as her hands curled into fists. It took all of her strength to keep from screaming at him. "Running from hungry hyenas. Fighting baboons for fruit, constantly covered in mud to conceal my scent from jaguars and cheetahs. Fight to survive where I'm the hunted more often than the hunter. All alone to suffer the loss of my mother, betrayal of my

66

father, and abandonment of my betrothed. No one to take a turn guarding at night so I can sleep. Yeah, it's been a fantastic adventure." She couldn't keep the snarl from her tone and stormed ahead.

"I'm sorry. I shouldn't have assumed you lived with Lainey, and I'm even sorrier you had to go through it all. How were you able to get sleep?"

She sucked in a deep breath and drilled him with her stare. "I sleep near the Azul. I take short naps there. Humans aren't the only ones to avoid that area. Very little game ventures to the far edge of the eucalyptus forest. I don't think they like to drink the warm mineral water. But it also means I have to travel long distances to hunt meat. It's an exhausting life."

Benjura kept his voice low. "Come back to the tribe, Jordana. You will be safe. You shouldn't be alone any longer."

Jordana shook her head. "I cannot. And this is not the time to discuss it." She straightened her shoulders. "Keep Lainey between us even after we enter the clearing under the Arrdock fortress." Jordana shook the adorned sash. "Stay on the leash, Lainey. It's just for show, so the villagers won't be frightened of you." Jordana pointed at the ram's horn dangling from Benjura's belt. "Will you sound the trumpet as we enter?"

"Yes. Twill be a full and proper display, so the Queen cannot find any excuse to deny your request."

"My request." Jordana halted. "What should I ask for?"

"You don't you know? Ask for acceptance back in the tribe." Benjura's bewildered face searched her eyes, as if flying questions at her.

Jordana shook her head. "It must be for something far more important than that."

Lainey's gaze alternated between the humans. "I don't understand."

"After presenting a miracle, you," Jordana pointed at Lainey, "one request will be granted to me by the Arrdock. I can ask for anything. Everyone will expect it to be admission back into the tribe. But that won't work for me. If the laws have not

67

changed, then next week I will be banished once more." Jordana bit her lip. "I shall ask father to dispatch warriors to stop Chinzu from defiling the Falls Territory. The purpose of my visit is to warn him. But with the presentation of a true wonder, I can ask him to stop Chinzu from defiling the Holy Land, instead of just guarding here."

"The Arrdock can't send the entire army and leave the village exposed." Benjura wiped his forehead with the back of his hand.

"The Queen will not want him involved in anything that has to do with me." Her lip no longer sufficient, Jordana raised one hand to bite her fingernails.

Lainey plunked her bottom down. "The Arrdock must *want* to help us and not be forced to do so."

"If only his heart could be made tender again, like when mother lived."

"He needs water from the Restoration Pool." Lainey moaned.

Both Jordana and Benjura's head snapped toward the leopard.

"Tell me of this water." Jordana stopped chewing her nails.

"A small pool lies high up in the Falls Territory near the entrance to the Holy Land. It is the only remnant from the inside garden that is found outside the sacred gate. When water falls from a cloudless sky, the pool churns. One can enter the water to receive restoration, whether to the body after an injury or to the heart after sinning. Tis why we call it the Restoration Pool, as it restores us to Elohim."

Jordana's arms dropped. "Let us go to this pool at once, fill my water skin, and come back to present the miracle. My request will be for the Arrdock to drink the water. Then his mind will be set free from the curse of Queen Brin. I do not understand her hold over him."

"No, child, tis not how it works." Lainey's tail swooshed across the ground stirring bits of dust. "Although it is good to drink the restoration water, one must dunk themselves into the deep. First, they beseech Elohim and declare their faith. If they do not believe in the power of the pool, when the water comes from the sky, nothing happens. Like if a non-speaking animal goes into the pool during the cloudless rain, there is no change. One enters the pool as a show of faith."

Benjura arched a brow at Lainey. "Animals sit around waiting for it to rain so they can rush into the pool?"

"I'm not talking about regular rain. Tis a mighty cascade falling from a perfect blue sky. It comes from so high up, no one can see the source. No clouds are visible. It might not happen for a full moon cycle, or it could happen many days in a row."

"Then I will ask my father to travel with me to this pool, pray, and enter when the waterfall appears. Perhaps if he sees it, he will have faith to dunk in the water." Jordana bit into her nails once more.

"And what if that takes a month? The Chinzu army could wipe out our village while you and the Arrdock are off sunbathing." Benjura grabbed Jordana's hand and laced his fingers through hers, stopping the assault on her nails.

She did not yank her hand away, as she considered his wisdom.

Lainey meowed. "I think the wisest request would be for a feast with the Arrdock. No one else except him and the three of us. We can visit about many things. You may tell him what you have seen and heard of Chinzu's army. I can share about the Falls Territory, Elohim's Holy Land, and of the Restoration Pool. We may need two nights of dining and planting seeds of truth to reach his heart. What the Arrdock does with this information will be up to him. If he rejects the honor of defending Elohim's land, then another will come forward." Lainey stood. "This is what you must request."

Jordana's heart pounded in her chest, drumming louder and louder. She tipped her head in agreement. "I will do as you say, Lainey. I will invite Granna as well. But no one else." She closed her eyes. "Soften the Arrdock's heart, Elohim, and grant us favor in his sight."

"Be it so." Benjura tipped his head back and gazed into the sky. "Now we must go. The sun is directly overhead. No more talking on the trail. Especially you, Lainey, our revered guest. Let no one hear you before we enter the Arrdock's presence."

Lainey nodded to Benjura.

Jordana stepped forward. Her toe caught on something and she stumbled. When she regained her footing, she gazed back at the path. Her foot had caught a thick black root. She followed its trail up the side of an apple tree. Part way up the trunk, the black root splintered into tiny webs. Near the top of the tree, the black web covered every bit of green. The upper third of the tree was dead. Not a single apple appeared anywhere on the once prolific fruit tree. "What happened? What caused this?" Her heartrate picked up speed, almost afraid to hear the answer. *Someone hurt a purple palm—a sacred Tamar.*

Benjura whispered, "Brin. You'll see what she did."

Jordana's fists clenched. "I will never return to this place and that evil woman." The venom in her tone could not be held back. She whipped her cape around and snatched up Lainey's sash. Teeth clenched, she strode forward.

As their group descended the path in silence, she searched for any other signs of the curse. She counted eighteen blackened fruit trees. Whatever Brin did to cause this, how could father allow it? Especially when it killed off food sources. *Please, Elohim, soften his hardened heart.*

At the distant sound of chatter, Jordana jerked her head toward Benjura.

He nodded and flashed a smile, as if to reassure her. Donned in ceremonial garb, Benjura did look handsome. The golden flecks in his hazel eyes seemed to sparkle at her.

Honeybees swarmed her belly. She didn't need any distractions, and Benjura's nearness certainly drew her attention. She forced her gaze away, and pictured her father in her mind. Had he changed, too? Some might think three hot seasons was a

70

short period of time. To her, it'd been an agonizing eternity.

The closer they crept to the village, the louder the racket grew. Her hand carrying the jewel leash trembled. She searched the jungle for signs of the village edge. Mamu's voice echoed through her mind. *Hold your head high. Let them see the whites of your eyes.* Jordana fixed her stare straight ahead as she strode forward. She stole a glance at Lainey and up to Benjura, but never high into the branches where her beloved kinsmen would soon watch her. And aim their arrows her way.

CHAPTER EIGHT

You are worthy. The words from Elohim breathed into Jordana's soul as she entered the outskirts of the village. They filled her with a peace she didn't think possible to possess. A lift of her chin and straightening of her spine, she slipped into the graceful walk of royalty. Just like Mamu had taught her. Excited chatter grew above her. Low murmurs rippled across the assembly, but Jordana didn't meet anyone's gaze.

Mother's words filtered into Jordana's mind. *Never forget you're a princess.* Jordana remembered. And more than ever, she needed the warriors to remember. Perhaps it would keep them from slaying her before listening to why she dared to enter the village. Banished or not, Jordana of Arrie, the first-born child of the Arrdock, would always be their princess. At the time of her exile, she was his only child. Perhaps Brin had given him a prince by now, and she lost her birthright. It wasn't stripped away at the Banishment Rite, which left her with a sliver of hope for a future return. And here she was, striding in to tell them of a coming war. Not the happy reunion she dreamed of.

Benjura raised the ram's horn and blew a strong blast. Ten seconds later he sounded another. People scurried down from their tree houses to stand on the labyrinth of swinging bridges. New homes built in the trees made the village larger than she remembered. Tribesmen lined up on the ground, all around the clearing. Children made wild gestures at Lainey.

A small boy pulled on his mother's tunic. "Look,

momma, a panther."

"Yes. They're very dangerous. Stay back."

Lainey's head raised a notch, but she didn't show any sign of understanding.

Jordana suppressed a smile. Good thing Beast wasn't there to roar at the child's mistake.

At the sight of her father's magnificent fortress, Jordana's pulse quickened. The stronghold expanded over a dozen baobab trees, and encompassed several kapok and jackelberries as well. A city built above the ground—bedrooms, dining rooms, meeting halls, a courtroom, decks, and balconies all connected by dozens of suspension bridges. Shiny wood structures carved with animal patterns, thick corded ropes, and lovely trailing vines. Purple and white wisteria, honeysuckle, fuchsia Bougainvillea, and climbing yellow roses weaved around the bridges and walls.

Her breath caught. It was more beautiful than she remembered. The old yearning for home—long buried—rushed back through her. She took in the scene, the colors and scents, memorizing every detail. No sign appeared inside the village of the curse for destroying a sacred palm.

Benjura sounded another horn blast, waited a few seconds, and gave the final moan, deep and strong, as the warrior custom to assemble the tribe had dictated.

Many of the baobab trunks had been hollowed out at ground level to provide shelter during a heavy rain, or recovery stations for the injured. The elderly moved into the trunks when they could no longer climb.

Finally Jordana gazed at her countrymen and didn't let any fear show. The multitude of warriors pulling their bows taut, or tree maidens posing daggers at the ready, stole air from her lungs. But many of them smiled at her. Some nodded. Their beaming faces eased her turmoil, even though none lowered their weapons.

Jordana scanned the group standing under the kapok trees. They glared at her, from fury or hatred, Jordana could not tell. They were Brin's kin.

73

When Benjura and Lainey stopped walking, Jordana did too. If they hadn't halted, she might have marched all the way out the other side of the village. The butterflies flitting about in her belly seemed to multiply as fast as rabbits.

Guards Jordana recognized stood on either side of the main tree untying ropes. Mother's guards, Henry and Zachariah, lowered a platform inch by inch from the tree top toward the ground. Their muscles strained as they struggled under its weight, yet they managed to keep it moving in a fluid motion. Brin's kin, Kai and Bootah, rushed forward to help. The entire crowd silenced.

When the platform reached Jordana's eye level, she scanned its occupants. Two shiny chairs sat in the middle, covered in sparkling black bark from the sacred Tamar. Her breath caught over the defilement. A handful of purple palms would have been stripped of their rubbery bark to cover the elaborate thrones. Didn't anyone care that they were sacred? Queen Brin sat on the right chair and the Arrdock stood between the abominable thrones, his hand resting on Brin's shoulder.

Surely Jordana would vomit at any second. She tried to zero in on Brin's attire. A high crown of rubies and amethyst, and a gable headdress dripping more jewels, sparkled across the expanse. A tight gown, beaten as white as clouds, hung low on her ample chest, leaving plenty of room for the jewel encrusted necklace she proudly displayed. The gaudy thing fanned across her pale skin. She looked ridiculous covered in so many jewels. She looked nothing a fierce tree maiden. The gown Brin wore covered her knees and legs. Why didn't she wear a short tunic for easy access to a harness of blades around each thigh?

Jordana had yet to lift her gaze to meet the Arrdock's eyes. Would she see fury for returning to the village? Would he accept her, or pierce her with his own blade? She tried to steady her racing heart as she finally shifted her gaze and met his stare. *Father.* His pinched forehead and the crinkles around his eyes, hinted at concern, but not anger. Did he care about what happened to her? Perhaps he even regretted sending her away.

When the platform met the ground, her father stepped off and strode toward her.

Both knees trembling, she focused on his tunic. More adorned than usual, but not as gaudy as Brin's, Father looked handsome with his beard shaved off. He stopped inches from her, towering almost a foot above the top of her head. The Arrdock placed his right hand across to her right shoulder. "Daughter, do you have a miracle to present?"

Jordana nodded, her attention frozen on the cleft in his chin. She'd forgotten he had one. Childhood memories flooded back to a time when he wore no beard. She lifted her finger to touch the line.

He smiled at her, his gaze penetrating deep inside her like before Mamu's fall.

"I forgot you had this."

"Seize them." Brin's voice shrieked from behind the Arrdock. "Kill her for breaking the sacred law. Benjura and the panther, too."

Locked onto her father's eyes, Jordana whispered so only he could hear. "Are you still the Arrdock of this great village? Or have you relinquished all of your power to that woman?"

Lainey's flickering tail hit the back of Jordana's cape. The cat had amazing hearing. Still, Jordana did not break father's stare.

His lips twitched, insinuating amusement, but a smile never claimed his face. When he released Jordana's shoulder, he inspected Lainey as he passed to stand in front of Benjura. Father whispered something in Benjura's ear.

Grinning, Benj nodded at the Arrdock.

"I said seize them." Brin jumped to her feet and motioned at two of her royal guards.

Bootah and Kai took tentative steps forward, but halted at the Arrdock's hand gesture.

"Sit, my Queen." He pointed at Brin's throne.

She opened her mouth, then closed it and tromped back to her nauseating throne.

75

Jordana let out her pent up breath.

The Arrdock spun around to the crowd and raised both hands. "Tree Warriors, this is my daughter, the Banished One. Ancient Law dictates death to any exiled person who attempts to return to the village." He held up one finger. "Unless they present a miracle. Then I can override the decree. From her grand entrance, I believe the Banished One has something to show us." His voice grew to a shout. "Who wishes to see it?"

Whoops and clapping erupted. From behind her and on both sides, villagers cheered. Above on the wooden decks and bridges, warriors rapped the butts of their weapons. The deafening sound brought warmth into Jordana's heart. Not even Brin's glower could stop Jordana from smiling.

The Arrdock clapped as well and grinned back at her. At last he motioned for everyone to settle down. When the warriors quieted, he pointed at her. "This better be good."

Chuckles rolled across the crowd.

Jordana stole a look at Benjura.

He gave her a wink.

The crowd's encouragement spurred her on and Jordana dropped the sash-leash. As she bent to pick up the edge of her cape, she whispered near Lainey's ear. "Wait here. I have an idea." Jordana stepped forward and swooshed her cape around in dramatic flair. When she picked up speed in her stride, she released the ends of her cape and lifted both arms. The cape floated in the air behind her. "Tree Warriors, I have missed you. I come with an urgent message from Elohim. But first, I shall show you a miracle." She took long, fast strides around the perimeter of the clearing, so her magnificent cape could be seen and appreciated by all. Perhaps it would remind them of her mother, and garner Jordana favor. Her mamu had been a wonderful Shedock, and dearly loved by the tribe.

Jordana made eye contact with as many of her countryman as she could. The anger she once held for them had dissipated. Her people had simply been deceived. *Please, forgive their actions of old. Open their eyes to Your truth.*

She raised her voice. "The miracle I am about to show you is not of my doing. I did not create it or discover it. Elohim sent this wonder to me in my time of need." Her un-used voice cracked from the shouting—solitary life didn't require loudness. It required hiding and silence. Jordana pressed on, forcing out more volume. "This miracle is not only for my need, but for yours as well. You shall learn of that later." Jordana whipped her cape in another direction—the feathered drape floated like birds soaring behind her as she crossed to the far side of the crowd. "I shall show you a miracle from Elohim, himself." Jordana shouted the last and raised her fist.

The crowd cheered and Jordana moved to her original place next to Lainey, and waited a few seconds until they quieted down.

"My Arrdock, my Tree Warriors, it is my great honor to present to you, Lainey, gatekeeper to Elohim's Holy Land!" Jordana stepped away and gestured to the leopard. "Lainey is the leader of the black leopard pride dwelling inside the Falls Territory."

A few people gasped, but most of the crowd remained silent.

Lainey slinked forward, her paw placement mimicked Tanga's crisscross pattern of walking. Her tail whipped back and forth above her head.

Jordana giggled and Lainey nodded at her before stopping short of the Arrdock. She lifted her silky head, and met the Arrdock's stare. "It is an honor to meet you, Arrdock, father of Jordana who is highly esteemed by Elohim." Lainey gave a fierce roar, like an exclamation at the end of her greeting.

No one could have been more shocked by Lainey's words than Jordana. *Elohim esteems me?* Instant tears welled in Jordana's eyes. It took all of her strength to stay upright and not sink to her knees in worship.

"A talking animal? I can't believe my eyes. And ears. Astounding!" The Arrdock's deep voice boomed above the gasps in the crowd. He crossed the distance in a few great strides and engulfed Jordana in his embrace. Picking her up, Father swung her in a circle, and kissed her cheeks. "You've done it, my daughter. A true miracle." He carried her up onto the platform and stood her next to him. Father faced the crowd and raised one of Jordana's hands into the air.

The crowd cheered even more. When at last they simmered down, the Arrdock shouted so loud, leaves on the closest branch reverberated with the sound. "This is my daughter. JORDANA!" The use of her given name meant his acceptance of her miracle.

"Jordana! Jordana! Jordana!" Her kinsmen chanted.

She stood numb, scanning the faces of her tribemates. Could it be over just like that?

Seconds ticked by until Father motioned for the crowd to quiet once more. When silence filled the area, he paced in front of her. "As is the custom and law, you shall be granted one request from your Arrdock. What have you?"

At the twinkle in his eyes, Jordana guessed at what he wanted her to ask. But she couldn't. She swallowed hard. He looked so happy. Now she'd disappoint him. Again.

Adjacent to her, Queen Brin glared. No attempt to restrain her hatred.

Ask him to banish Brin. A smile threatened to claim Jordana's mouth, but she wiped it away, and rejected the evil idea.

Jordana faced her father and bent to one knee. "My Arrdock. I do not ask for anything elaborate. I only wish to feast with you tonight and tomorrow night in my Granna's home. Come alone both nights. Lainey and Benjura are invited too." She pointed at Brin. "But not her. That is my request."

The Arrdock's brows collided, and his voice deepened. "You do not ask to return to the tribe?"

"No. I bow to Elohim alone." She stood and shouted. "I will never worship according to Brin's blasphemous law."

"This is an outrage." Brin flew out of her chair. "She has broken my decrees. The Banished One knows to call me Queen.

Seize her!"

Jordana clasped the Arrdock's forearm. "I have missed you, Father. Please. I only wish to dine with you twice. Then I will return to my banishment."

Brin entwined her arm in the crook of Father's elbow, smashing herself into him. "Please, my Arrdock. She disrespects me and breaks my laws. Make her obey."

Jordana bore her gaze into Father's. "It is my right to be granted anything from the Arrdock for presenting a miracle. I have made my request—two nights of feasting alone with you. My father." Jordana stepped closer to Brin, towering over the short woman. "But not you, Brin. You are not welcome."

Thick silence swelled the air.

The sudden heat radiating from Father seemed to singe the hair on Jordana's arms.

"Jordana. Come to me, child." Lainey's she-cat voice registered in Jordana's ears. "Now."

She pivoted and made her way to Lainey's side, hands trembling as she bent and picked up the sash. All of her bravado gone, Jordana could not lift her face to meet her father's stare. Why did the worst in her always surface when she encountered Brin? Could she not even bridle her tongue for one short assembly?

"Granted." The Arrdock pivoted around, and escorted Brin back to her throne. He motioned for the men to hoist them up. Father kept his back to the assembly as he disappeared into the fortress.

Benjura rushed to Jordana's side, squeezing her elbow. "Does that temper of yours get you into trouble every day of your life? How is it you still live? You know it's illegal to say the queen's name, and yet you repeatedly shout it for all to hear, as if you're above the law." He pulled her through the throng of people.

Jordana focused on the gatekeeper at her side. "Have I ruined everything, Lainey? Father is furious with me."

79

CHAPTER NINE

As soon as Jordana stepped into her grandmother's home, she collapsed into the old woman's arms. Granna now resided in one large room carved into a huge tree trunk at ground level on the far edge of the village. *Disgraceful.* Brin must have moved Granna there after Jordana fled.

At the shutting of the door, Jordana peered over her grandmother's shoulder at Benjura. He had held onto her as he whisked her through the crowd and onslaught of questions. Somehow he suspected the encounter had taken its toll, just like he could always read her before the banishment.

Jordana leaned into Granna's embrace, soaking in every drop of love. It must last through the lonely years ahead.

"My sweet girl is alive and back to me." Granna stroked the back of Jordana's head. "I missed you so much. Always before Elohim, I beseech for you."

"And I you." Jordana pulled back and wiped her nose. "I lionize Elohim for your long life. I had feared you would succumb to a broken heart. First mamu gone, then me. I should have known how strong you are."

Granna raised a bony hand to Jordana's cheek. "I died anew each day. But now you're here. Why only for two days? Perchance I will succumb to a broken heart after all."

"You heard?" Jordana examined her matriarch's face. "I searched for you in the crowd. I'm sorry I did not see you."

"I will never miss a ceremony again. Had I not been

80

there, I would have surely fainted when a black leopard entered my home." Granna rotated to face Lainey without letting go of Jordana. "I am honored to meet you, Lainey of the Forbidden Falls Territory. I am Kawbi. My daughter was Makani, first Shedock to the Arrdock, and the mother of this beautiful spit-fire." Grandmother stretched up and kissed Jordana's cheek.

"Lainey is very special, Granna. Thank you for welcoming her into your home. She's a lot bigger than the kittens I snuck into your tree house as a little girl. And Lainey's already housebroken."

Lainey pinned her ears back and narrowed her slanted eyes.

"I'm teasing, Lainey. Tis what we humans do with those we love." Jordana stepped to the big cat and pet her head.

Granna motioned to the table. "Let us sit. We have much to talk about. And preparations for tonight's feast will need to begin soon."

As Jordana crossed the small room to the table, she studied the round enclosure. It took mere seconds to scan every inch of the twenty foot circle that formed her grandmother's dwelling. Adjacent to one wall sat a narrow bed less than two feet off the ground. At the end of the bed, many trunks stacked high on top of each other. In the small expanse between them and the counters, short shelves attached to the curved wall from floor to ceiling. Various sized baskets occupied the shelving. A series of cooking counters took up most of the remaining wall space, adorned by pots, wooden bowls, and whittled goblets. A sparse amount of food sat on the shelf above the cooking area—two baskets of fruit, a cloth covered what appeared to be a single loaf of bread, and a plate of jerky.

Except for the door, a brick fire pit took up the remaining wall space. Numerous layers of bricks formed a barrier between the fire pit and tree trunk. A brick hood over the pit forced smoke to rise up and outside instead of into the living area.

In the center of the room sat the one thing Jordana recognized—a beautifully carved table with six chairs. A gift from Jordana's father to Kawabi after receiving her blessing to marry Makani. The exquisite table graced her grandmother's spacious tree house in the Arrdock fortress for as long as Jordana could remember. Today a bouquet of fragrant plumeria blooms decorated its center.

Jordana sunk into a chair, and ran her hands over the smooth surface. Her heart warmed as the memories flooded back, sewing and baking at the table with her mother and Granna. Jordana fought against the tears threatening to fill her eyes. "I love this table. I always wanted to raise my own family around it." She swallowed hard and tucked a stray lock of hair behind her ear. "So how long after I left before Brin had this trunk hollowed out for you?"

"Immediately. I do not think she wanted the Arrdock to ever lay eyes on me again. I might remind him of his banished daughter and late wife." The old woman held her head high. Long gray strands tied back at the nape, intermixed with red locks. She looked beautiful.

Lainey plopped onto the floor near the table.

"I want to know all about your life outside this village, but business first." The matriarch sat at the head of the table, her gaze bouncing between Benjura and Jordana sitting across from each other. "If we are to prepare a feast for the Arrdock, we'll need meat. Someone must go hunting. I want to bake bread. I'll get more wheat and will need help with the grinding." She held up her disfigured hands, large knots at each knuckle, and wiggled her index and middle fingers. Both were crooked with age. "I can barely prepare enough for myself, much less enough bread for a feast. I have plenty of fruit, though."

"My father does not provide you with food from the fortress?" Jordana fought the heat rising in her cheeks.

"I refuse it." Granna patted Benjura's hand and graced him with an affectionate smile. "This fine boy brings me meat each week."

Jordana should have known he'd never stop caring for her beloved grandmother. "Thank you," she whispered to the once

82

cute boy, and now handsome man across from her.

Lainey lumbered toward the door. "Benjura and I shall do the hunting. Jordana, you stay here and help your Granna. You two should be together as much as possible."

Jordana said, "I'd like that very much, but I worry for your safety. Perhaps you should stay here, too."

"The hunting will be much faster if I go with Benjura. I can keep your sash around my neck, so no one will mistake me for a wild predator. Can you shorten it though? I do not want it getting hung up while running."

"Yes. That will be easy." Jordana locked eyes with Benjura. "Promise you'll see to her safety?"

Lainey huffed. "I shall see to his safety."

Benjura tipped his head to Jordana then grinned at Lainey. "What do you mean it will be faster with you along? I'll have you know I'm one of the best hunters in the village."

"We shall see." She blinked her long black lashes.

So beautiful. Jordana pulled a short blade from her leather sheath and sliced off the end of the leash. Several feathers floated to the floor. "Oh no. I've ruined your beautiful cord. That wasn't smart of me."

"Nonsense." Granna waved her off. "It is my honor. I am overjoyed to give anything for whatever your cause may be. When it involves Elohim, and this talking miracle in my home, all I have is yours."

"Wise one," Jordana bent close to the cat's face. "Have I ruined any chance of gaining the Arrdock's favor by insulting his wife?"

"With Elohim, all things are possible. You know this, child. But..." Eyes intense, the black leopard plunked her hindquarter down near Jordana's feet. "You must humble yourself when your father arrives. Apologize and promise not to say one disparaging word against his queen. If you force your father to choose between you and his helpmate, he will choose her. His past actions have already made this clear. Settle in your mind that you'll never again push your father into a place where

83

he must decide between you and his Shedock." Lainey's voice deepened. "Do you understand me, child? If you do not learn to bridle your tongue, Elohim cannot use you for His greater quest."

The words stung like a scorpiowasp attacking her skin, but Jordana accepted the reproach and nodded. "I was just so repulsed when I saw Brin's throne from a sacred Tamar. How dare she! But I will purpose in my heart not to say anything bad about her in front of my father. Nor will I put him in an awkward position between us. To this I vow."

Benjura's rich voice sounded. "Why don't you prove your remorse to the Arrdock tonight by calling her Queen instead of using her name? You know it's forbidden, yet you seem to relish saying it as often as you wish because you think there are no consequences to you. But you are wrong."

Jordana nodded and began pacing. "You are right. Both of you. I'm grieved. By the time you return from hunting, my attitude will be as new as the forest after the rain." She stopped walking and faced the trio. "Thank you all so much."

"Let's get to work." Granna shoved herself up from the table. "We can visit while attending to our chores."

Benjura followed Granna's lead, and stood as well, eating up the distance between them. He embraced Jordana. "You have matured while you've been away. Although I have missed your fire more than you'll ever know, I like the changes I see in you." He pulled back, his gaze roaming over the length of her before resting on her face. "I will guard Lainey with my life. Do not fret." He moved to the door and escorted Lainey outside.

Once they were both gone, Jordana closed the door and grasped her granna's hands, inspecting her fingers. "Are you in much pain? Why has not cousin Letta or Tooki taken you into one of their homes?"

"They have asked." Granna pulled free and crossed the room, pulling a large basket off a shelf. "I am not so old I can't care for myself. When I'm ready, I will go. But not with one of the twins. I have something better in mind." She moved to the door.

84

"What, Granna? What is better?"

"I am not ready to tell you. Maybe I will before you leave. I do not promise, though."

Jordana let it drop. For now.

The old woman opened the door, then immediately snapped it shut. "If you wish to be alone a few moments to entreat Elohim, you best not come out. A large crowd has gathered. They're staying back—giving you time, but I don't know for how long. If they see you, they may pounce."

Jordana nodded. "Please thank them for coming. Let them know I will be out soon."

As soon as her grandmother departed, Jordana moved to the bed and kneeled. *Oh, Elohim, thank You for caring for my Granna. Praise to You for my father's acceptance of the miracle today, and agreeing to attend the feasts. With all that is within me, I repent for not controlling my tongue.* For several minutes Jordana poured her heart out to the Great Creator. She walked to the fire pit and dipped her finger in ash, wiping a stripe of gray soot across her forehead and down her nose, just like during the Atonement Season. She lay prostrate on the floor imploring Elohim to grant her favor in the Arrdock's sight tonight, and to soften his heart about traveling to the Falls Territory to engage Chinzu's army. "Please, restore Father to You, I pray." She stayed in that position until her granna returned.

The old woman heaved a large basket onto the table.

Jordana jumped up. "Let me help you with that, tis too heavy for you."

"Oh, cat fish. Tis good for me. I like to work." Granna's gaze froze on the repentance ash down Jordana's nose and across her forehead. She nodded, and patted Jordana's hand.

"Time for me to get us some help." Jordana pasted on a smile and stepped outside. "Hello, tribesmen. I've missed you all. Thank you for greeting me."

Granna was right, the crowd rushed to her. Many hugs, pats on the back, and stares at the ash cross on her face, but no inquiries about it. The other questions flew fast.

One person asked, "Where did you meet the black leopard?"

"Have you entered the Falls Territory?" Someone from the back of the crowed shouted.

"Yeah, have you seen Elohim?"

"What did you mean—"

"Make way. I'm her cousin." Tooki's familiar voice cut through the chatter.

Jordana searched around the sea of people. Braves and maidens parted, allowing Tooki to step through. She held a baby on each hip. Only then did Jordana remember Benjura saying her cousin had twins and Jordana never asked which one. Tooki and Letta were daughters to Zinjada, who was Makani's twin— Jordana's mom. Both sisters were now gone from this world. If the twin tendency ran in the family, perhaps Jordana would one day bear a set as well. She buried the idea, knowing she'd never find a husband while banished. Her only hope to raise a child rested in Zinnia. And that was a terrible thing to hope for.

Tooki rushed closer, her strawberry locks swayed behind her shoulders. "You sure know how to make an entrance, cousin. I had long given up hope of ever seeing you again, and then you strutted in wearing your glorious princess cape. And let me say, you were magnificent!"

"Yes. Here, here." Murmurs spread across the crowd.

Jordana embraced her cousin, then placed a kiss on each baby's forehead. "I see you two girls have strawberry hair like your beautiful mother." Jordana straightened. "They look just alike. What are their names?"

Tooki bounced the baby on her right hip. "This is Danna, after you, Jordana, only spelled a little different for a true pronunciation." Tooki shook the girl on her other hip. "And this is Kani after your mother, Makani."

Instant tears welled in Jordana's eyes. "Oh, Tooki. I'm honored. My mother is honored. Thank you." At least someone would be able to name a child after her precious mamu. Letta and Tooki seemed to turn their backs on her at the Banishment Rite.

Yet Tooki named her children after Jordana and her lovely mother. Had Jordana read her cousin wrong back then? Had something else held them silent on that awful night? Now wasn't the time to bring it up and Jordana dismissed her ponderings. "Deep in my heart, I am touched."

"I loved your mother. She helped raise Letta and I after my mamu fell prey to a lion. Aunt Makani was a perfect Shedock. Tis the least I could do."

Again Jordana embraced her cousin and the twins, before digging up the strength to let go and face the crowd.

Tooki pulled back and cleared her throat. "Okay, we all want to know what you meant when you said the miracle was for our need too."

Nods from the crowd gave Jordana an idea. "People." She raised her hands. "I shan't keep anything from you, but I must tell the Arrdock first. As you can see from my ash cross, I'm in mourning over my disrespect to him and Brin-" She paused, gulping the forbidden word down. "The Queen. I shall not dishonor them again. If I tell all of you about the trouble brewing before I inform the Arrdock, it would be a sign of impertinence. I hope you understand and will help me prepare a grand feast for tonight. On the morrow, I shall explain it all."

"I can help." One woman stepped forward. "You want me to grind your Grandmother's wheat for bread?"

"I can help with that too," said another.

"Me too." A third woman stepped forward with shoulders as broad as a man's. "My bread is always perfect."

"Wonderful, thank you." Jordana smiled at them. "Tooki, will you take these three ladies in to help Granna?"

Her cousin nodded and moved to the house, the ladies trailing behind.

Jordana raised her already-hoarse voice to the remaining tribesmen. "Who has a lovely cloth to adorn our table? We need plates, goblets, and fine silver fit for the Arrdock. Might we borrow from one of thee?"

"My wife has a cloth." One man pointed to the woman at

his side. "No one bests my Hakku when it comes to stitchery."

The woman elbowed her husband's side.

"I remember." Jordana smiled at Hakku. "Thank you."

"And mine with pottery." A tall tribesman draped his arm across an equally tall woman's shoulder.

His wife blushed. "Thank you." She kissed his cheek. "I will fetch them."

Jordana recognized the tall couple, and searched her mind for their names. She did not know them well, for they had lived on the village's edge, and she grew up in the center.

"I have fine silver." The blacksmith's wife stepped forward.

Jordana smiled at her. "I imagine you do, Avika. You and your husband craft the finest swords and knives I've ever seen."

Avika seemed to beam at the praise and pivoted away. "I'll get them."

Soon Jordana had enlisted the help of many families for various tasks. Friends of her late mother brought colorful flowers to cover the outer door frame. Jordana's teenage training mates, many now married with young children, gathered sprigs of pink honeysuckle and tied them on the back of each chair. They adorned the head seat with elaborate feathers and fresh flowers. Haku returned with a white table cloth. Tropical birds in bright colors were stitched around the border and in the center of the covering.

Jordana's aunts on father's side, led the cooking team down at the public kitchen. In the many ovens, various types of bread baked, along with potatoes, yams, beans, fruit pies, and tarts. The feast would be far superior to what Jordana had pictured.

"Thank you, Elohim." Jordana whispered as she fetched water. "Now if you can grant Lainey and Benjura success in their hunt, soften the Arrdock's heart, and help us win the war against the Chinzu army, maybe I can give You a respite from all my petitions." She smiled, but stopped when one more prayer filled her mind. A prayer she dare not say aloud. To even ask would give life to the dream. Jordana strolled back to Granna's tree-trunk with light footfalls to prevent spillage from the water jug, all while the yearning mounted in her heart. *To belong to a family again.*

CHAPTER TEN

Lainey's careful paw placements in the thick jungle produced no sound or echo, while Benjura's footfalls resonated as if he were stomping beetles. She halted and faced the human. "We need to split up. Twill be faster. Your noise is driving away my prey. How do you catch enough game to feed your mate and litter when you make so much noise?"

"Mate and litter?" He laughed. "I have no wife or children, but I do help feed several families in the village. I'm an excellent hunter."

"I have no doubt if given all day, you could find game deaf enough to kill. But I'd like to get back as soon as possible. I wish to speak to your townspeople."

He arched a brow. "About what?"

"Elohim." Lainey locked eyes with the tree warrior. "Meet me back here in an hour."

"Right here?" He glanced around as if to remember the spot.

Lainey sunk her claws into a tree trunk, scratching four long marks at the base. "Yes, right here."

"I hope that was for you. I know these woods like I know my own village."

"May your hunt be blessed." Lainey sauntered away from the human and into the direction of an aroma she picked up earlier.

"Yours too." Benjura moved in the opposite way.

Twenty yards through the jungle, and Lainey left her scent on a bush. Now she'd have no trouble finding the rendezvous point in the thick tangle of foliage.

After trotting dozens of yards away, she opened her mouth, lifted her head high, and breathed in the sweet fragrance of antelope. At least two were close by. She took to the canopy, climbing a white neplar and moving across its branch to adjacent limbs. From tree to tree, she followed the scent far above the ground, crisscrossing boughs through the dense forest. Thick moss along the branches absorbed any noise from her paws. The antelope smell grew stronger as she stalked the game, finally catching sight of them. Two females and a magnificent stag. Neither doe looked pregnant. She'd target the smaller one, pouncing from above.

The three animals nibbled plump red berries from a large bush, all of them munching and yanking. Thankful for their clatter, but still crouching low, Lainey took extreme care as she inched along a bough, praying no howler monkeys would give her away. At last she drew within range and sucked in a quiet breath, filling her wide black nostrils with oxygen. Lainey leaned back on her haunches, then flung herself through the air, pouncing on the back of the closest doe.

All three antelope sprang into motion, leaping and sprinting away. Running zigzag through the jungle and over bushes, the two larger animals left the smaller behind. She fought beneath Lainey to get free. The creature made up for her petite stature with strong, jerky movements.

As fast as a lightning strike, Lainey sank her fangs into the side of the doe's neck, puncturing the jugular, and clamping down on the windpipe. Blood oozed onto Lainey's tongue, and within seconds, the lovely doe collapsed. It took less than a minute for her to topple over dead. A quick and successful kill.

The animal's small size would make it easy to drag through vines and bush to meet Benjura. But Lainey decided to eat her fill where the doe fell. It might unsettle the humans to watch her shred and devour raw flesh. There would still be

91

plenty of meat left for the humans to feast upon.

After a prayer of thanks, Lainey devoured a hind quarter of the antelope, then drug the remaining carcass through the woods. Every so often she stopped, opened her mouth and inhaled, searching for the scent marker. After a quarter mile of labored dragging, she reached the area and found the claw-marked tree. Lainey plopped down and labored to catch her breath, just as she had the night she met Jordana and helped drag the human bodies to the river bank. And to their fiery graves.

Odd that Jordana had said her village might not want to help protect for Forbidden Falls Territory. Why wouldn't they consider it their highest priority?

Tongue moist and rough, Lainey licked every drop of blood off the pads of her feet and legs. She cleaned as much of her chest as she could reach. Long, wet tongue strokes on her front paws were transferred to her face and ears. When no taste of blood could be detected on her sensitive palate, she stretched out next to her haul, resting her head across its torso, and closed her eyes to rest.

In the distance, a leaf crunched—the unmistakable footstep of Benjura.

Although her ears twitched in the direction of the sound, Lainey didn't move or lift her lids as she waited for the noisy human to arrive. The edges of her lips curled up—Benjura had no wife and children as Jordana had feared, but was too afraid to ask. Lainey would pass along the information as soon as a private moment presented itself.

"Wow." Benjura entered the clearing. "You're sleeping? And you ate part of the antelope?"

"Yes, of course." Lainey stretched and yawned, then focused on Benjura. He carried a bird in each hand, one of them quite enormous.

Lainey pushed up and lumbered over to smell the fowl. She filled her lungs with the odor as she strode forward. "The smaller one is a turkey, but what is this giant feathered creature?" She planted her nose on the upside down bird and sniffed. After ferreting farther into the fluffy nape, she sniffed one more time. "It smells like some kind of goose, but I have never seen one this big. I don't think we have this species in the Falls Territory. What is it?"

His proud smile revealed a lot. "We call it an osgoose. My ancestors bred ostrich and geese for eggs and game. Both are delicious. For fifty years, they could only be found in the captivity of our village, but a great storm set the flock free a dozen years ago. My father started over and the tree warriors now have a great drove of osgeese supplying our village."

Benjura raised the osgoose and studied it a moment. "I'm surprised they breed in the wild. My people believed they would die out, once they returned to their goose or ostrich roots."

Lainey's ever-alert ear twitched toward a chirping, then relaxed. "Perhaps they were rejected by the geese and ostrich flocks. They may have been forced to stick together. Life fights to thrive. All creatures follow their Elohim-given survival instinct. Soon, every country on Tzuri could see sprinklings of osgeese."

He smiled at her, then jerked his head up to look at a branch. "Wow. Don't move." Benjura stooped, easing both birds onto the ground. From his crouched position, he sprung up, jumping over Lainey's head to grab a tree limb, and swung himself to stand. Benjura clambered to catch a giant tree frog. Bright orange with neon green spots covered the hopper's back. Benjura scooped up the funny-looking creature and held it with both hands as he dropped to the ground.

Lainey gasped at his legs when he hit the forest floor. Surely a fall from that distance would snap his sticks into many splintered pieces. But Benjura landed sure footed, a huge grin splitting his face.

He held the monster out for her to see. "This is an O'janga tree frog. Very rare."

"That's not a tree frog. It's a mammoth toad."

He gave a vigorous nod. "My three kills may not be as big as your one, but O'janga frog legs happen to be the

93

Arrdock's favorite meat. Let's get this big boy back for the feast."

"If I had hands, I'd clap for you like your tribesmen did for Jordana this morning." Lainey flicked her tail above her head.

"Thank you." Benjura took a little bow. "Praise Elohim for our successful hunt of rare game. He must favor your plan to host a grand feast for our Arrdock. I'll carry your doe and you carry my birds." He opened the satchel hanging at his hip and dropped the ten-pound jumper inside.

Lainey studied Benjura, pleased with his sincere thanks to the Great Creator. His jovial attitude and skill as a hunter might make him a good mate for Jordana. But bitterness remained in the girl's heart toward the man. Why? And if Jordana didn't get the strife out, it could take over her life. Consume her. Fill her with ugliness. Jordana was too lovely a human for that. Beautiful on the inside at least, for Lainey knew not if Jordana possessed any outward appeal.

As Benjura tied the feet of the fowl on each end of a small length of twine and laid it across Lainey's back, she prayed for wisdom and an opening to talk to him. Soon they set out down the trail, and Lainey mustered the courage to ask a benign question. "Is Jordana ugly?"

"What?" Benjura nearly tripped on the path and scrambled to catch himself under the antelope's weight across his shoulders.

"Doesn't anyone find her attractive enough to make her their mate?"

His brows shot up, eyes full of question. "What are you asking?"

Lainey tossed her head back. How could the man be so dense? "I do not know how to judge a human's outward appearance. Only their heart. I see Jordana as honorable, brave, and devoted to Elohim. To me, she is lovely. I assume you see the same traits, as you are her friend. But based on human standards, is Jordana ugly on the outside? Is that why no man wishes her for their mate?"

Benjura's face grew intense. "Jordana is the most beautiful woman I've ever seen. Tall and lean, but strong. The girl I grew up with has always been both smart and pretty. And now that she's a woman, her beauty is unparalleled and unique. Her eyes are different than most of the tribe, a soft gray-blue under long, thick lashes makes her lovely to look at. Her skin is perfect, as are her lips. Sometimes I can't breathe when she smiles at me." He swallowed hard, then pivoted, and strode forward.

Lainey fell in next to him.

While walking, Benjura stared straight ahead and spoke. "I haven't even mentioned Jordana's hair. Rich auburn waves that brighten when the sun shines on them, as if on fire. I've always said her hair matches her temper."

"Yes, a fiery temper. That makes sense to me." Lainey glanced up at Benjura. He seemed smitten with the girl, yet did not fight for her. Or challenge another. The ways of the humans made no sense. Perhaps in the days ahead on their journey back to the Azul River, Jordana could explain some human customs and traditions.

"I'm going to be covered in blood by the time we get back." Benjura adjusted the animal across his shoulders, as red ooze dripped from the chewed stump. His front and sheath of knives tied to his right thigh shined crimson.

"I thought you were a strong and mighty hunter. Or does the site of blood make you queasy?" Lainey's ear moved in the direction of the nearing village noises.

"Wow. I didn't know leopards jested. What a funny cat you are." He stayed beside her as they made their way back through the jungle.

Lainey debated which of her other questions to ask the man. Topping her list was why Jordana's father had banished his only child. But to ask Benjura seemed like a betrayal of her new friend. Jordana would reveal the mystery when ready. For now, Lainey would settle on other topics, as Benjura seemed willing to discuss his thoughts.

95

She stole a glance at the man. "Tell me about your Arrdock. Does he take good care of your tribe?"

"For the most part. The Arrdock does a fine job settling disputes and judging—assigning the watch tower schedule and approving the marriages. But I liked him better before."

"Before what?"

"I'm prejudiced. Not a good judge."

Lainey twisted her torso to gaze up at the human. "I don't understand."

"I grew up with Jordana. We trained together and I lived near her family. In a way, Jordana's mother helped raise me too, along with Jordana's twin cousins. Shedock Makani was mother to many of the village children. A rare jewel. She brought laughter, peace, and unity to our tribe. I loved her and when she died, I deeply mourned her. Our whole tribe did. We still do."

What he didn't say intrigued Lainey. Peaceful then, but not now? Liked the Arrdock better when married to Jordana's mother? Both seemed obvious. No need to ask.

Benjura cleared his throat. "When you first met Jordana, did you see where she lived?"

"No. I don't believe she has a permanent home. I think she's always on the move."

A groan escaped his lips. "I started searching for her after the banishment, but Elohim stopped me before I even got out of the Arrie Jungle. My mouth was closed at the Banishment Ceremony. I can't explain it, but I wasn't supposed to stand up for her. Then when I set out to find her, I was halted again. Elohim's instructions in both instances still baffle me. They went against everything inside me. Watching her flee the village all alone, twisted knots into my intestines that have never untied. But I knew the Great Creator forbade me to go along. I always strive to obey Him over my own will, so I stayed behind. I held my tongue and turned my back on her. It was the hardest thing I've ever done. Not a night goes by without petitioning Elohim for Jordana's safety and happiness."

The intensity in his voice tugged on Lainey's heart. The

young warrior's faith made him a brother. He may not understand the Creator's instruction, but clarity came to her, and Benjura should appreciate the reasons. She opened her mouth—

Wait.

The word filled Lainey's soul—a leading from Elohim. Someday it would all make sense to Benjura. But not from Lainey's tongue, and not on this day. She closed her lips.

"Have you ever seen Him?"

Lainey shook her head. "I've seen His light when He visits the Holy Land. But no creature can lay eyes on Him and survive. That joy is saved for paradise."

"You talk to Him though, right? Can you hear His voice aloud or just in your head like we do?" Benjura strides matched hers.

"Both."

"Wow."

"You say that word a lot. I have never heard it before." Lainey did not wait for his reply as she moved to more important matters. "Have your people fought in many battles?"

"A few."

"Will they be prepared for war?"

"We can be." His footsteps picked up speed, suddenly much faster than hers.

"What about you, Benjura? Have you fought in a war before?" Lainey called ahead to the tall human creating distance between them.

"No." His soft reply reached her ears.

For a talkative person, his answers became clipped, as his paced increased. The cause hit her like a cascading waterfall. "Your people have never fought a war, have they?"

He did not answer.

"Benjura! Your people have no experience fighting a great battle, do they? Answer me."

He spun around and faced her, his brows pulled together tight, a deep crevice forming between his eyes. "There's never been a need. Small squirmishes, yes. But never a full war. Don't let that fool you. Our village received its name for a reason. We are fierce warriors."

Lainey studied the man. How long ago did his people earn their reputation as mighty tree warriors? Could their skill be carried down generation to generation?

As if he read her mind, Benjura's gaze bore into her eyes. "From childhood, we are trained with all types of weapons— knives, swords, and bows. Our skill will amaze you. Have faith. We're capable of conquering the Chinzu army."

"If the Arrdock sends you."

"Yes. But if he refuses, it will not alter my decision to go with you. I will never again leave Jordana alone. Never."

"As long as Elohim permits it."

Benjura's whole demeanor fell as if he'd been hit by a tree. "Yes. I pray this time He does."

Lainey believed the human would leave his village forever behind to engage the enemy with Jordana and the gatekeepers. A great number of warriors would be needed to defeat an army. Though the Tree Warriors lacked experience, Benjura claimed they were well trained, and they would have power in numbers. It would not be enough.

CHAPTER ELEVEN

Jordana stood at the door directing Tooki, Letta, and the villagers when Benjura and Lainey stepped out of the tree-line. He balanced a large antelope across his shoulders. Blood dripped down his bare chest and stomach as he walked toward her. She scanned him, taking in every inch of his frame. His strong thighs hosted a sheaf of five knives on each leg, one crimson red. Jordana veered her focus to Lainey. A bird dangled on each of her sides as she sashayed forward, one bird much larger than the other. An osgoose.

The crowd parted for the hunters as they strode forward without stopping until they presented themselves to Jordana.

She smiled at them. "A blessed hunt." She reached out and lifted the chewed antelope stump. "Did you do this?" She arched a brow at Benjura.

"Ha. I'd at least have enough sense to do it after we carried the carcass back here." He swung the heavy load off his shoulders and dropped it at Jordana's feet, then motioned down his front. "I'm a mess."

Lainey's long lashes blinked at him. "I lightened your burden. Blood washes instantly. But without the Restoration Pool, an injury could take weeks to heal."

Jordana bent and removed the fowl from across Lainey's back. "I thank you both and commend you on your fine kills." She held up the osgoose. "A wild one?"

"Yes. And I have another surprise." Benjura opened the

satchel and pulled out the massive tree frog.

"Oh, Benj. An O'janga. Father's favorite. Thank you." Jordana rose up on her toes and brushed his lips with a kiss. When she pulled back, heat rushed to her face. *I kissed him?* Jordana spun away. "I better get this frog inside to Granna."

"I'll wash up and change. See you later this evening."

"Without glancing back at the handsome warrior, Jordana simply said, "Goodbye." She motioned Lainey inside, shutting the door behind them, leaving the fine game outside for now. It would need to be cleaned and cooked on the open pit down at the community fire pits.

"Wow, child." Lainey gazed around the room. "Tis beautiful and smells delicious. What is that aroma?"

"Bread. Granna's specialty." Jordana placed her hands on her hips. "Wow, huh? I see you've learned some of Benjura's slang."

"Yes. He says that word often." She opened her mouth and sucked in a deep breath. "I look forward to sampling some of your Grandmother's baking."

Jordana led Lainey to a mat near the bed. "Why don't you rest while we finish up? There's not much left to do but wait while things cook. I'll get someone to prepare the doe, then I'm going home with my cousins to change. Tooki and Letta have fine clothing for me and will arrange my hair."

At the thick wool floor covering, Lainey leaned back and stretched her front legs, opening the pads of her paws wide to spread each toe. Her claws darted out, two inches long, and razor sharp. As quick as they appeared, they retracted like a turtle sensing danger. Lainey yawned, her huge jaw opened wide, providing Jordana with a close-up view of her white upper fangs, twice as long as the bottom canines. The feline plopped down and closed her eyes. "Don't let me sleep long. I wish to speak with your tribesmen."

Jordana let out the breath she held. "Yes, ma'am." Could anything be more magnificent and terrifying than her new leopard friend?

* * *

Two hours later, cousin Tooki peeked through Granna's door, "He's coming." She snapped it shut.

Jordana's stomach dropped to her knees. She had to win over her father and convince him to help. Her hand trembled as she touched the flowers in her hair. They seemed to be in the right spots. She adjusted the tight bodice of Letta's dress. Dark magenta in color, rare and exquisite, the gown fit Jordana well, although it took some getting used to. Far more clothes than she normally wore, and no blades strapped to her thighs, awkwardness filled her gut. She tried to shrug it off, as she needed to concentrate on the evening—it must go well.

Tooki secured several beaded cuffs around Jordana's upper arm and ankles.

Did she now look fit to dine with the Arrdock? Would the elaborate fanfare please him?

"Go join Lainey outside and greet your father while we display the food." Granna brought the roasted osgoose over to the adorned table. Orange persimmons encircled the baked bird on the platter.

Several ladies ladled vegetables into shiny mahogany bowls skillfully carved in the shapes of giraffes, elephants, or cheetahs. Letta poured a mixture of fresh squeezed pineapple, orange, and guava juice into each goblet.

Jordana fought the lump filling her throat as every lady scurried to put the finishing touches on each dish and table setting. Jordana laid her hand over her heart. "Tree maidens, thank you. From the top of my head and deep into my heart, I am grateful."

The activity paused as the women smiled and nodded at her.

"Go, Child." Granna motioned her away. "Don't keep your father waiting."

Jordana opened the door a crack. Benjura stood talking to

101

the Arrdock, and blocking her view of Father's face. Would he still be angry?

Large crowds had gathered around Lainey. When she met Jordana's gaze, Lainey nodded at the people, and padded to the front of the trunk house.

Tribesmen and women dispersed, ascending the trees.

Jordana stood silent with the feline. Her voice box seemed to sink down her throat. Would she even be able to speak when Father came to her? She sucked in several deep, slow breaths to steady her racing pulse.

Seconds ticked by before both men faced the dwelling.

As soon as their eyes met, Benjura's gaze inched down, inspecting her from head to toe while striding forward in sync with the Arrdock. He wore a fine tunic as did Father, who's face softened as he made his way to her.

She gave a proper curtsey. "Welcome, my Arrdock. Thank you for coming. Everything is prepared." Jordana cleared her throat. "Before we go in, I wish to apologize for disrespecting the queen this morning. I promise this night I will obey the queen's law of not saying her name. No words of disdain will pass through my lips. I deeply regret putting you into the awkward position of having to choose between your daughter and your wife. I shan't do that again."

The Arrdock's brows rose. "It seems you may have grown wiser over the last three hot seasons." He stepped forward and pulled Jordana into his arms. He gave her a long, tight embrace, then kissed her forehead as he released her. "I have missed your spunk." His eyes twinkled at her, before he veered to Lainey. "I understand you had quick success while hunting today."

The black leopard nodded. "I would have been even faster if not for my noisy hunting companion." She shot a defiant stare at Benjura.

"Now I know why they call it leopard pride." Benjura sidestepped them and disappeared inside the threshold.

Father's deep belly laugh filled Jordana's ears for the first time since losing mother. "Let's eat the feast before it gets cold."

Jordana motioned Father and Lainey in first.

The maidens stood at attention against the far wall, ready to serve their Arrdock.

Granna and Benjura positioned themselves behind chairs sitting next to each other on one side of the table.

Lainey hopped up on the large trunk at the foot of the table. Jordana had scooted it over so Lainey could be at eye level during the feast.

Jordana pulled the chair out at the head of the table for Father, then took her own chair across from Granna and Benjura.

"This looks and smells delicious, Kawbi. I have missed your cooking." Father's deep voice filled the small room.

"Thank you, my Arrdock." Granna tipped her head.

Jordana reached for her father's hand. With the other, she laid her hand atop Lainey's shoulder and waited for the circle to complete. "Lainey, will you bless the meal for us?"

"My honor." Lainey closed her eyes and bowed her head. "Elohim, *barak* our substance and the human helpers. Shalom for the grand purpose you have *qudoshed* to the Arrdock and Tree Warrior Village, be it so."

Jordana smiled at Lainey's foreign words as she took her time opening her eyes.

The waiting ladies sprang to life—dishing, slicing, and serving the food.

Jordana unfolded her napkin. "Lainey, I am not familiar with a word from your prayer. What does *qudosh* mean?"

"Set apart for a special purpose." Lainey sniffed at the bread on her plate and licked a slice of pie.

"You think the Tree Warriors are set apart for a special purpose?" Father's voice rumbled from the head of the table.

"I hope so, as your daughter will soon explain."

When Lainey and the Arrdock's plates were piled high, each maiden waited on the remaining guests. Before long, they disappeared out the door, leaving the group of five alone.

"Jordana." Lainey's soft whisper barely registered.

Jordana turned to the black cat.

"I don't want any of the cooked meat I've been served, but I would like to try your Granna's bread and pies. They smell so good."

Jordana nodded and slid the osgoose and antelope off Lainey's plate, leaving it in a pile on the edge of one of the platters.

"So, daughter, explain this special purpose."

"I will. But first, may I ask about your health, Father? How you are? Do you have any other children?" Jordana already knew the answer, but wanted to prove her intent to accept his new life.

"I am very well. You are still my only child. Tell me now, daughter, why you didn't ask to return to our village as your reward for presenting a miracle?" He set his cup down and pinned Jordana with his gaze.

How could she explain without offending him, or breaking her new oath to not disparage the queen? Jordana grappled for the words.

Lainey's voice cut through the silence. "If I may, Arrdock. Elohim has a much higher purpose for Jordana's request. She could not waste her only reward on personal gain."

"So she asked for a trivial and temporary feast?" An underlying anger colored Father's tone.

Jordana held up her hand, stopping Lainey from replying, and rotated back to her father. "I love you. I love the Tree Warrior people, and I have missed my family more than you can know. But I love Elohim and continue to worship Him alone. I bow only to the Great Creator. I do not want to return to the village and disgrace you again, my Arrdock, when I disobey the queen's laws." She laid her hand on his. "I could not endure another Banishment Rite. But I do mean to keep my vow to show respect to the queen. I hope you understand."

They locked gazes a long time, his stone expression revealing little. At last he nodded and picked up his fork. "Tell me about your life outside these trees. I heard you were banished from the Garden Tenders. I had asked their Arrdock to look after you and was disturbed when you left. What happened?"

"You did? Thank you, Father."

"They wouldn't tell me what happened."

A giggle escaped her lips, for they would like this story and not think ill of her. She wiggled her brows. "Cannibalism."

Benjura choked on his juice, Granna's spoon clanked to her plate, and Father's fork froze half way to his mouth.

Jordana said, "Did you know they are vegetarian? No meat at all. I was caught eating a quail I had shot and roasted over a small fire. They consider it cannibalism to eat any animal, and acted like I had murdered the bird. I was asked to leave forthwith."

"Well, I'll be." Father gulped in the bite of O'janga.

Jordana nodded to everyone. "Tis true. And when I left them, I traveled around the various forests. The Great Eucalyptus Forest at the Azul's edge is the safest. That's where I met Lainey." She stopped and jerked her head to the Arrdock. "Do you remember my mother's stories about the animal whistle?" Jordana puckered her lips and blew out the tune.

Lainey's ears perked, each small orbit shuddering as if to capture every note.

Jordana grinned. "The stories are true, Father. When I needed desperate help and whistled the tune, Lainey came from across the Azul." Jordana regaled the group with her first look to the far side of the river, discovering many sets of eyes glowing at her. "When Lainey spoke, I did not know it was an animal who talked to me. Most of the big cats in Arrie have eyes of gold. But Lainey's eyes glowed like emeralds. Then when her—"

"Arrdock," Lainey interrupted. "If Jordana presented another miracle tomorrow, a similar miracle, yet a little different, could she be granted another request? Perhaps to visit your village for one month each year—for a little time with her beloved father and grandmother?"

"Oh." Granna cried out. She patted her former son-in-law's hand. "Please say yes."

"I think that's a fine idea." The Arrdock leaned back in his chair and flashed a knowing grin at the leopard. "Benjura, you shall blast the horn again at high noon tomorrow and gather villagers. Jordana, you shall present a second miracle with the petition Lainey suggested, and make an old lady happy. Along with your father." He reached to the back of Jordana's neck and pulled her forward, planting a kiss on her forehead. Once he released her, the Arrdock raised his goblet. "To the second miracle. May it be as tantalizing as the first."

Only then did Jordana realize how much her father had missed her. Maybe he had even regretted sending her away. She could only imagine his disappointment earlier that morning when his daughter didn't wish to return at all.

Lainey's idea would appease her father, and allow Jordana to visit him and Granna each year. Splendid. Why had she not thought of that earlier? *Oh yes. Because of Zinnia.* A piercing slice ran through Jordana's heart. From whence did the child come? Not from the Tree Warrior Village as she had first thought. *Please, Elohim, let Zinnia's mother and father live, and help me return the child to her rightful home.* If she failed to find Zinnia's family and returned each year with a growing child, questions would be asked. Somehow, Jordana must convince Father to let her raise Zinnia if the worst were true.

Jordana twisted the napkin she held in her lap. If the Arrdock refused to grant her wish to raise the child, would she have the courage to flee with Zinnia and never return?

CHAPTER TWELVE

At the trumpeting of the ram's horn outside, Jordana settled her gaze on each occupant in Granna's small home. "That's the first blast. Benjura will sound three more, then we'll go out and present ourselves."

They nodded at her, all so willing to help.

Humbled by their generosity, her insides warmed for the first time in years. How could she repay them? What would be a grand and special gift for each one? Lainey enjoyed the pies and tarts last night. Perhaps Jordana could bake them desserts.

Beast's tongue hung out of his mouth as he panted hard. "How can you humans stand to live inside walls?"

"We take off our coats." Jordana adjusted the princess cape around her shoulders. "But like you, I can't do that right now."

Granna knelt beside the magnificent male leopard and pinned on the headdress she had crafted last night. "I usually stay outside during this hot part of the day."

Kamali, already wearing her headdress, sat on the bed nursing Zinnia.

Jordana would like to curl up next to them for a few more hours of sleep. After Father left last evening, she and Benjura took Lainey out to gather Beast, Kamali, and Zinnia. Slipping them into the village and Granna's home without being seen took an enormous amount of time. They did not want Zinnia to cry. Darkness from the jungle canopy helped conceal them. Under the cover of her grandmother's quilts, Beast hid with Kamali and her charge the last hundred yards to Granna's front door. She had conceded to bring the baby as well.

The second blast from the ram's horn filled the air, although from much farther away. "Benjura must be at the center of the clearing now under the Arrdock's fortress." Jordana inspected the train of the princess cape, perhaps even more pleased to wear it now than she had been at her fourteenth birthday.

A swirl rolled through her stomach. Would her tribemates appreciate the second talking leopard and a talking patas monkey nurse? Or were they already accustomed to talking animals? The Arrdock would be the only judge, and had hinted at his approval last night. A yearly visit by his only child seemed to delight him as much as it did Granna.

After that, the Arrdock showed little emotions as she had shared about slaying the five giants in the eucalyptus forest, and Lord Joice's declaration of war upon her people. Tis why she returned—to warn them. But more than that, she entreated her father for help in stopping the Chinzu army from defiling the Forbidden Falls Territory. A scowl had filled her father's face as he listened without asking any questions. Before departing, he simply said Lainey had been wise to suggest two nights of feasting. *Whatever that meant.*

The final horn resonated through the trees, long and low. "Let us go." Jordana motioned for them to hurry. "After we get outside, I want Lainey and Beast side by side. Granna, you and I will flank them, okay?" Jordana didn't wait for her grandmother to reply. "Kamali, want me to lift you onto Beast's back?"

"Don't be ridiculous." The patas monkey swung up, while clutching Zinnia to her chest. She straddled Beast as if he were a horse, once again fisting handfuls of fur with her toes and free hand.

When everyone stood ready at the door, Jordana sucked in a deep breath. "Thank you all for helping me."

"It's Elohim's will, child. Let us be on our way." Lainey

twitched her whiskers.

Jordana led the group outside. Each one fell into the proper order, and Jordana set the pace. As they neared the clearing, clapping began from people lining each side of the wide path. Rumbles above them sounded as the stomping of feet and weapons escalated.

Nerves jumped inside the fibers of her skin, yet Jordana forced herself to maintain eye contact the villagers. Smiles filled their faces, as they waved at her. Not one person raised a weapon.

Granna's voice rose to reach her. "Be their princess."

Jordana glanced at her grandmother's face and understood. She lifted her arms and waved at the hundreds of tribemates gathering around. When she spotted her cousins, Jordana blew kisses to them. As she passed the ones who helped her prepare the feast yesterday, she motioned 'thank you' with her hand on her heart, then pointing out, as the old Arrie custom dictated.

Father stood akimbo in the clearing up ahead, smiling at her. Behind him sat Queen Brin, dark eyes glaring from beneath kohl-blackened lashes. They reminded Jordana of fat spider legs.

A giggle escaped Jordana's lips. For the hundredth time, she reminded herself to be respectful of the Shedock. No bitterness. No pride. And no saying her name.

Light glinted off the sparkling bark on Brin's throne.

Instant bile rose in Jordana's throat. What gave Brin the right? Did she have no fear of Elohim? Did she not understand the far-reaching consequences on their food supply? *Help me tame my tongue, Elohim.*

Jordana stopped several feet in front of her father and curtsied, then swept around to Brin. "Queen, you look radiant today." Jordana tipped her head. Not a bow to the ground like the worship rite of Brin's law demanded, but a respectful curtsy to the Shedock in accordance to the ancient custom. Mother had taught her the old traditions well. Jordana moved back in front of the Arrdock.

109

"I did not tell you yesterday how beautiful you look in the princess cape." He whispered before kissing Jordana's cheek. His voice lowered even more. "My daughter is as lovely as her mother was."

Warmth radiated into Jordana's cheek from where his lips had met her skin. The heat moved over to her shoulder when his fingertips squeezed through the feathers. It seemed to stretch down into her heart, and Jordana melted into her father's embrace, hugging him tight. His affection and acknowledgement of her late mother touched her soul.

A moment later the Arrdock released her and raised his arms, motioning to the crowd.

Jordana could never grow weary of watching her father command the people. He had a way of evoking affection and loyalty. People wanted to follow him. Jordana had feared it would be lost when he didn't stop Brin from going too far. But today and yesterday, the villagers displayed no evidence of dwindling devotion.

"Tree maidens and warriors of Arrie. Would you like my daughter to present another miracle?" His deep voice filled the expanse for all to hear.

The crowd erupted with hoots and thunderous applause. The Arrdock motioned with raised arms for the shouting to rise even louder. The people cheered, stomped their feet, and rapped their knife handles against posts or walls.

Jordana waved at her countrymen, motioning 'thank you' to each corner of the village, to those on the ground, and above on the suspension bridges.

After a minute or two passed, the Arrdock settled the onlookers.

Only then did Jordana hear Zinnia bawling. Kamali rocked the baby, patting her back without saying a word, just as Jordana had ordered.

When the crowd silenced, so did Zinnia.

At her father's nod, Jordana grabbed the edge of her cape and swung it around. Like yesterday, she swept around the

110

clearing with hands raised. "My Tribesmen, I present to you another miracle from Elohim. I wish to introduce you to Beast, a magnificent male leopard, who also speaks as a human." She pointed at him.

Beast opened his jaw wide and roared, then bent his front legs and bowed to the Arrdock, with Kamali still on his back. Upon rising, he spoke strong and clear. "I am honored to meet the Arrdock leader of the Tree Warrior Village, and the father of Princess Jordana of Arrie."

Whistles and more clapping filled the air.

When the people quieted, the Arrdock tipped his head at Beast. "It is I who am honored to meet you." He opened his mouth to say more, but Jordana cut him off.

"Wait. There is more." She swung her cape around and paced next to Beast. She lifted Kamali up and held her high. "This patas monkey is named Kamali. She is nurse to both leopard cubs and human babies. She too speaks."

"Put me down, Jordana. You are going to make Zinnia cry again." Kamali tried to peer over her shoulder at Jordana.

The Arrdock laughed and walked forward. He took Kamali from Jordana, handing the baby off to his daughter, but kept the monkey.

Kamali stared at him, their faces inches apart. "Yes? Did you want something?"

"She's kind of grouchy, Father."

"I am not." Kamali folded her long, hairy arms across her chest.

The crowd laughed, as did the Arrdock. He handed the monkey back to his daughter.

Jordana transferred Kamali to one hip, and held Zinnia on the other.

A grin filled the Arrdock's face. His voice lifted for all to hear. "I accept the second miracle."

The crowd erupted anew.

Jordana strode to her father, but the thunderous crowd drowned her out. She could only mouth the words. "Thank you."

At last he settled the crowd, then fisted both hands on his hips. "Now. What request make you today?"

"I would like permission to spend a month in the village each year." Jordana's voice was low and timid. She chastised herself. Mother's words rang clear. *A princess is a leader and must speak with authority.*

The Arrdock arched a brow at her and dropped his tone an octave. "Only once a year?" The corners of his lips hinted at a grin.

Father's suggestion tickled Jordana like a feather. Yesterday the man seemed angry at her miracle request, but last night and today, he seemed to be helping her. Jordana's heart soared. Perhaps some of her lamentations for Father's heart to soften had manifested. She opened her mouth and shouted. "Twice a year. I wish to spend a month in the village during the hot season and again during the rainy season."

Brin stormed forward, her screeching voice bringing the celebration to an end. "My Arrdock. Is the Banished One going to bring a different talking animal before you each day, requesting more and more things of you? I propose a law declaring that talking animals are no longer a miracle."

"I shall consider your request, and rule on it when I am next on the Judgment Seat." He took Queen Brin's hand in his, and kissed the back of it, before facing his daughter.

An arrow whizzed past Jordana's face, missing her nose by an inch and landing in the Arrdock's upper chest. For a second Jordana froze, baby and monkey still on her hips. A second arrow flew and stuck into her father under his left collar bone. Drips of red stained his leather tunic.

A war cry pierced the silence, as more arrows flew. Guards surrounded the Arrdock, covering him with their shields and pulling him back toward the giant hollowed-out tree trunk. Father locked eyes with Jordana, motioning for her to come under the protection of his guards.

Screams filled the air. Arrows and knives flew in many directions as Jordana held still, clutching Zinnia and Kamali.

112

Lainey leapt to Jordana's side. "Run, child. Take cover."
Granna fell to the dirt.

Beast jumped next to the old woman. "Grasp my fur."
Granna latched on, and stood up when he moved forward.

The tight circle of guards and shields around the Arrdock marched back toward the giant trunk of the baobab tree. It had been hollowed out for a covering during a heavy rain. That must be where the guards were whisking her father now.

"Let's go." Benjura appeared at her side, breaking her frozen stature. He pushed the small of her back. "Move!"

Jordana shot into motion. "Lainey, with me. Do not take to the trees. Beast, bring Granna." She couldn't let anything happen to the Elohim's special creatures. Jordana ran for the baobab tree, Zinnia and Kamali bouncing hard in her arms. Several knives sunk deep into the tree trunk near Jordana's head as she passed into the shelter. She blocked one of the guards from closing the door until the leopards, Granna, and Benjura slipped inside.

The heavy door thumped shut. Several of the Arrdock's personal guards leaned against it, their machete's drawn.

Brin's voice cut through the battle noise raging outside. "Get her out of here. Tis all her fault." The Queen pointed at Jordana.

Two warriors rushed forward, each grabbing a shoulder, as Jordana still clung to her two charges.

Teeth bared and fangs dripping with saliva, both Lainey and Beast growled at the men.

"Touch her again and you'll lose your hands." The Arrdock's shout echoed in the small enclosure.

The men inched away, their stares still locked onto the leopards.

Granna reached up and took Zinnia from Jordana, comforting the baby. She gazed at Jordana. "Are you injured?"

"No, I'm fine. And you?"

The old woman's wrinkled face nodded. "Fine."

Jordana set Kamali down as she scanned Beast and

Lainey. No signs of blood. She rushed to her father's side. The arrow in his collar bone area had already been removed. The tip of the second arrow stuck out an inch in the back.

"Push it through." Father gritted his teeth.

One of his men snapped off the back end of the arrow, then shoved it hard. When the Arrdock's screamed, the guard stopped pushing.

Father hissed through a clenched jaw. "Finish it."

Royal guard, Zachariah, grabbed the bloody arrow from behind. "Zarr, push hard on that side, while I pull it out."

Zarr nodded and shoved. The ghastly task was completed within seconds. The men tore their garments and pressed them into the Arrdock's wounds to stop the bleeding.

Father shoved them aside and unsheathed a knife. "Let us fight."

Jordana drew two knives, poised them above her shoulder, and moved with them to the door.

"Not you." The Arrdock glared at her.

"Now is not the time to argue, Father. I have fought and killed before."

"Jordana, stay here." Lainey drew everyone's attention. "Help Beast and I protect the Queen and Zinnia in this shelter."

Jordana nodded and rushed to stand in front of Granna.

The guards stepped aside from the door.

Before they had a chance to yank it open, the door crashed inward. A throng of warriors rushed in, long swords swinging, slicing flesh. Metal clashed against metal as the invading warriors fought with Father's men. The enemy's longer, thinner swords sparred against the shorter, heavier machetes of Benjura, Father, and his guards. In the center, Benjura's long auburn hair swung back and forth, matching the long red locks of his opponent

Wait? Jordana squinted at all men fighting. Each one had long red hair...both sides. These attackers were the same size and coloring of the Tree Warriors. They were not giants.

"Stop!" Jordana screamed as loud as she could. "We are

not the ones who raided your village." Jordana snatched Zinnia from Granna's arms and held her up high. "I rescued this baby from the dark giants. We all have red hair. We are not each other's enemy." Jordana lowered Zinnia, searching through the fighters until spying her father. "My Arrdock, this is not Chinzu's army. Command the Tree Warriors to lower their weapons."

A few men glanced her way, and the fighting slowed, but no one lowered their weapons.

Jordana set Zinnia back in Granna's arms and jumped between Benjura and his opponent. She jerked up her machete to deflect his sword. "Sound the horn, Benjura. Do it now!"

Without question or protest, her friend pulled up the horn dangling from his waist and blew a low moan.

Warriors on both sides hesitated, keeping their weapons poised.

"Please, listen to me. We did not raid your village. I saved that baby." She shouted as loud as she could muster. "Blow your horns to stop this battle! Look at each other. No one here is over eight feet tall with black hair and golden skin. Let me tell you what happened and who the giants are."

Both sides stepped back from the mirror image they fought and sized her up.

Jordana searched through the men for her father. She froze when she spotted him. Ice sickles prickled through her.

A young attacker held a blade to the Arrdock's neck, and a thin line of blood slid down Father's throat.

CHAPTER THIRTEEN

"Blow the horn again." Jordana commanded Benjura without shifting her gaze from the young man who had seized her father. The captor's eyes widened and his stare jumped around to the various people in the shelter. He did not glare at her with hatred, like the others did. Two skinny braids hung from the man's temples, a blue feather entwined at the base of each one. Thick leather covered his chest, while his comrades were bare-chested, and void of feathers. The man's gaze rested on Zinnia. And moistened.

As Benjura blasted a low groan from the horn, Jordana stepped in front of the young man poised to kill her father. She added kindness to her tone. "You must be the Arrdock of your tribe?"

The young warrior nodded, every bit of his fear splashing across on his face—pupils dilated and veins throbbing on his forehead.

Jordana rushed to lift Zinnia out of Granna's arms and present her to the young chief. "Was your village raided several nights ago by five dark-haired giants? They kidnapped this girl baby, didn't they? I encountered them in the Great Eucalyptus Forest and surprised them from atop a tree. I landed a blade in each one to rescue this child. I call her Zinnia. What's her name?"

"Taryn."

"Taryn." Jordana let the name float over her lips. "Tis a

perfect name for a beautiful baby." She kissed the child's cheek. "Taryn belongs to you, doesn't she? Is she your daughter?" Jordana held the baby out for the man to take. "I thought she came from this village, tis why I brought her here. I was trying to find her family."

"She's my only child." The young Arrdock shoved Jordana's father away, and snatched Taryn up.

Jordana's father whipped around and faced his enemy, pointing a knife at the young chief's belly. "Bootah." Her father commanded his sentry forward.

Bootah pressed the tip of his blade against the young leader's back.

Several of the young chief's men raised their swords to Bootah's neck and torso.

Seemingly oblivious to the standoff around him, the young Arrdock kissed Taryn's head and clutched her to his chest, a smile filling his face. "We've made a grave mistake." He closed his eyes as he spoke to one of his men. "Jasper, blow your horn outside. Stop the battle. This woman is right."

Jordana faced Benjura. "Go with him and blast your horn as well. Stop the fighting."

Benjura ignored her and focused on her father, waiting.

"Hurry. People are dying." Jordana snapped at him.

A strained silence filled the room until her father nodded at Benjura, approving the order.

Only then did Jordana glance around. Every warrior suffered a gaping wound somewhere on their arms, shoulders, or chests. One clutched his bloody stomach and two others lay dead on the floor. The stench of blood filled the heavy air in the hollowed-out baobab trunk.

Two different horns bellowed outside. Both sung two more times before the battle clangs silenced. Moaning floated in the distance, followed by weeping. How many warriors had died this day?

Father's evil hiss chased the quiet reprieve away. "You shall pay for this." He drew a narrow stiletto from his sheath and pressed the tip into the young chief's neck.

Despite the knife at his back and two at his front, the young man didn't quake. Instead he tilted his head to the side and rested it against Taryn's forehead. He patted her back, as if in sheer relief. The man appeared not the least concerned about the razor sharp dagger about to slice his jugular. Such odd behavior.

The baby cooed at him and kicked her feet, just like she had when Jordana took her into the river. The young father's face shined, and Taryn responded the same—love flowing between them.

Jordana glanced at her father. His lips held a grim line and fire shone in his eyes. She touched both of his outstretched arms and inched them down to his sides. "Another death will not make this right, my Arrdock. We need each other. Our tribes ought to unite against the Chinzu army, or none of us might survive."

Father did not reply.

The young chief handed Taryn to the brave who had returned from blowing his horn. "Care for her with your life, Jasper." At the man's nod, the young father inched down to one knee. "I am Chief Drongo, Arrdock to the Akimmi people. Five days ago, our village awoke to discover many men slain in the night. My parents, the Arrdock and Shedock were dead, leaving me to assume the throne. My daughter was missing, snatched from our fortress, along with weapons, and goblets of gold. Only the missing princess mattered. A lone survivor described the huge giants who had attacked us and kidnapped Taryn. I dispatched my army and we infiltrated your camp. When I spotted Taryn. I ordered the attack."

Chief Drongo did not break his stare from Father's face. "If my men return without Princess Taryn, it will mean death to my wife. I offer my life as payment for the warriors you lost in today's battle. Take me. Please allow my men safe passage back to the Akimmi Village with the princess. Let them return Taryn to the new Shedock."

Jordana browsed over the young chief's men. Muscular

and as tall as Benjura, the mighty warriors frowned at their Chief. One's jaw clenched and released over and over again. Moisture filled the oldest guard's eyes. Their love for the young man offering to sacrifice his life for theirs, displayed on each one's face.

"Chief Drongo, how old are you?" Jordana asked with as much authority as she could muster.

"I am eighteen."

Father returned his blades to their rightful spots in the sheaths at his thighs. "Your request is granted. I shall accept the sacrifice of your life in payment for the warriors you have stolen from me this day."

Jordana jumped between her father and the kneeling young man. "No, my Arrdock. Please spare him."

"You dare to argue with the Arrdock?" Brin flew to her husband's side.

Adding a softness to her voice that she did not feel, Jordana met his gaze. "Father, you never granted my request this morning after accepting the miracle I presented. I change my request to the sparing of this young father's life. I ask you show the Akimmi people mercy." She stretched as tall as she could make herself stand, stared at her father, and didn't allow even a hint of the fear coiling around her spine to show.

Father's eyebrow's collided and the lines across his forehead doubled. His face turned as red as the moons. As fast as a toad's tongue, he reached out and snatched Jordana up, grasping both of her shoulders, and jerking her up to him. Words hissed in her face. "You dare to interfere with the orders of your Arrdock? Again, you overstep your bounds!"

"I'm sorry, Father." Jordana whispered. "I know what it's like to lose a parent. Taryn needs her dad. This Arrdock is so young and not as wise as you. He was just trying to rescue his baby girl. Wouldn't you have done anything to rescue me at that age?"

Queen Brin's adorned hand slithered up Father's bare forearm. "Perhaps you should grant her request if the Banished

119

One agrees to trade her life for his."

Lainey and Beast each filled the room with a roar. They sprang forward and flanked Jordana. Beast growled, baring his fangs at the queen.

Queen Brin tucked behind the Arrdock, cowering from the leopards.

"Great Arrdock," Lainey hissed. "Jordana has a special purpose from Elohim. Please release her."

After a moment's pause, he nodded at Lainey, and let Jordana go.

Her hands rose to massage her upper arms where father's fists had squeezed her too tight.

The Arrdock gazed down at the wide-eyed young man, still on one knee. "My daughter has saved your life. Jordana's request is granted. You and your men are free to go."

"Wait!" Jordana shouted, motioning with her hands. "Both Arrdocks must come to the feast tonight. Our tribes must unite to stop Chinzu's army."

"No, Banished One. My husband will not dine with his enemy. These men tried to murder him. Have you no loyalty? You need to clear out of the Tree Warrior Village with these hideous swine."

If it were possible, more adrenaline surged into Jordana's veins. She faced the queen. "He granted my request for two feasts. Are you suggesting the Arrdock break a sacred oath? Is that your wise council to him?" She almost hoped it was, for it might open father's eyes.

Brin folded her arms across her chest. "I'm sure there's something in the ancient scrolls allowing an Arrdock to rescind a granted request when assassination is attempted by the one who presented the miracle."

"Assassination? By me?" Jordana jumped forward, towering over the Queen, her fingers tingling, but she did not give in to the temptation of wrapping them around Brin's evil throat. "Are you insane?"

"Enough." Father snarled at the women.

120

Lainey's smooth voice sing-songed through the thundering beat of Jordana's heart. "Child, you must release your father from his duty to attend the feast tonight. He is wounded and needs rest. It is evident the war with Chinzu's army is not your Tree Warrior's fight. We must go with the young Akimmi Chief. They are the humans destined to oppose the Chinzu raiders."

A lump formed in Jordana's throat. She wanted to scream at her father and beat her fists against his chest. Did he not see what an honor it would be to defend Elohim's Holy Land? She had never read about ancestors doing anything even close to this in the scroll history. "Please, Father." Jordana whispered through tears.

He spun and strode toward the door, but paused when a sob broke out in the back of the room.

Granna buried her face in her hands and wailed.

Jordana's heart broke along with the old woman's, for once again they'd be separated forever.

Benjura rushed forward, dropping to a knee before the Arrdock. "Please grant me your blessing to accompany Jordana."

She stared at her friend, but he ignored her, and focused on the Arrdock. Why did Benjura step up this time, and not the last?

Father searched Jordana's face before replying. "Granted." He rushed outside without saying goodbye or looking back.

Tears slid down her cheeks. *How could he do that again?*

Brin cast Jordana a wicked grin as she fell in with the departing entourage.

From a fog, Granna's muffled cry cut through to Jordana. She rushed over and enveloped her beloved matriarch. "I'm sorry I won't be able to visit. It was foolish to get our hopes up. I love you." Jordana whispered in the sweet woman's ear.

"My Lady." Chief Drongo came to stand in front of them. "Thank you, Princess. For saving my life and rescuing my daughter. Whatever you request, I will grant it."

"You must send your army to defend the Falls Territory. You will help us stop the Chinzu army from defiling the Holy Land." Jordana did not mince words. "Move your men to the north meadow. I shall meet you there in an hour."

"No, you must come to our encampment five miles northeast at the lake."

"I know the area well," Jordana nodded. "I will need some time to get there."

"As we will. We must evacuate our wounded." He gulped. "And our dead."

Lainey paced near to the entrance. "Let us clear out of here quickly. We will discuss the details when this village is far behind. Danger crouches at the door."

Jordana frowned at Lainey, but chose not to question her.

"You act as if you've seen many talking panthers, but to me, tis a miracle." A smile hinted at the young chief's eyes, who once again, held Taryn.

"We are black leopards." Beast growled.

Jordana helped Granna to the door. "Benjura, please go first and escort Chief Drongo. Make sure he and his men are not harmed as they depart."

The chief tipped his head. "We will need to gather our fallen."

"Of course." Benjura nodded, and slipped outside with Jasper and the others.

As the young chief moved away with Taryn clutched tight to his chest, Jordana sucked in a deep breath. The baby would not belong to her after all. And rightly so. Praise to Elohim for saving the lives of her parents. The good news did nothing to stop the throbbing of Jordana's heart. Despite a stab of sadness, she was delighted that Taryn would be well loved, and would one day rule the Akimmi people. Jordana might never be a mother, but she warmed at Taryn's beautiful future.

Granna's arm squeezed Jordana's waist, drawing her attention. Love shone in the old woman's eyes. It was as if Granna had understood. Only Jordana and her matriarch

122

remained in the tree trunk with the three talking animals. She bent down and hugged Beast. Then she moved over to Lainey. "Thank you both for your protection and assistance." Jordana hoisted Kamali up. "Let's take Granna home, and then be on our way."

Drained of all energy, Jordana shuffled out the door. Her free arm reached for Granna, clasping her hand as they snaked back through the village toward the elder woman's home.

Bodies sprawled everywhere. The casualties had been heavy. Slight differences in leather tunics and loin cloths helped her distinguish between her former tribemates and their attackers. Wounded warriors, severed limbs, and dead bodies strewn in odd positions littered the area. Nausea swirled through her tummy. The carnage caused silent streams to slide down her cheeks. Warriors and maidens alike lay slain. Children sobbed next to fathers and mothers. Some villagers already worked to drag victims away. A band of the Akimmi chief's men, led by the guard called Jasper, marched through, claiming some of the casualties as their own.

Outside Granna's home, Jordana pressed her back against the tree trunk and took in the ghastly scene. A tugging at her arm broke Jordana's stare. She followed Granna into the house, over to the bed, and flopped down. Granna sat beside her, and both women wrapped their arms around the other, and wept anew.

Lainey laid her head on Jordana's thigh. Wet fur shone under her slanted eyes.

A gritty tongue ran over Jordana's ankle as Beast licked her.

Fingers parted her hair as Kamali inspected every inch of Jordana's scalp. The group comforted each other as the minutes passed. Then Lainey led them in prayer, which only ended in more mourning.

The door burst open and Benjura rushed in, kicking it closed behind him. "We need to hurry." A heavy pack was strapped to his back, and Ladybug balanced on his shoulder. Poised in his bow, an arrow held ready under his fingers. Benjura

123

labored to catch his breath. "Many of the Tree Warriors are blaming Jordana for bringing war into the village. They want her head."

CHAPTER FOURTEEN

Jordana yanked off the princess cape as she ran to snatch her bag off a shelf. She grabbed her belongings and shoved them inside. How had she gone from the village darling that morning to a hated villain in a matter of hours? *Fickle people.*

"Leave your things, child. Let's go." Poised at the door, one paw hanging in the air, Lainey stood next to Beast, while Kamali clutched his back.

Jordana swung the long strap over her head and one shoulder.

Granna yanked open its top and dumped in a bowl of nuts and jerky. Her arthritic arms embraced Jordana before shoving her toward the door. "Go. Do not come back. When we see each other again, twill be in Elohim's paradise."

"I love you." Before her heart ripped any more, Jordana slipped out. She dare not glance back.

Benjura led the group to the rear of Granna's baobab trunk and pointed at a moose tree. "Climb. Everyone ascend to the top. We must make our way out of the village from above the jungle canopy." He set his falcon to flight with a command. "Scout."

Beast sprinted to the tree. "Up, Kamali. Climb."

The patas monkey scrambled off his back and swung up the tree.

Lainey sunk her claws into the fuzzy bark and heaved herself up as well, Beast trailing behind her.

125

Jordana gaped at the leopard's power clambering up the tree. Never before had Jordana been so thankful that leopards were the best climbers of all felines.

"What are you waiting for?" Benjura latched on to her waist and heaved her up to a branch.

Jordana clutched the limb and swung to stand on it. As shouts from the village grew louder, she flew into action. She and Benjura ascended at the same time, from either side of the tree. Soon the ground dwarfed beneath them, and lush foliage welcomed them in, as if to shield them from the danger below. While they traversed the canopy, Kamali swung across from vines or by jumping to branches. The rest of them made steady, but careful progress. All the weeping and shouting grew dim as they left the village far behind.

After a mile or more of painstaking progress across the trees, a loud caw sounded from Benjura's falcon.

"That means we're clear to drop to the forest floor. Let's make a run for the lake from down there."

Without hesitation, Beast turned and descended. Lainey followed, as did Jordana. Despite the fear she fought off while scrambling away from the village, Jordana admired Benjura's leadership. The carefree teenager she remembered had grown into a courageous and capable warrior.

Once their feet hit the jungle floor, they sped through the jungle. Kamali from the treetops, swooshing above their heads, Ladybug soaring over them, and the rest running in front of her. She soon lost sight of the patas monkey, and fought to keep up with Benjura and the leopards. After hurdling a fallen tree trunk, Jordana spotted Kamali on a branch, as if waiting for them. But when they drew near, Kamali swung into motion again.

Jordana pumped her arms and legs as fast as she could move. The others seemed to slow for her. She tried to sprint faster. Life as the hunted or the hunter shaped her into an excellent distance runner, but Benjura and the leopards could outdo her in short dashes. No doubt she could trounce each one if given a long vastness to cross, like to the lake.

126

As the village fell another mile behind, the heavy panting around Jordana grew louder. The others slowed, but Jordana kept her pace, unable to keep from trying to prove herself once again to Benjura.

Soon sunlight streamed through the sparse branches at the edge of the forest up ahead, beaming bright around the last tree before the meadow and lake. When Jordana closed in on the jungle's edge, Kamali scampered along a branch overhanging the path. She dangled by one foot, motioning with a hand for Jordana to come closer. Legs and arms pumping, Jordana sprinted straight at the patas monkey. A hair's breadth before reaching Kamali, the monkey let go and dropped. Jordana caught her without slowing, and a second later, burst out of the dense trees, and into the golden sunlight.

A sparkling aqua lake sprawled before her with a meadow to the right and thick jungle encompassing the region. A tent brigade dotted the shoreline with a makeshift horse corral occupying a corner. Inside, a hundred or more magnificent Clydesdales munched on grass.

Jordana shifted the monkey to her back and slowed her approach, so they wouldn't mistake her intent.

A long row of dead bodies—flies already thick around them—spread out to the side. Jordana veered right and avoided the area. As she neared the tents, several men pulled skinny logs from the tree line on the other side of the forest. Others worked to build something.

"Jordana."

The faint call brushed her ears and she twisted to face the meadow. Benjura motioned for her to stop. His face covered in a wet sheen. The two leopards staggered behind him, their tongues dangling from their jaws, held wide from panting. While waiting for them, Jordana scanned the other tribe's work. The Akimmi people had taken the wheels off their small cart, casting the frame away and worked to fashion some type of large flat-bed wagon. Must be to carry their dead home for burial.

Kamali leaned over the front of Jordana and pointed to a

large tent in the middle of the encampment. "I can hear Zinnia whimpering in there. I should nurse her." A banner waved from each of the four corners of the tent.

"I will take you to her." Jordana craned her neck to look at Kamali. "Remember though, her name is Taryn. She is a princess."

"What was that all about?" Heated words hissed her way.

Jordana pivoted toward Benjura. "What do you mean?"

"Sprinting ahead like that. We stayed with you when you could not keep up. Then when the cats slowed, you left them. Leopards aren't built for long distance running. You know that. We must to stick together. It's safer for you."

Guilt seized her over what she must have put the leopards through. She shouldn't have tried to show off for Benjura, but what did he mean? Safer for her?

"I can't protect you and both of them if we're separated." He stormed over to her, hovering inches above her head, his brow furrowed. "Don't leave us like that again."

"I do not need your protection." Heat rushed to her cheeks. "I've survived three years alone in the wild. Don't try to step in as my jira now. Out here, there is much for you to learn. I shall be the one to watch over you." Jordana zipped away, storming between the tents, and ignoring stares from the other tribesmen.

"Let it go, child." Lainey's melodic voice rang out next to Jordana. Its music eased the heat burning inside.

She hadn't noticed the leopard trotting to keep up. Jordana's heart squeezed at the sight of Lainey's wet back and nape. Too angry to speak, she bent and slid her hand down Lainey's back. What gave him the right to correct her? To step in as her protector after all this time? The man had the audacity to ask the Arrdock for permission to go with them, but he never asked if she wanted him along. Well, she did not, and marched to the royal tent near the center without looking around. She wanted to clobber the man walking behind her. He lost all rights to her three hot seasons ago. Later tonight, she'd make sure he

128

understood that.

Jordana forced her hands to relax. Once everything calmed down, perhaps she could get Lainey to intervene. As mediator, the leopard might be able to convince Benjura to return to the Tree Warrior Village. Jordana didn't want him joining their quest. He occupied her mind, infuriating her at every bend. They clashed far too often for the important job ahead. They must be separated for good. And this time it would be easy to say goodbye. They were different now. Older. Wiser. Innocence gone. Love faded. Yet, her heart squeezed inside her chest.

* * *

Benjura studied her back. Despite Kamali's vice grip around Jordana's waist, the princess kept her spine straight as a sword. Just like days of old, her temper flared high. The fire in her belly had always matched the flames in her hair. When the sun beat down on her cascade of ruby locks as she crossed the meadow, it nearly brought him to his knees. Her shimmering crimson curls in front of the turquoise water and the pale green meadow just now, would make an easy target for a warrior's arrow. If she had stay closed, he could have used his shield to deflect a projectile had anyone tracked them down. But he dare not leave Beast and Lainey's to run ahead to Jordana.

The leopards would be mistaken for wild animals if left alone to stroll into the young Arrdock's fortress. Who should he protect? His heart had torn in two directions—run ahead of the spent leopards to shield Princess Jordana, or escort two of Elohim's gatekeepers to safety? Benjura had judged the greater threat befalling the leopards and stayed with them. He could only pray for Jordana as she crossed the open field. Did she not understand how serious the threat was from the Tree Warriors? The Queen probably dispatched men to find and kill Jordana. Wouldn't be too hard since everyone knew they were heading to the lake to meet Chief Drongo.

Benjura's stomach churned over the carnage back at his

village. Dead bodies spread from one end to the other. Could his people recover from so many needless deaths? Would Jordana ever be safe in this world? As long as air filled his lungs, he would protect her and never leave her again.

Fingers squeezed tight around his bow, he extended his free arm and whistled. Ladybug landed and he transferred her to his shoulder. They followed Jordana as she neared an embroidered tent with flying banners.

As Jordana approached the opening, two guards pulled their swords.

Benjura snatched an arrow from his quiver, planted his feet and took aim.

"Put down your weapons." Kamali shouted at the guards while sliding off Jordana's back. "I'm here to nurse Princess Taryn. Out of my way."

The men spoke not as they stared wide-eyed at the talking monkey waddling past them.

Kamali's gruff voice sounded inside the tent. "I'm the nursemaid. Hand her to me." After a brief pause, Kamali barked again. "Do you want her to stop crying or not?" Seconds later, Taryn settled down.

Benjura moved alongside Jordana, aiming his arrow at the ground without slacking the line. "This is Princess Jordana of Arrie. She saved the life of baby Taryn and Chief Drongo. She needs to speak with him." The side of his cheek tingled as she glared his way, but Benjura did not tear his gaze away from the two sword-drawn sentries.

The tent flap opened and the young chief swept out. Jasper followed him. A smile filled Chief Drongo's face. "Malady, I am beholden to you for saving the life of my daughter." He tipped his head. "And my life. Come. Food is prepared. We have much to discuss." He motioned the humans and leopards inside.

The hair on Benjura's arms rose to attention. The guards didn't seem to share the young Arrdock's admiration. Although they did sheath their swords, both stood fingering their weapons as if anxious for action. Benjura slipped between them. Inside the tent, two other sentries watched from the sides, glares filling their expressions.

Were they safe in this camp? Perhaps these tribesmen blamed Jordana for their dead, as well. It seemed the woman wasn't welcome anywhere she went. Danger found her at every turn in life.

Woven blankets covered the floor, and oversized pillows surrounded a rug in the center. Several bowls of food sat on the mat—bananas, flat breads, and blackened chickens from roasting over an open campfire.

Benjura moved to the far side of the room, slapped his bow across a makeshift table, and set his pack atop his bow to anchor it. The end of his giant bow overhung the table's edge. After double-checking the bow's sturdiness, Benjura transferred Ladybug to stand on its end. Her talons added to the already numerous scratch-marks on his favorite weapon.

Chief Drongo motioned for everyone to sit. Kamali had already nestled into a pillow and helped herself to some bananas while nursing Taryn. One discarded peel sat at Kamali's feet, and a half-eaten banana rested in her palm.

Jordana and the Akimmi leader eased down onto cushions across from each other.

When Jasper, the youngest of Chief Drongo's sentries, moved toward the pillow next to Jordana, Benjura slipped onto the padding before the other man could.

Jasper shot Benjura a scowl but said nothing as he moved to the other side of the eating area.

A cloth covered a bowl near Benjura. He flipped off the towel. "Yikes." Several raw, but plucked chickens filled the bowl.

"Oh, those are for your talking leopards." The Akimmi leader pulled the bowl to him, and motioned for Lainey and Beast to come close. "Do you eat chicken? We weren't sure what to serve you."

Beast licked his chops. "We love chicken."

131

Chief Drongo tossed a whole one to the male leopard, who caught it in his powerful jaws, and gave it a vigorous shake, bones snapping one after another like finger knuckles cracking. His spittle flew through the air.

"Beast!" Lainey snapped at him. "Not here."

"That's disgusting." Jordana curled her lip.

Benjura would never admit to the ladies, but the gross sight was magnificent.

The mighty male leopard trotted to the tent's perimeter and plopped down near the falcon.

Benjura reached for some ribs, also blackened from an open fire pit. "When do we move out? Are we heading straight to the Falls Territory?" An excited itch crept through him. It would be a dream come true to cross the Azul River and gaze at the gateway to Elohim's Holy Land. But war and death lay ahead, too. Mustn't let his appetite for adventure influence him in any way. Remembering the tragic scene they had fled sobered him. A fierce battle loomed, and Benjura now knew how horrific it would be.

"In the morning, we'll move out. A small band will return our dead to their families and escort Princess Taryn home. The rest of us will go with you as promised."

"Very good." Jordana set her corn cob down. "We must find Chinzu's army and prevent them from defiling the Holy Land. Twill be a great honor. The ancient scrolls decree Elohim's high favor upon anyone who fights for His name." Her voice cracked. Every line on her face hinted at how badly she wanted that favor upon The Tree Warrior village.

Benjura shared the desire. Not that he coveted the Akimmi blessing, he simply wanted his tribemates restored to Elohim's protective covering. Now the opportunity was lost. How much further would their tribe fall under Brin's influence? He couldn't help but shudder.

"It is our privilege to fight for Elohim." Chief Drongo's words drew Benjura's attention. "We do it not for the prize, but for our love. The Creator has already done much for us."

"To be sure," Jasper said, his stare glued to Jordana. Jordana nodded at the men.

Passion filled the chief's tone. Perhaps it would give Jordana solace to know their motives were pure. Yet, the sadness on her face didn't fade. It tore at Benjura's heart.

As they ate, Lainey, Jordana, Chief Drongo, and Jasper discussed strategy, as if Benjura and Beast were mere bystanders.

Once the details were decided, Lainey purred. "Beast and I will leave tonight and scout ahead. In two days' time, we'll meet you at the riverbank where we first met Jordana."

A familiar look filled Jordana's eyes. She must have washed it away, for soon a stoic expression bathed her. "I understand. I want to go with you, but I must show the Akimmi warriors the way."

"Tis why I did not suggest your accompaniment."

Kamali pulled a mango pit from her mouth. "I shall see Taryn safely to her mother's arms, before returning to the Falls Territory."

"I thank you." Chief Drongo smiled. "You are an excellent nursemaid."

"Yes. I know." The patas monkey bit into a plum.

No one grinned at the funny comment. They finished the meal in silence.

At last, Lainey and Beast stood at the threshold.

With trembling arms, Jordana hugged Beast goodbye. When she latched onto Lainey, tears filled her eyes.

Benjura shoved the temptation away to pull Jordana into his arms and comfort her. Even though their time apart from the animals would be short, Jordana seemed overwhelmed.

Although tall for a female at five foot ten, Jordana had small bones. Narrow shoulders, small nose and chin. Even her hands and feet were petite. Her back bone, though, contained more strength than anyone he'd ever known. So why did a short separation from Lainey and Beast cause Jordana to almost come undone? Whatever the reason, it ate at him. He never had been able to handle her tears.

Benjura clenched his jaw and clasped his hands behind his back before he did anything to embarrass the princess. Or himself. He simply nodded at Lainey and Beast. "Safe passage, my friends."

A ragged scream pierced the silence. Before anyone could move, another one sounded from across the encampment.

CHAPTER FIFTEEN

Jordana launched herself toward the tent opening, but a handful of guards darted in front of her. Men rushed into the tent and surrounded Chief Drongo. More than a dozen warriors blocked the exit. She could see nothing around their tall, wide frames.

Another scream pierced the air, but not a woman's high pitch shriek. This came from a man, deep and guttural as if in agony. Shouting resonated through the enclosure. Jordana tried to squeeze between the guards to get outside, but they formed a crude blockade around the Chief.

Buzzing sounded in the distance. It grew louder, vibrating above the village clatter. Her breath caught in her throat. Locust plague? Killer bees, perhaps? Blood surged through her veins as she feared the worst—scorpiowasps.

Benjura's unmistakable figure pressed into her back. His hands resting on her waist as he drew her to the back of the room. Spinning her around, his gaze bore into hers. "Stay here and guard the animals while I go check it out." He shoved himself through the bottleneck of guards, using his strength to force them to make way.

Jordana stared at his back. Why had she let him take control? She should have asked him to stand guard, while she went to investigate. As a warrior maiden, she didn't need his protection. She sprang to the back edge of the tent, and pulled out a knife. If killer bees approached, they needed to get into the lake, and she ought to set the falcon free. Ladybug would make easy prey if trapped inside a tent.

"No, child." Lainey squeezed between Jordana and the thick leather wall. "Don't tear the covering. We may need it as protection from whatever is making that sound."

Jordana sheathed her blade. She always followed the leopard's instructions without question. Not her father's. Not Benjura's. Only Lainey's. Jordana shoved the realization aside and focused instead on the humming noise. How close were the predators? How much time did they have?

Beast stood in the center of the room. His ears twitched in every direction, and his jaw held wide as he sniffed the air.

Lainey joined him, opening her mouth too, and sucking in deep breaths, her lungs filling to capacity as evidenced by the rise and fall of her ribcage.

Both felines snapped their jaws shut and turned to each other. A silent stare passed between them.

"What? What's out there?" Jordana touched her knives, as if they would protect her from deadly insects. Her first thoughts should go to Elohim, and not her weapons. Another odd realization.

Benjura burst back in, his brows cinched together, and face drained of color.

Beast spoke first. "Scorpiowasps?"

Benjura nodded, his eyes big and round. "A swarm."

Jordana's stomach collapsed to the floor, her knees threatening to follow.

Lainey leapt for the back tent wall. "Cut it. We must find a fire pit for ash and hurry into the lake."

Benjura used his largest machete to slash at the animal hide wall.

Lainey leapt into the room's center. "Chief Drongo, you and Princess Taryn must come with us. Tis your only chance against the scorpiowasps."

Beast, with Kamali on his back, burst through the opening first.

136

Benjura straddled the hole and extended one arm to set Ladybug to flight, then turned and held out a hand for her. "Come, Jordana."

She could not leave Lainey or Taryn, and scanned the crowd behind her. When the chief and some of his men rushed her way, Jordana pointed. "Some go the front and some come this way." She spun back and latched onto Benjura's outstretched hand.

He lifted her outside with one arm.

Beast and Kamali were nowhere in sight.

"Which way to a fire pit?" Lainey leapt beside her and spoke to the young chief. "We must get ash."

Drongo held Taryn against his chest, protecting her with both arms. "I know not where the cooking is done."

"Ash?" Benjura shook his head. "We should go straight to the lake. Come on, we're wasting time."

"You know not about the repentance ash? How have you survived scorpiowasp attacks without it?" Lainey pinned her ears back and hissed. "Do not challenge me on this."

"I wouldn't dare." Benjura spun and scanned the area. "We've only been taught to use the repentant ash during the Season of Atonement. We will gladly do as you say."

Jasper pointed between two tents. "The cooking area is through there."

"Lead the way." Lainey whipped her tail in the air.

The Akimmi sentry sprinted forward, and Jordana followed him, along with the rest of their group, many guards and Chief Drongo cupping Taryn's head as they ran.

Beast shot out on the path up ahead. "This way."

The Akimmi warriors veered right to follow him, with Jordana close behind them. Lainey ate up the ground beside her, and Benjura brought up the rear.

Jordana's prior experience with a single scorpiowasp had brought terror and pandemonium to the entire Tree Warrior Village. Many people were stung before the insect was killed. Now a full swarm bore down on them. Could anyone survive?

Sparks shot through her nerves. Lainey seemed to know something the humans did not. It provided a glimmer of hope.

From behind her, the buzzing grew louder. Jordana glanced over her shoulder, half expecting to be overtaken. But the sky shined as blue as ever. Still, the unmistakable sound of a giant swarm approached. It was close. Too close.

Jordana zigzagged around tent after tent. Did Beast lead them in circles?

The wild shriek of howler monkeys in the nearby woods caused her to jump. Their cries almost drowned out the swarm. Bird caws joined nature's terrifying screeches, as the tree tops came alive with fowl taking to flight. Hundreds, if not thousands of birds vacated the jungle. Benjura's falcon might be among them.

Jordana and the group rounded a corner where men skedaddled in every direction, fleeing right past a smoldering fire pit.

"Why aren't they stopping?" Lainey shot up next to Jasper and the chief. "Command your people to scoop up ash and follow us. It's their only chance for survival."

He didn't question her and pointed. "Men. Come with me. Elohim's gatekeepers will keep us safe."

"No, that's not how it works." Lainey opened her mouth as if to say more, but Beast cut her off.

"Explain later." He dug at the edge of the camp fire, his massive paw scooting ash up and over the edge of the round pit. He buried his head in the mound. When he lifted, his face and skull were covered with a dusty gray grunge. The only color came from his guppy green eyes blinking under long sooty lashes.

Kamali jumped off his back and tested the ash, dabbing at it with her finger. "Tis not hot." She scooped up some soot and rubbed it on her head, grabbed another handful and climbed up the young chief's leg as if he were a tree. She smeared soot on Taryn's hair and wiped a dainty cross on the child's forehead, then proceeded to do the same to the Akimmi Chief.

If they weren't in danger, Jordana may have laughed at the expression on Chief Drongo's face, or those of his men, when the monkey plopped a big dollop of the dirty debris onto the chief's head. Everyone seemed to gawk at Kamali's gall.

Lainey roared above the approaching hum, drawing everyone's attention. "Wipe a repentance cross on your forehead, and make sure it matches your heart. Then get in the lake."

Task complete, Kamali swooshed around to the young chief's back and hung on. "What are you waiting for? Get us into the water."

Chief Drongo glanced around at his warriors. "Do as the animals say, men. Ash, a repentant heart, and in the water." He sprinted away.

Benjura appeared in front of Jordana with a handful of ash. He held it out to her. "Do you want to do it, or shall I?"

Jordana scooped up a fist full and plopped it on her head. "You help the others, I'll assist Lainey." As she bent to one knee in front of her friend, she wiped a cross on her own forehead, then rubbed some into Lainey's fur atop her head and down between her eyes.

"Here they come. Let's go." Jasper jumped up and extended his hand to her.

From her other side, Benjura grabbed her arm, pulling her to him. "Don't look back."

Too panicked to yell at him for bossing her again, Jordana did as she was told. She sprinted, pumping her legs and arms fast. If they survived this, she must make Benjura stop treating her like a child. At nineteen and on her own for three hot seasons, she was more than capable of caring for herself.

Beast ran beside her, roaring instructions to the group as they made a mad dash for the lake. "Wade into the lake and sink down to your jaw. Only your head can be left above the water. When the scorpiowasps come near, do not dunk under, as it will wash away the repentance ash when you resurface. That is when they will sting you. These monsters are smart. Only the praises of Elohim on your lips will save you."

139

At the water's edge, Jordana twisted her hand free from Benjura and tromped out to the chief. He had already sunk down to his jaw, clinging to Taryn and Kamali, the water at their necks too. "Get on me, Kamali." Jordana squatted at Chief Drongo's back and the patas monkey transferred over. Only then did Jordana glance around. Less than forty people accompanied her and the three animals into the lake.

Jordana scanned the shoreline and the makeshift tent village. A thick mass of insects swarmed at the right edge of their encampment as people fled into tents and secured their flaps. They could not be saved, but perhaps there was time to gather the warriors doing the same on the left side of the embankment.

"Chief Drongo, we must try to rescue those men." Jordana pointed at the far bank. "Kamali, get on Benjura's back." After the monkey latched onto him, Jordana reached for Taryn and passed her to the nursemaid. Jordana stood inches from Benjura. "Guard them." She ignored his protest and rushed after the chief, who had already darted away with Jasper and several guards.

Careful breast strokes so as not to splash any water on her face, Jordana swam to shore. Both men stood in ankle high water, shouting at their comrades, motioning with giant arm gestures. Very few on the shore even took notice. Those who did sprinted into the water. Most couldn't hear over the deafening sounds of buzzing, howling, and cawing. If they survived this, no doubt the ringing in her own ears would last for days.

Chief Drongo left the safety of the water and ran to the closest tent, ripping the flap open, and stuck his head inside. Seconds later, a mob of people descended on the lake.

Jordana stood up and shook her hands in the air as hard as she could, and blew on her fingers. She turned to others. "Dry your fingers and use some of the soot on your own heads to wipe a cross on each person."

When men entered the water, Jordana motioned to them. "Do not let this wash off, even when the swarm comes. Elohim will protect you if you praise Him with a repentant heart."

140

As fast as she and the others could move, they wiped crosses on the people joining them. A glance at the bank revealed Chief Drongo and Jasper sprinting from tent to tent, shouting commands. More people ran to the lake. Maybe twenty gathered in front of her to receive repentance crosses. Did she have enough for each one?

"Use our ash, too." Beast and Lainey had come alongside her.

Many warriors veered over to the cats, dipped their fingers into the thick ash atop their heads, and wiped crosses on their foreheads before wading out to Benjura and the crowd.

Jordana searched the shoreline. Where was the swarm now? A black mass moved from tent to tent on the right side, disappearing through the crack at the top where the walls met the roof. People screamed, and a minute later, the pests emerged and moved to the next tent. Somehow they knew which tents hid the Akimmis. Beast had commented about their intelligence. It showed.

Abruptly the cloud paused and hovered between shelters. Then with a jerk, it headed out again, but this time it shot straight at the shoreline. No blue sky could be seen in the center of the thick, dark cloud.

"Chief Drongo. Come!" She jumped up and down, waving her arms when it became clear the scorpiowasps meant to intercept his work.

No way could he hear her over the massive attack, but Jasper must have been watching. He grabbed the chief's arm, and both men dashed for the lake. It became a race between them and the swarm as to who would arrive first. A much shorter distance for the humans, but the insects possessed lightning-fast speed.

Could she do anything to help them? Despite her trembling, she did not wade farther into the turquoise liquid to sink down. Like boulders, her feet stuck to the lakebed.

Chief Drongo reached the edge of the water first and ran with giant steps straight at her.

Finally Jordana spun and rushed into the deep, sinking to

her neck. Only her face and skull remained above the waterline.

Close behind her, a man screamed. Jasper or the chief? Before she could zip around, the black swarm descended on her. A throng of giant insects so thick, daylight disappeared, and left her in darkness.

Yellow and black scorpion tails, with front pinchers and long paper-thin wings fluttered inches from her face. Black balls for eyes dotted their round heads. The body of a scorpiowasp looked the size of her thumb. But their tails…a three inch curvature tipped by a poisonous stinger, hung above their hideous skull, just waiting to pounce. They flew closer, their wings brushed against her skin.

A single sting would torture a person for months, leaving them in agony for the duration of a hot season. Multiple stings brought death.

Jordana couldn't stand to gaze at the dreadful insects and closed her eyes. It took all her strength not to dunk under the water. Her people used long reeds to breathe while staying underwater until they were sure a single wasp had passed, or had been killed. To face an entire swarm above the surface, trusting Elohim's ash cross on her forehead for protection, took every bit of faith Jordana possessed.

Beast's words rang in Jordana's head. *Only the praises of Elohim on your lips will save you.* Just as she opened her mouth to sing, a scorpiowasp landed on her skull. Then another. Their pinchers scratched her scalp as they walked, but they did not sting her.

"Praise, Elohim." She whispered through the crack between her lips, daring not to open her mouth very far. "Praise, Elohim. We lionize His mighty name. Praise, Elohim, the one who reigns supreme."

One by one, each scorpiowasp atop her head flitted away, and she opened her eyes. Others came to inspect her, their wings fluttering against her cheeks and hair. She shivered at the picture of one getting entangled in her long curls. But none landed on her. More importantly, none sunk their curved spike into her flesh.

"Praise, Elohim!" Jordana lifted her voice louder, and the thick blur of evil tormentors departed. A mass of insects surrounded the others in the water. For mere seconds they scanned their prey before moving to the next target. Seemed like hours, but in reality, their inspections took no more time than it took to swallow a drink.

Jordana waded closer to the group without slacking in her praise song. Was Princess Taryn unharmed, as well as the animals and Benjura? And what of Chief Drongo and Jasper? One of them had screamed before the swarm overtook them. She gulped, praying she wouldn't find either one, or both, face down in the water.

CHAPTER SIXTEEN

Zelle gave a violent shake to rid her leopard coat of the spray it absorbed when inching past the last waterfall. She trotted up the trail along the cliff's edge, thinking of her sister Lainey and Jordana. Shouldn't they be back by now? Her big brother Beast accompanied them, and would protect the two females with all his fierceness. Still, Zelle couldn't keep from fretting. As she sidestepped a jagged boulder jutting into the path, she whispered a silent prayer for the three, and the sweet baby. Kamali, too.

Farther up the passageway next to thunderous waterfalls, Zelle climbed toward Rojo's watch area. She was just a two-week old cub when the wolf pup was born. Against all odds, they'd become best friends and now she had exciting news to share with him.

A mighty howl sounded from above her, and Zelle gazed to the rock outcropping. Rojo's silver tips sparkled in the sun. His alert frame looked rigid as he raised his impressive head to the sky and howled anew.

"Hello, Rojo." Although Zelle couldn't see the young wolf's eyes at that distance, she spotted his wagging tail.

Rojo turned and sprinted from the crag onto the trail leading her way.

Once she lost sight of him, Zelle jetted to a mackelbush and hid underneath the forest green leaves and massive yellow flowers. The sweet fragrance would help hide her feline scent.

144

She crouched low, twitching her small ears to locate his canine steps.

Rojo burst around the corner and galloped down the path. When he prepared to pass her by, Zelle leapt out, pouncing on him. The two rolled on the dirt path. When she tried to get away, he gave chase, nipping at her hind legs.

Zelle twisted and swatted at his face, her claws fully retracted.

He feigned an injury and flopped to his side.

She giggled and butted his nape. "You're a terrible actor."

The wolf sat up and licked her face. "Are you here to help me stand guard? The mountain lions in the next sector are boring. All business and no games."

"No, but I might be able to come back. Have you heard? Ojai has returned from the outer rim."

Rojo's pale gray eyes, always wise and alert, widened. "What news did he bring?"

"I know not. I swung by here on my way home."

"Stop lollygagging and go. But please, if you aren't needed elsewhere, come back and share the information with me."

Zelle nodded. "I shall." She trotted backed into the jungle, leaving Rojo and the cliffs behind. His words dawned on her…*if you aren't needed elsewhere*…Her friend always put the duties of the gatekeepers above his own desires. Just like her sister. Perhaps Rojo would become their leader when Lainey grew too old. The wolf's sacrificial heart would make him an excellent commander.

Two eagles swept by, their piercing calls wafting through the trees. They flew in the direction of the gatekeepers' gathering place.

When Zelle gazed up, she spotted hawks and falcons coming in the distance as well, also aimed for home.

Not far from the dens, she'd arrive soon if she kept up the steady jog. Their caves dwelled in front of Elohim's Holy Land on the west. More cliffs and water cascades filled the east side. She'd visited that area once before, where the mountain lions, rams, and goats stood guard. The smallest of the animals patrolled the sheer rocks. And the birds patrolled everywhere.

The wet lands began at the southern tip of the Falls Territory entwined all the way to the outer rim. Otters, beavers, hippos, and elephants guarded the wetlands. Miles and miles of canyon swept up from the southern tip all the way east. It separated them from the rest of the world. Or so she'd been told, for Zelle had never been to the outer rim. Perhaps Ojai would have grand descriptions...or need help if he must return. She licked her chops.

Once again her thoughts turned to Lainey, Beast, and Jordana. Were they having good success at the human village? What took them so long? Zelle shoved her worry away. They were in the Creator's hands. She refused to give room for fear.

As she glided over a fallen log, she searched the bushes for Tut and Simi. They often played around the lair outskirts. No sign of them anywhere, nor of any flying squirrels in the trees. Everyone must be at the dens to hear Ojai's account. Zelle sprinted faster, trying to live up her to gazelle-like name.

Voices reached her first. She twitched her ears to capture some of the words. Her whiskers flicked at the scents bombarding her as she approached the gathering area. It seemed every species of gatekeeper had assembled.

Massive rumps greeted Zelle when she rounded the last bend. Gorillas, bears, rams, and elephants faced the center of the gathering area. On the far side, mountain goats, sheep, and leopards stood on the overhanging rocks. Hundreds of animals crammed into the small area. No one spoke, as they listened to the unmistakable voice of her older brother. Ojai must be standing in the center, but Zelle could not see anything around the sea of back ends.

She hesitated not, as she walked between an elephant's hind legs and out from beneath his front. She glanced up to apologize, but Logan, the big-eared patriarch, paid her no attention. She maneuvered around the wolves, pandas, and zebras before reaching the front. All the small m's occupied the first row—meerkats, minks, and monkeys.

Zelle spotted Ariel and Tanga on the rocks across from her. Neither sister glanced her way as they clung to Ojai's every word. Zelle zeroed her attention on him as well.

"We ought not to engage them until Lainey and Beast return with the human warriors. The tree woman, Jordana, was correct. The giants are huge in stature, and a great number of them have gathered. They work at the canyon's rim." Ojai paced in front of the den openings, where exactly sixty-two caves converged, for Zelle had them numerous times as a cub.

A mountain lion stepped forward, his paws twice the size of Zelle's. "Do you think they'll complete the bridge before Lainey and Beast return?"

What bridge? Zelle's stomach flipped in her belly. Could the Chinzu army be building a bridge over to the Forbidden Falls Territory? Surely not. She dismissed the idea as impossible. The canyon had been carved by Elohim's own finger. No human would dare to cross it. But Zelle had missed the first part of Ojai's story. She'd have to wait to hear the explanation. No need to panic before then.

"At most, they will complete it in another two or three weeks." Ojai let out a heavy sigh. His black tips appeared brownish gray. Dusty. Her brother needed a bath. And sleep as evidenced in his droopy eyes. "Lainey and Beast are due back any day. In the meantime, others should go and observe the giants' progress. Bring reports back here every two days. I want a twenty-four hour vigil at the outer rim."

A golden eagle standing near the front flicked a wing. "We shall go ahead of you and watch until the others arrive." The bevy of birds around him cawed their approval. Without a moment's wait, the whole flock took to flight. Six and seven foot wing spans flapping at once—a magnificent sight.

Zelle returned her attention to Ojai and bounded forward. "Rojo and I will go ahead as well."

147

Ojai narrowed his gaze, ears flattening back. In a blink, his features softened. "Thank you, Zelle, but that won't be necessary."

"Our pack will accompany them."

Zelle twisted to discover Rojo's parents, Buck and Dolly, trotting forward. The rest of their pack stood as well. The two huge grays were twice her size. Zelle twirled a circle, as if still a kitten chasing her tail. She smiled like Jordana taught her and shifted back to Ojai. Panting, she waited for his answer.

"Okay, but this is not a game, little sister. The giants mustn't see you. Their arrows have no trouble flying over the canyon to strike their prey. Those men kill for sport. Promise me you'll obey every order Buck and Dolly give you. Do not stray from their pack."

Zelle smiled at Ojai. "I promise I will. I mean I won't." She shook her head before straightening up and puffing out her chest. "I saw the giants Jordana had slain. Vile creatures, they were. Yes, I'm excited to see the outer rim. But I understand the seriousness of this assignment. I'll do our pride right. I promise to obey Buck and Dolly." She held his gaze a long time.

At last Ojai nodded, and spoke to the grays. "If you leave tonight, you'll arrive before sunset tomorrow. In two days' time, I'll dispatch another small posse. Twill take them a full day and night to reach you. When they do, return with an update. I'll continue this schedule and send relief every two or three days until Lainey returns and guides our next move."

Buck growled, shaking his head up and down.

Ojai's volume rose. "Who will relieve the wolf pack in two days' time, returning four days after that?"

The mountain lions roared and paced. They drew everyone's attention. One swiped a paw in the air. "Our pride will go next."

"And us after them." The gorillas beat their chests.

Zelle loved to play with the gorillas. Grouchy on the outside, funny on the inside.

"Very well. We have the week covered. Lainey and the

148

others will be back then. Let us all gather together when they arrive for final instructions. Thank you, Gatekeepers. We shall defend the Falls Territory. No human will ever see the entrance to the Holy Land!" Ojai lifted his head and roared loud and powerful.

Zelle joined him, opening her jaw wide to give her fiercest snarl.

Animals from every direction sounded off with howls, heehaws, hoo-hoos, and the like. Zelle smiled like Jordana at the impressive and wonderful sound.

* * *

Zelle fetched Rojo from his station and said goodbye to her family. She thanked her brother for letting her go with the wolves. They set off as the sky filled with blazing streaks of pinks and purples. Pleased that sunset was upon them, the nocturnal creature moved away from the dens.

Zelle had learned what she missed of her brother's speech. As the pack scampered down the mountains, she relayed the information to Rojo. "Ojai spoke to the northern gatekeepers. No one crossed from that direction. We guard the west, and know they didn't come from here. So Ojai went south, and worked his way up the outer rim on the east. Along the eastern canyon, he stumbled upon numerous slain zebras, pierced by many arrows, otherwise completely intact. They were killed for sport, not food. Finally Ojai spotted the Chinzu army working to build a bridge over the canyon. Men were working at the bottom of the ravine to build a massive foundation. Other humans dangled from ropes at the cliff-face to build along the rock wall. From the top of the canyon's ledge, more workers fashioned a wooden structure. They still have much to do before reaching our side."

Zelle paused to skirt an ant hill. Once back in pace with Rojo, she finished her tale. "Ojai said the dark-haired giants dressed the same as the men we helped Jordana cremate. Even

149

with their vast numbers, Ojai believes it will take them a couple more weeks to finish their project. Then the army of giants can march right over to the Forbidden Falls Territory." A shiver ran under her fur. "Have they no respect for Elohim's decrees?"

"I have often wondered about the stories of humans." Rojo trotted next the Zelle. "I'm *not* looking forward to meeting my first one."

"Don't judge the race by the golden giants you are about to see. Wait to judge them when you greet Jordana and Zinnia. She's the cutest baby ever. To lick her hairless skin delights the tongue. And her smell…"

Rojo laughed. "You've talked of nothing except Jordana and Zinnia since returning from the Great Eucalyptus Forest. I hope I'm not disappointed when I finally come upon them."

"You won't be." Zelle flicked her tail. "Impossible."

The two chatted endlessly as they traveled through the night. At day break, Buck and Dolly instructed everyone to get a few hours of sleep before completing the last leg of their journey.

Zelle climbed a tree and stretched out on a limb with the wolf pack cuddled at the base. Too excited to sleep, she scanned as much of the land as she could see. Orange poppies and purple delphiniums covered a field in front of her. A lake sprawled across the horizon in the south. Mountains filled the landscape to the north and trees dotted both sides of the river they had followed out of the marsh lands. There she'd seen a species of trees new to her. Sharp pointed leaves, if you can call them that, of deep green covered the pointed tree. Others had long needle-like bluish green leaves. The fragrance from the trees delighted her senses. That must be their purpose, for a leopard could never climb one of the needle-leaf plants.

Her lids grew heavy and at last she closed her eyes, still picturing the new discoveries she encountered that day. Elohim's creations danced in her mind, until she finally drifted off to sleep.

* * *

A bark jolted Zelle. She opened her lids, stretched, and scanned the area. The pack had taken down a caribou and ate below her. She lumbered down the tree, her own hunger gnawing through her belly.

"Good morning, sleepyhead." Rojo tossed a rabbit at her feet. "I saved that for you. Father says we slept too long and must hurry the remaining distance."

Zelle ate her breakfast, and in a short time, they departed. They kept quiet while traversing the remaining miles. The sun held high when the first human scent reached her. "Stop." Zelle spread her jaw wide and breathed in.

The wolf pack wiggled their snouts, raised and sniffed.

Buck broke the silence with a whisper. "We're close. Spread out and crouch low in the long grass. Absolutely no talking. We want none of their arrows aimed our way."

Each animal nodded and moved out in various directions. Zelle stayed close to Rojo and hunkered low, as if stalking mighty prey.

Distant shouts from the giants drifted her way. They were close to the rim. Zelle concentrated so hard on the words of the men, she didn't realize until it was too late that she stepped on something gooey. She glanced down, and froze when she discovered blood covering her paw. Jaws opened, she inhaled and followed the sent through the tall grass. The blades parted to reveal an eagle with an arrow in its chest, Zelle gagged. She ran over and sniffed the lifeless body of Sarah, a talking eagle from her sector, lay dead from a piercing. Zelle vomited, unable to keep her breakfast down. She scurried away and caught up to Rojo, whispering her gruesome discovery in his ear. Sarah had a kind heart, gentle voice, and graceful way about her. Zelle fought tears over Sarah, as she made her way toward a lone tree along the canyon's edge where Rojo hunkered down.

She inhaled several deep breaths to calm herself, and forced her thought to focus on task at hand. Sarah would have wanted that above all. Zelle leaned into Rojo. "I'm going up the back of the tree."

The wolf nodded, his gaze frozen on the scene ahead.

From the back of the trunk, Zelle sunk in her claws and climbed. She ignored the first two limbs, and moved up into the vegetation. At a third branch, she inched out. When the bough began to sway, she stopped. Second later she sprawled out and surveyed the activity.

From the top of the canyon, giants lowered supplies to the men dangling from heavy ropes at various lengths along the cliff's side. They hammered spikes into the rock face. Other builders at the top fashioned a staircase and eased it over the side. The structure was fastened to the spikes.

At the bottom of the ravine, a few hundred giants built a base, chopping logs and attaching them with rope. They used rocks and clubs to pound metal spikes into boulders and more logs. The base stretched across the entire canyon floor and grew wider as the labyrinth rose to meet the expanding canyon walls. Eventually the work of the three different groups would meet. Once the various sections were connected, the bridge would be complete.

Saliva caught in Zelle's throat as a lump formed. The giant's plan seemed clear. And doable. They were building a sturdy foundation from the bottom up, with stairs down the side, and the bridge in the middle. A smart plan. An enormous undertaking. If the giants weren't so vile, she might be impressed with their ingenuity. How could her small group of animals ever take down a bridge of that size and or an army of that magnitude?

The encampment on the mesa behind the workers drew her attention. Maybe a thousand tents filled the expanse. Blazing campfires dotted their village. She zeroed in on the fire. Weren't the men worried about sparks igniting their shelters while they slept? Only once had Zelle been close to terrifying fire. The memory sent jolts shuddering through her.

Just as fast, an idea struck. Zelle sunk her claws into the limb as she considered it. With a glint of hope, she scooted back until her rump met the tree trunk. Then she turned, and

152

descended. For more reasons than one, she must speak with Jordana.

CHAPTER SEVENTEEN

Jordana breathed in the cool morning air. Two hundred and eight men had died in the scorpiowasp attack and forty-seven more were balled up in agony. Add them to those injured in the battle with her former tribe, and half of the Akimmi warriors were unfit to fight.

She yanked hard on the rope, attaching a travois to a horse. For two grueling days, she helped the uninjured build a hundred horse-pulled litters, cared for the injured, and tore down the camp. Exhausted, but unswayed by the setback, they finally prepared to set out for the Akimmi village. No longer could they head straight to the Falls Territory. Replacements were required, the injured needed nursing, and the dead must be buried. The Akimmi braves refused to entomb their men away from the village cemetery.

Jordana clicked her tongue to set the horse in motion. She led the Clydesdale to a blanket where two of the cooks lay, both females. Good thing the elderly women only had one bite each, as a second might have done them in. They thrashed in torment. It would take several months for the poison to wear off. Jordana helped Agatha up, the older of the two. She whimpered as Jordana eased her onto the soft bed of the litter. Jordana had piled what blankets she could find to cushion the ride. Each of the massive horses would pull two or three people on a litter. As the only females, and because of their ages, Agatha and Marta each had their own.

"You'll be okay, ma'am. I'll take care of you. Can I get you some breakfast?"

"No, dear. Just let me die." The woman moaned as she rocked back and forth on the makeshift bed.

"Don't say that." Jordana ignored the tightening of her chest as she retrieved a second horse for Marta. The aged widow had been stung on the wrist. In her delirium, she begged for someone to cut off her forearm. Jordana believed if the woman were strong enough, she might attempt the grizzly deed herself. Only time could cure her from the venom surging through her bloodstream.

Marta shrieked when Jordana shifted her off the blanket and onto the travois. If possible, Jordana's ears rang even more. She picked the blanket off the ground, shook it, and secured it around the woman.

Jordana moved to stand between the Clydesdales, taking a bridle in each hand, she led them forward. Agatha and Marta cried out. The horses didn't flinch as they paced to the back of the procession.

Benjura appeared in front of her, setting his falcon to flight off his forearm, then offering her a small rag.

She stared at the extended cloth. Did he want her to wash something? Could the man not see she was busy? She blinked without moving.

He moved in close, mere inches from her face, and dabbed the cloth under her eyes. He dried her cheeks, and enveloped her in his arms. No whispers of comfort, just his strong hands running up and down her spine offering solace.

Jordana, so focused on her two charges, hadn't realized tears soaked her cheeks. The poor ladies' misery, and that of countless men from either battle wounds or insect stings, tore through her heart. "Why, Benj? Why would Elohim allow this suffering when important work is to be done? I don't understand." She melted into his embrace, resting her head against his chest.

"Elohim has not left us. He wasn't the one who told the

155

Akimmi braves to attack. Do not blame Him for human mistakes." His lips touched the side of her head as he whispered. "Perhaps only those with repentant souls can cross into the Falls Territory. The swarming plague could have been merciful for those not fit to enter the Falls Territory. Only two hundred and eight braves died from the stings. But with the size of the mighty swarm, we could have been wiped out. Yet two talking leopards knew what to do and saved many lives. Focus on the protection we received from the Creator. I do not believe our deliverance was by happenstance."

Benjura pulled back and rubbed her bare arms. "Every other year during the Season of Atonement we must bring forth a perfect sacrifice, an animal with no blemishes. Anything less is unacceptable. Right?"

She nodded at him. The Season of Atonement wasn't for another year. What had that to do with this?

"Well, I've been wondering about those who died. Were they blemished? I don't mean on the outside, I'm referring to the inside their heart or mind. Those stung and now unable to cross, might have been saved from bringing a curse upon themselves. Maybe this was more merciful."

Jordana shoved him back. "More merciful? No one's heart is blemish free. What a terrible thing to say."

Benjura dropped his arms and nodded. "I do not feel right to judge." He paused and folded his arms across his chest. "I only meant to share my musings, but I'm not explaining it well. We've never been allowed to enter the Forbidden Falls Territory before. Tis no small thing we plan. Before I step into the Azul, I shall make sure my heart is in right-standing with Elohim." Benjura sighed, his hazel eyes heavy. "Entering with a forgiven heart may be the key to a successful mission, that's all I'm trying to explain." He handed her the rag, turned, and left her alone.

For a long time, Jordana stared at his back. If he had doubts about crossing, he could stay behind. And yet, part of his words rang true. *Tis no small thing we plan.* Comparing it to the Season of Atonement sacrifice might be more accurate than she

156

dared to admit. She glanced around for Lainey—the Gatekeeper might know.

Jordana spotted Kamali up ahead, arguing with Jasper. Although too far away to hear their words, Jasper's red face could not be missed. Jordana left the horses in the procession line, and hustled forward. Kamali clung to Taryn. The monkey alternated between shaking her head and barring her teeth at the chief's royal guard. Something had really upset the monkey.

Jordana jogged up to them. "What's going on here? Can I help?"

"She won't give me princess Taryn." Jasper fisted his hand on his hips.

"That's right, I won't. No, no. Absolutely no!" She gave another violent shake, sending her lips flapping. "I am the only nursemaid here. I will care for the princess until she is safely in her mother's arms." Kamali adjusted her clutch on the baby. "This vile human wants Taryn to ride with her papa on the travois while he's thrashing in pain. He could hurt the child, or even drop her."

Red as a ruby, Jasper raised his voice. "Chief Drongo has improved and is asking for his daughter. I must obey his command and take the princess to him. I don't want to hurt this monkey, but I will if she does not follow my orders."

Jordana held up both hands. "You are both right. Chief Drongo needs to see his daughter to know she is well cared for." She held up her hand to stop the patas monkey's open mouth. "You are correct, too. Kamali. Taryn will not be safe on the litter." Jordana turned to Jasper. "Can you arrange for a calm and obedient horse to walk beside your chief?"

"Yes." He shrugged—his expression full of exasperation.

Jordana zeroed in on Kamali. "You will ride next to Chief Drongo and when he gazes up from his bed, he can find solace in seeing his daughter. It may comfort him to observe her safe in your arms. Agreed?"

Silence swelled between them. At last Kamali nodded, as did Jasper.

"Now," Jordana pointed at Jasper. "Please bring the sweetest mare you can find." She motioned to Kamali. "You carry the princess over to see her father. Keep her in your arms, but allow the chief to kiss Taryn's cheek if he's able to rise up."

Kamali harrumphed as she waddled away, the baby clutched to her chest.

Jasper smiled at Jordana, his eyes as blue as sapphires above prominent cheeks and a strong chin. Not nearly as handsome as Benjura, but attractive nonetheless.

"Well done, Princess of Arrie. You shall make a fine Shedock one day." He reached over and pulled a piece of straw from her hair.

Kamali called back to them. "Hurry up, brute. They're almost ready to move out. Fetch me a good horse."

Jordana opened her mouth to state once again that she'd never be Shedock to her people, but Jasper snapped away and jogged up to Kamali. He never looked back at her.

Jasper and Chief Drongo were not brothers, simply boyhood friends. When a scorpiowasp landed on the chief's back, raised its wicked tail, and came down on Drongo's skin, Jasper hit the creature off, cutting it in two. He risked getting stung himself to save his chief. The vile insect didn't have a chance to sink its stinger all the way into the chief's muscle. But the Akimmi leader got a small taste of poison and convulsed in Jasper's arms as they sunk to their necks in the lake. As the swarm inspected their heads, Jasper sang praises to Elohim and both men were spared.

Jordana admired Jasper's loyalty. A rare quality. All she experienced was abandonment. First by her mother, although not Mamu's fault, for death had stolen her away. Then by Father when he married young Brin and forgot all about his hurting teenage daughter. Lastly by Benjura who refused to stand up for her at the Banishment Rite, of which he had yet to offer any explanation. No one in her tribe came to her aid. Even the Garden Tenders did not want her. Would she ever have anyone she could depend on?

158

Back at the horses, Jordana picked up the reins, keeping them slack. She allowed the Clydesdales to munch on as much grass as they wanted before heading out. Benjura's words returned to her. Did he think the chief unworthy to cross the forbidden river, hence the partial sting? Chief Drongo risked everything to save his child, and even offered to sacrifice his own life to save his men. How much more pure-hearted could one get? The gall for Benjura to suggest otherwise…and yet he had a point about crossing. They ought to fast and pray before entering the Azul's current.

Would there be enough time? Everything took far longer than she anticipated. Jordana squeezed her eyes shut and held them tight, as she fought off memories of the dark giants, their hideous grins, evil plans, and declaration of war. Was the Chinzu army already on their way? A shudder ran through Jordana's tummy. Those monsters must be thwarted from bearing down on any village. They must be defeated before slaughtering men, and kidnapping women and children.

"We're leaving now and have come to say goodbye."

At Beast's unmistakable rumble, Jordana spun around. "What? No."

"Tis time, child." Lainey sat a good thirty yards away, Beast beside her. "I don't want to step any closer to the non-speaking horses. Leave them and come to us."

A glance at the mares revealed their ears perked and heads jerking up and down. So lost in thought, she hadn't noticed their agitation. Jordana motioned the felines to move farther away, settled the horses, then released their reins. She left them and rushed over to Beast and Lainey. Dropping to her knees, she said, "Please change your minds."

"We can't, child. We've been over this." Lainey's long lashes blinked.

Beast nuzzled his head under Jordana's hand and leaned against her body. For all of Beast's terrifying bravado, the pussy-cat loved for Jordana to rub his ears as if he were a little kitten. She gave them a deep massage while gazing at Lainey.

159

"You don't need our help at the Akimmi village. Our job on this side is done. Beast and I shall return to the Falls Territory at once. Kamali must stay with Taryn until she's back under her mother's care. Kamali can help you once you take the Akimmi people to the right spot on the Azul. Whistle your animal tune. I will post sentries to watch for you. I'll find out what Ojai has learned of the golden giants, and be ready with a plan when you arrive."

Jordana inched her chin up and down. "You are right, of course. But I will miss you both so much."

"And we, you." Beast blinked at her with a telling look in his eyes.

Jordana's throat thickened. How did she get so close to the leopards in such a short time? "Can I ask something before you go?"

Lainey nodded.

"Could the swarm of scorpiowasps been a plague from Elohim?"

Beast's whole body stiffened. "What makes you think that?"

"It's something Benjura said." Jordana relayed the conversation to the two gatekeepers, hoping they had special insight. When finished, the three sat in silence.

Beast rendered his opinion first. "It's an interesting theory. I don't agree or disagree."

"Neither do I." Lainey's whiskers twitched. "Benjura is wise to seek a clean heart. Each human should do the same, just as we prepared our hearts before crossing to you."

"You did?" Jordana arched a brow at Lainey. "I didn't know that." She had much to learn from the gatekeepers.

"Tis what took us so long." Beast flipped his tail.

"So you think Benjura is right?" Jordana studied their faces.

"Part of what he says is true. Tis not our job to understand everything. We are simply to love and trust Elohim."

Jordana did love Him—loved Him very much. It was the

160

trusting part that grew harder as more obstacles crashed into her life.

Beast stood and Lainey followed.

Jordana stayed seated on the grass, blinking at them.

"See you soon, princess. Do not lollygag." Beast ran his tongue from her jaw to her eyebrow.

She hugged him, rubbing her wet cheek on his silky fur. "I have grown to love you and will miss you deeply."

"And I you." He pounced away.

When Jordana twisted to face Lainey, she had trouble keeping eye contact. Tears blurred her vision and lumps the size of grapes filled her throat as if a whole cluster had lodged inside.

Lainey moved in and laid her head on Jordana's shoulder, her mouth close to Jordana's ear. "Oh, perfect Creator, protect this child and bless her quest. Comfort her. Give her wisdom. Bless her life, her heart, and soul. Bring us back together soon. Be it so."

Too choked up to whisper her agreement, Jordana simply nodded while clinging to her friend.

The blast of the ram's horn sounded up ahead to start the procession.

"I love you." Jordana let go. "Be safe."

"And you." Lainey pulled back without stepping away and stared at Jordana, her paws rooted in the grass.

"What?" Jordana raised her eyebrows. Indecisiveness wasn't a common expression on Lainey's furry face.

"Tis not my place to say." Lainey's head drooped low.

"Nonsense. You're my friend. I want to hear your thoughts."

Lainey's head lifted. "Even in regard to Benjura?"

Especially in regard to Benjura. Jordana stopped herself from saying it aloud. Her curiosity increasing by the second. "Yes."

Lainey plunked her bottom down. "The man has a good heart. He had special reasons for his actions—the ones that hurt you. You should know he's suffered for his obedience. Benjura

161

has earned a fresh start."

Suffered for his obedience? What about how I've suffered? Jordana's tongue stuck to the roof of her mouth as if covered in sap.

"Goodbye, child, I shall miss you." Lainey ran ahead to Beast, and disappeared over a slope.

Jordana flopped back on the grass and gazed into the blue sky. A single cloud floated overhead, dainty and insignificant in the big firmament. It looked out of place. Just like her. Though she traveled with a crowd of people, she didn't fit in with any of them. And when this ordeal ended, she would be alone again.

At the Akimmi village, she'd only serve as a daily reminder of the men they lost. The idea of causing more pain to the widows and orphans, sliced into her heart. Not to mention the need to become an expert at deflecting Jasper's attention. Moving to the Forbidden Falls Territory was not an option either—Lainey had said Elohim set the gatekeepers apart from humans after the fall for specific reasons.

A blast from the ram's horn jolted her.

Perhaps she should accept the truth. She didn't belong with anyone. She didn't belong anywhere.

CHAPTER EIGHTEEN

Jordana inched along in the procession. Damp from sweat, she longed for a cool river. Moisture even dripped from behind her knees. Benjura had checked on her after their late lunch, but she hadn't seen him since. Perhaps he could scout ahead for a water source. How was Taryn faring in the soaring temperatures? No baby cries echoed from the front—Kamali must be doing something to keep the child cool. How soon before the sun would dip below the horizon? When could they stop for the night?

"M'lady, might I walk with you a while?" Jasper spoke as he maneuvered between the two litters to stand on her right, trapping her between him and one of the Clydesdales.

She nodded.

He slipped one of the sets of reins out of her hands and led the horse beside him.

She glanced at the position of the sun in the sky. "We've been traveling southeast of the Tree Warrior Village for the last two days. I've explored down here many times. I've never seen any signs of a village."

"That's because we conceal the entrance to our city."

Jordana arched a brow at him. "A mysterious passageway?"

"Exactly. But I'm sworn to secrecy, so I shan't tell you more." Jasper grinned at her, the cleft in his chin visible under whiskers.

"If it's so secret, how did the five giants find you?"

Jasper rubbed his jaw. "That topic has been on our tongues since the morning we woke to discover the raid. Maybe one spied an Akimmi hunter entering our secret passageway, and that's how they found us."

She nodded, considering his explanation. Very disconcerting how giants from a foreign land could find the Akimmi fortress when she, a native of the area, had not.

Jasper lowered his voice and leaned her way. "There is great debate among the warriors about permitting you and Benjura to enter our city."

"Even after what we've been through together with the scorpiowasps? Surely they know we pose no threat."

He smiled at her. "Shielding our village goes back three centuries. Some want you blindfolded before we get close, others wish to make you leave and wait for us in the Eucalyptus Forest. Others say you must swear oaths first."

"And what do you say?" Jordana studied his strong and masculine face. The leeriness of the Akimmi people differed from the confidence of the tree warriors in so many ways.

"The Akimmi dead and wounded, coupled with the prospect of war, demands an exception. I say you will be the most beautiful addition to our village in decades." Jasper's fingers brushed against hers as they walked.

Jordana reached to clasp the reins with both hands. She shifted to gaze at the grass they traversed.

"Sorry if I overstepped my bounds. You are a lovely princess, and I do not wish to embarrass you. I shall take my leave. Before I go, let me assure you. There is no need to fret over the warrior's worry. Chief Drongo is beholden to you for saving his daughter's life. And his. You are welcome in our city any time you wish, and can stay as long as you want. No one will ever challenge the chief's decree." Jasper held out the reins for her to take.

She should let him take his leave, but her craving for conversation made her push back his offering. "Will we arrive to your secret entry during the day? I wish to view it in the daylight."

Jasper smiled and fell in beside her. "Oh yes. I promise there'll be remnants of light on the morrow for our entry. You'll not be disappointed."

She continued leading her horse while asking Jasper many questions about his village. His hearty laugh and funny stories of growing up with their chief, made the miles pass quickly.

Soon they stopped for the night. No doubt the journey could have been made in half the time, if not for the injured. She slept between her two charges on the ground, and not in the trees. Such an odd feeling, but she wanted to be close if the ladies needed her.

The next morning, Jordana rose early, along with the encampment. Traveling on the final day proved to be less difficult. They departed at dawn and rested during the hottest part of the day. After eating a late lunch, the large procession headed out.

On the final leg, Jordana replayed Lainey's words in her mind. *Benjura deserves a fresh start*. Obviously he had spoken to Lainey about his motive for not standing up at the Banishment Rite. Why would he speak to a stranger and not to her? Shouldn't he explain to her above anyone else? The two were betrothed, yet he said nothing, and did nothing to help her. Best friends since age six, training partners, hunting buddies, and at the end, sharing stolen kisses, and declaring their love.

As future Shedock, Jordana's childhood training included much more than that of normal village girls. Cooking and sewing were mastered by age eight. Knives, snares, and hunting by ten, putting her a year ahead and into Benjura's age group. He learned how to shoot a bow alongside her, and protected her from older kids. As if the Arddock's only daughter needed a jira protector.

Combat training came next, along with scroll study. For her alone, the ancient laws were memorized. Benjura helped her

165

study and quizzed her. He knew the history and decrees as well as she. By the time she turned fourteen and he fifteen, their bond was so thick, other teens couldn't penetrate it. That is when she asked Father if Benjura could study the leadership duties alongside her. Jordana announced to her parents that Benjura would either be her husband or trusted advisor when she became Shedock, so he must prepare, too. Father and Mother grinned, nodding their approval.

Knowledge of the future responsibility to rule had matured Jordana at an early age, Benjura too. He attended every one of Father's Judgment Seat sessions. And when people criticized her for only seeking her own pleasures, and not looking out for others, Benjura defended her. He knew how hard she studied to memorize the law. He took his future job as seriously as she took hers.

But months later, when Mamu fell and died, Jordana lost interest in her studies. She trudged along, barely able to concentrate, not caring if she passed or failed.

Absorbed in thought, Jordana strolled between the massive steeds without glancing around. As so often with memories, the best one flooded her mind. Heat rushed to Jordana's cheeks, and her lips tingled. She could still feel the touch of Benjura's first kiss. On the eve of her sixteen birthday, she slipped out of the Arrdock fortress and across the canopy to the eastern guard tower where Benjura had served since turning seventeen two months earlier. Most evenings, she'd slip out to help watch. Of late, the boy had been moody—brooding over something. She planned to make him talk. They didn't keep secrets from one another. Everyone else yes, but not each other.

Jordana had dropped from a branch onto the outer decking of the watch tower where Benjura stood motionless—studying her. She searched his eyes, trying to read his expression. His eyes roamed over her in a way she noticed only a few times before. The look on his face caused her heart rate to jump. Finally he rushed forward and raised both hands to her cheeks and stared into her eyes. At last Benjura's mouth covered her lips

166

for their first kiss.

Jordana didn't know how long they stood there on the open deck for anyone to see while nature's music serenaded them…croaking frogs and crickets, the call of owls. When he finally pulled back, she grappled to catch his arm. Her legs wanted to sink to the floor, and he grabbed her, grinning. She'll always remember the cute smile on his face when he said the most amazing thing to her.

"I have always loved you."

"I love you, too." It poured out of her. Never before had she realized how much she loved him. Husband it would be, not just an advisor. She deepened their kiss, burying her hands in his hair.

When Benjura broke their hold, he pressed his forehead to hers. "You must go now. Tomorrow I shall speak to your father about our betrothal and a chaperone until we wed."

She nodded at him, unable to speak over the heaving of her chest. It took longer than usual to return home. Her limbs shook as she traversed the moose trees. Her focus away from her lost mamu for the first time in a year. She couldn't wait to tell Granna what just happened.

As future Shedock, laws required her to complete her training before marrying. If she doubled her studies, they could marry once she turned seventeen, and he, eighteen.

A blissful week followed that night, with secret whispers to Granna and sewing plans made. Their betrothal was announced and Benjura worked out details for a new tree house in the Arrdock fortress. For the first time since mother's fall, and father's marriage to Brin, hope for a happy future filled Jordana. Back when father had married a young wench and doted on her every whim, ignoring his only child, Jordana cried daily in Benjura's arms. Now she laughed in them.

Most girls married at sixteen or seventeen. None waited until their eighteenth year. Jordana had no intention of doing so either, and set a strict study schedule. But before getting half way through it, the tribe gathered to banish her. Jordana would never be Shedock, and Benjura could never be Arrdock. All because she refused to bow to the ground before the Queen and attend her birthday party over Elohim's Atonement. How could her tribemates go along with Brin's new decree? Why didn't Benjura rebel? He claimed to worship the Great Creator, and should have fled with her.

Jordana blinked to clear the memories. She exhaled a deep breath to calm herself and stop the sharp prickles in her heart. Before the Banishment Rite, Jordana would have dismissed any suggestion of Benjura marrying her for the Arrdock title alone. Yet his actions that night suggested otherwise.

If he had vouched for her on that day, they could have married and moved outside the village. She could have lived a semi-normal life as long as she never tried to enter the city—that would bring certain death. However, Benjura could enter as often as needed and Granna could come out to visit. Jordana would have been safe, instead of battling in the wild to keep from becoming someone's supper. Perhaps she could have become a mother. Surely Father would venture out to greet his grandchildren and daughter.

Jordana shook her head. Benjura had made his choice. She must accept his decision and move on. Explanation or not, she forgave him and would find a way to be his friend. She'd never trust him as jira, but she could fight side by side with him in the coming war. She wouldn't want anyone else at her back during a battle. A brother-in-arms—that's what he'd be. Lainey had urged her to look at Benjura with a fresh heart. For the holy gatekeeper, Jordana would do as requested.

"Jordana?" Jasper called from the front of the procession and motioned her forward.

She shoved the memories back into the recesses of her mind and closed heavy gates around them. Shoulders pulled back, and a thrust of her chin, she dropped the horses' reins, and slowed her gait. Both horses passed her and continued to trudge forward. A glance at the two old cooks, revealed one asleep and

168

the other whimpering. Both horses stayed in the procession without her guidance.

Jordana ran ahead to Jasper. Not an easy dash, as they'd been ascending a gentle slope for the past mile. A quick swipe under each eye, and hands smoothing her mane, she slowed her approach.

Jasper faced the front of the line as she came up behind him. Broad shoulders, tapered waist, and thick muscles formed the man's physique. The closer she inspected him, the more attractive she realize he was. When Benjura was present, she didn't notice other men.

The brave glanced over his shoulder and they locked eyes. A smile filled his face and he held his hand out to her.

Jordana stared at his palm. Should she grab hold? Would he get the wrong idea? Despite his pleasing looks, she had no intention of accepting his advances or staying in the Akimmi village. When all of this ended, she would return to the Great Eucalyptus Forest.

"Come on. I won't bite." Jasper wiggled his fingers.

Jordana shook away her hesitation and latched onto his palm. He pulled her to him, tucking her hand around to the crook of his elbow as if to escort her. She stiffened, unsure what to do.

"You're the oldest young-person I have ever met. How old are you?"

"Nineteen."

"You're so serious. Try to enjoy the small things in life. Like a beautiful view." His free arm swung across the space in front of him, drawing her attention.

A gasp escaped her lips as she took in the scene. They stood at the hill's crest, and below them sat a sprawling valley filled with vibrant wildflowers. Faint scents of jasmine floated in the air. The long slope down to the valley floor spanned a quarter of a mile and ended at the foot of a mountain range. Red rocks formed the rugged cliffs. Giant willowy trees the color of limes dotted the mountain side. White flowers or bushes of some type filled the landscape.

The most spectacular part of the scene fell over a crag. A wide cascading waterfall dropped into a turquoise river. Tropical foliage and forbidden purple palms lined both sides of the river. Their shimmering bark sparkled under the setting sun. No sign of damage or defilement appeared anywhere.

"This is the most beautiful valley I've ever seen." Jordana exhaled a deep sigh.

"I thought you'd like it." Jasper patted her hand.

Even the sky cooperated by displaying streaks of pink and orange amongst white clouds and a still blue sky.

"This is my home. Can you see the secret entrance to our city?" Jasper arched a brow at her.

"What city?" Jordana scanned in every direction. No people. No houses in trees. No caves carved into the crimson rocks. Although she had never been to this particular spot before, she wouldn't have spied any hint of civilization if she had. "I see no sign of human life."

"Good. Soon you will." Jasper unclasped her hand from his elbow, and motioned to a young brave riding horseback. "Devin, find the cooks. Their horses are unmanned. Take the old women home. Make sure they aren't dumped as we pass through."

The skinny kid nodded and galloped his Clydesdale up the line.

Jasper left her to bark orders at his countrymen.

Jordana found Kamali and Taryn, and strolled along with them as they crossed the meadow. Baby and monkey were well. As for Chief Drongo, in the three days of traveling, he had improved a great deal. This morning he even walked a few hours. By his furrowed brow and curled position on the travois, she assumed the torturous pain had returned. Still, he was one of the lucky ones.

At the base of the mountainside, the Akimmi braves positioned their caravan into a single line. She left them and moved to gaze into the water. The pounding waterfall drowned the tormented cries of many in their procession. She hadn't realized how much they bothered her until only cascading water noise filled her ears. Eyes closed, she breathed in the fresh, misty air. The dirt on her skin itched. Did she have time to jump into the river? She pivoted to go ask and smacked into Benjura's thick chest.

"Whoa." He caught her, a chuckle escaping his lips. "Sorry about that. I guess it's pretty loud over here."

She lifted her voice above the din. "A welcomed relief from the wincing and buzzing I can still hear."

He nodded, and bent close to her ear. "Do you think they'd notice if we dove in? I could use a bath."

They always did think alike. *Give him a chance to be your friend.* Jordana broadened her smile. "I was just going to ask if there was time."

"We can be quick and join the end of the line." He arched a brow at her. "Unless you plan to skinny dip again and make me cry for a week."

Jordana socked his arm. "I was seven. I didn't know it would send you running like a wild zebra back to the village." Jordana soaked in his deep laugh until she caught sight of a horse and travois disappearing into the brush and seemingly over the edge of the embankment. She leapt forward. Did they fall off the cliff and into the water below? Jordana searched the water, ready to dive in to save someone before they drowned.

CHAPTER NINETEEN

Jordana peered over the embankment—only a ten foot drop to the churning river below. No sign of horse, stretcher, or victim appeared anywhere. They hadn't fallen over the edge? She pivoted around to the giant shrubs next to the mountainside where the Clydesdale and travois had disappeared. Tall, thick bushes butted up to boulders forming the side of the cascading waterfall.

Before her, another massive steed and makeshift gurney stepped into the vegetation. She veered her gaze at the waterfall. Perhaps the bushes led to a passageway behind the falls? But no. Nothing emerged on the other side. Points from jagged rocks poked through parts of the cascading water. There was no opening behind these falls.

"Where are they?"

Benjura stood next to her. "These bushes are huge. Perhaps they're concealing a cave large enough to fit horses and people."

She searched the brush. Small, pointed green leaves and giant white blooms covered the plants standing twenty feet tall and just as round. Thick layer upon layer of leaves and flowers blocked the center of the bush. When she parted the greenery to peer inside, the shaking of the flowers sent sweet smells her way. More lovely than the fragrance of a rose or honeysuckle, Jordana inhaled until her lungs were full. *The scent of Heaven*. Almost as large as her hand, the pointed leaves were fuzzy. And prolific—

growing as close together as blades of grass. But the flowers, the magnificent flowers were the size of iceberg lettuce heads. Layer upon layer of petals formed their blooms. Their tips were not pure white like their center, but a soft blush color. They were the prettiest thing she'd ever seen. Or smelled. Eyes closed, she bent and sucked in another deep whiff.

Jordana cocked her head to the side to ask what they were, and discovered both Jasper and Benjura gaping at her.

Jasper licked his lips, but said nothing.

Benjura swallowed hard, his Adam's apple jutting out for a quick appearance, then back in.

Jordana released the bloom and straightened up. How foolish to get side tracked by flowers. "What is the name of this plant?"

Jasper smiled. "My people call it Pure Abeda."

"It's nice." *Nice* didn't come close to describing it, but she wasn't about to say more, afraid they already thought of her like a silly girl. "I've never seen anything close to it in all my travels."

Ten feet to her left, another horse and rider plodded straight into the dense foliage. A second one followed close behind, pulling a travois.

Jordana zipped over to gawk at the feat, Benjura at her side.

Jasper emitted a hearty chuckle. "Do you see the entrance now?"

"No." She studied the greenery as it closed around the big rump of the Clydesdale, then over the patient on the litter.

"That's amazing. Even close up, it's unseeable." Benjura turned to Jasper. "I take it a cave is on the other side of these plants. These bushes conceal a path into the entrance. Do you train your horses to trudge right through the foliage?"

"Yes. Exactly." Jasper gave an enthusiastic nod. "Shall we?" He held up his hand stopping the procession, and motioned her and Benjura to cut in line.

Jordana went first, pushing back heavy limbs stocked

with fuzzy fronds and stunning flowers. When they brushed against her, they seemed to sooth her, as if caressing her skin. The leaves may be shaped into sharp points, but they were velvety soft. Puffs of flower pollen filled the air. *Lovely.* No wonder the horses did not object. "Does the Pure Abeda have any medicinal properties?"

"It makes a relaxing tea. Aids in rest, but that's about all."

She strode forward the length of three steeds before blackness fully engulfed her. She must have entered the mouth of the cave, but her outstretched hands still touched foliage. She continued to wave them in front of her as she inched forward. After another ten or twelve feet, and her waving arms only met air.

A strong hand slid around her waist and pulled her in.

Jordana leaned into Benjura, not minding the intimate embrace. Not that she was afraid of the dark—she just needed a second to get her bearings. And pray for no spiders.

"Don't be frightened. I'll escort you."

At the sound of Jasper's whisper in her ear, Jordana shoved away.

His voice turned cold. "Pace another twenty steps and the cavern will curve to the left. It's a slow and wide bend. Just skim your fingers against the wall and you'll have no trouble following it around." Footsteps echoed past her.

Jordana spread her arms wide to the opposite side of Jasper's voice. She touched a torso and whispered. "Benjura?"

"Yes. I'm here. I can't see a thing."

"Me neither." She reached up to find his arms waving out in front of him, too. Jordana latched onto one of his palms, lacing her fingers between his. She pulled his arm toward her and clutched his bicep with her other hand. Positioned more behind his shoulder than next to him, and whispered. "Lead me."

She knew not if he nodded, for he strode forward without a word. The clip-clop of horse hooves sounded behind them. How on earth did the Akimmi people teach their horses to traipse

174

through such blackness? As they moved forward and the temperature dropped at least twenty degrees. "Are you skimming the wall with one hand?"

"Yes," Benjura said. "It's cool to the touch. Slick and smooth. Granite perhaps."

"Do you feel any spider webs?"

"None."

"This cave is kept clean and pristine." Jasper's words bounced off the walls. "It's a duty of every village boy to take turns maintaining this cave. We cannot allow manure to build up, or allow snakes to enter and spook our horses. The floor is swept to keep it free from any trip hazards. This is our lifeline to hunting in the valley we just crossed. Not that we need to. We have plenty of chickens, turkeys, and crops."

A pinhole of light appeared directly ahead. "Is that where we're going? It looks so far away." Her racing heart settled as she zeroed in on the white spec at the end of the deep cavern.

Jasper spoke, "We have completed the turn and are heading toward the mouth now. From this spot, it will take fifteen minutes to reach that opening."

Benjura whistled. "How did your people ever find this cave? I can't wait to get a torch and explore it tomorrow. What kind of rock forms the walls? It's like nothing I've felt before."

"The cave is cut through black onyx, which adds to the darkness, and makes the walls smooth."

"Are there other paths spinning off in here?" Jordana kept her voice low to keep it from echoing around the vast space.

"No other paths are carved through this mountain. Ancient legend claims Elohim created this cave and the valley ahead for the Akimmi people and placed us here in safekeeping."

"Do the Akimmi people record your history in scrolls?" Jordana's favorite Shedock training included study of ancient history and customs. Even the census fascinated her— discovering who descended from whom.

"Yes, we have hundreds of scrolls."

"Can we read them?" Benjura asked in unison with her.

"Are they public?" Jordana remembered how Benjura tried to out-memorize her. He had excelled in the scroll study of their laws.

"I suppose. No one purposely studies them once they complete their schooling. I'm sure any request you make of the chief would be granted, Princess."

"Please, Jasper. We've been over this. I am not the future Shedock of the Tree Warrior Village. Call me Jordana."

"Yes, m'lady, but you are still the only child of your Arrdock. You will always be a princess, even if not the Shedock."

"For once, Jasper, you and I agree on something." Benjura's voice rang an octave louder. And merrier.

Jordana stared at the increasing bright spot ahead. Soon the outline of the first horses exiting the cave appeared. The echo of many horse hooves bounced on the walls behind her. She didn't glance back, but focused on the growing light. At last she shielded her eyes and stepped outside, sucking in fresh air. The sky seemed so bright, but upon closer inspection, dusk had encased the valley. Dark outlines jutted high into the sky in every direction. She pointed at the shadows. "Does a mountain range surround you? Are we in the center?"

"Yes. You are correct again." Jasper stared at her, his month held in a grim line.

"What's the name of this region?" Benjura asked.

Jasper never broke his narrowed glare. "The Valto Mountains shield us in every direction. There are only two ways into our village. The cave we just passed through from the Shando Valley leading to the Arrie lands. And the one on the far side of our city leading to Snake Valley."

"Snake Valley?" She shivered. "I shan't be going there."

Jasper zipped around and marched forward leaving them behind. "It's named for its shape. No more snakes there than anywhere else."

Benjura stepped forward to follow Jasper, pulling her along.

Realization dawned on her. She still clutched Benjura's arm, while tucked into his shoulder. She let go and stepped away. "Sorry. Or thank you. I'm not sure which, or both."

His voice lowered. "I wish you to hold me like that every day of our lives."

A horse galloped past and laughter filled the air. People came running up the slope toward them. A vast structure sat on the opposite hillside, with hundreds of horses grazing in the adjacent meadow. Stripes of varying shades of green crisscrossed the expanse of land. The Akimmi people grew crops like the Garden Tenders. But she didn't see any shelters scattered about. Movement in the trees caught her eye. Shadows descending the trunks. Something swung between the trees. Bridges perhaps? There looked to be a labyrinth of them around the thick grove in the center of the valley. They must live above ground like the Tree Warriors. Too dark to make out any details, she'd have to wait until the morrow to fully view the Akimmi village.

A scream pierced the air, then another, followed by crying. Jordana had almost forgotten about the dead they hauled back for burial. Mourning and devastation would overshadow the joy of their chief's return with Princess Taryn. Families would need to care for the many soldiers suffering from war injuries and scorpiowasp bites. Perhaps she should find Kamali, Taryn, and meet Chief Drongo's wife.

Jordana spied the patas monkey atop a Clydesdale and made her way over. Her eyes widened at the sight of the chief standing next to the stallion, Taryn in his arms. "Are you feeling better?"

His chin inched up and down. "Despite the aching in my joints and no appetite, I hurt less today than I did yesterday. And certainly less than the day before that."

"Are you strong enough to hold the baby?" Benjura's voice held genuine concern.

"No. I told him that." Kamali slid off the back of the horse, fisting its tail to climb down.

The Clydesdale shuffled a foot in the dirt, but did not

kick at the primate.

"I am fine to stand here with her, but I will not attempt to walk." Chief Drongo kissed the top of his daughter's head. "I wish to be the one to place Taryn in my wife's arms."

Jordana nodded at him, joy rushing through her over the peace on the man's face as he gazed upon his baby girl. Devoted and loving just like her mother and father had been as she grew up. She had no idea how special and important it was until she had lost it.

Villagers rushed by, stopping to curtsey or bow to their chief before continuing on to the various stretchers. Chatter filled the air. People darted in various directions and others led the horses away.

A boy of eleven or twelve approached. "Welcome back, Chief Drongo. Do you wish me to attend to your horse?"

"Yes, Kona, but in a few minutes. I'm not ready to release him. Would you like to wait with me for the Shedock?"

A smile split the boy's face. "Yes, sire." He moved to stand at the horse's head.

Few remnants of blue remained in the pink-streaked sky.

"I see her." The boy gave a wild gesture through the crowd. "Shall I fetch Shedock Jada for you?"

"No, thank you." The chief grinned.

Jordana reached down and picked up Kamali. Perhaps they should make themselves scarce for a few moments. She nodded at Benjura and the two stepped away.

"Don't leave. I want you both to meet Jada, my wife." The man lifted an arm and waved.

A woman sprinted forward. Long hair, almost to her knees, fanned out behind her.

As she neared, Jordana sized the woman up. Petite. Not even five foot tall. Jordana had never seen a red-haired woman so short before. Could she be a descendant of the Garden Tenders? Shedock Jada looked older. Twenty-five perhaps, and lovely. Round face, high cheekbones.

The woman cried and smiled at the same time. "You did

178

it. You found her." She latched onto her husband with such force, he might have fallen to the ground if not for the massive stallion at his back. Shedock Jada stretched up to kiss her husband, and slid Taryn from his arms. She clutched her daughter and sank to her knees. There she wept and praised Elohim a loud.

The woman's sobs tore at Jordana, as did the helpless look on Chief Drongo's face. He stood still, unable to move. Jordana set Kamali down and sunk to the weeping mother. She wrapped an arm around Shedock Jada and led them in a prayer, thanking Elohim for Taryn's safe return.

At last Jada moved upright and faced Jordana. "Thank you." She turned to her husband and her eyes widened. "What's wrong? Why are you just standing there? Are you injured?"

"I'm fine. I'm very sore. Much has happened. But first, I wish to introduce you to the Princess of Arrie." He gestured at Jordana.

Jordana gave a full and proper curtsey. "I am honored to meet you, Shedock Jada of the Akimmi people."

The woman arched a brow at her. "What is your name?" An odd expression flew across the Shedock's face.

"Jordana." She would have missed the familiar look if she hadn't been studying the shade of Jada's brown eyes. *Jealousy.* Pure jealousy. Jordana didn't want to give the Shedock any reason to feel that way, and reached for Benjura's hand, pulling him close. Once again she laced her fingers through his, sending a clear message. A little misleading, but not as bad as Jada's first impression. Jordana cleared her throat. "Please allow me to introduce you to Benjura, high watch guard of Arrie."

The Shedock's gaze bounced between them. At last, her eyes brightened and a smile overtook her face.

"She saved Taryn's life. And mine." The chief grinned at Jordana.

Jada's gaze darted over to her husband's admiring face, then back to Jordana—a wary expression reclaiming her.

Jordana frowned. Why was the Shedock so insecure?

179

Benjura released Jordana's hand and pulled her in front of him, wrapping both arms around to hug her. "Actually, chief, I think Jordana saved your life more than once. Three times, was it not?" Benjura moved her hair back and leaned in to kiss her neck.

Jordana froze. She did not want to push Benjura away in front of the Shedock. He, too, must have read the woman's envy. But he took it too far. How dare he manhandle her like that, especially in front of royalty! It wasn't proper. His breath brushed against her ear. Heart rate accelerating, Jordana tried to focus on the chief's words as tingles ran up her spine.

CHAPTER TWENTY

A rooster's crow woke Benjura with a jolt. For the second morning in a row and hours before dawn, the evil fowl began its daybreak routine directly below him. He stretched on the straw-stuffed mat near the center of the shelter. Positioned closest to the chicken pens, he questioned why the tree house was built for anything but a guard tower. Its location made for an awful guest house.

Another cock-a-doodle-do cut through pre-dawn's light.

He swung around to the floor and reached for his moccasins. Might as well let Ladybug out of her cage and sneak out to the river for a bath. Today they'd set out for the Falls Territory. Yesterday had been spent gathering weapons, food, and new recruits. Jordana insisted they stay no more than one day at the Akimmi village before departing for the Great Eucalyptus Forest. In accordance to the Akimmi custom, they'd have an early breakfast feast and blessing, before marching out.

When Benjura descended the trunk, a bonfire blazed in the center of the camp. Meal preparations must be underway. He headed that way and snagged a log from the edge of the fire. One end burned bright—a perfect torch. Yesterday, he made time to explore both the cave they passed through and the one leading to Snake Valley. For three hundred years, the Akimmi tribe, over five thousand strong, dwelled in the shadow of the Valto Mountains. They outnumbered the tree warriors by double.

A most shocking discovery occurred late last night. He

and Jordana read the Akimmi scrolls by candlelight. According to the writings, twin brothers divided households, livestock, and workers, then set out in opposite directions. The older one would establish a settlement on the edge of the Shando Valley and the younger at the end of the Arrie Valley. Together they'd rule all of the land in between. But when the younger twin plotted to kill the older in order to rule everything, Elohim raised up the Valto Mountains, hiding the eldest twin, his family, and livestock in the center. There they thrived and multiplied for the past three centuries. Jazeal and Jarrus, the founding twins, never saw each other again, or knew of each other's destiny. Benjura now knew, and so did Jordana.

Jazeal founded the Akimmi village, naming it after his eldest daughter, who was just a baby at the time. Chief Jazeal had twelve daughters. The oldest married a shepherd and ruled forty years as Shedock, bearing many sons and daughters, teaching them all to worship Elohim. Both their produce and livestock thrived.

The greedy twin, Jarrus, founded the Tree Warrior Village, teaching them to become mighty fighters so they would be prepared for war once he found his brother's hiding place. He spent his life searching, but never finding. All these years, the Tree Warriors prepared for battle allegedly to protect their people. In reality, they were preparing to kill their own kin.

Since childhood, Benjura had sung praises about their founding father—the entire tribe did. "Powerful Jarrus, loving and true, founded their tribe in a peaceful coup." All of it a lie. Jordana, a direct descendant of Jarrus, seemed punctured by her family's heritage, swearing she'd never go back.

Benjura ran a hand over his head. How could he sway her? Was he the only one who understood how much the Tree Warriors needed her? Benjura emerged from the cave and pushed himself through the last of the foliage.

Kona jumped up and blocked Benjura's path. "Stop, sir. The ladies are bathing. We must wait here."

Seems Benjura wasn't the only one getting ready for the

long march. He nodded at the boy. Yesterday Kona had followed Jordana around like a baby elephant using its trunk to tag along with its mother. Jordana had developed quite a few admirers in the Akimmi village. While Kona's devotion made him smile, Jasper's attention caused thorns to poke up on Benjura's skin. His fists clenched at the memory of Jordana laughing with the other warrior.

She'd reach for Benjura's hand or kiss his cheek in front of the Shedock, her intent clear, but when he tried to do the same in front of Jasper, Jordana acted as if his touch bit her like a cobra.

Kona scratched his chin. "I'm sure the Shedock and Princess Jordana are almost done."

"Yes, we are." Jordana passed him on the narrow trail, the Shedock close behind her. "Thank you, Kona. Good morning, Benjura." Jordana tipped her head.

Damp hair hung around Jordana's face, eyes sparkling in the dawn's light, and her smile already bright. She smelled of lavender.

The Shedock smiled at him, too. "Good morning, Benjura. Thank you for waiting. And thank you, Kona, for halting him."

The boy beamed, but said nothing.

Several wet maidens trailed behind, all wielding bows. Obviously they had surrounded the Shedock in the river with their weapons at the ready while the two monarchs bathed.

Benjura nodded at each one as they passed. No one in the female parade compared to Princess Jordana's beauty. He stayed motionless until they all disappeared through the foliage. After tipping his head to Kona, Benjura rounded the corner, leaned his torch against a boulder, and plunged into the cool water. He swam on his back and gazed into the dawning sky. His falcon circled far overhead. He must take a cage for his bird when they entered the battle.

Despite floating on top of the water, his stomach flip-flopped at the thought of war. Was he ready to fight? To kill or be killed? Could anyone ever be fully prepared for death?

* * *

A growl ripped through Jordana's stomach. After the huge breakfast feast that morning, she thought she'd never be hungry again. But the past seven or eight hours of traversing the jungle had long since digested her food. She led four hundred Akimmi warriors, two hundred Clydesdales, dozens of wagons full of weapons, and many more filled with supplies toward the Azul River.

Kamali provided little help. Her home was in the Forbidden Falls Territory, not the Eucalyptus Forest. Kamali couldn't be expected to know a direct route. The decision at every fork fell to Jordana. No wonder her stomach had grown ravenous. At first nothing looked familiar, but for the past hour, she recognized various landmarks, a rock outcropping, and a group of sacred palms. One of them even showed signs of defilement. Father probably had no idea how far the effects of Brin's desolation had reached. No doubt the Queen didn't care.

Benjura came alongside her, passing over a banana and piece of jerky.

"You read my mind." *Again.* She tore into the banana, gobbling a quarter in one bite.

"Everyone is hungry and tired. The horses need food and rest. Let's find a place to stop," he said.

After finishing the last bite of banana, she held back several giant fern leaves and pushed herself into a small clearing. She glanced around. Scents from the rainbow eucalyptus filled the air. A white neplar with beautiful sapphire leaves stood opposite her. "We're here. This clearing isn't very big, but this is where we'll make camp and prepare ourselves. The Azul is right through there." She pointed at the path she had formed during her three years of banishment.

"Oh, thank Elohim." Benjura grabbed her shoulders, pulled her forward, and gave her a quick kiss. When he broke

184

away, he paused a few seconds, then inched back down and kissed her again—slow and tender. At last he pulled back.

Unable to move, Jordana stared into his eyes. Finally her gaze dropped to his mouth. When it did, Benjura moved in and brushed her lips with another kiss, this one soft and tender.

At last he released her. "I'll let everyone know to set up camp here. They'll need to clear some brush between the trees." He strode away.

Jordana's fingers rose to touch her tingling mouth. Like a meteor shower, thoughts soared across her mind. *He kissed me? And I let him?* More than let him, she had kissed him back and would have done so again, had he not darted off. She didn't need this distraction. She shook her head. She could not let herself fall for him again. Benjura had so many ideas for when he returned to the Tree Warrior Village. Topping his list was taking her with him. He talked of little else. But she'd never go back. Jordana must send Benjura away before her heart broke anew.

A horse drew alongside her and a brave dropped his pack to the ground. It landed with a clang, jolting her.

Jordana searched the crowd as they moved in. It had been slow going through the thick forest the last few hours. The braves had spread out as they maneuvered around trees and bushes. Jordana spotted Chief Drongo riding a horse, Jasper walking beside him. She high-stepped through the vegetation to them, and motioned. "This is a small clearing. Have your men fan out and set up camp. I'll take Kamali down to the river. She alone should cross."

"I wish to go with you and see it." From atop his horse, the young chief motioned to Jasper. "See to it everyone is fed and the horses are cared for."

"Yes, sire." Jasper nodded—his eyes hinting at disappointment.

Benjura appeared next to Jordana. "I don't see Kamali anywhere."

Jasper pointed at one of the Clydesdales. "She rides."

Jordana chuckled as soon as she caught sight of Kamali.

"You mean she sleeps."

The monkey lay on her stomach, arms and legs dangling on either side of the horse, her mouth open and snoring.

Jordana strode to Kamali and tickled the bottom of her foot. "Wake up."

Kamali yawned and pushed herself to a sitting position. "What do you want?"

"We've arrived."

"Finally." Kamali reached for Jordana. "Carry me across the river." Kamali's head jerked around as she studied the area. "Where is the river?"

"I shall take you." Jordana found her trail and paused by the bush where she had buried the giant's weapons for later. So much had happened since that day. She shoved the hideous memory away, as led Drongo and Benjura to the Azul.

If she got a private moment with Benj, should she say anything to him about those kisses? Ask him not to do it again? He had nuzzled her neck at the Akimmi village, and kissed her cheek. But those were only for show—to dispel Jada's jealousy. But his kiss on the lips just now contained passion. Intimacy. A promise of something more. But there would never be more between them. Should she try to convince him, or just forget the whole thing? And yet, the warmth of his lips on hers still lingered. She could not have it both ways, and must settle the matter in her mind, then address it with him.

Once they reached the river bank, Jordana stepped close to the water's edge and spoke. "The Azul is fed by hot springs, so it's very warm. There's a mineral taste, but drinking it won't make you sick." Jordana set Kamali down and used her hand to cup water for a drink. She splashed some on her face to wash the sweat away. And wash away Benjura's kiss still tingling on her mouth. Upon straightening, she puckered and whistled her mother's animal tune.

Kamali, who had bent over and slurped water, stopped and gazed at Jordana. Her ears twitched.

Chief Drongo slipped off his horse and bent to drink as

186

well. His Clydesdale sloshed forward and nudged his big head under Jordana's arm.

She laughed and wiggled her brows at Benjura. "It works."

"I never doubted you." Benjura puckered his lips and sounded the animal song as well.

"You two stop that." Kamali lifted her hands to Jordana. "Carry me over."

Jordana hesitated. Was she ready to set foot on the forbidden side? Reminded of Benjura and Lainey's warning, Jordana planned to beseech Elohim first. Yet her mind had been on Benjura. She needed to shift her focus before stepping near the Holy Land. They all needed time to pray before risking their lives with a single step on the sacred ground.

Jordana cleared her throat and gazed at the two men. "A wise leopard warned me—tis no small thing we do—to enter the Forbidden Falls Territory. Each one is to make sure their heart is right and their motives pure. I wish to pray and use the repentance ash before crossing, like Lainey showed us for protection against the scorpiowasps. We should explain this to the warriors who dare to journey with us."

Both men gave a somber nod.

Jordana swung the monkey up to sit on her shoulders. "I shall take you close to the other bank, but not all the way over. You'll have to finish the crossing yourself. Only your legs shall get wet, although I do believe you could benefit from a bath."

The loud hoo-hoo shriek above Jordana spoke volumes.

At the music of Benjura's deep laugh, Jordana smiled. Her focus stuck to him like honey on her fingers. How could she be so conflicted about the man? The way he glared at Jasper whenever she talked to him was intolerable. As if Benjura had any claim on her. And yet when Benjura smiled her way, the spark in his golden eyes warmed her heart. His kisses seemed so natural. Yet he acted oblivious to the fact she'd face death by returning to the Tree Warrior Village. The constant war within drained her strength. She must ask Lainey to intervene, and send

187

the man away. Maybe then she could get some peace.

Jordana shoved the thoughts away and entered the river. She strode toward the bushes where Lainey's emerald eyes had first appeared. Once she passed the middle and rose to knee deep water on the other side, she stopped. "This is as far as I go." She lifted Kamali off her shoulders and set her down. "I'll make camp on the other bank and wait for Lainey. Please send her to meet me."

"Of course." Kamali waved over her head as she waddled out of the water and raced into the foliage.

Jordana stood still, unable to move as the last of talking animals disappeared into the jungle. She whistled her mother's animal tune. Sounding it twice in a row, she blew as loud as she could. From behind her, Benjura whistled it as well. He had followed her lead in so many instances these past few days, it was almost like they hadn't spent all these years apart.

Glowing eyes in the bushes caught Jordana's attention and she froze. Not green like the leopards, these eyes shone as orange as tangerines.

"Hello?" Jordana whispered. "Who's there?" Her heartbeat migrated up to her throat.

Fronds slashed and bushes rattled as something stomped and tore leaves from branches. In a giant leap, a huge gorilla jumped out and stormed into the water at Jordana, baring his teeth.

Jordana tried to scramble back but slipped on the slick river rocks. Flailing, she fell into the water and rolled over. She tried to kick her feet to swim away, but something caught her ankle. Adrenaline shot through her veins, and she struggled to get free.

In a swooshing jerk, Jordana flew through the air and hung upside down by one leg. The massive gorilla dangled her by the foot. She sucked in several deep breaths. Didn't Benjura have his bow with him?

The gorilla cupped the back of Jordana's head and pulled her toward his face. His lips curled back, and the gorilla bared

188

his teeth. Four massive fangs, two on top and two at the bottom, each as long as her fingers, hovered inches away.

She opened her mouth to scream, but no sound escaped. Frozen inches from the gorilla's jaw, she could only stare at the drool dripping from its sharp fangs. Had she come this far only to die in the mouth of a gorilla? *Please, Elohim, forsake me not.*

CHAPTER TWENTY-ONE

Jordana's pulse raced as she tried to push back, but the gorilla's powerful hand held the back of her head.

An arrow whizzed through the air and landed in the gorilla's shoulder.

A frown filled his face and the gorilla closed his mouth. His stare veered to the opposite bank. "Ouch." He whispered so low, Jordana wasn't sure if he spoke a word, or grunted.

Two more arrows swooshed from behind, the first missing her captor. The second landed below the animal's collar bone.

"Why are they shooting me?" The gorilla implored her with his eyes.

"Stop, Benjura!" She managed to get her voice box to work again. "This gorilla speaks. I'm fine." She narrowed her gaze at the giant creature holding her upside down, his front paw still cupping the back of her head. "Let me go."

The gorilla did as told, releasing Jordana's foot.

She landed with a splash and scrambled to stand, brushing her hair back and spitting out water. Jordana glanced behind. Benjura and Chief Drongo stood waist deep in the river not twenty feet away. They had rushed in to help her. The chief wielded a machete and Benjura aimed an arrow straight at the gorilla's chest.

The gorilla plopped down on his bottom in the water, a great splash hit her. He fingered the two arrows poking out of his upper left side. "Why did you whistle the special call, and pierce me when I came?" The tone of his voice was deeper than any human's.

"I'm sorry." Jordana stepped forward. "They were protecting me. Why did you scare us like that? I thought you were going to eat me."

"Eat you? Don't be ridiculous. I don't eat humans. Elohim forbids it." The gorilla tapped his mouth. "I was smiling at you the way Zelle showed me."

"Smiling?" Benjura stood at her side now. "Is that what you call barring your fangs?"

"Did I do it wrong?" The gorilla curled up his lips, thrusting his jaw out to reveal his massive teeth.

Jordana giggled. "No, you did it perfectly right. I'm sorry we didn't understand." She flashed a big grin at the gorilla, and twisted to beam at the chief. She elbowed Benjura, and nodded at the primate. "Smile, gentlemen, and introduce yourself."

Teeth gleaming, the chief dipped his chin. "I am Drongo, chief of the Akimmi people. It is nice to meet you, gorilla."

"Name's BoBo. The honor is mine." The gorilla fisted the arrow as if to yank it out.

"Wait. Don't do that." Benjura stepped forward. "I am Benjura. I'm Jordana's—" His grin faded as his gaze shifted to her.

"Friend." Jordana kneeled in the knee-deep water in front of BoBo. "I'm so sorry they shot you. I'm Jordana of Arrie. We're going to pull these arrows out, okay? It's going to sting."

"It might not be wise to yank them out the front." Benjura bent to examine the wounds.

"Hold my hand?" BoBo reached his palm to her.

"Sure." Jordana clasped it. "But don't squeeze too hard and crush my bones."

He nodded. "Smile at me again. Your tiny teeth are pretty."

"Thank you." Jordana did as asked while stroking his furry arm. The back of BoBo's hand was covered in wiry hair down to the first part of his webbed fingers. Only the end of his digits separated and were void of hair. Thick, leathery skin covered his palms and fingertips. Although his hands were huge in comparison to hers, the wiggly parts of his fingers were short and stumpy.

Chief Drongo positioned himself behind of the gorilla.

Benjura stopped inspecting the wounds and straightened. "The tip under his collar bone will hit the shoulder blade if we try to push it through. It needs to come out the front. But the arrow in his shoulder is closer to the rear. Chief, come around here and push this arrow out the back as fast as you can. At the same time, I'll yank this one out of the front." Benjura pointed at the protrusion in BoBo's shoulder area. "First I'm going to break off the end of this arrow so Chief Drongo can push it through." Benjura snapped off the end before the gorilla had a chance to object.

"That was the easy part." Jordana caressed BoBo's cheek. "Try to remain very still. Ready?"

His big head bobbed up and down, then BoBo squeezed his eyes shut.

"One, two, three." Jordana counted off and both men yanked or pushed.

The fingers on BoBo's free hand fisted, but the rest of him remained motionless. His front paw holding Jordana's hand didn't so much as flinch.

In seconds, both arrows were free. "That wasn't so bad." Benjura swished the intact arrow in the water, and slid it back into his sheath.

"You did very well." Jordana pat BoBo's forearm.

"I'm woozy." He reclined on the river bank, his barrel chest heaving.

She scooted behind the gorilla, placing his head in her lap, and scooped water over his wounds. The river around him turned red, as she rinsed the blood away.

BoBo moaned two or three times with his eyes shut tight.

Who knew giant apes were such big babies? She smiled

192

up at Chief Drongo, suppressing a giggle before settling her voice. "BoBo, tis not yet time for us to get out of the water and stand on the Falls Territory side. We will not be able to help get you back to your family. We'll call for help though. Whistle the tune, Benjura." Jordana leaned forward and stared at BoBo's face upside down—for the second time. "Do you know Lainey, the black leopard?"

At last he lifted his lids. "Yes, of course. She's the leader of the eastern gatekeepers."

Leader? Jordana shot a look to Benjura. His eyes widen, probably matching hers. She knew Lainey led her family, but had no idea the leopard commanded an entire group of watch guards. "The eastern gatekeepers? Are there more of you in the west and south?"

"Oh yes. Each quadrant of the Falls Territory is filled with hundreds of gatekeepers. Lainey is the leader of the eastern sector."

Jordana rinsed the gorilla's forehead. "When you get home, will you please tell Lainey I am waiting on the banks of the Azul?"

"Certainly, but I'm sure she already knows." BoBo pushed himself up and faced the vegetation. "I'm going to the Restoration Pool." Twisting back, he pointed at Benjura. "You better not shoot me oncest I see you again."

"I'll try not to." Benjura smiled, then turned somber and bowed. "I'm sorry I hurt you."

"Tis forgiven." BoBo curled his lips up to reveal his teeth before lumbering into the tree line.

Once the jungle concealed all hints of the gorilla, Jordana gazed at the two men and broke out in laughter. They chuckled along with her as they waded back across. "We need to warn everyone about the animals' attempts to smile at us."

* * *

Jordana sat on the bank, eating the fruit Benjura brought

her from the camp. Ladybug circled overhead in the sky alive with sunset. As twilight took over, she whistled her late mother's tune. No sign of animal life appeared on the other side. What took them so long? How far was it to Lainey's den? Did BoBo go straight to the Restoration Pool without delivering her message first?

At least she was able to speak to the warriors back at camp and explain about the animal smiles. Benjura addressed the men, encouraging each one to cross the Azul with a pure heart. The warriors took time to seek Elohim. At the end, Chief Drongo led everyone in prayer. Someone started to drum and another joined with the lyre. Benjura sounded his ram's horn at just the right spots in the tunes. Jordana picked up one of the tambourines, and their camp resonated with music and praise. One by one, the warriors stepped to the campfire and wiped an ash cross on their foreheads as a sign of repentance. She and Benjura did the same.

Jordana's heart swelled. How many years since her beloved tree warriors conducted such a worship ceremony? Could she ever convince her father to reinstate them? That would require returning with a new miracle. And frankly, after reading the truth about the founder of the Tree Warrior Village and all the lies her ancestors told, she didn't want to go back to that heritage.

"You're quiet. What's captured your attention?" Benjura reclined next to her on a mat of leaves he'd fashioned for them atop the sand.

"You've been quiet, too. Seems we've both been buried in thoughts." Now alone at the river's edge, she should tell him not to kiss her anymore. And yet his nearness made her wish he'd do it again. Jordana swallowed the words and cleared her throat. "The Akimmi worship ceremony was beautiful. I miss those times of joining voices with tribemates to sing praise. Do you think the Tree Warrior Village can ever be like that again?"

A faraway look filled Benjura's face. "It's what I've been waiting for. Or perhaps planning for is a better way to say it."

194

"Planning for? You're not thinking of trying to overthrow my father, are you?"

"No. Nothing like that." Benjura tossed a pebble into the river.

"Good. It'd be suicide."

"Not if Elohim designed it." His gaze locked with hers.

Jordana leaned forward. "Okay, what's going on inside that brain of yours?"

He let out a heavy sigh. "Just desire and earnest prayer."

She always admired his great faith. It united them years ago.

A rustling sounded across the river and Jordana jumped up, Benjura joining her. She searched the vegetation. Dark shadows filled the underbrush.

The tip of a tail swooshed back and forth above the vegetation.

Jordana cupped her hands around her mouth. "Tanga is that you? I think I see your pretty tail."

Three leopards slipped out of the jungle and sauntered to the water's edge. The middle cat had the unmistakable gait of Tanga.

"Greetings, Jordana. Tis nice to see you again." Tanga swayed her tail like the slow graceful brush strokes of a village artist.

"Remember me? I'm Ariel." The feline on Tanga's right had the low-handing stomach of a still-nursing mother. "This is our cousin, Dahlu."

"I remember you, Ariel. Thanks for coming. And it's an honor to meet you, Dahlu. This is Benjura." Jordana motioned at him.

When Benjura bowed, dark auburn hair fell around his tanned face. His bangs swooped back into place as he straightened. "It's an honor to meet you…girls."

Each feline acknowledged him, Tanga with a flick of her tail, and the other two tossed their heads back.

"Is Lainey coming?" Jordana strained to view around

195

them, aching to see her friend.

"No." Tanga's moss-green eyes shone bright, just like they had on the day of their first meeting. "Lainey sent us to fetch you. There's no time to waste. We found your enemy, and the battle shall soon begin."

"We're ready." Jordana motioned with her thumb. "We have an army waiting." She hesitated, wondering if they had rested long enough. Meals, lodging preparations, and the worship ceremony had kept everyone occupied for hours. Jordana touched Benjura's arm. His warmth radiated under her fingers. "I must talk to Tanga. Are you ready to cross?"

"I've been ready for this my whole life."

She smiled, understanding the feeling, yet wondering if there was more to his statement. So often he hinted at grand notions.

Benjura left her side and strode into the Azul.

Jordana hurried to catch up, and the two waded across. The thump of her heart matched the pounding drums back at the camp. As she rose up on the other side in ankle deep water, Jordana held her foot over the dry bank, as if mere inches made any difference. Basically, she already stood on the forbidden side. Still she closed her eyes, whispered praises, and took the final step. For seconds, Jordana stood basking in the blessing of standing alive on the Forbidden Falls Territory side, gateway to Elohim's Holy Land. When at last she opened her eyes and twisted to face Benjura, his expression of pure pleasure must have matched hers.

His white teeth gleamed as his lips stretched up. "Praise Elohim."

Jordana nodded and rushed to Tanga, bending over and hugging her. Then Ariel. "I have much to ask. Please, sit with me a moment." She moved to a fallen stump and sat down.

Benjura joined her and the leopard trio plunked their rumps down.

Jordana searched their eyes. "Our human army has traveled far today. They need a good night's sleep before engaging the Chinzu warriors. How much longer do you wish them to travel tonight? Humans aren't nocturnal. Should they wait to cross the Azul in the morning? Is it a long distance to the Chinzu camp? How large is their army? If more fighters are needed, we have a rider prepared to fetch another two hundred warriors. We weren't sure how many braves to bring." Questions flew from her lips. She had more to ask, but Benjura laid a hand on top of hers, halting her barrage.

All three leopards gaped at her, their long lashes blinking over slanted eyes.

Dahlu spoke first. "We know not the size of the giant's army, as only Ojai has reported back with his findings. It will take two sunsets to reach the Chinzu encampment. They are building a bridge to cross the canyon. We mustn't allow them to complete it. As for the rest of your questions, you may present them to Lainey. We are only here to retrieve you."

Benjura exhaled a deep breath. "Is Lainey at your home? Is it on the way to the Chinzu encampment?"

"Not really." Tanga's long tail swept across the pebbles and sand behind her.

Jordana leaned forward, elbows on knees. "We have four hundred men and two hundred horses with us."

Ariel's whiskers twitched at Tanga and Dahlu. "That is too many to take to our dens. The non-speaking horses will not like it there."

"I agree." Tanga gazed back at Jordana. "Have your men and horses rest here tonight. On the morrow, I'll lead you to the southern sector." The feline spoke to Dahlu. "Escort Ariel home. Have Lainey, the prides, and packs meet us down south mid-morning tomorrow." Tanga faced Jordana and Benjura again. "After sunset in two days' time, we shall launch our surprise attack. It is time to fight."

Jordana's mouth ran dry. Were they really about to declare war on an army of giants?

197

CHAPTER TWENTY-TWO

Jordana crouched in the tall reeds, unable to see more than a few feet in front of her. Clouds blocked the stars and moons above. Darkness concealed their painstaking approach to the canyon's edge, now just four feet in front of her. Bears and wolves intermixed on her right, with Benjura in the lead. Lainey, Ojai, and sweet Zelle stood to her left with the various prides of tigers, leopards, and lions. A sprinkling of Akimmi braves flanked her, but most of them took up bows in the back.

Directly behind her and the rest of the frontline, elephants sat side by side. Packed together, they formed a wall without cracks. Their massive bodies blocked the view to three hundred Akimmi archers with blazing campfires and stockpiles of arrows. Everyone waited. Ready. Jordana's heart throbbed. At any second, they'd engage the giants. Jordana prayed for success. Surprise and darkness would aid them, as if Elohim had given them every advantage to win. It was time. They might not get a better chance.

A mile back, the Akimmi cooks and a few monkeys stayed with the Clydesdales. The horses grazed in a makeshift pen, innocent and oblivious to the coming deaths. The non-speaking steeds would only be used in case of retreat and to haul back the injured. And the dead.

She had spent the first minutes of the journey with Zelle.

"Above all, you must burn down the bridge, just like you burned the platform when cremating the giants." A somber expression had replaced Zelle's usual impish look.

The young cat was exactly right. As they traveled, a plan began to take shape with Chief Drongo, Benjura, and Lainey all setting forth the details. Beast and Jasper made suggestions. The many ways things could go wrong rumbled through her mind. She inhaled and released a deep cleansing breath.

Flocks of eagles and hawks had already crossed to the other side and waited behind the Chinzu camp. The brave fowl exposed themselves to the most danger. They had insisted upon going. Their purpose in life was to protect Elohim's Holy Land. They'd gladly give up their lives to fulfill their mission. The faith and courage of the birds inspired Jordana. The whole Akimmi army had been electrified by the eagles and hawk's sacrificial determination. If the flocks could do it, so could the humans. Still, acid bubbled up in Jordana's throat.

Smoke blew her way, filling her nostrils. She inspected the scene behind her, searching for any space between the elephant bodies. No visible flickers from the fires. Gray billows rose into the sky like a line of trees. Perhaps the night air would conceal the smoke.

Across the canyon, numerous Chinzu campfires dotted the mesa. Small orange fire-glows appeared between the enemy's shelters. Their smoke faded into the night sky—a good indication the line of Akimmi bonfires behind the elephants would do so as well. Not that it mattered much longer.

A sharp whistle sounded from the Akimmi archers. Seconds later, a hundred flaming arrows flew over her head. Before landing on the opposite side, another round of burning darts shot off, then a third. Jordana followed the arc of the fiery projectiles. Dozens hit their marks as tents went up in flames. Just as many arrows missed and stabbed into the ground. Shouts and screams echoed. Another two rounds of burning weapons flew over her head at the giants. More and more shelters were set ablaze, and seemingly many giants pierced as evidence by the screams.

At last the battle had begun.

Jordana and the rest of the frontline stayed low at the canyon's edge, while the Akimmi archers rained down fiery darts upon the enemy.

Soon arrows whizzed at them. Several elephants cried out. A wolf yelped, but Jordana couldn't see it in the dark. She focused on the warriors across the way. A flaming arrow headed straight at her spot in the front line. Jordana clenched her shield. At the last second, jumped up and knocked the arrow away. It fell to the bottom of the ravine. A quick glance around did not reveal any more fiery ammunition. Very smart of the enemy to shoot back one of the Akimmi's burning arrows.

More darts flew at them. Some on fire, some not. Upon landing, many animals cried out. Jordana traded her shield for her bow and squinted to find a target on the far side. She took careful aim and eliminated a brute before he could take down another gatekeeper.

Loud caws and thumps sounded on the far mesa. Giants cried out. Hawks and eagles pelted them with rocks as large as their talons could carry. If not dead from the stoning, many giants fell to their deaths when they slipped over the cliff's edge. They screamed all the way to the bottom of the massive cavern, landing on the unforgiving boulders.

Soon birds careened to the canyon floor as well. The Chinzu archers had switched their aim to the fighting fowl. Thank goodness Benjura had placed his falcon in a basket back at the Clydesdales' pen. Still, Jordana's heart ached at the number of birds falling victim to the Chinzu army. She objected to this part of the plan when the flocks suggested it. Her fear over their safety came true before her eyes.

As fast as Jordana could nock her bow, she fired at the Chinzu archers who shot down her feathered friends. Jordana spotted one giant releasing arrows as fast as Benjura did. She took careful aim and sunk her weapon in his chest. He pitched forward into the canyon's abyss.

Dozens of birds pelted toward the ground. She couldn't watch them hit the bottom. Fingers flying, she loaded her bow and fired at an aggressive giant. And then another. Still another. But it didn't seem to slow the slaughter of the birds.

Why didn't the flocks retreat? Would the talking eagles and hawks be extinct before sunrise? *Please, Elohim, save the courageous creatures. Keep a remnant unto Yourself.*

In a flash, she emptied three quivers, and reached for a fourth. A total of seven full quivers had lain ready at her station. She scrambled to poise another arrow and take aim. But the opposite side was no longer visible. A heavy fog rolled up from the canyon floor and billowed over the rock wall. It blocked her view of the Chinzu camp.

Overhead, the clouds split open, as if parting to let the partial moons gaze at the battle below. Their light, along with billions of sparkling stars, reflected on the white haze curling up and over the canyon's edge. How odd that none of the eerie fog swelled her way.

Lainey and Beast crouched nearby. Jordana kept her voice low. "Do you think Elohim is concealing the eagles and hawks from the giants, in order to save them?"

"It seems so," Lainey said.

Beast pawed at the dirt, as if anxious to join in the battle. "I hope they fly away and aren't too stubborn to see the means of escape set before them."

"Let it be so."

More fiery weapons shot off from behind her, slicing into the white clouds sitting on the far mesa. If they struck anything, she could not tell.

"Hold your fire." Benjura's voice echoed from somewhere on her right.

The fighting screeched to a halt, as all visibility had been lost.

Jordana dropped to her stomach and inched forward. She peered over the cliff's edge. Dense fog filled the ravine. It engulfed the platform built up from the valley floor. Not even the top of the structure could be identified. Her heart sunk. No fire appeared below. They needed to burn the bridge. Even if the

201

battle ended now, at least the Chinzu's progress would have been destroyed.

Jordana shoved herself up and jogged back. "Jasper?" She whispered, not wanting the Chinzu men across the canyon to hear her and fire at the noise. She received no reply and raised her voice a notch. "Jasper?"

"Yes."

Jordana couldn't see him through the elephant wall. She tapped two of the mammoths' backs, instructing them to stand, and let her pass. It took at least a minute for them to heave out of the way. Many elephants lumbered to their feet, causing a ripple affect down the line.

When she moved in to find Jasper and Chief Drongo, Benjura came alongside her. "There's too great a fog to see the bridge at the bottom, but we can still burn it down. Aim your fiery arrows at the canyon floor."

War cries sounded all around her. On instinct, her hands unsheathed knives as she whipped around.

Along the cliff's edge, Chinzu giants hoisted themselves up. From where had they come? Could the workers at the bottom of the ravine actually scale the cliff face? A shudder ricocheted through Jordana over the sheer strength such a feat required. The brutes were built for war. Did the Akimmis even stand a chance?

The giants wore leather covers and strapped heavy weapons on their backs. The first arrivals attacked with their long battle axes, swinging them wildly at anything that moved. Wolves, cheetahs, even mighty lions fell dead. Sliced through their chests and heads. A few giants fell prey to attacks from the packs. But like ants, more enemy warriors crawled up the cliff face, wielding five-foot swords and even longer battle axes.

Before her eyes, the gatekeeper casualties mounted. Jordana's muscles twitched, ready to fight and as she selected her target. A nearby foe thrust his sword at a cheetah and she flung her knife into his neck. Both she and the cheetah were onto their next encounter without a moment's pause.

Arrows shot from the Akimmi archers, striking both the

enemy and the gatekeepers. They were too close for a massive arrow launch.

"Archers, halt!" Chief Drongo's scream pierced the air. "Swords! Attack!"

The Akimmi braves rushed forward with weapons drawn.

The giants retaliated like angry rhinos. They raced to eliminate anyone in their path. War cries pierced the air. Metal clanged. Growls and screams mounted to a never-ending fury.

Steps away, Jasper dueled a Chinzu warrior. The giant stood two and a half feet taller than him, but was no match in speed.

As the two parried, Jordana flung one of her blades into the giant's unprotected thigh.

When he glanced her way, Jasper thrust his sword through the man's stomach, all the way to the hilt. He wasted no time in tugging it out, nodding at Jordana, and moving to another bout.

Jordana swung her machete at a nearby giant, cutting him down. Blood spatter flew at her. The smell of it, and death, hung in the air.

Ojai and Lainey attacked a mammoth man when he paused to unwedge his weapon from the skull of a bear. Lainey's powerful jaws clamped around the giant's hand. Ojai bit into his neck. The leopards killed the foe quickly. When they moved to another, blood dripped from their fangs.

Jordana flung her daggers at two different giants. The one causing carnage against the elephants with his extra-long battle axe, fell first. Her second blade went into a giant's eye when he raised his sword over his head at an unsuspecting gorilla. The man toppled backwards, leaving the gorilla unharmed.

Jordana unsheathed more knives, and flicked her weapons at two more giants. Her blades penetrated deep into the giants' necks, bringing both to their knees. She didn't wait to see them fall. Only her smallest, pointed daggers where left and she gripped them while searching for more targets. Two Chinzus fought animals twenty yards apart. She flung her first knife, and

203

pivoted to aim her second. It pierced the fighter's temple. When Jordana spun to see if her first dagger had hit its mark as well, she discovered her intended victim pulling his sword out from a lion's side. She had missed. The lion paid for her failure with his life.

No time to mourn. Jordana rushed to retrieve her blades, sheathing several. She knew not where her missed shot had landed. When an elephant-slayer turned his back to her, she sunk a machete into the evil giant's spine. She squeezed her eyes shut. Unable to watch her own carnage. She couldn't pull her machete out fast enough to flee. All her blades must be located before rejoining the fight—one of the few disadvantages of fighting with knives. Around her the clash of metal rang out, along with panting animals and moaning. She found and sheathed two more blades, and searched for the lost one.

Many elephants stampeded forward, using their trunks to knock giants off the cliff. The brutes retaliated by swinging their battle axes at the elephant's legs or trunks. Many had been sliced off. Mammoth bodies lay around her, their chests heaving. A front foot missing. Those with no trunks struggled to breathe.

Tears stung Jordana eyes. How could this happen to the gatekeepers? She swallowed hard to force back the nausea. She knelt next to a giant clutching one of her daggers in his neck. She slid it out. The man's mouth filled with blood, just like before when she had killed Lord Joice. Jordana couldn't watch again, and twisted away. She had no desire to see a man die, even if he was an enemy.

Jordana rounded an elephant and came face to face with a Chinzu giant.

He bore down on her, raising his sword overhead as if to slice her in two.

She screamed and scooted back, but fell on a slain elephant. More adrenaline surged into her throbbing veins.

A sinister grin filled the giant's face. But suddenly his eyes grew huge, like two round river rocks. The sword slipped from his fingers and his arms inched down. His gaze fell to his gut. Out the front of his stomach, the white point of an elephant tusk emerged.

The elephant raised his head, lifting the giant, who slid farther back on the impalement. His body went limp. A flick from the big elephant's head, and the giant flung off the tusk like a rag doll.

Jordana didn't know if she should vomit or thank the elephant. At least they had found a way to defend themselves. Their curved tusks almost equaled the length of the giants' battle axes. But they were far heavier. Perhaps now it would be a fair fight between the magnificent creatures and the evil Chinzus.

A glance over her shoulder didn't reveal any more ascending fighters. Their number and size were staggering. Animal and Akimmi bodies lay everywhere. Many slain giants sprawled among the dead. But not nearly as many as Jordana's comrades. Were they losing? Was Benjura alive? And what of Lainey? Jordana pushed away her fear, willing strength into her trembling heart. She must get back in the fray.

The distinct sound of swooshing filled her ears. Arrows fell all around her. They landed in giants, animals, and Akimmi braves alike. The thick fog on the opposite mesa didn't stop the Chinzu archers. They bombarded her side with razor sharp tips. The arsenal kept coming and stabbing, wave after wave. One grazed Jordana's shoulder, slicing a gash down her left triceps. She bit her tongue and ducked next to a fallen elephant, using his body to shield herself. She needed her bow and shield.

What should she do? Watch the sky to deflect fiery projectiles, or the ground to parry with attacking giants? Jordana's stomach sunk to her knees. Had they engaged a superior army? The opposition had a greater number, better skill, and heavier weapons. Did the gatekeepers and Akimmi braves have any chance of winning?

"Please, Elohim. We can't do this without you." Her hoarse voice whispered aloud as she crouched behind the dead animal. "Give us victory for Your glory."

A war cry drew her attention as a giant leapt over the

elephant. He flew at her. The point of his long sword aimed straight at her heart.

Jordana's sharp intake of air muffled her scream. Heels dug into the dirt, she shoved back as hard as she could, scooting into the crook of the elephant's massive front leg. She thrust its heavy limb over her shoulder, and kept it between her and the giant. Her gaze darted to every direction, searching for a way out. *Trapped.* Once the word filled her mind, it writhed through her, accelerating her heart to a wild pace.

CHAPTER TWENTY-THREE

A small dagger clutched in each fist would be no match for the warrior's sword. Still, Jordana pitched them up. Hard and under-handed at close range. Both knives lodged in the man's leather breastplate. The thick layer of protection covered his chest and stomach down to his hips.

A flick from the giant's fingers, and one of her daggers hit the dirt. He pulled out the second—puny in his massive hand. No blood on the tip. She hadn't even penetrated his leather covering. The hideous swine laughed and tossed away her precious weapon as if it were worthless.

A quick jab, and the tip of his sword entered the elephant's leg held in front of her chest. If the giant shoved it though. It would pierce her heart on the other side. The giant paused and gazed into her eyes.

Jordana slipped another blade from its sheathe. She should have aimed at the man's thighs. Below his leather covering, fringe hung halfway to his knee. All his internal organs were protected, but not his important leg muscles. A blade there might slow the man. Or down him if she managed to slice the main vein.

Before she could aim the blade, a booted foot kicked her wrist. Her arm flung back so hard, pain shot from her hand to her shoulder. Cast off, Jordana had no idea where her dagger had landed.

The goliath wagged a finger at her and clicked his tongue,

the corners of his lips rising to reveal black rotting teeth, just like Boar's. He pulled his sword out of the elephant and twirled the tip in circles, narrowing down to zero in on her chest.

As he toyed with her, Jordana gritted her teeth and scowled. He seemed entertained by her fear. She fought tears, and jutted her chin, refusing to give him the pleasure of seeing her desperation. Boiling blood now tore through her veins. "What gives you the right?"

His watermelon-sized head bent close. "We answer to no one." Rounded nose the size of a small banana sniffed her hair. End to end, his fat eyebrows could have matched a village cat's tail. He stunk like sweat and rotten meat.

Something flashed behind him. A loud battle cry drew Jordana's attention.

Benjura flew from atop the elephant's hind quarters. Raised above his head, Benjura swung his sword down onto the enemy. Every muscle flexed on Benjura's blood-speckled arms and chest. Even his thighs bulged. The fierce look in his eyes stole Jordana's attention. She'd never seen that look before. His blow landed across the giant's neck with all his weight behind it.

Although thankful for the rescue, Jordana squeezed her eyes shut, unable to watch the beheading.

Benjura pointed at her gash. "Are you okay?"

She touched her upper arm, blood moistened her fingertips. "I'm fine." She pushed up, refusing to dwell on her injury or the close call. "I need to find my knives."

"No time. I've gotta get you to safety." He pointed across the field. "Run!"

"We're retreating?" She glanced at the raging battle. Gatekeepers and Akimmi bodies sprawled everywhere. Arrows continued to rain down on them. Where had all the giants come from? Had the majority of their army been at the bottom of the ravine? Did they all scale the canyon wall?

Benjura clasped her uninjured arm. "Come on. Let's go."

"No." She wrenched free. "Why are we losing? Lainey said Elohim willed our attack on the Chinzu army. Did she get it

208

wrong?" Her voice cracked.

"Do not doubt the wisdom of our Great Creator."

"Elohim must be the one to win this battle. We cannot succeed without him." She rushed to a nearby bonfire and grabbed some ash, wiping a cross on her forehead. She fell to her knees and raised both hands over her head, stretching to the sky. "I beseech You, Creator, to help us. Let not Your gatekeepers perish, or the Akimmi Braves. Save us. Create a means to achieve victory for the sake of Your Holy Land. I have faith in You. This battle is Yours."

Thunder crashed above them and Jordana ducked. That's just what they needed—a rain storm. She gazed heavenward. No clouds blew in to shield the two moons and their shimmering rings.

Another mighty rumble rolled overhead, as if mere inches above them. No clashing swords echoed as the battle seemed to pause. Fierce cracking shattered the silence and reverberated around them.

She reached up to Benjura's leather vest, and tugged him down next to her. "Pray with me." She gazed back heavenward. "Send down Your mighty power, oh Great Creator."

Benjura raised his arms too, and called for Elohim's will to be done.

Deafening booms sounded as the ground shook in waves. Not like prior storms, the clear sky seemed to shout at the earth below in a cacophony of noise.

Benjura grabbed her shoulder and pointed across the canyon. Above the Chinzu encampment, bright orange balls the size of large pumpkins shot down from the firmament. Almost like falling stars, each one left a glowing tail in its wake.

Screams cut across the gully. Jordana couldn't see what transpired on the other side. When she rose to her feet, half of the fire balls dissipated before fading into the fog.

Benjura pushed up from the ground and the rest of the fiery downpour dissolved.

Realization struck her and she grabbed his wrist. "We

need to keep on our knees with our hands lifted in prayer. This is how we are supposed to do battle." She sunk while stretching both arms to the sky. "Send down Your power, oh, Father Elohim. This triumph is Yours, not ours. This battle is Yours, not ours. Forgive us for doing it wrong. You shall be victorious!"

Thunder rumbled again, jolting her. But Jordana didn't slow her worship and petitions. Benjura had joined her, shouting praise. More fire balls formed in the cloudless sky and barraged the Chinzu army. A gigantic explosion sounded at the bottom of the ravine. Flames licked up the side of the rock-walls, their fiery tips visible ten feet above the ledge. Even at a few hundred yards, heat warmed Jordana's face. "The bridge and its foundation has been demolished by Elohim's own hand."

"Hallelujah to the Great Creator!" Benjura cheered along with many Akimmi braves.

A beam of light came from behind Jordana, so bright she flinched. It passed right by her, not two feet away. She shielded her eyes and squinted at the amazing sight.

A man in a long white robe shone brighter than anything humanly possible. Tall as the giants, but with short glowing hair, he carried no weapon. Every inch of him shimmered as if he'd swallowed a beam from the sun. His pores glistened out light. He nodded at her and Benjura, then strode to one of the Chinzu fighters and touched his shoulder. The man's eyes rolled back and he collapsed to the ground.

The bright being stepped to another giant and did the same, then another. Each foe toppled dead.

Could the man be Elohim himself? Jordana considered falling flat on her face to worship, yet she couldn't tear her gaze away from the man's glistening skin. Even his feet cast rays of light as he walked.

Voices sounded around her. Several Akimmi braves dropped to their knees when the man-of-light passed them. Other Akimmi warriors shouted at their tribemates to stand and fight. Those yelling seemed oblivious to the amazing sight standing inches from them.

210

The Being touched no gatekeeper or Akimmi as he meandered through the crowd. His hand landed only on the enemy.

As if a veil lifted from Jordana's face, she blinked at the scene before her, gaping into the spirit world. Dozens of shining men snaked through the fighters. *Angels*. One by one, they touched every giant, tumbling them over like chopped trees.

Jordana softened her prayers to a reverent whisper. Continuing her worship, she ignored the prickles in her knees from kneeling on the hard soil.

Soon the angels stopped and glanced around as if searching for something. More Chinzu braves? Jordana hunted to find one on the illuminated battlefield. She could see all the way to the canyon's edge thanks to the amazing radiance from all of the angels. Not a Chinzu giant in sight.

The first guardian who had nodded at her and Benjura made eye contact again. He drew close with his quick strides but at the last second, he veered to a moaning elephant. One of the animal's front legs had been hacked off. Several arrows protruded from its body. The angel ran his hands across the creature's back and side, causing each arrow to fall away. Every puncture wound closed. The glimmering man picked up the amputated paw and held it to the bloody stump. "Elohim." The word swooshed through the air like rushing wind, and light flashed. The animal's leg reattached and healed whole.

The elephant rolled to his feet. He tossed his great trunk over the bright-one's shoulder, and stood rocking back and forth.

Benjura laughed, as did Jordana.

Even the angel chuckled. After petting the elephant and whispering something in its ear, he moved away.

Jordana locked eyes with the heavenly being, longing to speak to him. Could she please stay with the gatekeepers? Would Elohim make an exception?

Shallow, labored wheezing of a nearby panda caught Jordana's ear. She pointed at the suffering creature barely clinging to life.

211

The guardian rushed over to the animal covered in sticky red and whispered Elohim's name again. The gatekeeper sat up, its fur returned to black and white, all crimson stains gone. The panda hugged the shiny-one.

Before her, angels healed in Elohim's name. Every injured gatekeeper and Akimmi brave was made whole. As the miracle-workers methodically wove through the battlefield healing all the injured, they touched no dead bodies and carefully stepped over pools of blood.

Questions raced through Jordana's mind. Did the sunrays glistening from their bodies come from Elohim? If the angels were this beautiful and amazing, what did the Creator look like? How much brighter He must be. How could anyone survive in His presence? Jordana did not want to slow the angel's work and shoved her curiosity aside. Unmoving, she continued her worship and made petitions for Beast, Zelle, and Lainey's safety. *Please restore them if they are wounded.* Jordana prayed for Chief Drongo and Jasper. She hadn't seen them since the fight begun.

At last the first angel came and stood before her. He motioned for her and Benjura to rise, and they obeyed. *Daughter, be of good cheer. Your faith turned the tide of this battle. Moved by your love for these animals, Elohim healed them and the Akimmi men.* The angel's lips did not move, and yet his words penetrated her mind.

The guardian's gaze ventured over to Benjura. *Faithful son, well done. Your unyielding belief in Elohim's unmatched power helped win this war.*

His words to Benjura rang in her ears, too.

"Who are you?" Benjura's voice quaked.

Heart thumping madly, Jordana squinted at the lighted being. Diamond eyes stared into her mind and soul.

I am a servant of Elohim. He approves of your desire to glimpse His Holy Land. You may not enter, but as a reward, you may view what lies beyond the gate. Lainey shall take you both. This gift is for you two alone. Afterward, you must leave this side.

"Forever?" Jordana bit her bottom lip. Excitement, along with a wave of panic surged through her. Oh to see Elohim's Holy Land, but could she not stay with Lainey? "Please tell me, sir, must I leave? Will I ever return?"

The guardian cocked his head. After a brief pause, he leaned in and spoke out loud. "It is necessary for you to leave now, but you will soon cross again. Beyond that, I do not know. Go in peace." He tipped back head back, fixing his eyes heavenward. A gust of wind carried him up. High above, he floated and faded. All trace of his radiance disappeared.

Jordana searched the crowd. Not a single angel remained visible. She had so many unasked questions.

"Wow!" Benjura squeezed her hand. She hadn't even realized her fingers were laced with his.

"Wow, indeed." Lainey sat at Jordana's other side.

"I didn't know you were here." Jordana dropped and hugged her friend. "Praise, Elohim, you're okay. What of your family?"

Lainey nuzzled into Jordana's neck. "I don't yet know. I've been here worshiping with you and Benjura."

Zelle bound in, skidding to a stop in front of Jordana. "That was so scary! Every one of us would be dead if not for Elohim's servants. I had never seen one before. Tanga didn't see them at all. One saved Beast. He had stabs everywhere on his back and sides. A bad slice tore his ear and it dangled by fur. All were restored. Beast saved my life twice tonight. An angel saved his. Rojo was rescued too. Could you see the angels, Jordana?" Zelle twirled a circle and curled up her lips. Beyond her, sunrise hinted at the eastern horizon. They'd been fighting all night, but Zelle showed no signs of it.

"Yes," Jordana warmed at Zelle's exuberance, but it did not last. Standing, she wiped her forehead, her arm as weighty as a cow's full udder. She witnessed many wonders this night and should be dancing over the victory. But a heaviness rolled in and covered her. She must say goodbye to Lainey and the gatekeepers. Someday *soon* she'd cross again. Was *soon* the same to her as to the Creator? Would her friend's still be alive? Did the gatekeepers live as long as humans, or only a dozen years like the village cats?

"We get to see the Holy Land." Benjura enveloped her in a bear hug.

She stiffened. Together they would have the honor of glimpsing Elohim's remnant of paradise lost. But then they must separate. Wonder and dread raged within. Jordana stepped out of his embrace.

The deep voice of Beast rumbled. "You are bleeding, Princess." He sauntered into their group and sniffed the back of Jordana's wrist where a line of blood dripped from her upper arm. Beast ran his rough tongue across the back of her hand, licking away the red.

Jordana had forgotten about her triceps cut and the pain in her wrist.

"Elohim restored everyone except Jordana. Why?" Zelle asked Lainey.

"She was given a reward instead of healing."

"I'm not seriously hurt." Jordana rubbed the welt on the back of her hand. Now that she focused on where the giant kicked her, it throbbed as if it were a second heartbeat.

Zelle sniffed Jordana's angry red wound, then plunked down. "Why didn't the angels heal the dead? We lost Dahlu."

"Oh no." Jordana covered her mouth. She had only known Lainey's cousin a couple days, but found her devout and kind.

"The angels didn't heal the wounded, Elohim did." Lainey moved closer to her sister. "He did not give the guardians authority to raise the dead, as they were already in His paradise. We shall see them again one day."

Zelle nodded.

Jordana marveled over Lainey's ability to explain things in a few simple words. If only she could decipher the writhing emotions within herself as clearly. She'd been trying to figure them out her whole life.

"One of them spoke to us," Benjura said. "I just stood there gawking at him. I should have at least asked his name."

"It's Obadiah." When Lainey answered, all heads turned her way. "He said I am to escort you to the entrance of the Holy Land. After that, I shall send you back across the Azul."

Send you back. A cold flush coursed through Jordana. See the Holy Land, and leave Lainey. Jordana's stomach soured. She couldn't even muster enough curiosity to ask Lainey how she knew the angel's name.

CHAPTER TWENTY-FOUR

Jordana's arms throbbed and her feet ached as she trudged back to the cooks, Clydesdales, and monkeys waiting at the edge of the field in the shade of the trees. The noon sun beat down on her and the others, as they made the long trek across the barren region. For hours, they had cleaned up the mess at the canyon's rim. No enemy corpse was left on the Forbidden Falls side of the canyon. Tossed into the burning bridge below, each Chinzu carcass met a fiery demise. The work consumed every ounce of Jordana's strength.

Jasper and Chief Drongo received many wounds in the battle, but both were healed. Not a single warrior or gatekeeper had been left with even a scar. Except for Jordana, though her minor gash and welt didn't really count as serious battle wounds.

The gatekeeper death toll nauseated her. Members from every species had died—two dozen wolves, sixteen lions, seventeen elephants, twenty-eight bears, thirty-four cheetahs, forty gorillas, and eleven leopards including Lainey's cousin, Dahlu. The greatest number of casualties came from the hawks and eagles. Out of two hundred and sixty birds, only fifty-one returned.

The Akimmi tribe lost one hundred and twelve braves. This time the chief allowed them to be buried at the battle site, partly because it was in the Forbidden Falls Territory and partly because it was side by side with the gatekeeper. Everyone worked hard to dig over two hundred graves. The large elephants were covered with stones. More and more rocks were piled atop, forming great cairns. Row upon row of rock pilings would serve as a reminder of Elohim's sovereignty.

Jordana used the back of her hand to brush her hair out of her eyes. It stuck to her sweaty forehead. Caked dirt and dried blood covered her hands all the way to her elbow. No skin showed. Dirt wedged under every nail.

Chore finished, Lainey paced alongside Jordana as they traveled back to the encampment. "Child, I sense a heavy spirit within you. You're more burdened now than when we first met. What troubles you?"

Jordana shook her head, not trusting herself to speak. Her sunburned lips and parched throat added to the misery. "Later," she whispered.

When her foot stepped into cool liquid, Jordana glanced around. The procession had entered a river, and she hadn't even noticed. Braves and animals alike dunked into the water. Bending, she cupped some water and brought it to her mouth, but stopped short of drinking. Only dirty red water filled her hands. She waded to the center and dove under. The stream was far cooler than the Azul. She swam to the opposite bank and sat on the edge using handfuls of sand to scrub her skin and the tunic. All around her, red and brown swirled. She washed her hair as best she could without lavender or aloe, then swam upstream to find clean water to drink. After gulping and gulping, she rolled to her back and floated.

She let herself float downstream, past laughter and the splashing of animals and men. Ignoring them all, she drifted until everything grew silent. Only then did she let the tears fall. After what seemed like an hour, everyone was gone and she washed again, then floated some more. Awareness crept over her and Jordana glanced around. Four leopards—Lainey, Beast, Zelle, and Ojai—waited on the bank as if guarding her. Their devotion warmed Jordana, but the ache in her belly intensified, too. "Thank you, everyone. I'm okay. I wouldn't mind talking to Lainey, though." She lowered her voice. "In private, if that's okay."

Three of the cats nodded and slunk away.

Jordana climbed out of the river. As she wrung her hair, she grappled for the right words. Nothing made sense. She wanted to be alone, yet dreaded returning to her solitary life. A heavy sigh escaped her lips. How could she explain her feelings to Lainey if she didn't understand them herself?

"This way. We shall visit as we journey." Lainey led her.

"I don't know where to start. Or even what to say. I don't know what's wrong with me."

"Your exhausted and in mourning. Just speak your jumbled thoughts, and we can sort them out together." Lainey's slanted emerald eyes blinked up at Jordana. The cat's fatigue showed in her heavy lids and slow paw placements. Yet, Lainey acted more interested in helping Jordana, then hurrying to their camp to eat and sleep. The feline's kindness warmed Jordana.

"Leaving you cuts me to the bone, Lainey. I don't want to be alone anymore, but I'm not permitted to stay with the gatekeepers. I can't return to the Tree Warrior Village and I don't fit in with the Akimmi people." Jordana's throat tightened. "I don't belong anywhere. Or with anyone. I'm going to be alone again."

"Why not go with the Akimmi people? Tis smart to stay where you will be safe."

Jordana lifted a brow. "I'm not sure I would be safe in their village. It's complicated, but Jasper pays me too much attention. I do not desire him. It will only lead to trouble. Chief Drongo's wife looks at me with jealousy in her eyes. Eventually she will want me gone, but the Chief feels beholden to me. It will cause a rift between the royal couple. I spent two days in the Akimmi village dodging Jasper and deflecting Jada. It drained me. I can't do that long term."

"If you married, the Shedock wouldn't have an issue with you. I know Benjura loves you very much."

Jordana drew in a slow breath. "I know he does, but I don't trust him. I'm not talking about with my life or in battle. I

218

mean I don't trust him with my heart. I can't marry a man who won't stick by me no matter what. I must respect a husband to make wise decisions and to be my jira. Past experience with Benjura gives me many reservations."

She ran a hand through her wet hair, spreading her fingers wide to smooth out the tangles. "Honestly, Lainey, my greatest desire is for Benjura to go back to the Tree Warrior Village and tell what he's seen here. Testify to my father on the Judgment Seat. Share how Elohim rained hail of fire onto an army of giants and wiped them out."

Tears welled in her eyes, as she finally figured out the source of her turmoil. "Elohim is real and my father must reconcile with Him. Benjura should bear witness to how the angels healed gatekeepers and Akimmi braves simply by whispering the Creator's name. My Arrdock will listen to Benjura. The miracles we've seen this night are proof of Elohim's majesty. Perhaps Father will let go of his hardened heart and restore the seasons of atonement. Elohim worship must be reinstated in the Tree Warrior Village."

Jordana's voice cracked. She stopped walking as her heart broke anew. She feared for her father's soul more now after seeing the reality of the spirit world. Her own happiness didn't matter. Her knees weakened, and she sank to the grass next to Lainey. "Please, will you help me convince Benjura to go to the Tree Warriors? He won't want to go because he swore an oath to never leave me again. But I did not ask for his oath and I do not want it. The only thing that matters is salvation for my father and our people."

Lainey whiskers twitched. "I agree. Let us pray about it tonight."

Jordana hugged her before rising and heading out.

"I, too, am sad you cannot stay with me. But I shall see you again someday. Obadiah said it would be necessary for you to cross the Azul again. He did not say if it would be only once. I pray it is often. I shall miss you, child. My heart will break when I see you go off alone." Lainey spoke in a shaky voice, obviously

219

struggling to hold her emotions in check. "I will beseech Father Elohim about your future. No doubt He has great plans for you. Tomorrow, we'll speak to Benjura. He should witness to your Arrdock and his people."

"Thank you." Would Elohim really have something great planned for her? It seemed too much to dream for. And yet, hope swelled within. After a quick swipe to erase her tears, she pulled her shoulders back and entered their encampment. Sick of her own misery when she should be praising Elohim for their great victory, Jordana focused on unrolling her mat over leaves on which to sleep. She'd feel mentally and physically stronger after a good rest.

The fragrance of a campfire and baking bread wafted her way. Could she muster the strength to chew? Did she deserve to eat a nice meal, when so many had died this day? It didn't seem fair. Yet food was needed for the journey back to the Azul River tomorrow. They must send the Akimmi army home.

* * *

Jordana covered her mouth, sealing in the scream.

A wide sword slashed across Benjura's stomach, slicing deep into his torso all the way to the spine. Hazel eyes glazed over, her love sank to the ground.

Shiny steel swung her way, hacking back and forth in the air, fast and purposeful. Jordana went for a knife in her sheaf, but it was empty. She tried the other side but her frantic fingers found nothing. Without protection, she must flee. She pivoted, but her foot caught on something and she fell face first into the dirt. She lifted her head to meet Lainey's eyes—fixed and wide open just like her mouth, gray tongue hanging to the side. Lifeless. Dead.

Jordana opened her mouth to scream, but someone jerked her up by the back of her hair. Fire sliced across her scalp. Jordana writhed to get free.

"Shh. It's okay. I've got you." Benjura whispered, "Wake

220

up, Jordana. You're having a nightmare."

Inch by inch, an awareness crept into Jordana. She lifted her heavy lids, each one weighing as much as a basket of fruit. Darkness filled the wooded encampment. Benjura kneeled on one knee and caressed her cheek. Overhead, Lainey slept on a tree limb, her paws dangling on each side of the branch. Last night, the various prides took to the trees, as the Akimmi braves spread blankets and mats on the ground. Jordana laid hers near the only other human female in the camp. The cook sprawled next to Jordana, the woman's plump figure not three feet away.

Benjura clasped her hand. "Are you okay?"

"Yes." Her voice sounded hoarse. When had he come to her? She hadn't seen him before going to bed.

"Did you dream of the battle?" Benjura's released her hand and leaned back on his haunches.

"Yes." She cleared her throat. "Did you dream of it as well?"

He nodded. "I think everyone is having nightmares. Even the wolves. You can hear them yipping in their sleep and their paws twitch as if they're running." He pointed to the foot of her bedding.

Jordana lifted her head. A mass of limbs, bodies, and tails intermixed where a pack of wolves cuddled by her feet. Several paws convulsed, just as Benjura had said. She rested her head back on the soft pile of moss under her bedding and peered through the branches at the star-dotted sky. Everything from the past twenty-four hours flooded back. Despite the beauty of the angels yesterday, it was the worst day of her life. More horrible than being exiled three years earlier. She prayed she'd never see such carnage and death again.

"I'll go now, since you're okay." Benjura stood.

A rush of panic surged through her. She wanted to ask him to sit next to her until she fell back to sleep. Or perhaps they could go on a walk. But she bit back the ideas. "Thank you."

"Goodnight." He said nothing else and left.

If he had suggested it, she would have asked him to stay.

221

She didn't want to be alone. How could she feel so safe in his arms and yet not trust his decisions? Even more perplexing was her growing desire to spend time with him. Her heart leapt. Did she really want him to stay? She squeezed her eyes shut, admitting the truth. And yet, her desire wasn't as important as a city of people who needed rescuing from evil.

She blew out a slow breath, noting every aching muscle in her body. Sleep would bring strength for the important job ahead. A job she dreaded to the depths of her soul. Tomorrow she must make Benjura leave her once and for all.

* * *

"No! I shan't. Do it yourself." Benjura crossed the distance between them in a few long strides and stared into her eyes, as he continued to process her words. "I can't believe you would send me away." He hands squeezed into fists. "I swore an oath to never leave you again. You have no right to ask me to break it."

"I never asked for that oath. You made it up yourself. I am asking you to do something for me instead." Jordana frowned hard. "I'm banished. I have no other miracle to present. I'll die if I return. But you can go back without any opposition. You need to testify about all you've seen. It will restore my father to Elohim. If the Arrdock repents and changes the law, every tribesmen will follow. Nothing is more important!"

"I'm not a preacher, or a medicine man, or a teacher. They'll not listen to me. I'm just a watch guard who's pretty good with a bow. That's all." He wasn't afraid to stand in front of a crowd and testify as to what he'd seen in the battle. But how could he leave Jordana? He couldn't go through that again. It was too great a request.

"They will listen to you," Jordana said. "You studied the scrolls alongside me. You know the law. You're eloquent and well respected. Witness to them. I'm asking you to at least try."

Lainey volleyed in, the two had badgered him for at least

twenty minutes. "If you request an audience with the Arrdock, I do not believe he would deny you. Especially when it concerns his daughter. Anyone could see the look of pure joy on his face when Jordana returned. Out of his love for her, the Arrdock will hear what you have to say."

"Yes, I'm sure he'd grant me audience. That's not the issue." He paced in front of the exasperating females. Jordana going to the Akimmi village without him sent shudders through his body. Did she not see how Jasper drooled over her? Benjura couldn't lose her to him. At least Lainey should understand that. Yet she parlayed with Jordana against him. Perhaps this was a test of his devotion. One he wouldn't fail. "My answer is no. I will not leave Jordana. Find someone else to send."

"Think of your sisters, Benjura. Do you want them to know the truth and one day enter Elohim's paradise?" Jordana laid her hand on his arm. "I beg you to speak with my father. It's the only thing I ask. Isn't your faith stronger now that you've actually seen the things we've read about?"

He inched his chin up and down. "But what of you? I promised to protect you."

She lifted her chin a notch. "Jasper will protect me. I'll go with him to the Akimmi village."

Benjura ripped his arm from under her fingertips, blood burned in his veins. After all they'd been through, she'd choose Jasper over him? "Do you love the man?" The words burst from his mouth before he could stop them.

Jordana lowered her gaze and moved to sit next to Lainey. "I've only known Jasper a short time, but I like how he makes me feel."

Benjura's mouth drained of all moisture. He'd already lost her. How had he not seen it?

"I think it's better if you don't come to the Akimmi village with me and Jasper. You journey to your people." Jordana stared at the ground. "I am asking my childhood friend to please speak to my father. Just share from your heart about what you've seen." Her face lifted, the moisture in her eyes

223

sparkled like the sun shining on a lake. "Will you please do this for me? It's my only request?"

Never had he been able to refuse her anything, especially when her lovely gray-blue eyes fought tears. Unable to speak, he nodded, and stormed away. If Jordana loved another man, he mustn't stand in her way. On the morrow, they'd glimpse the Holy Land, and he'd depart for the Tree Warrior Village. Stomach roiling, Benjura tried to push the sickening picture of Jordana kissing Jasper out of his brain. Throughout her banishment, he had stayed true to her. Devoted and waiting, just like he'd been doing since childhood. Praying and hoping. But now, after more than a decade, he had to let her go. Completely. Forever. The girl no longer belonged to him.

CHAPTER TWENTY-FIVE

At the bank of the Azul River, Jordana shielded her eyes from the sun. She stood with Benjura, saying goodbye to the Akimmi braves as they entered the water. Cooks, warriors, and horses filed past as they exited the Forbidden Territory for good. Some men kneeled and kissed the holy ground before crossing over. If only her tribe could have such reverence for the Creator.

In her regal stance, Lainey thanked the Akimmi braves and gave each one a blessing as they left.

Nerves sparked inside Jordana's belly, as if fireflies flitted about. Soon, she'd leave, too. If only she could receive the blessing of staying with her friend. She'd choose it over the high honor of gazing into the Holy Land.

"I guess this is the end." Chief Drongo bent to one knee in front of the black leopard. "The things I have seen this past week have strengthened my devotion. I've learned much from you. I'm grateful for your wisdom, and indebted for your assistance in protecting my village from the giants." He stroked Lainey's neck. "If you need anything from the Akimmi people, we are at your call." The chief rose. "If not, I will see you one day in Elohim's paradise."

Lainey nodded. "Be it so."

Chief Drongo moved in front of Benjura, placing a hand across to his shoulder. "I am honored to have fought alongside a skillful warrior. I wish you blessings in your return the Tree Warrior Village. If you ever feel the need for change, please come to us. You will always have a place among my guards."

Benjura tipped his head. "You honor me. Thank you." His jaw muscle tightened, flexing and relaxing.

Jordana guessed at how much Benjura wanted to accept the Chief's offer. Misleading him regarding her feelings for Jasper was the only way she could get Benjura to return to the tree warriors. Jordana shoved the sickening feeling away. She did what was necessary for the good of her father and tribesmen.

When Chief Drongo moved in front of her, Jordana dipped into a full curtsey.

Chief grabbed her up and into his arms. He hugged her tight, and then drew back. "I owe you my life and my daughter's. I will spend decades repaying you. Hurry up and come along to our village. I'll have a special tree home prepared just for you."

She could only nod, unsure how to explain that she wouldn't be staying. Especially with Benjura standing so close.

Jasper walked past Benjura and positioned himself behind Chief Drongo. He didn't look at Benjura, and neither man spoke to the other.

Jordana focused back on the chief when he clasped her hands like a wise father would, not like a boy just one year younger than she. They had all aged in the past week. "I worry about you traveling alone to our village. Perhaps I should have Jasper wait here for you." The chief arched a brow, his lips twitching as if he said something funny.

"It's not necessary. I wish to be alone on my journey to the Akimmi village." Jordana didn't want to go there at all. But since she told Benjura that was her plan, she had to keep her word. Otherwise she'd be a true liar. Was not correcting someone's assumption the same as lying?

"Very well. Make haste." He strode to the water's edge and waded in.

Jasper moved before her, unblinking and still like a great boulder carved into a cliff.

Jordana stole a glance at Benjura. Did he watch her interaction with Jasper? *Yes.* He stared straight at them. How

226

could she put on a convincing show for him without sending the wrong message to Jasper? The man finally believed she loved Benjura, and had backed off. Not an actual lie, since she had once loved him as her future betrothed. So why did her insides scream at her? She clenched her fists. If the two men would just do as she asked, none of these games would be necessary. Yet if they led to her father's repentance, and the tree warriors' restoration, it would be worth it all.

Jordana stepped forward and laced her arm inside the crook of Jasper's elbow. Into the Azul, she escorted him. "Thank you for all you've done for the gatekeepers." He mumbled some sort of reply, but she paid no attention as she tugged him farther out to the river's center.

As soon as they were far enough away, she interrupted his words, her voice barely above a whisper. "I look forward to visiting your village again, but please do not let your chief build a tree house for me. I am not staying. Benjura and I have other plans. Can you tell your chief for me?" *Other plans separately.* Another mislead. Or was it an actual lie?

Jasper nodded.

She rose up on toes and gave him a peck on his cheek. "That's for Taryn. Please deliver it for me. I miss her." She kept her back to Benjura and Lainey as she scooted away from the Akimmi brave. She had no smile for him and simply nodded. "Safe journey." The hurt in Jasper's expression could not be mistaken. Did Benjura's face host the same pain?

Gooseflesh sprouted on her arms, sending a shiver through her. She debated calling both men over to confess the truth. Of course she had tried that approach initially, but each one only laughed as if she didn't know her own mind. They did as they pleased; flirting and competing with one another for her affection. Her wishes did not matter. The knowledge strengthened her resolve.

Jasper's face sagged. "Good day, m'lady."

She folded her arms across her chest and watched him catch up to the chief.

227

Drongo and Jasper turned, tipping their heads before disappearing into the jungle.

Jordana remained in the river's lazy current until nothing could be seen of the Akimmi clan. When she strode back to shore, she inspected her two friends. Benjura didn't make eye contact with her, but Lainey's gaze burned holes across Jordana's scalp. The jowls covering Lainey's fangs twitched, as if begging to rise and hiss. Jordana fought the instant welling of tears, for she had let her friend down. The cat's superior hearing probably allowed her to hear every word. The tangled web she created seemed the only way. If there had been another option, she'd have taken it. Couldn't Lainey see that? Jordana would sacrifice anything to rescue her father.

* * *

Jordana's thighs throbbed and her lungs strained for air as she climbed. The trio picked their way along a narrow trail cut around boulders, over rocks, and sometimes behind waterfalls. Strong from chasing down prey these past three hot seasons, this ascent should be a breeze. Different muscles must be needed for mountain climbing than ones for distance running, because she fell way behind the other two. From time to time, they'd pause so she could catch up. Such as now. They conversed without glancing her way when she approached.

"There are hundreds of waterfalls on the west side of the Falls Territory." Lainey motioned with a head bob. "These seven falls converge into a giant pool two thousand feet below. From there it flows downstream a quarter mile, and over a massive waterfall spanning a hundred and seventy yards before dropping six hundred feet." Even with Lainey shouting, Jordana strained to hear her above the thundering cascade.

"The lake at the bottom splinters into dozens of rivers, which drop over more mountainsides, becoming more waterfalls. This is the edge of the Western border of the Falls Territory."

Jordana stopped on an overhang and absorbed the view.

228

Numerous waterfalls streaked the rock face across a gully. A great mist filled the expanse. A rainbow shone through the spray. *Breathtaking!* Elohim's creativity demanded her praise. *You are an amazing Creator.*

A knot snaked through her intestines. She was about to receive Elohim's blessing as a reward for her great faith yet she had just deceived two men in order to get them to do her bidding. The depth of her unworthiness couldn't be denied.

All morning, Lainey acted cold and aloof to her, but friendly to Benjura. Jordana didn't know how much more she could take. And yet if she confessed the truth to Benjura, he'd stay with her and never return to Father. Jordana pulled her shoulders back. No matter the cost, she must stay the course.

After a deep sigh, she left the overhang, and veered up the mountainside behind the others. She made no effort to keep pace. Creating distance made it easier.

One foot after another, Jordana pushed herself higher and higher along the path. Although she remained silent, the other two prattled on as if they didn't know she followed. Their voices echoed off the jagged boulders they traversed. Temperatures dropped the higher they went. The chilly air against her sweaty skin helped cool her over-heated body. But the thin oxygen made it impossible to catch her breath.

"We're at the top." Benjura called down to her, his voice strong.

Why did this climb seem so easy for him and so hard for her? By the time she crested the mountain trail, both lungs threatened to burst. In a grassy patch next to the trail, she flopped down. She spread her arms wide and labored to fill her lungs with air.

Benjura walked over and extended a hand. "You need to stand up. You might pass out if you stay on your back."

If filled with energy to speak, she'd tell him how wonderful being unconsciousness sounded. And since she was already lying down, fainting wouldn't injure her.

Benjura grabbed her hands and tugged her up.

229

Back on her feet, the trees spun and stars twinkled in the daylight.

Benjura bent her at the waist and rubbed her back. "Take slow and shallow breaths. When you're able to walk, it's a short distance to a pool. We can drink and rest. No more climbing."

Hallelujah! Seconds grew into minutes before she breathed normally. The stars had disappears, and nothing spun out of control. Jordana attempted to break the silence with Lainey. "I understand why they call this the Falls Territory. Rocky paths, steep mountains, and thin air—one slip or a fainting spell, and over the edge you'd fall."

Lainey's gaze pinned Jordana to a tree. "That's not where the name stems from. It comes from the fall of mankind. Humans turn from Elohim's ways as often as the leaves turn red and fall off the trees."

Jordana held the leopard's stare. Was the cat insinuating Jordana had fallen away from Elohim? Nothing could be further from the truth. Everything she did was to bring her people back to Him. How could she make Lainey understand? With Benjura only two feet away, for now Jordana could only chew her lip.

Lainey led their group across a meadow and into a forest. A hundred yards into the woods, and they emerged at a clearing. Sapphire-leafed trees, bamboo, and purple palms surrounded the perimeter. No sign of damage on the sacred Tamars. In the middle of the meadow, a round pond glistened in the sun. They moved toward it in silence.

The water's color reminded Jordana of the turquoise stones in the riverbeds back home. But the pond's edge looked odd. Small and large boulders circled partial sections of the banks. Someone rolled the rocks close for sitting near the water. On the far side, two ferrets cuddled on a rock. Next to them, an albino squirrel sat still. Only his white fur moved as a breeze brushed over him. The squirrel did not gaze into the water, nor did he glance their way. Instead, the little animal stared straight up. He seemed to search the sky.

Like a falling pine cone, the truth hit her. She jerked

around to Lainey. "Is this—" Jordana's breath caught in her throat. "The Restoration Pool?"

"Yes. It heals physically or restores one spiritually to Father Elohim." The leopard's ears twitched. "If they have sinned."

CHAPTER TWENTY-SIX

Jordana inched closer. The aqua pool stood out against the backdrop of white, purple, and green trees. It was almost as if the colorful trees had been chosen specifically to highlight the water. Nothing about the pool suggested an offering of more than a cool drink, except for the rocks rolled around the perimeter.

Benjura rushed to the water's edge, shrugging off his leather vest. "You said it's good to drink. Can we swim in it, too?"

"Yes." Lainey entered the water and lapped up drinks. "The water is like any other. Tis only miraculous when rain falls from a clear blue sky and churns the current."

After removing his moccasins, Benjura waded in and sank to his neck. "What fills the pond if no rivers lead here?"

"Underground streams perhaps. Or another miracle." Lainey backed out of the pond and sat on the bank.

Footwear off, Jordana stepped toward the center. At a drop-off, she dove down, kicking hard and swimming toward the bottom. The clear water did not sting her eyes, and visibility extended at least thirty feet. Not a fish in sight. Neither was the bottom. Pressure built in her ears and she turned for the surface. She eased above the waterline, rolled onto her back and floated. As she gazed into the sky, water fell straight toward her—gentle and sparse at first. She squinted as several more drops hit her face. *Healing rain.* "Come!" Jordana motioned to the albino squirrel and ferrets. She had no idea what their injuries were, or how long they waited for healing, but the miracle had arrived and she wanted the creatures to receive answers to their prayers.

The flying squirrel leaped off the rock. As he passed her, Jordana noticed an awful crook in his tail. Broken or dislocated? The squirrel landed in the pond behind Jordana. His high pitched voice cried out to Elohim for healing.

Benjura kicked hard over to the rock hosting the ferrets. He stood up and reached out to them. "Let me help you in."

"Thank you." One of the ferrets ran up his arm. "Mingo fell and can't use his back legs."

The female's delicate voice might have been the sweetest thing to have ever reached Jordana's ears.

Benjura eased both of the slender creatures into the water.

The female swam, but Mingo clung to Benjura's hand.

"My tail. My beautiful tail. Look. It's healed." On the bank, the albino squirrel held up his white tail, rubbing his tiny hands along its length. "It's straight again and doesn't hurt anymore." After a quick twirl and roll on the sand, he scurried away. "Praise, Elohim." He disappeared into the woods.

Healing rain continued to shower down from the sunny sky. Jordana tipped her face up and squinted, trying to see the source of the sprinkles. Droplets pelting her, she closed her lids. When she opened them, she found Lainey in the water near Benjura, who still held a ferret. Lainey spoke in a low tone to the male, and he finally let go of Benjura.

"Swim, Mingo, swim!" His mate squealed at him.

Soon the little critter paddled around with no assistance. He laughed and kicked. "My legs are working. I'm healed." He aimed at Lainey, shooting atop the water toward her. "Thank you, my dear."

"Thank Elohim. Not me." She turned and exited the pond. Upon hitting dry land, the leopard shook hard, ridding her fur of seemingly every drop of water.

Benjura's deep chuckle warmed Jordana's heart. He smiled at the ferrets running for the trees. When the two critters stopped and waved at him, Benjura lifted a muscular arm and motioned farewell.

Then the rain stopped.

Her heart ached and her feet stuck to the bottom of the pond like roots of a tree. Jordana couldn't move—pinned by the hollowness of her soul.

"I would never leave this place, if Elohim permitted it." Benjura dunked under the water and came up flicking his bangs back before exiting the pond.

Skin burning, she met Lainey's eyes. Every chastisement Jordana could think of ran through her mind, as if Lainey had spoken them in her glower.

What kind of faith did Jordana possess if she always took matters into her own hands? If she manipulated people to get her way? Her insides burned. How could she gaze into the Holy Land as a reward for great faith in battle, when she only demonstrated cowardice afterwards? The three tiny animals had more faith than she. Her heart thundered anew.

Jordana held Lainey's gaze. "Okay. You win." The word eased over her lips. She'd trust Benjura to do the right thing, and more importantly, she'd trust Elohim to make it happen.

Out of the pool and over to rock, Jordana sat and wrung her hair. When she flung her wet tresses behind her, she finally spoke. "Benjura, can I talk to you a minute? Will you sit with me?"

He nodded and eased onto the bolder beside her. In the sun, the gold and green flecks in his eyes seemed to dance. So beautiful. Too beautiful for a man's eyes. Shirtless, he leaned back on one arm, every muscle showing in his biceps and torso.

"I'll give you two some privacy." Lainey rose. "Remember one thing, Jordana. Elohim cared about these tiny animals enough to send the healing rain. How much more does the Father care about those created in His image?" Lainey lumbered a good distance away, and plopped down in the sun.

"What was that about?" Benjura arched a brow at her.

Jordana bit back the pebble-sized lump in her throat. Memories from her life in the Tree Warrior Village flooded

234

back—the many times she gripped her problems tight in her fists instead of releasing them to the Creator. What did that say of her faith if she believed herself more capable than Him? How had she not recognized this failure in herself before now? And yet, Elohim loved her.

"You look like you're about to cry. Is everything okay?" Benjura reached for her.

Jordana pulled back, resting her hands in her lap. "I must confess something to you. I misled you on purpose, so you'd do something for me. Tis why Lainey has been angry with me since yesterday."

"I've noticed her attitude, but I'm having a little trouble believing you'd lie. You're the most honest person I've ever known. No matter the cost, you've always been truthful."

"No matter the cost." She whispered his words and met his gaze. "Please keep that in mind." The fireflies returned, flitting every which way in her gut. Jordana pushed to her feet and paced in front of him. "Understand that what I'm about to tell you changes nothing between us. I don't believe we're meant to be together. Do you understand?"

He stiffened and sat up straight, his jaw clamping down. "Perfectly."

The harsh words tore through her heart, but couldn't give him false hope. She'd always love him, but not trust him. A heavy sigh escaped her lips. "I'm not interested in Jasper. I have no desire to live with the Akimmi people. I don't even want to go there, but I must keep my word."

Light returned to his eyes as the corners of his lips lifted to grin, just as she feared.

"I only let you believe I was interested in Jasper, so you'd leave me alone. I don't want a life with you." The bitter words coming out of her mouth soured her stomach. Jordana eased down on the rock next to him. "Oh, Benj. I don't want to hurt you, or fight with you. Honestly, I don't know what to do after this is over. I have no idea what Elohim has planned for me. I'm worried, and would love to talk to you about it as my friend. But

I don't feel that freedom. You vowed to never leave me, and that's exactly what I want you to do. I *need* you to go back to the village and speak to my father."

She ran a hand across her wet hair. "You look at me as if you want to be my jira. And if I tell you my true thoughts, you'll swoop in and never return to the Tree Warrior Village. But more than anything on Tzuri, more than I need air for my lungs, I want you to go back to our people. Share about the things you've seen. Nothing else is as important. I am not important."

His body leaned toward her, but his face remained emotionless. "You're important to me."

"Stop." She shook her head. "I'm sorry I misled you about Jasper. I'm sorry I—" she could barely get the word out, "lied. But do not let it change your plans. Go back to the tree warriors. Speak to my father." Totally spent, her arms flopped to her lap. The collapsing feeling she experienced at the top of the mountain returned, and she struggled to remain upright.

Benjura reached for her cheek and ran his thumb across her jaw, but did not speak.

She wished she could read his thoughts. His solemn expression gave nothing away. Before she changed her mind and gave in to his caress, she pulled back and focused on the bird calls resonating all around them. Whistles from cookoos, toucans, and blue magpies filled the air, along with numerous others she didn't recognize. Overhead, a blue macaw flew. It didn't have a lovely sound, but no songbird could compete with its colorful tail and wings.

Try as she might, the birds couldn't hold her attention. As last she gazed back into Benjura's eyes. "I'm sorry I hurt you."

His Adam's apple wobbled as he swallowed. "I'm sorry I put you in a position where you couldn't be honest with me. We've always told each other everything. I never wanted that to change." He leaned forward, elbows on knees. "I'm glad you aren't going to marry Jasper. He's not good enough for you. The man is full of himself." Benjura's rose and picked up pebbles, skipping them across the pond. "I'm not an eloquent speaker like

236

you think, but I promise to get an audience with your father. I will testify about the things we've witnessed. After that, I make no promises to you. If the village does not change, how could I stay with them after what we've seen? I'll never again hide my Elohim worship from Queen Brin."

Jordana nodded. She hadn't thought of that. *Please, Elohim, reach my father. He must circumcise his heart and reconcile to you.* If Father led the way, perhaps the whole village would return to the Creator. And just maybe, she could dwell there once more.

Heavy rain poured into the water, pounding on the Restoration Pool's surface. As fast as she could move, Jordana jumped up and dove in. When she popped up, she lifted both hands high in the sky. "Please forgive me. Forgive my lack of faith. Forgive me for manipulating others to do what I wanted. Forgive me for trusting myself over you." Jordana dunked under many times as she repented.

* * *

Benjura hiked behind the two females as Jordana and Lainey prattled on about food in the Falls Territory. Thirty minutes prior, they left the gatekeeper dens after feasting on fish caught by the bears and venison from the prides. Benjura built a fire to cook some of the meat, which Zelle sampled. No other animal had any interest in eating his barbeque. Stuffed, he fell asleep for a short nap after the meal. When he woke, Ariel's triplets were cuddled around him purring.

Jordana's revelation at the Restoration Pool replayed in his head. She wasn't falling in love with Jasper. Relief wasn't an adequate word to describe the deep respite he felt. But why did she have such an aversion to a life with him? Heartache had been his companion these last three years. Looks like it would continue. At least she opened up with the truth. A good step toward rebuilding their trust. How could that grow if they parted ways on the morrow? Did he have the strength to let her go?

A sharp rock in the path caught his toe and Benjura stumbled. When surefooted again, he looked back. A jagged bluish stone poked out of the ground. He squatted and used a knife to wedge it out and toss if off the walking path. It rolled under a bush.

Benjura purposed in his heart to do his best with Jordana's father. She was right—if the Arrdock changed, so would the rest of the tribe. For a time, he'd witness to as many tree warriors as he could. Once he fulfilled his promise, he'd leave. He would seek Jordana out, now that he knew where to look. Perhaps he'd have excellent news to share. Maybe she could even return. Somehow Benjura knew he wasn't supposed to be without her. *Please, Elohim, show her Your plans for us.*

It wasn't easy to shove aside thoughts of the girl who occupied his mind for a decade and a half, but he ought to think about what he'd say to the Arrdock. Jordana could speak from her heart and ignite people's spirits. Sometimes in fury, sometimes in joy. He'd never been able to do that. *Please, Elohim, give me the words.*

"We're here." Lainey stopped in the middle of path.

He moved in next to her and Jordana. Nothing around but jungle trees and vines. Same thick foliage they'd been traveling though since leaving the dens. A huge shadow passed overhead, and Benjura gazed up. Several large birds circled above, their wing spans exceeded those of eagles. He squinted, but the sun at the flock's backs made it impossible to see clearly.

Jordana gasped and Benjura swung his attention to her. She pointed at a bush in front of them. A giant bird hovered above it. Again, light at the fowl's back kept its front in shadows.

Wait. If the sun shone directly overhead, it couldn't shine from behind the creature standing in front of them. Right? Something moved on bird's wings. Its flapping slowed to reveal a body like a lion. When the creature lowered to the ground, its wings stopped fluttering and separated. Two curled around to cover its feet, two stuck straight out, and two held swords above its head. Something moved on the wings. Eyes. Dozens of

238

blinking eyes on all six wings. They gazed around, searching in every direction. Blinking beautiful shades of iris. Could it really be?

"Seraphim."

CHAPTER TWENTY-SEVEN

Jordana squinted at the shiny swords the Seraphim yielded. Two golden blades so pure and clear, perhaps they were forged in rays from the sun. No metal on Tzuri gleamed as transparently gold.

The Seraphim raised both weapons high in the air, shifting light as the blades captured and refracted beams in every direction. A ray fell onto a gate—tall and wide, it sparkled like diamonds. When the creature swiped one blade down and back up again, and the gate swung open.

Lainey whispered, "The Seraphim has opened the entrance so you may see, smell, and hear what lies beyond."

Jordana couldn't speak as she struggled to absorb everything before her. Benjura must be doing the same thing, for he had yet to utter a word. She dare not glance at him or Lainey, for she might miss something. Her heart throbbed like she'd been sprinting, yet she stayed still. Reverent. As if any movement might chase away the breathtaking view.

Purple palms lined a wide path on the either side of the gated entrance. Their sparkling trunks shone brighter than the ones near her village. Light shimmered on black bark as the trees swayed in the breeze. Not just their bright amethyst fronds, but their whole trunks bent over. Palms on both sides of the path bowed until their fronds touched the ground. Upon rising, wind rushed through their leaves and they moaned a single breathy word. "*Rapha.*"

More palms bent to the ground, then swooshed up forcing wind through their fronds. "Praise, *Rapha.*" They spoke one after another. "Praise, *Rapha.*"

Lainey whispered. "*Rapha* means healer." She kept her voice low. "Purple Tamars are sacred because they edify the name of the Creator. They never stop praising Him. Elohim has opened your ears to hear them this day. I know not if you will hear the ones on your side when you return."

"Can you hear them?" Jordana asked without veering her gaze.

"Always."

Jordana fought to keep her tears at bay. Mamu was right—someday had come—they never cease praising Him. Queen Brin's destruction of the ones back home sickened Jordana even more. No wonder signs of defilement extended all the way to the Great Eucalyptus Forest.

The Seraphim swiped down the other golden sword and lifted it up again, opening Jordana's eyes to what lay beyond the palms—a lush garden with a fountain in the center. Fashioned from mother of pearl, the shiny, white fountain swirled with subtle hues of pink and green. Water poured from it and into a creek that meandered through the grounds.

Jordana zeroed in on the stream. Prisms of color beamed out of the clear water along the entire length of the brook. Emeralds, rubies, and amethysts. All manner of precious stone lined the creek-bed. Not a single dull rock in sight. Light refracted, casting beams of opaque, purple, and other colors into various directions. Like a rainbow. Only more vibrant and more amazing.

A strong breeze blew past, filling the air with gardenia. The fragrance, lovely and pure. All the while, purple palms continually bent and moaned, "Praise*, Rapha.*"

Flowers of fuchsia, violet, yellow, and tangerine filled the garden. Oh to see them up close and smell each one...Jordana grappled for descriptive words to memorize. Beautiful and exquisite fell short of describing the flora. No human word would ever be sufficient.

A light at the far end of the garden drew her attention. Burning bright and inching closer, she tried to focus on the form. But the light beams intensified too bright, and she had to shield her eyes.

Just then the six-winged creature slashed both golden swords down, crossing their points at the ground and held steady.

Wind picked up and the purple palms blocked her view. Jordana strained to see around the amethyst fronds, her heartbeat pounding in her ears. Inch by inch, the gate of shimmering diamonds drew together, shutting everything away.

"Wait." Her heart sank and moisture rushed into her eyes. *No, please. I'm not ready.*

The Holy Land closed away. In a flash, every trace of the gates disappeared into the foliage.

The Seraphim raised both of his swords, pointing them to the sky, and flapped its center wings. The creature lifted, all six wings flew into motion and it joined the others in the air. The flock flew to and from each side of the expanse before fading from her sight.

Jordana stayed motionless as she studied the sky. "The Seraphim are still up there. Aren't they, Lainey? Guarding the Holy Land. But we can't see them anymore."

"Yes. They circle without ceasing. I'm allowed to see the Seraphim and speak to them, but the other gatekeepers are not."

Jordana shifted to study the foliage. "I can't see one bit of the gate or the garden beyond. What would happen if I walked forward and tried to peek through the bushes?"

"Do not try. The Seraphim have it blocked. They will not allow anyone to get close."

Jordana used both hands to swipe her cheeks.

"Wow." Benjura spoke for the first time. "Did you notice the different fruit in the trees, and the throne?"

"No." Jordana jerked toward him. "Did you see the fountain and jewels in the creek?"

242

"No." He pushed himself up and extended a hand to her.

She latched on and they meandered down the path. "The creek bed was full of emeralds, pearls, and topaz—all kinds of precious jewels, casting prisms of light in every direction. It was spectacular."

"Tanzanite?" he asked.

"Yes, I'm sure there was tanzanite too."

Benjura stopped on the path and kicked at a small hole. He moved off the trail and dropped to his knees. He rubbed the ground under the brush and pulled something out. Standing, Benjura handed her a large rock. "Something like this?"

Jordana wiped dirt off the jagged rock, revealing purplish-blue underneath. Not as shiny as the tanzanite in the creek tumbled for a millennia by water, but nevertheless clear and lovely. "Yes. Just like this."

"You may keep it." Lainey strolled on ahead.

"It's marvelous." Jordana held it out to Benjura. "You found it."

He held up both hands and stepped back. "A beautiful jewel for a beautiful lady." He gave her a mock bow and came up grinning. White teeth, tanned face, and long dark eyelashes framing his hazel eyes. Benjura was still the most striking man she'd ever seen.

"Thank you." She place the stone in the satchel always at her hip.

"Tell me everything you saw as we walk back, and I'll tell you what I saw."

"Okay." Jordana grinned at him, his excitement matching hers. Every fiber in her body tingled, more alive with energy and faith. The images from the Holy Land etched into her brain. And the light in the back of the garden...what was it and where had it come from?

* * *

The moment had arrived. The ghastly moment she'd been

243

dreading. Jordana stood at the Azul with Benjura, facing Lainey, Beast, and Zelle. That morning she'd already shared a tearful farewell with Ojai, Ariel, and Tanga after spending the night at the dens. She even choked up when Kamali wiped Jordana's kiss off her cheek and kicked up dust as she grumbled away. But now Jordana must separate from Lainey—her dearest friend. Nausea swelled within. Even the morning sky turned gray, releasing buckets of rain as if weeping along with her. The rainy season had begun.

Benjura hugged Zelle and Lainey, bowed low to Beast, and retreated to stand near Jordana. Compassion shone in his eyes, as if to comfort her.

It didn't. She bounced her gaze between her three leopard friends, soaking in every nuance of their lovely faces. Unable to move or say goodbye, numbness filled her as she stared at them.

Zelle came forward and rubbed her head on Jordana's bare leg. "I will listen for your whistle and run to this bank whenever I hear you. I hope you call me often. Maybe we can converse as long as we stay on our own side."

Jordana's head snapped up. "That's the answer. I shall visit here each month when both moons are full and whistle for you. Maybe we can swim to the center and meet there?" She raised her brows at Lainey, praying she'd agree.

Beast visibly shuttered. "Cats hate getting wet."

"I don't mind." Zelle curled her lips up over her long fangs to smile at Jordana. "I will meet you in the Azul's center on the nights of full moons."

Jordana dropped and hugged Zelle. Upon rising, she approached Lainey. "Is it permitted? Will you come, too?"

"Perhaps." Lainey wrapped her tail around Jordana. "I shall beseech the Creator concerning this matter."

As her heart swelled, Jordana smiled. *Please say yes, Elohim Rapha.* She bent and hugged Lainey. "The angel Obadiah said I would cross over again one day soon. I hope it's not a long wait."

"So do I, child. So do I." Lainey backed away and padded

to the tree line. "I will pray for you daily. Especially for you, Benjura, and your task ahead. Blessings to you both." The cat sauntered into the jungle.

"Goodbye. I love you." The lump in Jordana's throat drew to the size of her tanzanite.

Lainey's melodic voice rang from the brush. "And I love you, child."

"Goodbye. See you next month." Zelle trotted into the woods. "Whistle your tune. I'll be waiting."

The drizzle increased as Jordana kneeled in front of Beast. "I was afraid of you when we first met. Now I don't want to leave you. I owe you much and will think of you every day."

Beast's voice sounded like gravel. "I shall miss you, Princess. May Elohim keep you safe." He licked her cheek before trotting into the rainforest.

All three cats disappeared. No sign of any animal moved in the foliage. No glowing eyes. Jordana covered her mouth to muffle her cry. She let Benjura steer her into the river and lead her across. Before stepping out on the other side, she splashed river water on her face and washed the tears away.

By the time they entered the Great Eucalyptus Forest, thunder pealed from the overcast sky, as it gushed with warm rain. She didn't stop to find shelter and kept moving, picking her way due west. Benjura followed in silence. For at least an hour, they sloshed through mud puddles and swollen streams—the rainforest now living up to its name.

Their path squeezed between trees, and the screech of howler monkeys rang through the jungle canopy. At last the rain faded and beams of light filtered through the branches casting shadows on trunks. The trees grew thick in that area, but when she tipped her head back, a few patches of clear blue sky could be seen. For the moment, the downpour had ended.

Jordana pivoted around, swallowing hard. Once she said goodbye to Benjura, it'd only be a matter of days until she was truly alone again. She'd make an appearance at the Akimmi camp as promised, and tell about her glimpse into the Holy Land.

Maybe she could write it on one of their scrolls for future generations. And then she'd leave. Her solitary life would begin anew.

"I guess it's time." She rested her hands on her hips.

Benjura frowned. "Let me escort you to the Akimmi camp. I'd like to make sure you're safe. Then I'll continue onto the Tree Warrior Village."

Jordana shook her head. "No need. I've been alone a long time in this jungle. I can take care of myself" She pointed north. "Their mountain range is straight that way. And the Tree Warrior Village is way up there." She pointed southwest with her other hand. "Tis time we moved in opposite directions." She lowered her arms.

"Don't be surprised to find me one day on the banks of the Azul whistling your mamu's tune during the full moons."

She laid her hand on his chest. "No, Benjura. Go and make a happy life for yourself. Forget about us." She embraced him. "I will pray for you, and the hearts of the tree warriors. May they receive your testimony." When Jordana pulled back, she fought against the agony in her chest and tried to smile. "Just be yourself. The villagers have always loved you." A piece of her heart still loved him, too. These last few weeks, she'd grown to admire the man he had become. "Goodbye." She moved back several feet, trying to hide her internal torment.

Benjura studied her. Still, unmoving, except for his jaw flexing and releasing. His hazel eyes shone with moisture. Did he fight tears? She hadn't seen him cry since her mamu died, when he had wept alongside her.

He stepped in and encircled her with one arm. His other hand cupped the back of her head. Benjura spread his fingers through her hair. In the next second, he pressed his lips on hers. The man kissed her as if starving for her mouth. He had never kissed her with such passion before.

Jordana's brain struggled to formulate a coherent sentence. His warm touch brought life to her senses. She should stop him, but didn't want to and circled her arms around his

246

neck. Her heart beat a little faster.

His hands raised to her cheeks. "I love you, Jordana. I will never love another. You mean more to me than my own life." His mouth claimed hers once more.

Seconds ticked by as she kissed him back—kissing like they never had before. Finally, she reached deep inside and mustered the strength to push him away.

Benjura stepped back.

Out of his embrace and tempted to pull him back, she blinked and forced steel into her spine. "The task ahead holds more importance than anything else. I thank you with all of my heart for doing this." Although the words, *I love you,* teetered on the tip of her tongue, she couldn't voice them. He'd never leave if she did. And she might not have the strength to make him. "Goodbye." She spun and sprinted away, arms and legs pumping as fast as she could run. She must put distance between them before she changed her mind.

CHAPTER TWENTY-EIGHT

A week had passed in the Akimmi Village. She had written her story on the scrolls. She took her time with great renderings of the Restoration Pool, the Seraphim, and Holy Land. Now free to leave, Jordana's solitary life called to her. It burned within. *How odd.* Moccasins laced up, she stood and folded the blanket over the fluffy mat on the tree-house floor. Today she'd venture into the Snake Valley. A tingle of excitement swirled within her over what the unknown territory might hold. The pull to leave gave her hope of what might lie ahead.

Parchment in hand, she jotted a note to the villagers thanking them for hosting her. She promised to visit again someday. And she would, although it might not be until many hot seasons had passed. Jordana bent and propped the note on her bedding, picked up her satchel, and swung it over her head. The heavy tanzanite rock at the bottom bounced against her hip. She touched its outline as she strode to the window, running her thumb over the worn leather to trace the edges of the jagged jewel within.

Red moon slivers shone above, adding little light to the ground under the tree houses. No muffled voices drifted. Quiet. Empty. No guards mulling about. If she could make it to the northern cave without detection, no one would know which way she ventured. *The cave.* Alone in pitch blackness. A shiver raced down her body. She couldn't risk taking a torch. The guards would see the light. If she helped fight an army of giants, she could certainly make her way through a clean, but very dark cave.

Another twinge pierced her chest. Was she being deceitful by sneaking away in the middle of the night? Never again would she mislead anyone. Yet, all week long, Jasper wouldn't heed her rebuffs. Without Benjura at her side, the man's advances unsettled her. Stealing away to discover what dwelled on the far side of Snake Valley seemed the best way to keep him from chasing after her. She re-read her note. Nothing deceptive. All from her heart.

Quiet foot placements, she hurried to the trap door and descended the ladder. When her feet met grass, she crouched next to the trunk. Sure of no movement in the distance, she slipped to the next tree, and the next. From inside the shadows, she methodically worked her way toward the southern tip of the village. Like the other end, a long meadow lay between her and the cave. Just as she rose to sprint across the clearing, muffled voices floated in the air. She pressed back against a tree trunk and froze.

Two men led horses along the outer edge of the village. Bows strapped to their backs, each had many quivers of arrows tied to the sides of their steeds.

"I'm hoping we find elk this time."

"I'd be happy with anything except fowl."

The other man chuckled as he fisted the horse's mane and jumped up, swinging himself atop the large Clydesdale. The other hunter did the same.

Jordana blinked at the sight. It didn't seem possible to mount a horse of that size without help. Of course, Benjura could probably do it. Jumping had always been easy for him. Once again the man's handsome face filled her mind. Of late, she couldn't keep him out of every thought in her brain.

Galloping hooves drew her gaze. Four more braves joined them. The hunting party rode to the southern cavern. They traveled the same way as she. Her heart sunk. Should she wait until tomorrow to execute her plan? A pull to leave burned in her gut. She mustn't stay another day. From shadow to shadow, she rushed back the way she came and into the southern cave, and out to the Arrie Valley.

* * *

A light sprinkle accompanied her since morning. Hunger now tore through her belly. She left the Akimmi village with only two oranges. Long since eaten. She spotted a patch of huckleberries and ventured over. Picked clean, not a single red berry remained. Unable to shake the urgency to create distance between her and the Akimmi village, she kept moving—choosing not to stop and hunt. Several small creeks served as her trail, no longer dry beds, the water concealed her footprints.

Eyes focused on the canopy above, and a knife in each hand, she waded through the area dubbed jaguar territory. The wind at her back made it impossible to go undetected through the most treacherous part of her crossing. Soon she'd be at the edge of the Great Eucalyptus Forest.

Hours later, she stood in the mango grove near the Azul River. First she'd eat, then she'd unearth the Chinzu weapons and supplies she had buried so many moons ago.

Void of the baboon troop, Jordana searched and searched until she found a few ripe mangoes. Three were deposited in her satchel. She fisted the last one to eat as she left the grove and meandered back to the spot where she must dig. After biting in, she pulled the peel back with her teeth. A putrid rotten smell assaulted her nose. Thick, black veins ran through the orange meat. She lobbed the cursed thing away, and prayed one of the others would be unspoiled. How many more fruit-producing trees would be destroyed because of Brin's defilement?

Stomping drew her attention, and Jordana froze. From which direction had the noise come? Bushes rustled on the opposite side of the clearing. The top of a young tree swayed. A large animal headed her way. She ran to a rainbow eucalyptus and climbed. Not since the day she fled the Tree Warrior Village after the mistaken battle, had she scaled a trunk so fast. The thrashing grew louder. Wind came from the south, meaning the animal had probably caught her scent ages ago. *Please be a rhino or an elephant.*

Jordana sat on a branch thirty feet above the ground, wrapped both legs around it, and split open a mango. Perfect orange meat greeted her, but she hesitated not and squeezed juice on her tunic. She mushed the fruit on her bare skin, arms, and face. Sticky juice covered her hands and fingers, she'd never be able to throw a blade with accuracy in that condition. Her hair served as a cloth to dry her hands. Fingers spread wide, she forked them through her mane.

More slashing and crackling of brush echoed as the animal took its time on the far side.

A blade in each hand, she poised them above her shoulders, ready to fly if needed. She zeroed in on the noise. It sounded more like hacking than an animal passing through. At last, the vegetation parted and two sets of feet stepped into view—human feet. Branches blocked their upper bodies, so she couldn't see their faces.

"We're through." Two feet pivoted back. "We made it to the clearing. Just a few more yards to the Azul."

Gooseflesh covered Jordana's skin. She'd recognize that voice anywhere. *Benjura.* But why did he bring others with him?

Four more sets of legs entered the area. Two in front and two in back carrying something between them.

Jordana didn't reveal herself. Knives sheathed, she stretched out on her stomach and peered under the limbs at the people.

Four men carrying a litter joined Benjura and his companion. A large form sprawled under a blanket on the litter. Who was hurt? As the group moved closer, Jordana zeroed in on the injured man. Something familiar about him... When they cleared the trees, she had an unobstructed view of his face.

"Father!" She launched herself down the tree.

"Jordana, is that you?" Benjura raced forward.

She dropped the final few feet to the ground and sprinted to them. "What happened?"

"He's ill."

Her gaze ran over the sentries as she moved in. Two of her father's long-time guards carried the back poles, while the queen's brother and cousin carried the front. Lester, her mother's favorite guard, stood next to Benjura. The men lowered father's stretcher to the ground as Jordana slid in, grabbing the Arrdock's hand. "He's burning up."

"Yes, Princess." Bootah, Queen Brin's brother answered. "He developed an infection from the arrows that pierced him weeks ago. It's getting worse."

"What's that stench?"

"His wounds. We wash it often, applying aloe or olive oil. Nothing helps. His fever grows higher every day." Henry kneeled next to her and pulled back the animal skin covering the Arrdock.

Bare chested, the wound under Father's left collar bone had grown from a small red hole to an infected mass larger than her hands. Black spider veins splintered out from it, covering his chest, just like in the rotten mango. Jordana crinkled her nose at the smell, and covered him. "Did my Granna not work her healing on him? She has better herbs than aloe and olive oil."

Kai, Brin's cousin, met her gaze. "The queen would not let your kin near her husband."

Father opened his eyes. "Jordana, is that you I hear?" His face softened. A small smile lifted the edges of his lips.

"Yes, my Arrdock. I am here."

"You look terrible."

She choked back tears. "So do you, Father. Are you okay?'

He lifted a shaky hand to her cheek and pulled off a large chunk of mush. "What's this?"

"Oh." She let of go his hands and wiped off her face. "I

smeared mango all over me when something approached. I hid my scent in case it was a jaguar."

"My smart girl." His words came out slow and soft. "Despite your temper tantrums, you've always been so intelligent. I'm proud of you." He closed his eyes again.

Despite my temper tantrums? The man must be delusional. Did he think her still a small child? Yet his words of pride warmed her heart. Jordana kissed his forehead and stood up. She grabbed Benjura's arm and yanked him aside and out of earshot. Hands curled into tight fists, it took all of her strength to keep from bursting into a tirade. "Why did you bring Brin's family here? We need to get my father to the Restoration Pool, but then they'll know the way. The first chance they get, and they'll lead Brin straight back here."

"Don't be angry with me." Benjura reached forward and pulled fruit from her hair. "Believe it or not, they're the ones who came up with the plan to sneak him away from Brin. I told as many people as I could about all the things we witnessed. About our need to worship Elohim alone. Some listened, some did not. I visited the Arrdock several days in a row, sharing about our experiences. I don't know if he listened to me, but his guards did. Then Bootah and Kai came to me, asking to get the Arrdock out of village without the Queen's knowledge, and to the Restoration Pool for Elohim's healing. They seem different now. Genuine."

Jordana studied the two men in the distance.

Benjura touched her shoulder. "The angel Obadiah said you would cross again *soon*. Could this be why? To save your father?"

"We must assume so. What greater reason could there be?" The sense of urgency she had to leave the Akimmi village now made sense. She peered again at the men as they helped her father take a drink. "I don't trust Brin's kin. They do her bidding. Bootah and Kai are the ones who took down Elohim's altar. And when Brin commanded it, they charged at me. How can we trust them?"

Benjura lowered his voice even more. "I'm leery, too. Lester and I are keeping a close watch. We've seen no secret whispers. Nothing untoward. Both men ask many questions about the Holy Land and angels who healed in Elohim's name. Even how to repent. Their questions appear sincere, as does their concern for the Arrdock. Lester and I, along with your father's guards, Henry and Zachariah, outnumber Bootah and Kai. We're on high alert."

Benjura moved toward the group. "Lester and Henry told me how none of the guards like Brin ordering them about. Especially her family. They dislike all her changes. Perhaps my testimony has reached Bootah and Kai's hearts. Anyone can change."

"Yes, with Elohim Rapha's help." She squinted at the sun. "If we leave now, we can make it there before dark. But we'll be climbing the cliffs during the hottest part of the day."

"Yes, but perhaps it will rain." Benjura's lips hinted at a grin. "You have gunk all over you."

She nodded and swiped her arms.

He gazed around the clearing, his expression fading. "Have you been living here all week?"

Fire flooded her veins. "I've been living here for three years." She stormed past him and back to the guards. How did Benjura make her blood boil so easily?

"After everything, have you not yet released that temper?"

His words echoed behind her, but Jordana ignored them and closed in on the guards. She forced her muscles to relax. "Thank you for helping. We must get the Arrdock to the Restoration Pool. After we cross the Azul, it is a long way up several cliffs. It will not be an easy climb. Hopefully, we can get help from the gatekeepers. Are you willing to continue until dark?"

"Yes, Princess." Henry nodded at her. "We will not stop until we are there. We've pledged our lives to the Arrdock."

She nodded and pointed at a narrow trail between two

pecan trees. "That way."

Benjura blew out the animal tune as he paced behind them. He didn't stop whistling all the way to the river.

Jordana stood at the bank, raising her face to the sky. She prayed for help and worthiness to cross. "Wait here." She instructed the men and ran to where the Akimmi's had camped before crossing. She found remnants of their fire and scooped a handful of soggy ash, carrying it to the shoreline. There she rubbed a cross on the Arrdock. As Benjura explained her actions to the guards, she moved to each one and smeared a repentance cross on their foreheads. The men closed their eyes and whispered prayers.

When done, Benjura pointed at the water. "Jordana, you need to rinse off while we carry your father across. I'll get some ash for when you're done."

The men raised the litter up to their shoulders and waded into the river. Jordana followed, stopping in the middle to dunk under. She rubbed her face and limbs, then swam underwater to rinse her hair. By the time she finished, the men stood on the other side, dripping, but very much alive. Perhaps they had listened and experienced a circumcision of the heart.

Jordana wiped water from her eyes, gave her hair several violent shakes, then moved in front of Benjura, bowed her head, and closed her eyes.

As his fingers moved slowly between her eyebrows and up to her hairline applying the Repentance Cross, Jordana prayed. *Please, make me worthy to cross again. Heal my father. Send help for this journey.* At the feel of Benjura's hand in hers, she opened her eyes and followed him to dry land.

"Last time we did this, we journeyed southeast. But this time we need to head straight north. Should we wait for escorts?" Benjura let go of her, and stepped in to trade places with Zachariah. Benjura now carried one pole of her father's litter.

Jordana broke her stare. "They probably already know we're here. Let's not waste time, and get started." She pointed uphill. "That way."

The group climbed a narrow path in silence. Every so often, she blew out the animal song. The men rotated carrying the litter, so each one had a short break every hour. They never asked to stop and rest. Perhaps the few sprinkles they encountered helped cool them during their fast ascent. After crossing a stream, they climbed several steep boulders to a smooth path. It meandered through a wooded area, all while climbing higher.

Growling drew her attention, and Jordana gazed into the rainforest. Eyes glowed at her, fifteen to twenty sets surrounding them. Inch by inch, a pack of wolves closed in with teeth bared. A silver tipped wolf, the largest gray in the pack, trotted forward, lips curled up over its fangs.

Jordana motioned for the guards to stay calm. "It's okay. They're just trying to smile at me." She pasted on a big grin and faced the canines. "Hello. It's me, Jordana. I'm Lainey's friend."

The snarling increased. Wolves barked. Drool dripped from their sharps fangs. A few wolves charged them, skidded to a stop, and scooted back. Others did the same.

Jordana's stomach dropped into her feet. Why were the gatekeepers acting this way? Did they not recognize her? She blew out her mamu's animal tune while squeezing the daggers in her fists. When had she drawn them?

A roar cut through the barking, and all heads turned toward the source. Beast rushed in front of Jordana, standing between her and the pack. A line of hair down his spine stood up. "Do not attack." He twisted, narrowing his slanted eyes at her and the others. "Put away your weapons. You'll not need them."

Beast faced Jordana. "Why are you here? You cannot waltz to this side any time you feel like it. This is the Forbidden Falls Territory. That means forbidden to humans. You must leave and never cross again without an invitation. Buck's pack had every right to tear you to pieces."

"I'd like to see them try." Kai raised his sword.

Jordana faced the guards. They had surrounded the stretcher on the ground, each one wielding a weapon. Except for

Benjura who had moved beside her—arrow taunt in his bow. She shuddered to think of what would have happened if the guards had slain the gatekeeper wolves. "Please, men. Put your weapons away." She slid hers back into place and bent on one knee in front of Beast. "There's an emergency. My father is dying and needs the Restoration Pool. Obadiah said I would return to this side soon. I think that's now. Please, Beast. Help me get my Arrdock up the cliff."

Beast's green eyes blinked at her, their gazes locked.

"Princess, Jordana." Henry kneeled next to her father's cot. "The Arrdock has stopped breathing."

CHAPTER TWENTY-NINE

Jordana sprinted to her father. "No. Wake up." She gave his shoulders a hard shake.

The Arrdock opened his eyes. "Stop. Hurts."

"Father, stay with us. Hold on. We'll soon be to the Restoration Pool." She laid her hand on his cheek. "Elohim can heal you." Jordana shot a glare over to Beast. "Can you not see the urgency?"

Beast nodded. "Yes, but hear me now. Never again can you enter the Forbidden Territory without our permission and escort. If you attempt it, you will be attacked."

She shuddered. "I understand and promise I won't. Can we now go?"

Beast turned to the pack. "Get Lainey and some of the donkeys. They can pull a litter up this mountain faster than the humans."

Several wolves sprinted away, but one approached Jordana and bowed low to the ground. "Sorry I frightened you, Princess. The smell of sickness overwhelmed your scent. Zelle will have my hide for this."

"Rojo, right?" She tipped her head to the silver tipped gatekeeper. "You were just doing your job." Upon straightening, she snapped her fingers at the guards. "Okay, move out. We've no time to waste."

Everyone swung into motion and hauled the Arrdock up

the mountainside. When several donkeys arrived, the travois was rigged to one. The donkey zipped up the mountain with amazing speed. At a crest, they switched to a fresh donkey and again after sunset. Despite only half-moons, both red orbs appeared unusually bright, as if helping to light their path. The donkeys had no trouble keeping away from the cliff's edge, and the nocturnal animals led the humans.

The air grew cooler as they ascended higher. The mild temperature kept her from overheating like last time. At every change, she spoke to her father and made him sip water. When the air tore ragged at her chest, Benjura shouted from up ahead.

"We're at the top. Only a little farther."

The spent donkey did not waste time switching when they crested the mountain, and trudged on to the pond. Their large group gathered at the water's edge.

"Benjura, will you help me float my Father in the water?" Jordana led the donkey into the pond, travois and all, and rolled her father off the litter.

She reached under him and clasped one of Benjura's hands under Father's shoulders and the other at his low back. He floated easily, and they were careful not to step off the drop near the pond's center.

Each of the guards splashed water on their faces and the back of their necks. Along with the gatekeepers, all drew in long drinks. Then each one sat on the bank facing the center. Soft at first, the men prayed aloud, but their volume grew when Lainey arrived and led worship. She nodded at Jordana, but didn't approach.

Jordana studied her father's face in the moonlight. Eyes closed and seemingly peaceful. Praise Elohim for Father's lack of pain.

"Daughter, bend close. I have something to tell you."

The group's worship hushed.

"I'm dying."

"No. Don't say—"

"Listen to me. I've not much time." He paused to suck in

259

a shallow breath. "I want to tell you where the Arrdock's ring is hidden. You must get it and rule." At last he opened his eyes. "Even from within a fog, I can see Benjura's stories are true." He licked his lips. "I hereby grant you immunity from your banishment. After I lost your mother, I didn't think Elohim was real. You shall lead our people back to Him. I was a fool to grant Brin's childish requests."

Jordana's heart soared. He had been listening and desired change. This had been her prayer for so long. But the Arrdock's other request? Return and rule a tribe who wanted her dead? Who blamed her for the mistaken battle? She met Benjura's stare. The expression on his face told her he had heard as well. She glanced at the shore. Henry, Lester, Kai and the others were nodding.

"Jordana." The Arrdock's raspy voice grew stronger. "I must know if you understand the devastating consequence of a fast temper. Do you still put your desires first, or the needs to our people? Have learned to bridle your tongue?"

She searched his face. "My tongue's been bridled these past years." Who did father think she'd been arguing with out in wilderness all alone? He was delusional. Jordana laid her hand on his cheek. "I've learned what a precious thing it is to belong to a family and a community. How valuable each member is."

"A wise Arrdock never rushes to a conclusion and always puts the tribe first."

"Yes, Father." A drop of rain landed on the part atop Jordana's head. She lifted her face to the sky. Another drop landed on her nose. "It's raining." She raised her voice. "My Arrdock, Elohim Rapha has sent his rain to heal you. Believe in him."

"I do believe, Jordana. But I need healing for my soul and forgiveness from the evil I committed. Tis my only prayer— restoration to Elohim, as Benjura has spoken."

Tears filled her eyes. Elohim answered her prayers before her very eyes. But He can do so much more than what Father asked. "Listen, my Arrdock. You can have both bodily healing and heart restoration. You must be the one to lead the people back."

"No. I had my chance and failed. Tis your birthright now. As I had hoped, you matured in these many seasons and seem wise. You are ready."

Fat rain drops pelted harder and harder, pounding the top of her head and shoulders.

Lainey appeared in the water at Jordana's side. "Dip him under. Submerse him in the deep."

Benjura did not hesitate and placed a hand on the Arrdock's chest. "Hold your breath, sire." He pressed down, dunking the Arrdock, then rushed him back up.

The Arrdock's eye's widened, and he lifted a shaky hand to point at the sky. "I see them." He turned to Benjura. "Make her do as I say." Father's head rotated Jordana's way. "Your mother has the Arrdock ring. Tis yours now. Rule with patience, honesty, and kindness. No temper tantrums. No manipulation. Rely on those around you. Put their needs above your own." He smiled. "I love you, daughter. And now I give myself fully to Elohim." Father closed his eyes and whispered, "It's time." His body relaxed and his mouth fell ajar.

"What?" Jordana shook him. "Wait. I'm not ready. I need you."

Benjura grabbed the Arrdock's arm and gave him a violent jolt. "Open your eyes. Please, sire. Breathe."

Jordana strained through her hoarse voice. "Please, Father, receive all of your healing. You need only to believe." Seconds passed before Jordana realized the rain had stopped. No more drops floated down from the clear night sky.

Lainey's smooth voice washed over Jordana. "He received restoration for his soul, child. That is the most important healing. Your father is now in paradise. Tis a wonderful thing."

Several guards entered the water, and eased the Arrdock out of Jordana's arms. They carried him to dry land.

Benjura embraced Jordana, pulling her to his chest.

A searing stab scorched her heart. The pounding inside

her head increased. Both legs weakened. Jordana buried her face in Benjura's neck and sobbed.

* * *

Birds sang their morning songs. Loud and cheerful. They woke her. Distant voices drifted past, and Jordana lifted her head. Why did she sleep in the grass and not up in trees? As soon as she spotted the pond, it all flooded back. Father had died. Now he dwelled with Mamu in paradise. Her prayers for him to turn from his hardened heart had been answered. So why did her stomach roil with nausea? Why did she feel like uprooting every red poppy on the slope and throw them into the pond? And didn't those birds know it was a day for mourning?

"I'm glad you're awake." Benjura plopped down next to her. "Did you sleep well?"

She shrugged, afraid to use her voice.

"We have some food for you. Can you eat?" He rubbed her back.

She shook her head. It'd been twenty-four hours since she ate her oranges, but the thought of food made her queasy.

Benjura pointed at the litter. It hosted the large form of her father, nothing visible under the cloth wrapping him. "The Arrdock has been prepared, and we need to get him back to the village for burial. The guards are anxious to go this morning. You and I can follow them at slower pace. Do you want to say goodbye to your father before they leave?"

She nodded and pushed herself up. Her feet trudged to the lifeless form on the stretcher. At her approach, every guard bowed at the waist and held the position until she passed.

Jordana knelt next to Father, laying her hand atop his chest. "I was so angry with you for forgetting mamu so easily. I hated you for banishing me. Now I'm angry that you chose to die. It didn't have to be—you could have received healing, too. I'll never understand your choices." She exhaled a deep breath. "But I love you, Father. I forgive you." Both her hands fanned

262

across him. "I'm sorry for hating you. I didn't mean it. I promise, I didn't. You told me to let go of my anger. I didn't know I had any. I promise to work on it daily."

Jordana choked up several times, but aimed to finish. "Yesterday you said you were proud of me. Last night, I have never been more proud of you. Confessing Elohim in front of your men took great courage. I love you, Father. When I see you again in paradise, I will tell you I forgive you face to face. Kiss mamu for me." She brushed the tears from her eyes and took her time standing. At last, she straightened and pivoted around.

All five sentries and Benjura lined up, each one knelt on one knee.

Zachariah held up his sword, extending it to her. "I pledge my life, my allegiance, and my sword to you, Shedock Jordana."

Next to him, Henry stretched his battled axe out to her. "I pledge my life, my allegiance, and my axe to you, Shedock Jordana."

Brin's brother and cousin did the same, extending their weapons and repeating the oath, as did mother's favorite guard, Lester.

Last in the line, Benjura knelt, his expression solemn. "On the way here, your father gave us instructions. He spoke them again to you last night. Jordana of Arrie, you are a princess no more. You are the Arrdock's choice for heir-successor. From this day forward, you are Shedock of the Tree Warrior Village. We will stand with you, as you retrieve the Arrdock ring and challenge Queen Brin."

A smile chased his seriousness away. "Since I was a boy, I've dreamed of one day kneeling before you and swearing my oath. I used to practice it. I do not delight in the loss of your father, but I am excited about the changes you shall bring to our village. I promise to fight for you. To die if needed. From this moment on, you are my Shedock." Palms up, he presented his bow. "I pledge my life, my allegiance, and my bow to you, Shedock Jordana of Arrie."

Touched by their sentiment, albeit premature, she could not be Shedock. How could she make them understand? Not just because she couldn't be inaugurated without the Arrdock ring and the special ceremony, although Father told her where to find it. *Mother had his ring.* Whatever that meant. Even if Jordana strolled into the village wearing it, Queen Brin would never step aside. To challenge her meant another battle. A civil war within the tree warriors. Would anyone fight for her when so many blamed her for the death of their loved ones in the mistaken battle? Could she ask them to raise swords against their fellow tribemates? Jordana couldn't be the cause of more deaths. Tears stung her eyes, as her heart tore anew.

Benjura tossed his bow to the ground and jumped up. In a few fast paces, he closed the distance between them and gripped her upper arm. The man practically drug her to the far edge of the clearing, his hand squeezing her biceps.

She refused to wince or rip free, and steeled herself. "Let go of me."

He dropped his grip, stopped in front of her bending close, and placed both hands on her shoulders. Anger spiked his tone as his drilling stare bore into her. "Don't even think about refusing. I see it written all over your face. How dare you snub the oaths of these men. You are the only child of the Arrdock. You have the royal bloodline. Not Brin." The frown between his brows deepened. "Our people need you. You forced me to go and witness to them because they needed to turn from their wicked ways. Some have." He stood upright and motioned at the guards. "These men have sacrificed everything for this moment. Now it's your turn to go back and lead. Like it or not, it's your job to challenge Queen Brin." He folded his arms across his chest. "Have you matured one bit, or do you continue with your childish ways?" He spit it out like venom, stinging her.

She pursed her lips as she searched his face. Never before had Benjura spoken to her in such a manner. She had no idea he harbored such feelings. As she blinked at him, her hands curled into fists. Tempted to beat them against Benjura's chest, she

264

fought to keep still—to not boil into anger. Couldn't she have time to grieve, time to think? She exhaled a slow breath. "The villagers hate me. If I challenge Queen Brin, will they even fight for me? And if they did, how can I be responsible for more deaths? We just witnessed a bloody battle. I will not rush into another one."

"I understand your concern. But it doesn't change the law or their need." Benjura ran both hands over his head, smoothing out his dark auburn curls. "They do not hate you. They loved your father and will follow his dying declaration."

Jordana shook her head. "You don't know what you ask of me. None of those people stood up for me. The queen has poisoned them, and I shan't force them to yield if they don't wish me as their leader."

Benjura cut back and forth across the grass before her. "You are stubborn and selfish. You're used to getting your way all the time, and refuse to consider someone else's point of view. You want to do everything yourself and don't accept the help of others. I see now why Elohim did not allow me to stand up for you at the Banishment Rite. He stopped me from finding you when I searched, because you needed to learn total dependence on Him. Stop looking at what you want. Look to the greater needs of others. We cannot bring all the people here to this Restoration Pool. Tis forbidden. You must guide them back to Elohim, even if it means war. Their salvation is worth the fight. But you say no without even asking for Elohim's guidance. You don't know what He has planned. Perhaps it's a peaceful coup. Have you not yet learned to rely on His wisdom over your own?"

She frowned hard at him. "What did you say?" She licked her lips. He tried to find her but Elohim stopped him? Jordana couldn't absorb the thought. No, no, no, it could not be.

"I said you must learn to seek Elohim's wisdom and guidance above your own."

"No, before that. You searched for me? And Elohim stopped you from standing up for me at the Banishment Rite?" It could not be true. The Creator wanted her to be banished for a greater reason?

Benjura released a heavy sigh and clasped her hands in his. "To see you standing there enduring Brin's ridicule shredded my heart into a thousand pieces. When Brin tore off your princess cape, I wanted to rip her throat open. But Elohim closed my mouth and nailed my feet to the floor. I was not allowed to speak or move. I did not understand why. After you left, I cried like a child. I filled my pack, said goodbye to my family, and set out to join you in a life of banishment. Before I got past the outer guard towers, Elohim stopped me. He turned me around and forced me to march home. I did not understand why and beseeched Him daily to allow me to find you. Always, I tried to pick up your trail while hunting, venturing farther and farther away. I never saw any signs. I fumed for a long time—angry with the Creator. But I yielded to Him even when I could not fathom His purpose. Now I finally understand."

His eyes showed truth. Jordana fought against the swirling of her own turmoil. How could spending years alone be part of Elohim Rapha's plan for her? "What do you now understand?"

"Even a short time ago, I still did not and asked Lainey if she knew why I wasn't allowed to go with you."

At his pause, Jordana shook his hands. "Tell me what she said."

Benjura moved away from her and gazed across the clearing at the Leopards sitting amongst the guards. "That one day Elohim would make His reasons clear. Five minutes ago He did. Clear to me, anyway. Not to you."

"What is clear to you and not to me?" She gave her arms an exasperated toss. "I don't understand."

Benjura's tone calmed. "Elohim had to prepare you to rule. You needed to learn to seek His wisdom above your own. To rely on Him and stop manipulating others to get your way. To commune with Him over every aspect of Your life. To hear his small whisper along with His roaring fire balls. As ruler, you must seek His will, value the opinions of others, and put their needs first."

Put them first? Hadn't she done that her whole life?

He held her gaze. "Above your own desires, even your own needs, you must put the needs of the village first. Even if it costs your own life to restore them to Elohim, it's a sacrifice a ruler must make. That is the job. Obviously I do not think it will come to that, but people must know that their ruler will sacrifice their own life for the greater good of the tribe.

He paused and ran a hand over his head before gazing back into her eyes. "Jordana, you must stop trying to control everything or manipulate people to do things your way. A good leader sees the gifts in others and appoints them jobs where they can best serve. People need to be useful and valued. A good ruler will seek Elohim's will above their own. You are His overseer, peacekeeper, and delegator. I don't know anyone as passionate for Elohim as you. You are well spoken. Truthful and brave. Dedicated to law and justice. Our people will follow you, if they trust you to care about them. You must learn to serve those you lead. That is the attribute of a good Shedock. Our people need to repent and seek Elohim. There's no one better than you to show them how."

Skewered by his words, she studied him until at last she tore away. She marched across the field and straight into the Restoration Pool. She swam and prayed. No rain came, only a small whisper to sear her insides. Banishment made her stronger and resourceful, as there were no servants around to help her. It took away her pride. She had learned to depend on Elohim for every morsel she ate—and every night she slept. More importantly, she learned to talk to Him about everything. There was no one else to talk to, so she talked to Elohim about every little thing. She'd never did that before. "I am sorry, Elohim. For all of it, especially not valuing my tribemates." What a horrible sin to be guilty of.

Compassion and respect of others fills you now. I am with you if you seek My ways before your own. You are ready.

Jordana gulped over Elohim's words to her soul. "I will

obey You in all things." She whispered so low, she knew only He could hear.

Jordana exited, shaking off the water, and marching past Benjura. When she approached the still-waiting sentries, they dropped back to one knee.

In front of Brin's brother she stopped. "Bootah, why do you pledge to me and not your sister?"

"Brin will have the village stop growing food, stop training, and making weapons. She'll have us mine for jewels to fashion her more crowns, while our crops wither and die. She does not have the interest of the people in her heart. Her ways will lead to our demise. I see that now. So does the village."

Kai rapped the butt of his axe on the ground several times.

"You agree?" She veered to him.

"Yes, m'lady. She'll destroy us." His words came out with ferocity. "Did you know my cousin asked your father to declare her a goddess? Full deity?"

Jordana's hand shot to cover her mouth. "Please tell me he refused." The woman's blasphemies were far worse than imagined.

"He had yet to rule on the matter," Bootah said. "M'lady, I will die before I pray to my sister. By month's end, I shall either be banished, dead, or serving you. My life is in your hands." He tipped his head toward the ground and did not raise it.

"And mine." Kai lowered his head.

"Mine too." Henry again held out his battle axe.

Lester thrust his sword to the sky, repeating every line of the oath. Zachariah did as well, followed by Kai and Bootah.

Choked up, Jordana noted each man's countenance. True sincerity could not be faked. She nodded and walked to each one, kissing their weapon according to the accent custom, and accepting their life and loyalty.

She saved Benjura for last, and her hands trembled when she reached for his bow. "Promise you'll never desert me. I can't do this without you."

"I promise to be at your side helping you at every juncture. And loving you. Always. You are exactly what the village needs. You are not only the Arrdock's chosen, but Elohim's chosen. And mine."

His words curled around her like the wisteria vines climbing the structures back home. She tugged him up to stand next to her, stretched up on tiptoes, and kissed him on the lips. Without shame, she hugged and kissed him in front of the others. When she released him, Jordana smiled. "I have never stopped loving you." She moved to his ear and lowered her voice. "More than ever before, we shall require chaperons."

He laughed and engulfed her.

Cradled within his arms, Jordana addressed the men. "As Shedock, my first order is this: Never bow to me again. Bow only to Elohim."

The men shouted war cries as they rose to their feet, whooping and hollering praises to Elohim.

Bootah raised his weapon. "Let us take the throne for Shedock Jordana."

She gulped. Hard decisions now fell to her. She purposed in her heart to seek Elohim Rapha first in all things and sacrifice her own desires for the greater good of the people. Even if it meant declaring war on them and causing more bloodshed.

CHAPTER THIRTY

Jordana studied Henry as he jumped in to take sides with Lester and Bootah. Those three argued with Zachariah, Kai, and Benjura. Evenly split. She'd have to cast the deciding vote. Incumbent Shedock for less than an hour, and already expected to rule on an important issue. A life and death issue. Her own.

Bootah stood with arms akimbo. "I believe we can do this peacefully. Only a few will join arms with Brin. We can take them down easily enough."

Benjura's red face competed with the bright crimson poppies growing wild. "By then it will be too late. One loyal guard is enough to land an arrow in Jordana's heart before she even finishes her petition."

"Not if we're there to stop it." Lester paced.

Henry, father's trusted guard since before Jordana's birth, moved before her and clasped her hand. His grandfatherly pat did little to give her clarity. "If you allow it, they'll go on like this for days. Your job as Shedock is to gather the information, make the final decision, and issue our orders. We will do as you say."

Jordana stared into the man's deep-set eyes, full of wisdom and experience. If only he would tell her what to do. But if she asked, it'd start another round of bickering. They'd been debating this one issue for the past hour.

Lainey lay in the grass near Jordana's feet. Her head turned back and forth as the two men volleyed. Perhaps the leopard had insight from Elohim.

"Silence." Jordana pulled her hand free from Henry and moved to the center of their group. "I appreciate your opinions and am ready to make my ruling. But first." Jordana zeroed in on Lainey. "What say you?"

Seconds ticked by as Lainey's whiskers twitched. "I have listened to these humans debate. They know your people better than I. And better than you. Your absence during Brin's time as queen has placed them in a good position to advise you on the overall culture of the Tree Warrior Village. I suggest you shove all personal feelings aside and take in their full counsel. Tis best to resolve issues peacefully as long as it's not a foolhardy act. I suggest you seek the will of Elohim while traveling. Waste no more time arguing, tis time to go."

Jordana nodded. She shouldn't have expected any other reply from Lainey. After giving each man her attention, Jordana issued her ruling. "I agree with both sides. Tis not my wish to come this far, only to die in two days' time. On the other hand, if a peaceful takeover is possible, we must attempt it. Bloodshed should be minimized. Let us be prepared if it tis not. Arrange your people at the ready."

She glanced at the sun's position in the sky. It would be directly overhead within a couple of hours. "As we journey, each one should seek Elohim's wisdom. If we leave now and travel through the night, we'll arrive at the western caves by nightfall tomorrow. A few of you shall sneak into the village while I wait in the cave. See what kind of support you might gather for my challenge. If the tree people still blame me for the Akimmi attack, I'll stay in hiding until we have swayed enough tribesmen to launch a civil war. But if our scouts learn the people prefer me as Shedock over Brin, then I'll join in the sunrise procession for my father's burial. At that time, I'll declare myself." She swallowed down the rattling in her throat.

Jordana paused in front of Benjura. "I have no desire to be run through before the funeral even starts. But I must try for a peaceful coup. Accompany Bootah into the Arrdock Fortress and speak to the other guards. See how many will support my challenge."

Benjura's stare narrowed as if trapping her in the center of a target. His hazel eyes sparked with opposition, but he tipped his head to yield.

Henry started clapping.

"Well done, Shedock." Zachariah joined in the applause. "This is a wise decision. The best of all advice."

The other guards nodded and joined in the merriment.

Silly, they'd applaud such a simple ruling. Jordana motioned for them to stop as she fought the heat seeping into her cheeks. "I haven't said the most important part. Elohim may have a better plan, just like when we engaged the giants. During our journey, let each one earnestly ask Him for guidance and favor."

"Agreed."

"Here, here."

Henry clapped once more.

Benjura clutched her hand. "Perhaps we can make the song historically correct after all. *Shedock Jordana, loving and true, restored our tribe in a peaceful coup.*" He pulled her wrist up to his lips and kissed the back of her hand.

Could it be possible to take over without shedding a drop of blood? *Let it be so.* She stepped over to Lainey. "Tradition dictates a coronation ceremony immediately following the burial, so there's no gap in leadership. I'll have a better chance of slipping into that spot with you at my side. Can you return with me? And Beast?"

"Yes."

Jordana nodded, then motioned the men to huddle in. "Lainey, will you pray for us?"

Her cat eyes closed. "Elohim, please grant us speed as we journey, and favor when we arrive. Our greatest desire is to peacefully restore the Tree Warrior Village to You. Your ways are higher than our ways, so if the plans these humans have made are flawed, reveal to us the better path. May it be so."

272

"May it be so," Jordana echoed her wise friend.

* * *

Once again Jordana stood in the Princess cape between Beast and Lainey. She closed her eyes and tried to dissolve the bees stinging her insides. *Please, let this work.*

While Benjura and all five guards had spent the night spying in the village and gathering followers, she remained in the cave with the leopards, and her father. She gathered fresh jasmine blossoms to cover his body. Still, it was unbearable to be in the cave with him. No daughter should have to go through that with a parent.

When the men returned in the wee hours of the morning, each had a good report. Inside support awaited them. The men caught a couple hours sleep before midmorning. Upon awakening, they dug a grave in the cemetery next to her mother.

Jordana searched her mother's burial site for her father's Arrdock ring. How odd that Father hid it in her mother's plot. Despite banishing Jordana, the Arrdock never told Queen Brin where to find the official ring. This fact revealed her father's desire for Jordana to succeed him. Each Arrdock or Shedock wore the heavy ruby and diamond ring for their coronation, then hid it during their entire reign. The ring only came out for an intended heir's coronation. Jordana had never actually seen the ring, but Father had described it to her.

She had dug around the base of her mother's headstone. Buried under several inches of dirt, she found a metal sleeve displaying the royal crest. Once opened, the precious jewel slid into her palm. Its oval ruby was at least an inch long. Diamonds encircled it. Too big for her middle finger, she slid it onto her thumb.

Their solemn group had washed and dressed for the burial procession. Four new guards had met them on the village outskirts with the Arrdock's ceremonial litter. Father had been dead three night falls and they must get him in the ground today. After crossing the Azul, she had unearthed the zebra hide, and wrapped it around Father. Now he lay on the ornate litter, covered in fresh bouquets to confuse the flies. Four new sentries, one positioned at each corner, hoisted the litter over the shoulders and led the way when the sun shone directly overhead.

From behind the royal guardsmen, Benjura blew his ram's horn. He walked directly in front of her, instead of out in front of the procession. His closeness calmed her nerves. Another low, long moan filled the air. Not the short spurts to sound an alarm or the sharp blast for announcements. This time he blew the deep extended funeral call.

She stared at the back of Benjura's head as they moved forward. Beast and Lainey flanked her, with Henry, Zachariah, and Bootah guarding them. The warriors donned their full breast plates and carried their battle shields and swords—each one a faithful bodyguard when she needed their loyalty the most.

Lester and Kai were not with them. Those two intermixed with the Queen's sentinels. From inside the Brin's inner circle, they'd have the best chance of preventing any shots at Jordana.

Families made up the rear of the procession. Granna, Tooki, and Father's sisters lined up behind her with cousins from Mother's side of the family behind Father's side. More warriors were behind them, along with all of their families. Henry had seen to a strong gathering in support for Jordana's petition.

She jumped at the second blast from the ram's horn, and rubbed the ring jostling around her thumb. Upon entering the village, she settled her hands at her sides and gazed into the trees. Eyes alert, she searched for any threats. Would arrows aim her way? Without the Arrdock to protect her and without a miracle to present, this could be a disaster. But she had the ring. She had Elohim's blessing. And she needed to bury her father.

People lined up on both sides of the path. Others came out of their treehouses and stood on bridges. Some wept and pointed at the obvious body on the royal litter adorned by colorful plants. Murmurs erupted across the awakening village. People ran to toss flowers and ferns on the ground as her father's body passed. Hundreds of people crowded in. More flocked to the trees and gazed at them. Soon all two thousand tribemates would be gathered. None raised weapons. Was that a good sign? She ought not to assume so, since she had yet to declare herself.

As they arrived to the Arrdock fortress, dogs barked and roosters announced the day. The platform had not been lowered. Where was Brin? Why hadn't she come? Jordana shot a frantic look to Benjura when he glanced over his shoulder at her.

"Tis fine." He mouthed before blowing the short blasts of the horn to announce a burial.

She fixed her gaze on the Arrdock fortress and the platform high up in the trees. A ray of sun caught on one of the thrones. They sickened her more now than the first time she laid eyes on them. If Jordana survived this day, her first order as Shedock would be to burn the blasphemous chairs on the restored altar.

Movement caught her eye as people scurried to the platform. It inched down. Before touching the ground, Jordana locked gazes with the Queen. Would the woman follow custom today, or would she speak out? Palpable hatred seemed to burn in her eyes, searing Jordana's flesh.

Benjura moved to Brin and motioned for her to take her rightful place as widow—at the head of the procession.

Queen Brin swept up her long gown, gliding to the front of the Arrdock litter. She uttered not a word as she led the funeral procession to the royal graveyard.

Jordana imagined what Brin must be thinking. The woman would be furious when she discovered where the men dug the grave. Brin must be in a panic over not having the Arrdock ring. Law didn't allow any speaking until the Arrdock was in the ground. A tongue lashing from Brin would surely follow.

The guards stopped next to the open grave, pivoted, and set the litter down crossways over the hole. Feet shuffled as the villagers crowded in. Minutes passed as more and more people circled. The smell of fresh dirt lingered in the air.

At last, Queen Brin took her spot at the head of the litter

and Jordana moved to the foot. They turned their backs to each other with the Arrdock between them, as was custom.

People came forward to hug Jordana. Many patted her cheek or squeezed her arms. Men reached across to grasp her right shoulder and nod at her. Each silent, more and more villagers lined up to offer their touch of condolence. Minutes grew to an hour as Jordana stood, receiving the people. Moisture filled the eyes of men and women alike. It was expected when Jordana's mother died—her father stood at the head with Jordana at the foot for what seemed like half a day. But it wasn't expected today. Not because Father was unloved. But because she was a banished maiden, hated by Queen Brin, and responsible for the mistaken battle. Yet a crowd of people lined up in front of her. Did they clamor to the queen as well? Jordana dare not peek over her shoulder to find out.

At long last, several guards moved in and lifted the litter parallel to the grave.

Jordana turned around to face the Queen. The woman clutched a huge bouquet of flowers. No tears ran down her cheeks as she glared across her husband's corpse at his only child.

Brin didn't drop to her knees to roll her husband into the grave like most spouses did. She snapped her fingers at the guards, and they moved around to conduct the grizzly task.

Jordana dropped to the dirt and helped them roll Father's body into the final resting place. She would not be denied this one final touch. She flinched when he landed with a thump at the bottom, hating that part. Moisture filled her eyes and she whispered, "Goodbye, my Arrdock. I love you." She made no attempt to dry her cheeks as she pushed dirt into the grave.

Hands covered in dark soil, she stood and stared at the flowers and zebra fur at the bottom of the hole. *He's in paradise now with Mamu. Only his body is at the bottom of this pit.* The truth gave her comfort. Villagers moved in and tossed handfuls of dirt and flowers over her father before filing out of the graveyard. The dirt at the bottom grew thicker as the people thinned out. This was it—a final glimpse as every trace of the shape at the bottom became buried.

Stillness encased the area. No more shuffling feet. She stood and tried to remember happy times with her parents.

An arm clutched her waist and led her away. "It's time." Benjura whispered in her ear. "We shall mourn him on the morrow. But today, we must be alert. Can you pull yourself together for what comes next?"

Jordana glanced around. Tribe gone, she stood alone at the gravesite with Lainey, Beast, and Benjura. "Where's Brin? What happened to Henry and the other guards?"

"Queen Brin left ages ago. Your royal guards have gone ahead to prepare. We need to get you cleaned up." He led her to a bucket of water.

She washed her hands, then wiped her eyes and face on a clean cloth. Benjura extended her mother's jewel encrusted dagger. It had been strapped to Brin's thigh these last few years. "How did you get this?"

"Seems your Granna confiscated it when Brin started wearing gowns instead of tunics. I suspect Henry helped as her inside man. Apparently Granna's been saving it for today, which she claims to have known was coming."

Jordana brushed her fingers across the intricate handle. White ivory carved like a leopard. Emeralds for eyes...like Lainey's. The feline's tail came down to form the sharp blade. The steel shone as if it had been recently sharpened and polished. Jordana spun the knife in her palm and with a flick of her wrist, caught the handle and sliced through the air. After removing a blade from her right harness and doubling it with a blade on her left, she slid her mother's dagger into the vacated slot. "I'm ready. Though I pray no blood will be shed."

He nodded. "Okay, then. Let us take the throne for Elohim."

Jordana nodded. "For Elohim."

CHAPTER THIRTY-ONE

Jordana met many of her relatives and the guards at the cemetery's edge. They had waited while she said a final goodbye to Father. She studied them as she approached. Uncles sporting furrowed brows, aunts nipped at their fingernails, and antsy cousins pacing. Henry and Kai grasped their sword handles. Lester and Zachariah's hands hovered over their knife harnesses, as if ready to fling a blade at any second. Benjura's friend, Tubow had joined them, also donning his breastplate and battle axe. The man had a new wife. *Keep him safe, Elohim.*

Jordana locked eyes with Zarr. She had not seen him since he helped pulled the arrow from Father's chest. She nodded at him, and he tipped his head back at her.

Beast and Lainey sat amongst the people. Their ears twisted in various directions to capture every sound.

Jordana headed straight to the leopards. "I want you both to walk with me in the procession. Okay?"

The felines nodded.

Benjura stayed close as well, his knuckles white from squeezing the massive shield's handle in his grip.

She searched the group. "Where's Bootah?"

"Summoned by his sister."

Jordana's heart fluttered as she pinned Kai with her gaze. "Is his treason caught? Would your cousin slay her own brother?"

278

"Aye, she would. But I don't think she suspects him. Brin has the whole household searching the fortress for his majesty's Arrdock ring. She sent for Bootah to find out where the Arrdock would go to fish or swim. Did he have a secret cave? She grows desperate."

"Good. It will keep her occupied." She laid her hand on Kai's left shoulder. "I can't imagine how you must be torn between your own blood and loyalty to your Arrdock. Thank you for honoring my father's wishes."

Kai tipped his head. "I do what is best for our people. Your father chose his successor wisely. My cousin oversteps her bounds. She is no goddess."

Jordana prayed to be worthy of the man's sacrifice. All the guards risked much for her, and she couldn't let them down. She swept up her feathered cape and took her spot at the front, Beast and Lainey flanked her. The guards closed in around them.

Benjura sounded the long blast of the ram's horn, announcing the time to gather, although there wasn't a need. Every tribesman knew the coronation would follow the burial. All villagers would be crammed around the Arrdock's fortress.

If the horn had not been in one hand and the shield in his other, Jordana would have pulled Benjura to her and laced her fingers in his. The guards marched forward, jolting her. She stayed in their midst as they traveled to the clearing. Many heads hung low in the crowd. No one met her gaze. Were they burdened by grief? Everyone loved her father. Or perhaps they dreaded crowning Brin as their ruler. Jordana could only hope.

Under the kapok trees in the center of the village, the three vicars lined up. Each wore a long tunic dyed blue like the sky. Two held candles, their wicks flickering. One of the holy men held a pillow hosting a single crown. Her mother's crown.

The sharp intake of air caught in Jordana's chest. She hadn't seen it since Father's wedding to Brin. The jeweled tiara wasn't oversized like the one Brin later fashioned. Jordana never knew what had become of her mother's diamond tiara. She always suspected Brin of melting it down for the jewels. Perhaps the royal guards had rescued the precious memento. They probably guessed Jordana wouldn't touch Brin's gaudy crown today and would want her mother's. Jordana couldn't keep from smiling at the sight of Mamu's crown intact and sparkling.

When the procession stopped, so did Jordana, staying behind the guards.

Benjura moved closer and nudged her with his shoulder. "You can't stay back here. Take your place before the vicars."

She shook her head. "Let's wait for the call."

He tipped his chin and stayed at her side with shield ready.

A low murmur erupted across the crowd. The tribesmen acted anxious to begin. A few met her gaze, casting questioning stares at her. Did they wonder why she was still there? Did they want her to leave? Or perhaps word had spread and they knew her intentions. Maybe the sight of her mother's crown and not one of Brin's, caused them to guess about what would happen next.

Please, Father Elohim, if there is a way to do this without bloodshed, let it be so. Help the people to forgive me for the mistaken battle. Don't let them blame me for Father's death. She gulped. How could she ask them to not blame her, when she blamed herself? If she had kept Taryn in the Great Eucalyptus Forest, Father would still be alive.

If so, he wouldn't be restored to Me.

The gentle whisper touched her heart. How dare she question Elohim's ways. They are higher than her own and led to Father turning from his hardened heart. They stopped the Chinzu giants from building a bridge into The Forbidden Territory. Perhaps even stopped them from enslaving the Akimmi women. She must never criticize the Creator's methods. He had all the knowledge. She did not. *I'm sorry. Again. I wish it could have been achieved with my father alive, but I trust Your will as far better than mine.*

One of the vicars broke the silence. "Sound the call. The coronation shall begin."

280

Benjura blew the ram's horn. Three strong blasts.

At last the queen emerged and sat on the platform. It lowered bit by bit. When the platform came within a few inches of the ground, Brin jumped up and swept to the ground. She stormed straight to Jordana, pointing. "Seize her. She's to be executed for breaking the law. No banished person is allowed to return without the presentation of a miracle. And I, the Goddess Brin, shall never accept a miracle from the likes of her." Every vein in Brin's forehead protruded and pulsated. Her big lips had been stained red.

None of the guards moved toward Jordana.

Brin whipped around and screamed at them. "I said, seize her!"

Lester rushed forward and knelt in front of the queen. "Your majesty, something has transpired. I have a message from your late husband as witnessed by the Arrdock's royal guards."

Brin lashed out at Lester, slapping him across the face. She stumbled forward in her follow-through. The violent strike echoed beneath the trees and several maidens gasped. "I will not hear the message until she is dead. Obey me!" Again the queen pointed at Jordana.

Lester didn't flinch and stayed in position on one knee. Bright red finger prints welted on his cheek.

Bootah rushed forward. "Queen, please stop. The message must be delivered first." He moved in closer. "My sister, you must accept this."

"How dare you call me anything but Goddess? Are you asking to be put to death, as well? Bow!" She pointed at the ground in front of her brother.

Bootah lowered to one knee, but lifted his head and shouted in a loud voice. "My queen. Before your husband died, he granted immunity to Jordana. He decreed her banished no more. The Arrdock issued this order while he was very much alive and in front of many witnesses, including myself. You cannot put Jordana to death, for she breaks no law."

Brin's hands curled into tight fists as cheers erupted

across the village. Feet stomped and clapping thundered from the bridges. A crimson-faced Brin stormed back and forth inside the perimeter, her body rigid. "Silence!" She screamed, but the crowd would not be quieted.

Joy filled Jordana's soul. Her tribemates did want her. Perhaps they had loved her all along. Would they be open to her rule? As fast as Brin had changed things after marrying the Arrdock, Jordana would change them back. Would the village embrace her then? Many of the people blew kisses at her from up on the bridges. Flower petals floated down from the trees as people tossed them from the bouquets they had gathered for the coronation.

A flash of metal caught her eye, and Jordana pivoted toward it.

Brin grasped a knife and thrust it down at Jordana's chest.

She screamed, one hand raised to block the blow, the other going for her mother's blade.

Beast leapt forward, coming between her and Brin's blade. He knocked the queen down, landing square on top of her chest and went for her throat. His powerful jaws closed around the queen's milky white skin.

"No, Beast. Don't kill her." Jordana pulled him away.

When Beast released Brin's neck, no blood showed. He had held her in his powerful jaws, but did not bite in. Beast collapsed onto his side.

Jordana's eyes settled on the knife handle protruding from Beast's front shoulder. Brin missed his chest, but had sunk the blade to the hilt in the leopard's body.

Jordana shouted, "We need the healers! Granna. Please help."

Several men and women rushed forward, including her grandmother.

Benjura pulled Jordana back. "Give them room to work."

"Pray! Everyone pray." Jordana pleaded with the villagers, as she sank to embrace Lainey.

Near to her ear, the feline whispered a soft prayer. Above

her, Benjura's deep voice led the villagers in a prayer for the brave gatekeeper who saved Jordana's life. The crowd grew alive with fervent prayers from every direction of the Tree Warrior Village. They hadn't forgotten how to pray. Even the vicars came forward, their candles flickering, as they reached out a hand and prayed for the gatekeeper.

I beg of you, Elohim, do not let Beast lose his life because of me. Jordana huddled on the ground with Lainey, her arms wrapped tight around the leopard. Acid bubbled inside her as the minutes passed. This could not be happening. A holy gatekeeper killed by a human. What kind of curse would it bring upon her village? *Please, Elohim, do not take vengeance on the tree warriors for one person's actions.*

Benjura finished praying and she motioned him over.

"We can't see anything. Please ask my Granna if Beast will live." When he walked away, Jordana rebuked the temptation of burying a blade in Brin. *Forgive her, Creator, and heal Beast.*

At last Benjura returned. "Beast is alive, but not conscious. They soaked up the blood, stitched him inside and outside. The knife appears to have penetrated the tendons and bones in his shoulder. He should survive, and maybe walk, but he'll never jump or run again. Your Granna poured plenty of wine on the wound to keep infection away. They're packing it now with herbs. Do you wish to see him before they carry him to your Granna's house? She insists on being the healer to care for him through the night."

"Yes." Jordana jumped up and followed Lainey who trotted ahead.

The feline sniffed Beast's wound and face, licking his eyes. She whispered something in his ear.

Jordana ran her hand through the fur on Beast's head. "You will not die. Do you hear me? You will live to proclaim the works of the Lord." Her voice cracked. "Thank you for saving my life, Beast. I love you. But you are not allowed to die." Jordana let go and faced Lainey. "As soon as he is strong enough, my men will carry him to the Restoration Pool if you will allow it."

"Yes. I'll need help getting him to the Azul banks. The gatekeepers can take care of it from there. Thank you." Giant tears soaked the fur under Lainey's eyes.

Jordana didn't know a leopard could cry.

Benjura pulled Jordana up and several men lifted the black leopard onto a litter and carried him away. Beast's massive paws dangled over one side. His lids never lifted.

Jordana lost sight of him and spun around, searching through the throng. Brin sat on her sparkling throne. Booth and Kai stood on either side of her. When she met Jordana's gaze, Brin's chin lifted and something akin to amusement flashed across her face.

Jordana wrenched free from Benjura and sprinted after the evil woman. No need to dodge any guards, for not one person stepped in her way. By the time she reached the platform, Jordana had flung off her princess cape and grasped her mother's dagger. She lunged at the queen, pressing the tip of the blade against the wretched woman's jugular. "Get out of that chair!" Jordana fisted the queen's strawberry locks and drug her off the platform. Brin fell to her knees, and Jordana stood behind her, still holding a blade to Brin's neck. "You have wounded a holy gatekeeper of Elohim. You sit on sacred purple-palm bark. You think yourself a goddess when you're a mere girl born in this tribe like all the rest of us. Have you no respect for the Creator? No fear of Him at all?"

"Let go of me. I shall have your head for this. Guards!"

No sentry marched forward.

Jordana held up her hand displaying the ring for all to see. "I wear the Arrdock ring. I am his successor. Not this greedy woman." She flashed it at the vicars and Brin's family.

Lainey circled Jordana and Brin. Drool dripped from her fangs. Obviously the feline struggled to control her temper as well.

"Release her, child." Lainey hissed, her words not

284

matching her blood-thirsty appearance. "Do not slay this woman in your holy rage. Use restraint. You have a higher calling on your life. Do not begin your reign with a rash decision leading to bloodshed. Tis not the right way to rule."

Jordana twisted Brin's hair in her fist, pulling the woman's head back, her blade still pressed against Brin's throat. The queen winced, but didn't struggle against the knife. Drips of blood slid onto Jordana's fingers. Still, the people remained frozen. Watching. No one aiding Brin.

Only Lainey moved and spoke. "I, too, am tempted to rip open this woman's throat. I wish to keep her from doing any more harm. But vengeance belongs to Elohim. Tis not ours. You must let her go." Lainey's pace slowed as she came to a stop in front of them. Her powerful jaw opened and hovered inches from the queen's face. Lainey let out a powerful roar.

Jordana wanted to scream and bury her blade in Brin. She wanted to banish the woman forever. As soon as that temptation hit her brain, Jordana's blood ran cold. She dropped the knife as if it burned her fingers and stepped back. Not too long ago, she cried to Elohim, claiming she'd never wish banishment on anyone, not even her worst enemy. And here she was thoroughly tempted to banish her father's wife.

Benjura's hands around Jordana's forearm drew her gaze. Sticky red blood slashed across her thumb and index knuckle. He led her to the basin of water on the Arrdock platform and rinsed her fingers. He washed her mother's dagger and slid it into Jordana's harness. From within a fog, she let Benjura lead her back to the vicars.

Brin hadn't moved, and for once, the woman seemed frozen with fear, her wide eyes and staring at Lainey's bared fangs hovering centimeters from the queen's face.

Lainey hissed, but did not back away. "You will answer for your sins, your blasphemy, cruelty, and greed. I suggest you prepare your heart for judgment. Tis wise to spend the rest of your days wearing repentance ash." Lainey sauntered away.

Brin took her time in standing. She jutted up her chin and

smoothed her gown, before a guard clasped her hands and gazed back at Jordana as if waiting for orders.

Jordana didn't wait for the crowning before dictating instructions. She pointed at Brin and raised her voice for all to hear. "I want her to stay right there. Front and center for my coronation ceremony. I, Princess Jordana of Arrie, am the Arrdock's choice as Shedock of the Tree Warrior Village. I shall put the needs of my people before my own. I will destroy Brin's abominations and return Elohim worship." Jordana zeroed in on Brin. "You are queen no more and everything you tried to do shall now be undone. Front this point forward, you are to be called Brin. Nothing more."

Jordana motioned to the guards. "Tie Brin to the kapok tree, so she may watch the celebration. Do not harm her or allow anyone to hurt her. Tonight she is to be jailed until the next Judgment Seat after the full moons. I will seek Elohim's instructions for what to do with her after that."

The royal guards pulled their former queen to the giant trunk and bound her with rope and sashes. She spat at them, but didn't try to wrestle free.

Jordana's chest heaved as turned her back to the woman, willing her pulse to slow and her insides to stop churning. Perhaps humiliation would put Brin into a pit of despair, leading to repentance. Jordana had weeks before the next Judgment Seat. Right now she must focus on the ceremony.

Again, she shouted for all to hear. "Tree warriors and maidens, I'm sorry for the events of this day. Do not let this woman ruin our memory of my father. He was a great Arrdock and will be sorely missed." Her voice cracked, and she displayed her hand once more. "I wear my father's Arrdock ring and accept his designation as successor. But I want there to be no doubt. Before we proceed, I wish you to hear the testimony of my father's royal guards."

Jordana motioned to the men. "Henry, Lester, Zachariah, Bootah, and Kai. Come forward and give witness to the vicars and this great village." She purposely left out Benjura's name and moved next to him. As she had wanted to do all afternoon, Jordana laced her fingers in his. The warmth of his hand soothed her as if she could absorb his strength and know everything would be all right.

The crisp voice of Bootah sounded first. "As we carried the Arrdock to find Jordana, he made me and my fellow guards swear an oath to see his only child on the throne. The Arrdock named Princess Jordana as his heir successor. He pardoned her and told her where to find the Arrdock ring. I witnessed this with my own eyes and ears. I swear it as truth before my tribe." Bootah raised his voice. "And before Elohim!"

One by one, each of the other men stepped forward and proclaimed the same.

Benjura leaned over and whispered. "I debated whether or not to let you slit Brin's throat. That was a hard temptation for me to overcome. I can only imagine how hard it was for you. Looks like you're already behaving like a Shedock."

She arched a brow. "Still is hard. I might slit her throat after dark."

When he laughed, many heads turned their way.

"Shh. The men are bearing witness."

He gave her hand another squeeze. "I have missed your clever jokes. I hope your humor is returning. It has been many hot seasons since I have heard your laugh."

She took in his smile, his handsome face framed by dark auburn curls. "I'm ashamed at how I've acted toward you—like a crushed teenager. I only focused on my sorrow. I should have known you had a good reason not to help me at the Banishment Rite. I'm sorry for not trusting you."

"You are forgiven. And I hope you have forgiven me for not being able to leave with you. It was not my choice, and it was torture."

"I wish you to always obey Elohim over me and over yourself. I promise to do the same." When he smiled, she resisted rising up on toes to kiss him. Jordana forced her attention back to the holy men just as the last of the guards finished speaking.

287

The vicars called Jordana forward.

"Are you ready?" Jordana faced Benjura.

A huge smile filled his face. "I've waited to see you crowned since I was eight years old."

"I have waited the same. Well, since I was fourteen anyway. I'm slower than you." She took a step forward and Benjura released her. She jerked around and grappled to catch his hand. "Come on. I'm not doing this without you." The crowd grew so quiet the pounding of her own heart filled her ears. Even the jungle birds had stopped their racket.

Benjura's forehead wrinkled. "You want me to stand up there while they coronate you? That would deviate from custom." Benjura clicked his tongue. "Princess, I'm shocked. You are such a stickler for tradition." He covered his heart in mock surprise.

"Very funny. Let's go."

His eyes widened as he stared at her, smile fading. A confused look filled his face.

Jordana frowned at him. *How could he not know this?* "I shan't rule without you. Arrdock and Shedock. That's what we've always planned."

The space between Benjura's lips widened as a flash of surprise flitted across his eyes. "You wish to marry me?"

Her stomach dropped to her feet. He hadn't actually asked for her hand since their reunion. She had only assumed they were picking up where they left off three years ago when they had become betrothed. Perhaps he meant to serve her, not to love her as his wife. Never to be her *jira*. How had she not realized this? Heat rushed to her cheeks. All the townsfolk stared at her. She meant to humiliate Brin, and instead, she had humbled herself. *Forgive my foolish pride, Elohim. I thought he still wanted me. When will I learn not to assume things?* She turned and took a step toward the vicars.

Benjura let out a loud whoop that caused her to jump. He encircled her, and spun in circle. Setting her down, he pressed his lips to hers. In front of the whole tribe, he raised both hands to

288

her cheeks and deepened their kiss. "I love you." He whispered before lifting his face to the sky and shouting. "I love Jordana!" He scooped her up and carried her to stand before the vicars. "A wedding and coronation. Let the ceremonies begin."

Laughter rang through the village as whistles erupted. People shouted well wishes. Applause filled the expanse. The rapping of weapons drowned everything out. More flowers rained down, thick in the air.

Heart soaring, Jordana clutched Benjura. He did want to marry her after all. She leaned in and kissed him. When cheering crowd seemed to reach its crescendo, she pulled back and laid her hand on Benjura's cheek. Was she ready for this? To be Shedock and Benjura's wife? With Elohim's guidance, she would do her best.

And to think she almost ruined it seconds ago by giving in to her fury. As ruler, Jordana could never let her anger influence decisions and ruling. Use restraint, as Lainey had said. Bridle her tongue, as Father had chastised her. Mamu always tried to teach Jordana to serve the tribe. She finally understood what everyone meant, and Jordana purposed in her heart to serve those she must lead. *Only with Your help, Elohim Rapha, can I be a wise Shedock. Rule through me, I pray.*

Benjura's hazel eyes sparkled at her before turning to face the three vicars.

At long last, she was right where she belonged. Benjura at her side, marrying her true love, wanted by her people, and starting the job her parents had prepared her for since birth. In total devotion to Elohim, she and Benjura would rule as Arrdock and Shedock of the Tree Warrior Village.

~ THE END ~

Made in the USA
Columbia, SC
01 January 2019